KT-161-904

The Giant Book of
STORIES

The Giant Book of
STORIES

Galley Press

© Copyright original Text IPC Magazines Limited 1976

© Copyright this compilation 1976 The Hamlyn Publishing Group Limited

© Copyright this edition 1986 Hamlyn Publishing,
a division of The Hamlyn Publishing Group Limited

Published in this edition 1986 by Hamlyn Publishing for Galley Press
an imprint of W.H. Smith and Son Limited
Registered No. 237811 England.
Trading as WHS Distributors, St John's House,
East Street, Leicester, LE1 6NE

All rights reserved. No part of this
publication may be reproduced, stored in a
retrieval system, or transmitted in any
form or by any means, electronic, mechanical,
photocopying, recording or otherwise, without
prior written permission from the publishers.

ISBN 0 86136 683 2

Printed in Yugoslavia

Contents

DEADLINE FOR DANGER

The villagers disliked Ginette. They supposed that because her aristocratic guardian was over-friendly with the Nazis, that she too must be a willing collaborator.

Little did they dream that Ginette was prepared to risk her life for her beloved France and strike a blow for freedom.

"There she goes! And if you ask me, she's as big a traitor as her uncle."

"Of course she is. They both toady up to the Nazi officers so as to get extra rations and privileges. I hear there's fresh cream on the table every day at the chateau."

"And no one else around here can afford to keep horses. It's only because they're allowed a special ration of grain — and in return they let that old bully Colonel Fischer and his officers go out riding."

"Shame on them, I say!"

It was June, 1943, in the little French village of Nanquette, during that grim period when the whole of France was occupied by the Nazis. A group of villagers was standing on the pavement glancing at the slim, dark-haired girl who was trotting up the street on a sleek chestnut mare. They watched her draw rein as an army car stopped close by.

From the car stepped the bulky figure of Colonel Hugo Fischer, the Nazi commandant.

9

His face as black as thunder, he swung round towards the villagers.

Clicking his heels, he bowed to the smiling girl in the saddle.
"Bonjour, Mam'selle Ginette.*"*
"Bonjour, M. le Colonel.*"*
"Your uncle, the Count has been good enough to invite me to lunch at the chateau. A good opportunity for you to continue with that so-excellent portrait of me you are painting, *nicht wahr?"*
"Of course, monsieur. It will be a pleasure."
"Excellent — excellent!"
He clicked his heels again and was just going to climb back into the car when he noticed something pasted on an old brick wall across the road.
It was a fair-sized poster, and on it was an unmistakable caricature of himself!"
His face as black as thunder, he swung round towards the villagers.
"See that that poster is pulled down before I pass this way again," he shouted, "or you'll suffer for it, the lot of you. Pigs!"
Shaking his fist at them, he bundled into the car and was driven away.
"Whoever stuck up that poster was a friend of France," growled old Lucien Devray, a veteran of the 1914—18 war. "Not like that treacherous little snob on the horse. Let's show her what we think of her, comrades."
And as Ginette shook the mare's reins, preparing to ride on, a sound reached her from that little group on the pavement — the sound of a scornful, angry hiss, growing louder and louder. Her cheeks grew pink, but without turning her head, she urged the mare into a canter that sent a cloud of white dust drifting up from her hooves.
"Old Lucien holds the croix de guerre," thought Ginette. "No wonder he despises me."
There was a strange gleam in her eyes — almost a gleam of laughter — as she turned her mount into the lane that led up between the poplars to the gates of the White Chateau.
On the terrace of the house the Comte de Chauvet was pacing, smoking a cigar. He was a fussy, self-important little man and from the first he had made a great point of being friendly with the Nazis because, as he said, it was good for business. He had been made Ginette's legal guardian when her mother had died six months before. Seeing her slide from the saddle he came bustling up.
"Lucky you have a talent for painting, my dear," he exclaimed. "Our Nazi friends never seem to get tired of seeing themselves on

canvas. How is the colonel's portrait going?"

"Nearly finished, Uncle. He'll come to the chateau an hour before lunch to give me a chance of working on it."

Her uncle nodded. Then, as he turned to look towards the village, his puffy face twisted into a sneer.

"Those dolts of villagers," he said. "They'd have a much better time of it if only they'd co-operate with the Nazis instead of trying to resist all the time. They don't know which side their bread is buttered. Fools!"

Ginette said nothing, but that same little smile played about her lips as she led the mare to the stables.

An hour or so later, in a trim lunch-time dress, she was waiting in the little room she used as a studio. At exactly twelve o'clock Colonel Fischer arrived, striding across the room to gaze at the canvas on Ginette's easel.

She had certainly flattered him. She had made him look slimmer and had toned down his thick lips and bony nose.

"*Gut — gut!* A splendid likeness!" he beamed. "I may have a chance to show it to General Seidel — he is visiting our troops here tomorrow. We are arranging a big parade for him soon after dawn in the meadow just north of the old Nanquette Mill."

"Indeed? How interesting, monsieur!"

That hint of a smile still showed on Ginette's face as she worked away at the portrait until the lunch gong sounded and the Nazi officer strutted away for the excellent meal which the Comte de Chauvet would provide.

Left to herself Ginette opened a cupboard and took from it a mask. It was cleverly made to represent the face of Colonel Fischer, but — unlike the picture on the easel — it certainly didn't flatter him. It made him look extremely comic.

Chuckling, Ginette held the mask beside the portrait for a moment, comparing the two faces. Then she slipped the mask into a haversack.

"It may be useful tonight," she said to herself, "when the Invisible Three take the midnight trail again!"

The Invisible Three — who were they? That was a question many of the local Nazis would have liked to answer.

They suspected that a trio of youngsters was often abroad after curfew, distributing copies of a forbidden Free French newspaper, pasting up unflattering caricatures of Nazi officers, laying booby traps in the path of Nazi patrols. But so skilful were these daring three that the enemy rarely had more than a passing glimpse of them in the shadows.

No one knew who they were and nobody dreamed that their leader was dark-haired Ginette de Chauvet, niece of the unpopular owner of the White Chateau.

Ginette had to live at the chateau, but she didn't share her uncle's views. She was playing a double role. By day she was the demure girl whom the villagers thought so snooty and so friendly with the Nazis — and by night she was the leader of her own daring little gang, doing all they could to help their country.

Frequently she was able to glean scraps of information from the Nazi officers which she was able to pass on to the Resistance.

And so that night, as the moon swung up over the poplars, Ginette was once again clambering over the wall that surrounded the chateau gardens. As usual she wore jeans and shirt, and had a haversack over her shoulder.

Tu-whit! Tu-whoo-whoo!

An owl's hoot sounded weirdly nearby.

"Marcel's signal," she thought. "They're waiting for me."

She slipped noiselessly through the shadows to the moss-grown oak which was one of their meeting-places. Marcel Lebrun and Mimi Fabre were already waiting and she saw that Marcel had brought the life-size dummy of Colonel Fischer which he had been making.

"Good hunting, you two!"

"Good hunting!"

It was their usual whispered greetings. And now Ginette brought the comic mask from her haversack.

"How will this do for the dummy's face?" she said, holding it so that the moonlight showed it clearly.

"What a joke!" Mimi giggled. "It'll make old Fischer burst his buttons with rage."

"Marvellous!" agreed Marcel. "Now we've got to decide where to put the dummy so as to get the best effect."

"I know the very place," Ginette told him. "The old Nanquette Mill. There's going to be a big Nazi parade soon after dawn tomorrow to welcome a Nazi general. Fischer told me about it when I was finishing his portrait. Just imagine their feeling if they see a dummy of their famous colonel hanging from a pole at the top of the mill!"

"Come on! Let's go!" Mimi laughed.

They sped away, keeping to twisting woodland paths unlikely to be known to Nazi patrols. Soon the dark shape of the mill loomed up against the moonlit sky.

"Mind how you go," Marcel warned, as they entered. "The ladders in here are pretty rotten."

Batteries were scarce in wartime France, but Ginette had a torch in her haversack and shone it cautiously as they hauled the dummy up through the trapdoor to the first floor.

"When we come down again we'll jam the trapdoors and smash the ladders, so it won't be easy for them to get at the dummy," Ginette whispered. "They'll be blazing mad, and . . ."

"S-s-sh! Listen!"

The low-voiced warning came from Marcel. Ginette had switched off the torch and they froze into silence, their ears straining.

Then all three of them heard it — a sound, like a stifled groan, coming from the darkest corner. Click! Ginette had switched on the torch again and its wavering beam travelled around the dusty walls until . . .

"Oh-h-h!"

The choked-back cry came from Mimi. She had been the first to see the figure lying on a pile of old flour sacks in the corner.

"Ma foi! His sleeve — look — it's soaked with blood," she whispered.

She wanted to be a nurse when she grew up, like her elder sister who was caring for the wounded in a Resistance camp far to the south. She knelt down beside the man on the sacks, gently feeling his shoulder.

"I believe he's been shot. Help me draw his jacket off — carefully, Marcel . . ."

In her haversack Mimi carried a first-aid kit and skilfully she bound up the stranger's arm. He was only half conscious and weak from loss of blood, but for a few moments he opened his eyes. Ginette, bending low, caught his muttered words.

"Midnight . . . midnight . . ." And then, so low that she could hardly hear it: "The Nanquette lock . . . I must . . ."

His eyes closed, and the words tailed away. Marcel, meanwhile, had picked up an object that had been standing on the floor close to the wounded man.

"It's a tin of substitute coffee," he murmured. "That awful stuff made from acorns that they dish out in the shops now." Carefully he unscrewed the lid. "Yes, it's quite full — up to the brim. The poor fellow must have brought it with him, whoever he is."

For the time being their own mission was forgotten as they knelt around the wounded stranger. His eyes opened again and this time he seemed to realise that he wasn't alone.

"We're friends," Ginette told him softly. "Who are you? What has happened?"

"I'm from Paris. A special mission . . . you see, we learnt that a string of barges will be passing up the canal tomorrow loaded with vital raw material and they've got to be delayed. My job was to blow up the Nanquette lock, but an hour ago I ran into Nazis — a whole truckload of them. I dodged away and took refuge here, but not before I'd stopped a bullet . . ."

In the torchlight he suddenly noticed the tin Marcel was holding. "Put that down, please. On the floor."

Wondering at the sudden urgency in his tone, Marcel obeyed.

"You spoke of blowing up the lock," Ginette whispered. "But — how?"

"The tin," he muttered. "I just had to drop it in the water by the lock."

They stared in surpise.

"You mean this tin?" Marcel exclaimed. "But it's full of coffee. I looked inside."

He shook his head.

"Only an inch or so of coffee," he said. "The rest — well, it's part acid, part explosive. You see? When the acid eats through the partition it goes off and it's timed for midnight — more or less . . ."

He gave a deep sigh and his eyes closed again.

"I think he's fainted," Mimi said. "His pulse is weak but fairly steady. It's just the loss of blood . . ."

They were all three now gazing at the tin of substitute coffee, thinking of the acid slowly eating away at the partition somewhere inside there.

And Ginette made her decision.

"We've never done anything as big as this before," she told them.

"But — well — it's up to us. As your leader I'll take the — the tin to the lock, now."

But Marcel was ahead of her. He was already picking it up, preparing to stow it in his haversack, even though his hands trembled a little.

"I know I'm a year younger than you," he muttered. "But I'm the man, after all — and my dad's in the Resistance. I'll take it."

"We'll go together," Ginette said. There was no point in arguing. "If Mimi will stay and look after the patient."

It would take them perhaps forty-five minutes to reach the canal and it was now ten o'clock, so they had a fair margin of safety. Marcel knew that his father, out on another mission, would be home in the early hours of the morning and would be able to arrange for the wounded man to be taken to a place of safety.

"Bonne chance — good luck," Mimi whispered, as they began to climb gingerly down the ladder.

"Wait, Ginette. I thought I heard a sound — ahead of us . . ."

They were in deep shadow, for the moon was temporarily obscured by drifting cloud. But there should be a rutted lane not far ahead that would take them part of the way to the canal.

"I'll tiptoe forward and reconnoitre. If you hear the owl-hoot, you'll know all is well."

Marcel glided forward into the darkness before Ginette could stop him. She waited tensely. Then it happened — without warning. A glare of light ahead. A harsh voice.

"*Ein knabe* — a boy! A young lad breaking curfew. It's time these local brats were taught a lesson, eh? Hold him, Karl!"

Ginette drew a trembling breath. It was clear that Marcel, too impulsive, had run straight into an enemy patrol! As a ray of moonlight filtered through the leaves she dropped on hands and knees amongst the long grass, then began to crawl cautiously forward, trying to forget how dizzily her heart was beating. And now, at last, she could see the lane.

There were three Nazi troopers in the patrol, with a jeep. Mindful of blackout restrictions they had dowsed their lights again. She could see one of them pushing Marcel into the vehicle.

"You'll spend the night in the guard-house at Marville, you young scoundrel." She could hear that same harsh voice again. "Kicking your heels in one of the cells for twelve hours will teach you a lesson. Drive on, Karl."

The jeep moved away taking Marcel with it.

Even in the midst of her despair, Ginette knew a sense of relief that these Nazis were stationed at the neighbouring town instead of in the village. They wouldn't be so likely to know Marcel by sight.

"But the bomb," she whispered. "It — IT'S STILL IN HIS HAVERSACK!"

She glanced at her wrist-watch. It was twenty past ten. Marville was less than two miles away and she knew where the guard-house was — an old building on the outskirts.

Without further thought she stepped out into the lane and began to run. She could reach the town in fifteen minutes if she wasn't stopped. Then, when she saw how the land lay, she would have to decide what to do.

Would Marcel have told them about that fateful coffee-tin? If not, she would surely have to go in and tell the Nazis herself, for of course she couldn't allow her friend to stay in the cell with a bomb that was timed to explode at midnight — or before.

"And then?" she breathlessly queried. "What will happen then?"

She could picture the scene. The harsh interrogation — the blows — as the Nazis tried to force them to tell where the bomb had come from. It might lead to everything being discovered, including that wounded man in the old mill with Mimi. She almost groaned aloud at the thought.

There it was at last — the square stone house standing a little way back from the Marville road.

The windows were blacked out, but she could hear voices and laughter inside; probably most of the troopers in there were at supper. She guessed there would probably be two or three small rooms used as cells.

Luckily there was no one on sentry duty outside and noiselessly she tiptoed round the building. Down one side were three small barred windows, tightly closed and blacked out, and she guessed these were probably the cells. Was Marcel in one of them?

Tu-whit! Tu-whoo-oo!

She gave the owl call and then waited tensely. She had almost given up hope when, faintly, she heard the answer; almost certainly it came from the middle cell. Marcel had heard, and risked a reply. He knew she was outside.

She tiptoed round to the back. Here she found a window which, on this summer night, was slightly open at the bottom, so that she could touch the blackout material inside. Quickly she brought a clasp knife from her haversack and made a slit in the black stuff so that she could peep cautiously through.

The window opened on a corridor. Halfway along, a fat Nazi trooper sat slumped on a bench, a greasy dinner plate beside him. To the left were three doors, each with a square grille in the middle.

"The cells!" she thought. "And that trooper's on guard outside. He's probably just had his supper and looks half asleep."

Close to the window another passage branched to the right, running along the back of the house. She noted, too, the position of an electric light switch, near where the corridors met.

Ginette had always been a fast thinker, which helped to make her such a good leader for the Invisible Three. Now her quick wits came to her aid once again.

She took something else from her haversack and busied herself making certain preparations. Her plan was risky — foolhardy perhaps — and yet she told herself that it just might work.

"Now for it!"

There was a back door close by which she had already tested, to make sure it was unlocked. Carefully she opened it, shivering as it creaked a little, and stepped into the second passage. The kitchen must be near at hand, for she could hear a clatter of dishes — but she tiptoed to the left, towards the angle which this passage made with the cell corridor.

Slowly, holding her breath, she risked a peep round the corner.

The sentry still sat slumped on his bench, half closed eyes looking straight in front of him. She could see the numbers on the cell doors — 1, 2, 3. By the sentry's shoulder was a wooden board on the wall, where keys hung from numbered hooks.

For one tense second Ginette waited. Then —

Click!

She had switched off the light in both corridors. In the blackness she sprang sideways, grabbed hold of the blackout curtains and with a terrific tug ripped them away from the window.

"Himmel! Was ist das?"

The spluttering gasp broke from the guard. Was he dreaming? The whole place was in blackness and from the end of the corridor a weirdly glowing face was peering at him.

His hand groped for a shelf, picked up a torch. Switching it on he lurched down the corridor towards the window. That eerie face was still out there — glowing, mocking. With a curse the man put the torch on the sill and grasped the window frame, struggling to open it, forgetting that for days it had been so tightly jammed that none of them had been able to shift it.

So he did not see the slim figure dart noiselessly down the corridor behind him.

"Number two cell — Marcel should be in number two!" Ginette thought.

She risked a gleam of her torch to find the right key. Marcel must have been waiting by the door, haversack over his shoulder, for he darted out the instant she threw it back.

"Ginette! Thank heavens . . ."

"Quick! Make for the front!"

They heard an angry shout as the fat sentry at last realised what was happening, but by that time they had reached the front entrance without being challenged. Discipline here seemed lax and the other occupants of the guard-house were still at their late supper.

Even some miles from their own village, the Invisible Three had always tried to memorise the lay-out of the country. Though the alarm had now been raised the two fugitives fled silently up a narrow alley opposite the house, crossed a farmyard, dropped into a dry ditch which, roofed with brushwood, gave them cover for a half-mile as they headed towards the canal.

"The plan worked!" Ginette explained breathlessly. "The mask for the dummy was still in my haversack — I smeared it with some of that luminous paint we used last week — lured the sentry away . . ."

They scrambled out of the ditch, took a woodland path leading towards Nanquette.

"The coffee tin!" Ginette gasped. "You've got it still?"

"Yes. They never guessed . . ."

They were running recklessly in the dark, and even as he spoke Marcel caught his foot in a trailing root and fell heavily. A ray of moonlight showed up his dismayed, puckered face.

"My ankle — I've twisted it," he panted, pulling himself to his feet.

I'll only be able to hobble from now on, Ginette. I can't run."

It was then that they heard the clock over the Marville town hall chime the quarter hour.

Time hadn't seemed so important during that mad rush from the guardhouse. Now their thoughts came back to it with a jolt and Ginette's cheeks paled as she glanced at her watch.

"Quarter past eleven — but mine only says five past. That town-hall clock is never wrong. I've been ten minutes slow all along."

Ten minutes that might make all the difference between safety and destruction!

"You make for home, Marcel," she said quickly. "When your father comes back, arrange for that wounded man at the mill with Mimi to be taken somewhere safe."

She had already opened the flap of Marcel's haversack and was lifting out the tin.

"Ginette! Wait — think!" he whispered hoarsely. "I know this sort of bomb, my dad has used them. They can't be timed within half an hour — it could go off at eleven-thirty as easily as midnight. And however fast you run you couldn't reach the lock under twenty minutes."

"I must try. It's for France."

She was already moving away down the path, the "coffee tin" in her haversack.

"Come back, Ginette — please —"

Her friend's voice died away behind her. She forced herself to quicken her speed, though her knees felt weak and her throat dry. It seemed as if a clock inside her brain was ticking away the seconds that separated her from that fateful moment when the wafer-thin partition in the bomb would finally give way . . .

She had been running for eight minutes when the path emerged from the trees.

"The Nanquette Road at last. Thank goodness!"

Half a mile along the road, then she would have to turn aside again taking the track that led directly to the canal. She ran steadily, her face damp with sweat, resisting the temptation to glance at her watch every few seconds.

"There it is — the signpost!" Ginette gasped.

It marked the track she must take and she turned down it, stumbling over the rutted surface, feeling physically sick as she plunged on. And now, to her straining ears, came the distant chime of the half-hour.

The deadline had been reached. At any moment now it might happen . . .

She had an awful fear that she might collapse, fainting on the track. She was moving almost like a sleepwalker and when at last she reached the canal bank close to the lock she almost pitched headlong into the dark water, not realising where she was.

Here hands were trembling so much, she could hardly open the haversack. Somehow she found strength to lift out the tin and with a supreme effort toss it into the canal close to the lock.

Next afternoon the sun was shining as Ginette rode the chestnut mare down the hill. She still looked pale, but she was smiling to herself.

Everything had gone well. The lock had been destroyed and a vital consignment of Nazi war material delayed. Later in the night Marcel's father had smuggled the wounded Resistance man — who had been carefully tended by Mimi — away from the mill.

"I expect I'll get the usual sour looks from the villagers," she mused, a little wistfully.

She could already see old Lucien Devray and his friend Fernand. The two old men had strolled out from the village and were standing beside the road, almost as if waiting for her.

She tensed in the saddle, for it wasn't easy to bear the contempt of those two, who had both distinguished themselves in the previous war.

Then, suddenly, she gave such a start that the mare tossed her head and whinnied softly.

The two old men had straightened their shoulders as she approached. Their hands came up in a military salute and Lucien spoke.

"Mam'selle Ginette! The word has been passed round to some of us," he said softly. "Your secret will be safe, but we know what you did last night and — well — we're sorry we misunderstood. I want you to take this."

She could hardly believe her eyes.

"Your croix de guerre! Your medal! Lucien, I couldn't . . ."

"I insist, mam'selle — please. Keep it till the war is over and the Nazis have gone, then you can hand it back. It will remind you that some of us here in Nanquette honour you as a true fighter for France."

He pressed into her hand the bronze cross with its green and red ribbon, then stepped back beside his friend and once again they raised their hands in salute. Ginette, a blur of tears in her eyes, could only smile at them.

And there was a great happiness in her heart as she rode on.

ANNA'S FIRST JOB

by Hilary Bailey

Anna wanted very much to be a buyer at Webber and Nunn's one day. But first she had to gain experience as a salesgirl. It was a pity that she made her ambition known to Claire Holliday for Claire was spiteful and jealous.

Then came the day when Anna was accused of stealing from the store. Dismissal followed and Anna was in despair.

Anna Hill stood behind her counter at Webber and Nunn's, the second biggest store in London. It was four o'clock on a hot summer's day and her feet were aching in the new black shoes her mother had bought her, but the excitement prevented her from feeling the pain, or the heat, for it was her first day as a salesgirl in the dress materials department.

Everything was so new and interesting that she had to force herself to concentrate on her job.

Anna wanted very much to be a buyer at Webber and Nunn's, but until she had proved her worth and done some training in actually selling materials in Mr. McAlister's department, she could not hope to be promoted.

The girl next to her expertly rolled up a bolt of wool ready to put back on the shelf. Watching her, Anna felt she would *never* learn to roll the wool so perfectly and at such high speed. The girl's name was

Claire Holliday. She had lank, mousy hair, a pale face and a small, hard mouth.

"Everything all right?" Claire asked.

"Oh, yes," Anna smiled. "I'm really and truly enjoying my first day here — though I feel a little scared, you know. Who was that woman who was so rude to you just now?"

"Old Mrs. de Courcy. She's always like that. But she's very rich and her family have shopped here for years. So she thinks she can do just what she likes."

Anna busily set to work, rolling up the heavy bolts and putting them back on their shelves. Claire was in charge of her during her first week and she was trying to learn all that she could.

"I had the whole stock out for that last silly woman," Claire grumbled, "— she didn't seem to know what she wanted!"

Anna said nothing, but went on rolling up the lengths of cloth and putting them on the shelves. Secretly she glanced at the other girl, noting the ugly frown and the angry eyes. Claire had not been nasty to her so far, but she could be bad-tempered and unhelpful with the customers. She was definitely not a girl to quarrel with.

The next morning, Anna arrived in the department and began dressing a model on a stand near her counter. She arranged it in bright scarlet jersey wool, as Claire had done the day before. Just then, a tall, bowler-hatted gentleman walked up to the counter. As Claire had not yet arrived and all the other assistants seemed busy, Anna decided she ought to serve the customer herself.

She hopped behind the counter and looked up at the man. He was handsome with a pleasant smile and candid grey eyes.

"Can I help you?" she asked.

He looked slightly surprised to see her bob up like that. "Yes," he smiled, "I'm looking for a length of tweed to send to the wife of one of my American friends."

"Have you any idea what colour she'd like?" asked Anna.

"Well —" he hesitated. "I'm not quite sure. She's very fair and has blue eyes."

Anna pulled down two rolls of tweed material. "Either of these might do," she said. "This dusty blue is very nice — or, this cream-mixtured tweed. Both are very good quality."

"Yes," he agreed and had just decided on the cream tweed when Claire rushed in.

Anna turned to her. "This gentleman," she began to explain, "wanted to —"

"Yes, *thank* you, Miss Hill," Claire said in a cold, angry voice. *"I'll look after this gentleman, if you please! Go away!"*

Anna bit her lip and turned away but said nothing in front of the customer. She thought angrily — *how dare she order me about in that way. I only served him because she was late — and I helped him to find what he wanted!*

A little later, the man passed by, his material wrapped in a neat parcel, was tucked under his arm. He glanced at her, and seeing her upset expression, he winked encouragingly.

Unhappily Claire noticed the sympathetic exchange. She came up to Anna, hissing angrily: "Keep away, Anna! I'll serve the customers in future — you're only a learner, remember!"

"I know," Anna said quietly, "So shall I leave the customers to form a queue in front of your counter until you get here in the morning?"

Claire was just about to give an angry reply when Mr. McAlister walked into the department. "Just keep your voice down," she muttered to Anna.

Claire's snappiness went on all morning, and Anna, in spite of the interest she felt in learning a new job, began to feel very unhappy. Claire was obviously jealous of her ambition to become a buyer.

Things were no better during the afternoon either. In fact, they were far worse because Mr. McAlister praised Anna and told her that she was making such good progress that she could begin to serve the customers the following morning. However, that same evening, when she and Claire came to add up the money in the till against the bills of sale the till was short of £15!

Claire was furious. "That's what comes of letting learners ring up an item or two. What Mr. McAlister will say I just don't know. But I do know that it's not my fault, so you'd better tell him yourself."

Mr. McAlister was very concerned when Anna told him. He looked at her sternly and said:

"Of course, I know this is only your second day here, Miss Hill, and I'm inclined to believe that the £15 is not missing but that you rung up £15 too much — twice maybe in error. This time, we'll overlook your mistake. But don't let it happen again!"

The morning of her third day at Webber and Nunn's, Anna went to work in a wary mood, nervous that she might unwittingly make other mistakes.

To her surprise and pleasure, her first customer was the man in the bowler-hat whom she had served the day before — at least — was serving when Claire had rushed in to take over. But today, she was permitted to serve customers. It was official.

"Good-morning," she smiled.

He raised his bowler-hat and returned her greeting, adding:

"My sister liked the cream-tweed I bought for my friend's wife yesterday, if you remember? She liked it so much that she asked me to get her a suit length. Is there any left?"

"Yes, sir," said Anna eagerly. She cut him the length he required, wrapped it, took the money, gave him his change and wished him a cheery good-bye. The day had started better than she had anticipated.

A little later, Claire came up, glowering.

"I'm going to lunch at twelve today," she said. "So you'll have to wait until one o'clock before you take your lunch hour."

"All right," Anna said. She didn't mind, but she did find Claire's rude tone somewhat annoying.

Twelve o'clock came round and Claire went off while Anna served the stream of lunch-hour customers.

By one o'clock, Claire was not back and Anna had to stay on feeling emptier and wearier with every passing minute. Mr. McAlister didn't seem to notice that Claire was missing, which was lucky for her, since it was two-thirty when she finally showed up.

"Did old Mac say anything about my not being here?" she asked.

"No," replied Anna.

"Thank goodness. Well, you'd better hop off and have your lunch now."

"But it's long past my time," protested Anna.

"Don't worry. I'll cover for you," said Claire.

Anna walked away, furious with Claire for leaving her all that time. She was tired and hungry and very disgruntled. But there, thought Anna quite suddenly, if you want to become a buyer, you'll have to put up with a little discomfort now and then. Hurriedly she ate her lunch and then went into the Food Hall to get some shopping for her mother, who was in bed with a severe cold. After that, she hurried back to her department.

Her philosophic mood was broken almost at once.

"Miss Hill!" shouted Mr. McAlister, his voice booming in the empty department. "Where have you been? It's well past three o'clock!"

"I've been at lunch," replied Anna timidly.

"Your time is from twelve until one o'clock — not from twelve until three!"

Anna was about to explain what has happened but thought better of it. She could hardly tell him that Claire had got back late as well as herself! No, that's not right, she told herself. *I'm* not back late. This is all Claire's fault. It's a misunderstanding but she couldn't explain it without giving Claire away although Anna thought the girl didn't really deserve to be shielded.

Mr. McAlister continued: "If this happens again, I shall report you. Is that clear?"

Anna nodded and took up her place behind the counter, thinking she might not now have the chance to become a buyer — and all because of Claire!

All that miserable afternoon, Claire kept up her usual trick of barging in front of Anna to serve customers. She ordered Anna about in front of them and interrupted while Anne was helping someone with an order.

Anna longed to go home. At a quarter to six she tidied up in the cloakroom. At five to six she hurried back to the department and at six o'clock she hurriedly flung the dust covers over the display stands and at two minutes past six she was once again hurrying to the cloakroom to collect her bag and shopping basket.

Salesgirls from all departments were there, putting on their hats and coats and seemingly in no hurry to leave. At least, they weren't dashing out as usual for there was a hold up in the passage outside.

"What's up?" Anna asked a girl from the linen department. "What's the big hold up?"

"There are two detectives at the door, searching everyone's baskets and handbags."

"What? Has someone been pilfering from the store?"

"Looks like it."

Anna joined the queue and soon it was her turn to be searched. She emptied out the contents of her handbag and then all her food parcels from her basket. The detectives looked inside each bag and then unwrapped one parcel that Anna didn't remember seeing before.

"*I didn't buy them,*" replied Anna uncertainly. "*I didn't take them. I just don't know how they came to be in my basket.*"

Inside was a length of jersey wool; a tape measure and a large pair of scissors such as are used in dress-making.

"Have you got bills for these, Miss?" enquired the detective.

"No!" declared Anna. "I haven't because I didn't buy them."

"No?" replied the detective. "Then why are you taking them home?"

"I'm not," replied Anna uncertainly. "I — I didn't buy them. I didn't take them. I just don't know how they came to be in my basket."

'I see," said the detective slowly. "Well, I'll just keep them over-night and tomorrow morning, bright and early, you report to me, Miss, and we'll get to the bottom of this as soon as we can. My name's Jenkinson. I'll see you at nine o'clock."

There was a low murmured buzz of conversation as Anna pushed her way down the corridor and made for home.

She didn't tell her parents what had happened. Not feeling able to eat her supper, she went to bed early and lay awake all night, torturing herself with worries and doubts.

The next norning, in Mr. Jenkinson's office, she told her story to the detective and Mr. McAlister and the assistant store manager. Even to her own ears, it sounded so weak to say she had no idea how the goods came to be in her basket. She knew only too well how weak it must sound to them.

She was sent outside the room to wait until they had discussed the matter between themselves.

It seemed like years before she was called back in and told to sit down while the assistant manager spoke for the rest of them.

"I'm sorry, Miss Hill," he began, "but things look pretty black against you. In a sense, you've convinced us of your honesty, but you must understand that when a new employee is found coming out of the store with goods she has not paid for — well, we have no other course but dismissal."

"You're sacking me?" said Anna, hardly able to believe what was happening.

"I'm sorry, yes. We shall not inform the police and we shall not mention this in your reference because we are sure that from the manner in which you told your story, that you are basically honest. We realise this must have been a first and sudden temptation. Nevertheless, I am sure you will see that we cannot possibly keep you on in our employ. Now, I suggest you go back to your department and work for the rest of the week and tell your colleagues on Friday that you are leaving for another kind of job."

Anna said nothing as she got to her feet as if in a trance and left the room.

When she got back to her department, Claire stared at her and said: "You look pale."

Anna gasped as she sat down on her stool while the whole horror of the scene she had been through washed over her.

Very near to tears, she was still sitting on the stool when up came her friendly bowler-hatted customer. He smiled at her as he placed his briefcase on the counter and took from it a piece of yellow silk.

"I wonder if you could suggest a suitable material to go with a blouse of this colour?"

Wearily Anna rose to her feet. "Yes, sir," she said. "I'll do my best."

She found just the right material — a deep amber jersey wool — and was making it into a parcel for him when, quite suddenly, she burst into tears.

He looked at her sympathetically and was about to ask what was wrong when Anna forestalled him.

"Please excuse me," she said, "Miss Holliday will give you your bill."

Anna rushed blindly out of the department and within minutes had managed to control herself.

When she returned to her counter her customer was still in the department, talking to a burly man at the door. Then they both went out.

"So what's all the rushing about for?" asked Claire.

Anna shrugged her shoulders and shook her head, far too upset to tell her troubles to the cold, unsympathetic Claire — or to anyone else for that matter.

Ten minutes later Claire was called to the Superintendent's office, leaving Anna in sole charge.

Half an hour later, Mr. McAlister called to her: "Come with me, Anna. Someone in the office block wants to see you."

As she entered the office, there, behind a large desk sat her friendly "customer" and on the peg behind him hung his familiar bowler-hat.

His smile was a friendly as ever.

"Yes, Anna. I am the new Chief House Detective."

Anna gasped and before she could speak he said:

"And I've got good news for you. We know you didn't make a mistake on your till money. We know you didn't take the materials from your department and we know that you weren't really late back from lunch that time, either."

"Phew!" cried Anna in relief, adding, "But how do you know?"

"We would never have been certain but for one thing — the person who tried to frame you, tried to frame *me,* too! Of course, she had no idea who I was."

"Well, who on earth —?" began Anna.

"Claire Holliday caused all the mischief. She rang up the extra money on your till while you were at tea. She put the material and things into your basket and she even rang us up to suggest that you were stealing from the store. She deliberately came back late from lunch that time to make Mr. McAlister think that *you* were the one to blame, knowing you would not be so disloyal as to involve her in any explanations.

"But why?" asked Anna.

"She was jealous of you. You were popular with the customers and she wasn't. You were training with a view to becoming a buyer — and she wasn't."

"How did you find all this out?" Anna wanted to know.

"She made one mistake too many. Apart from being jealous of your popularity and possible future success — she was jealous of *our* friendly relationship as salesgirl to customer. So, she tried to frame me, too! Her chance came when you burst into tears and left the department. She took the money for the material you had sold me and then phoned for one of the detectives to say that I had not paid! Of course, she had no idea who I was. When that happened, we called her up here and told her what we guessed to be the truth. She broke down and confessed."

"Oh," said Anna and as an after thought she asked, "Am I still sacked?"

"No," grinned her friend, "Your job is quite safe. We hope you will stay with us a long, long time, don't we, Mr. McAlister?"

Mr. McAlister smiled at Anna. "We certainly do," he told her. "I'm sure you'll get your promotions quickly in this firm. You've got the makings of a real buyer. You may well be our Chief Buyer one day!"

Anna could hardly restrain her happiness. "Oh, do you really think so?" she cried. "Oh, I'm so glad."

"Meanwhile, young lady," began Mr. McAlister in mock severity, "You've got a job to do so you'd better get back to your counter. I'll be keeping a close watch on the staff to ensure that in future you are helped and not hindered."

Anna walked back to the department as though she were walking on air. The future looked bright and very promising and Anna felt very happy about it. In the midst of her great happiness, she had a thought for Claire. Poor, unhappy Claire. Anna realised that people as bitter as Claire were always trying to make others bitter too, whereas if only they would try to be cheerful, everyone's lot would be that much better!

HESTER AND THE HIGHWAYMEN

by Nita Nevison

For six months Hester Mayhew and her father had striven to make a success of the Black Dog Inn. But all to no avail. The trouble was the tavern was too far away from the coach road.

"We'll have to sell up and start afresh, maybe in a big town like Portsmouth," said the innkeeper and Hester's heart sank. She loved her life in the New Forest with her faithful ponies.

Then deep in the forest she came across a wounded man.

"Leave off polishing the tankards! They'll not be wanted tonight or any other night for that matter!"

The harsh words echoed under the ancient, smoke–blackened timbers of the Black Dog Inn, situated close to the New Forest. Hester Mayhew, an attractive brown–haired girl, turned to look at her father who had just entered. It was the year 1760 and Hester and her father had run the tavern since the death of Mrs. Mayhew, six months earlier.

"Still no sign of anyone, father?" she asked.

"None!" he grunted, staring through the leaded windows of the small, snug room that looked out across a lonely forest track. "We're

33

too far from the coach route, that's the trouble."

He shrugged. "If things don't improve. I'll be obliged to sell up and start afresh, maybe in a big town like Portsmouth."

"I'll miss the country if we do," Hester said forlornly. "The fresh open air, the forest and . . .

"And your ponies, lass!" Her father's voice was suddenly tender and his arm went around her waist. "I know how you love them and how they trust you in return." He went on with an attempt at cheerfulness. "There now, these are sad topics for a January evening. You said something about going to feed them, nigh on an hour ago."

"I felt I could not go and leave you here by yourself — that is why I delayed," she said.

"You go, my dearest," her father replied. "Happen there'll be snow tonight and we don't want those ponies going hungry if it freezes hard. Take some sacks of hay and load them into the trap."

As she slipped outside, Hester found that her parent's gloom had added to her own wintry mood. She went to the livery stable and with practised hands, harnessed Timothy, the steady reliable old cob, to the shafts of the cart.

"Oh, Timmy," she whispered. "I hope father doesn't have to sell and move. My poor ponies — who will look after them when I've gone?"

Soon the trap was loaded with its six sacks of hay. Hester clicked her tongue to Timothy and with only her mournful thoughts for company, drove off along a rutted track towards the New Forest. The sky was darkening, the air freezing as she urged the cob along at a smart clip, anxious to finish her task and be indoors before the snow caught her halfway.

Before very long, she was followed by half a dozen ponies, ghostly forms who had drifted from the forest. They formed up on either side, trotting to keep pace with the longer strides of the bigger horse.

"As if I'd forget you on a night like this," she chided them. "But where's your leader, Whitey? Perhaps he's waiting at the ruined barn by the clearing. He knows I always stop there."

Suddenly, she gave a gasp and strained her eyes through the gathering gloom. Ahead of her, a man staggered from the shelter of the trees, his head lowered. He waved from side to side, his arms held in a strange way behind his back. She pulled on the reins as he blundered into the side of the cart, recoiled and fell on his face.

"His arms! They're tied behind him!" ran through her mind as she scrambled down from the driving seat.

She turned the man over and from a deathly-pale face, blue eyes blinked open to look into hers.

"Help . . . help me!" The whispered words barely reached her ears. In the cart was a knife used for ripping open the hay sacks and in a trice, she had used it to cut the stranger's bonds. Wincing, he sat up, rubbing fresh life into his cramped wrists. She noticed a large, dark bruise on his forehead.

"I thank you, mistress," he breathed. "I apologise if I startled you, but I was looking for assistance. I was trying to reach the Black Dog Inn hereabouts."

"I come from there! I am the daughter of the landlord!" cried Hester. "But what has happened? Who has tied you up so cruelly?"

"Ben Searle, the highwayman!" the man panted. "My name is Dick King of the London Bow Street Runners. I trailed Searle and his gang to their meeting place in a ruined barn yonder. I managed to overhear their plans to rob the west bound coach in an hour's time. Thinking I was unobserved, I backed away, fell and twisted my ankle." He shook his head as if to ward off an upleasant memory. "They heard and were on me in a flash — three of them. When I came to my senses, I was tied by a thong to a tree outside the barn. They hadn't tied me up very well and at last I managed to wriggle free and set out to find help," he continued. "We have to warn the coach before Searle and his men carry out their plans!"

He got to his feet, only to reel against the trap as his injured ankle gave way.

"You must rest in the cart," Hester said firmly. "I will drive towards the coach road and alert the driver."

"I fear . . . we . . . may already be too . . ." the Runner's voice tailed off as he clambered painfully into the cart. With a groan, he fell forward and fainted, his face pressed into one of the sacks.

Hester made him as comfortable as she could and looked wildly around, her mind racing.

"I will get him to the barn first and there decide what is best to be done!" she thought.

She shook up the reins and with the ponies keeping pace, she reached the clearing, the barn looming up on her left.

Only yards away, a branch cracked!

Her head swung towards the sound. A dim shape appeared and then another. Hester uttered a gasp of relief. The rest of her beloved ponies had arrived at the place where so often in the past she had fed them. Heading the small herd was her own favourite, Whitey,. so-called from the streak of white running down his muzzle. He lifted one hoof as if in greeting.

"There's no time to feed you just now," she explained breathlessly. "Some highwaymen are going to hold up the coach and . . ." A snowflake fell on the back of her hand and she realised that the snow, so long delayed, was upon them.

Hester's mouth set in a firm line. Dick King was better where he was and it was up to her to take on his role. She led Timmy under the shelter of the barn and tied him to a pole.

"I'll take Timmy and try to reach the coach before Searle and his rascals," she told the pony. "You'll look after him, won't you, Whitey?"

It might have been her imagination, but her favourite seemed to nod his head up and down. Together he and the rest of the shaggy troupe crowded into the barn and gathered about the cart. Hester hastily released Timmy from between the shafts. The snow had now begun to fall thickly and quietly. As a last thought, she picked up Dick King's cocked hat and cloak and donned both of them for warmth and protection.

Mounting Timmy, she nudged him outside. She looked back once to see the ponies crouched around the cart where the wounded man lay.

"He'll be safe until I get back, whenever that will be!" she thought.

The snow fell ever thicker, but in her journeys with the ponies, the girl had come to know every inch of the New Forest. She made good time along paths untouched as yet by the downpour and shortly came out on the main highway.

"I'll make for the cross-roads," she thought. "That ought to be a good place to hail the coach!"

It was Timmy who saw the danger first and not Hester, with her head bowed against the blinding wall of white flecks. He stopped abruptly and the girl saw that she was too late! Ben Searle and his band had already struck!

The coach was 50 yards off, its side lanterns burning. Two burly figures stood beside it with a line of passengers, faintly seen, their hands in the air. Timmy had spied a third man standing back from the

Two burly figures stood beside the coach with a line of passengers, their hands in the air.

others, holding the reins of three horses. The soft snow had muffled her mount's hooves so that they had almost blundered into the group. As one of the horses whickered softly, the man looked over his shoulder, showing her his startled face.

His hand groped beneath his cloak and came up with a pistol. Hester's heart seemed to rise into her throat with sheer fright. Instinctively, she kneed Timmy forward and the horse reared, its fore feet flailing. An iron-shod hoof caught the highwayman a glancing blow on his head and he fell heavily, dropping his weapon. Hester leaped from her saddle, snatched up the pistol and made a grab for the trailing reins of the horses. But they backed away and she was forced to follow, clicking her fingers and hoping that the other two highwaymen would not look around.

She set her foot on a trailing rein and bent to gather the other two. Then a hoarse voice shouted:

"Jem! What are you doing, matey? Catch hold!"

As she glanced from beneath the brim of her cocked hat, a small, laden sack sailed towards her and landed at her feet.

"We'll be off in a minute, now that the pigeons are plucked!" came the raucous tones.

Thanks to the hat and cloak, the thieves had taken her for their companion. But her disguise was short-lived. From behind her, the highwayman who had been guarding the horses had recovered. She saw him plunging through the snow, waving one arm.

"Ben! Arty! It's a girl! Stop her!"

His bull-like bellow brought the two men to the alert. They raced towards her, shouting with rage. Then from behind the guard, Timmy made a rush and charged into the man, knocking him on his face in the snow.

Hester shouted and yelled at the other horses which backed and scattered in three different directions. She held the bag in one hand and snatched at Timmy's mane with the other. She swung herself on to his back and jerked his head away from the stationary coach and the furious bandits. Timmy stretched his legs as if recognising the need for instant flight.

A pistol cracked dully and Hester felt, rather than heard, the bullet whistle over her head. Then the darkness and the snow swallowed them up. Behind her, she heard the bandits whistling to their mounts and an outbreak of cries.

"She's got the blunt! She's getting away with it!"

"Then what dolt gave it to her?"

"Stop squabbling! Find the horses and give chase!"

As soon as those rascals have recovered their horses they'll be able to follow our tracks before the snow can fill them in!

These were Hester's rapid thoughts as Timmy ploughed through the snow.

"I must get back to Dick King!" she said aloud. "At least there's safety in numbers — if I can find him, that is!"

Because of the darkness, she would have galloped past the barn, but for a welcoming whinny from Whitey who came trotting out to meet her. Behind him, limped the still dazed figure of the Bow Street Runner, a hand to his head.

In a few quick sentences, Hester explained her adventures and handed him the pistol. But half-stunned as he was, he did not seem to grasp what to do next.

"We . . . we could leave under cover of the snow," he said, his voice stumbling on the words. "But we might bump into them and then . . ."

"There is a way!" Hester interrupted. "If we work quickly, we may manage to bluff them and win clear!"

She ran to the cart and lugged out the sacks of hay.

"Whitey!" she called. "I want you to carry this on your back — just for a little while. If you do it, the others won't mind. Over here, boy!"

The animal stood patiently and with the aid of some short lengths of rope from the cart, Hester was able somewhat clumsily to secure the sack to his back. Dick, imitating her example, did the same with five more ponies. He was chuckling to himself as he worked for he had understood Hester's plan.

"Now clap your hat on top of one sack while I drape your cloak around another!" Hester said tensely. "Hurry! They'll be upon us any moment!"

Even as she spoke, three horsemen appeared through the swirling flakes on the edge of the clearing. The leader pointed and shouted at his confederates. It was then that Hester in the lead with Dick just behind her, burst from the barn. Dick waved the pistol on high and behind them followed what looked, in the snowy murk, like six mounted riders on sturdy ponies. The highwaymen came to a sliding halt, their courage rapidly fading.

"She's led us into an ambush!"

"It's a plant, lads! Better lose the loot than our lives!

As the cavalcade closed on the brigands, Dick fired his pistol and the threatening hum of the bullet decided the highwaymen. They wheeled and putting spurs to their steeds, vanished into the trees.

Hester, breathless and excited, pulled Timmy to a stop and dropped the rope on which she had been leading the other ponies.

She broke into a merry laugh.

"Just as well they broke when they did!" she cried. "Another few seconds and they would have guessed!"

Already the sacks were awry on the backs of the ponies, one trailing in the snow, another dragging at the heels of a second.

"Mistress Hester, you are a marvel!" commented Dick admiringly as he helped the inn keeper's daughter to dismount. "You did the work I should have done and you did it well!"

"But my task is not finished yet," said Hester reprovingly. "Those poor ponies haven't had their hay and that is what I set out to do!"

The coach passengers were delighted to have their stolen property restored and lost no time in telling of their adventures when they reached the next stop. Dick King put in a full report to his superiors, stressing the courage of the young girl and soon Hester found herself the heroine of the area. Ballads were written about her exploit and broadsheets were printed, telling — THE TRUE AND FAITHFUL HISTORY OF HOW YOUNG HEROIC HESTER MAYHEW OF THE BLACK DOG INN, NEAR THE NEW FOREST, DID PUT TO FLIGHT THE VILLAINOUS HIGHWAYMEN, BEN SEARLE AND HIS BLOOD-THIRSTY GANG OF RUFFIANS!"

People came from near and far to catch a glimpse of the famous Hester and for Mr. Mayhew there was no more talk of shifting to Portsmouth. He had quite enough to do coping with the extra trade and telling enquirers:

"Well, now, if you want to see my Hester, you'll have to wait a bit. She's off feeding those blessed ponies of hers!"

NINE WEEKS' WONDER

From out of savage Africa, where she had spent her life on a big game reserve, came high-spirited Andrea Landen. She was looking forward to her new role as a schoolgirl at Baronscourt.

But Andrea's amazing talents and uncanny ways completely baffled the other girls. Truly, never before had they ever met such a strange and intriguing person.

I'll admit I wasn't in the best of tempers as I walked to the station that day. For one thing it was raining hard. And for another . . .

"Why can't new girls arrive on the first day of term?" I grumbled. "If they come a day or two later it means that some honest hard-working schoolgirl like me has to take time off to go and meet them. Drat it!"

Anyway, there was no difficulty in picking out Andrea Landen when the train rolled in. She was wearing our Baronscourt green kit, carrying a tennis racquet in one hand and a kitbag in the other. Blonde hair hung to her shoulders, her face was suntanned — and at sight of me she fairly galloped down the platform.

"Andrea? I'm Judy West. Welcome to Baronscourt —"

"Gosh! Am I glad to be here!" she exclaimed, hardly giving me time to utter my little speech of welcome. "And what a gorgeous day, too! I hope it's a good long walk to the school. When I was abroad I loved walking in the rain, it's so clean and fresh and —"

"Well, I'm sorry to disappoint you," I said as I steered her towards

41

the exit. "But rain in England is different from rain abroad. It's inclined to be wet and to trickle down the back of your neck. So I'm afraid I've booked the station taxi to run us out to the school."

I was trying to be sarcastic, but it was no use. You just couldn't get peeved with Andrea — at least *I* couldn't. Most new girls are naturally a bit subdued, but Andrea seemed just gloriously happy to have arrived.

"You've got your own swimming pool, haven't you?" she chattered as the taxi trundled on its way. "And of course you play tennis and hockey at the school . . . What about athletics? Have you a decent track? And netball, riding, lacrosse?"

"Hey, steady on!" I grinned. "You'll find out in good time. Meanwhile I'd better break the news that you're sharing a study with me, as my old study-mate left last term."

"Lovely! Couldn't be nicer!" she beamed.

A sudden rain squall lashed the taxi as it turned into Waggoners Lane.

It was then that I noticed a change in Andrea — difficult to describe, but a sort of tenseness came over her. She leant forward and called to the driver.

"Stop, please. Stop!"

The taxi jolted to a halt. Mr. Scarfe, the driver — an old pal of mine — looked over his shoulder.

"Anything wrong, miss?"

Andrea was already opening the door.

"Well — er — I thought I heard a call from that cottage over there. Perhaps someone needs help. Wait here — I shan't be a second."

The cottage gate was only a few yards away. Blonde hair gleaming in the rain, Andrea charged through it, ran like a flash up the garden path and vanished somewhere round the back.

I half-rose to my feet.

"Perhaps I'd better go after her, but — honestly — I didn't hear a thing."

"I shouldn't worry, miss," Mr. Scarfe said. "I happen to know the folks who live in that cottage and they're both out all day working in the town so there's nobody there. That new chum of yours must have been mistaken."

We waited a couple of minutes, while the rain pelted down. Then Andrea appeared again, loping up the garden path.

"Who said English rain wasn't lovely?" she laughed.

"Glad you enjoyed it," I replied as the taxi moved on. "But what did you find? Mr. Scarfe and I didn't hear a thing and there's no one at the cottage in the daytime. Were you mistaken?"

"Oh, well, not exactly. A little spot of bother which I was able to put right."

"Spot of bother? For goodness sake, Andrea, what on earth do you mean?"

"Don't worry, Judy," she said. "I want to concentrate on getting my first view of Baronscourt, so please — please — don't interrupt!"

That was all I could get out of her. She started craning out of the window, evidently dying to catch a first glimpse of her new school.

The rain had eased up and there was a gleam of sunshine. I must admit the school buildings did look rather impressive as we saw them from the top of Waggoners Lane against the dark pine trees beyond. Andrea gazed, thrilled beyond measure.

As I expected, in those first few days she took to school life as a duck takes to water.

I'm not specially athletic myself, but rumours of Andrea's prowess soon started floating around. It was said she'd already knocked a second and a half off the school's record for the 220 yards backstroke, and within a week she had beaten Susan Perry, our top tennis girl.

And she was the nicest, friendliest person to share a study with.

I'd almost forgotten that odd incident during the taxi ride when, about a fortnight later, something else happened — even odder.

We were walking down one of the corridors together. Andrea chatting happily as usual.

"Believe it or not, I'm in the school's first swimming team," she told me. "Imagine — swimming for Baronscourt! I've already written to Daddy to tell him the good news. He'll be as thrilled as I am, and —"

Suddenly she put a hand on my arm and stopped short. Glancing at her, I saw on her face that same tense expression I'd noticed in the taxi.

Before I could stop her, she had swerved to one side and tapped on a study door bearing the words "Miss Miriam Rapp."

Miss Rapp is our history mistress. When I tell you that, even in her sunnier moments, her temper is not unlike that of a grizzly bear with the toothache, you'll understand how startled I was.

"Andrea —!" I hissed.

But already a sharp voice had called "Come in!" and Andrea had stepped into the study, leaving the door partly open behind her.

"Well, girl, what is it? As you see, I'm busy."

Andrea's glance had turned to where, in a cage by the window, a green and scarlet parrot was rocking solemnly on his perch.

"I'm so sorry to interrupt," she said, "but I'm afraid your parrot isn't happy."

"WHAT?"

If you think I'd politely moved away so as not to overhear what was going on, I'm afraid you'd be wrong. I was rooted to the spot!

"Your parrot is rather distressed," the amazing Andrea went on. "He's not showing it outwardly at the moment, but — ah, I see! There's an old cage here and he's now in a new, larger cage. That might be the reason — in fact, I'm sure it is —"

Miss Rapp had risen to her feet.

"Never, in all my experience as a teacher," she said icily, "have I met with such brazen impertinence as this."

"But, Miss Rapp —"

"SILENCE! You, a new girl who has never set eyes on my parrot before, have the effrontery to march in here and tell me how to treat a bird I have kept in perfect health for two years. GET OUT!"

"I feel sure you'll find that —"

"OUT"

Andrea left, closing the door quietly behind her.

"Sorry about that, Judy."

"Sorry! It's a wonder you got out of there alive," I told her, as we walked on. "Bearding Rapp in her den is about as dangerous as dancing a jig on an unexploded bomb. And anyway, she was quite right, you know. You've never set eyes on her parrot before, so how could you tell it was unhappy?"

She put an arm round my shoulder.

"Forget it, Judy," she said.

That was all I could get out of her, but three days later that startling incident was followed by an even more startling sequel.

Our form mistress had asked me to return a book she had borrowed for Miss Rapp. As I neared the study door it opened and a bearded man in tweeds stepped out, talking to Miss Rapp. The tweedy man was, I knew, our local vet.

"Parrots are queer birds in some ways," he was saying. "Even giving them a different-coloured drinking cup can upset them. The reason why poor old Pompey has turned so mopey is, I feel sure, the new cage. Medicine won't help. I can only suggest that you put him back in the old cage."

I could see Miss Rapp was shaken — and so was I.

Andrea had been right! She'd known that Pompey was unhappy in his cage!

I tried to tackle her about it at dinnertime, but I might have saved my breath. She was bubbling over with the news that she'd been chosen as our backstroke swimmer in the big match against Redbridge Grammar.

Then, the following afternoon — another odd little happening.

I was in the town buying films for my camera when I spotted Mr. Scarfe on a taxi tank. He beckoned me across.

"Remember that ride in the rain with your new chum the other day, miss?" he asked. "Funny thing, but I was talking to Mrs. Thornton who lives in the cottage we stopped at. She told me that on that particular day she'd forgotten to shut her pet rabbit in its hutch — she'd left it to scamper around the garden. But, strange to say, when she got home she found the bunny safely shut in the hutch — and what's more, her husband noticed the paw-marks of a fox under the hedge. If some kind person hadn't shut the rabbit up, he'd have made a fox's dinner for sure."

Mr. Scarfe grinned.

"Know what I was thinking?" he chuckled. "That new girl of yours said she heard a call for help. You don't think she heard the rabbit calling that a fox was after it, do you?"

We both laughed at the idea, but as I walked on, I wasn't so sure.

If she could tell through a closed door that a parrot was feeling unhappy, perhaps —

"Oh, come off it!" I told myself. "You're getting fanciful notions about Andrea. She's an amazing girl — and one of the nicest you've ever met — but she isn't a magician!"

When I returned to school I ran into Carol Harper, our swimming captain. She was looking vaguely worried.

"Judy, I wish you'd have a word with that study mate of yours," she said. "She's a real bombshell of a swimmer — a marvellous addition to the team — and I don't want her to get into trouble through breaking school rules. She might be banned from one of our matches, which would be a disaster."

Carol was called away before she could explain, and I spoke to Andrea about it over our study tea.

"Breaking rules?" she murmured. "Oh, she was probably thinking of last night. One of the prefects caught me at the far end of Long Meadow just after midnight. It was nothing really."

"Just after midnight! But why — ?"

Andrea jumped to her feet, drinking off her cup of tea.

"As I say, it was nothing," she said hastily. "The Head keeps her horse in a stable down there, as you know, and a strange cat had got in and was upsetting him. Just a spot of bother, but I sorted it out. And now, Judy, I've got swimming practice, and if I don't fly I'll be late. 'Bye!"

A spot of bother in the stable — at midnight! I was more mystified than ever. And then, about a week later, came the amazing affair of Waggoners Folly . . .

Once a week I have to go into the town for a special violin lesson with Professor Harschmann. Not bad really, because it means missing most of the ordinary morning classes. I take my time getting back, usually strolling through the wood if it's fine.

It was as I stood on the woodland path, watching a pair of squirrels frisking about, that I heard the kitten mewing.

Pushing my way through a clump of bushes, I found myself quite close to Waggoners Folly — an old ivy-covered tower that has stood for centuries in the wood, about half a mile from the school. Twenty feet up, a kitten was clinging to the ivy, mewing frantically for help.

As I've said before, I'm not really the athletic type and I could no more have climbed up the ivy than flown to the moon. But I saw there was a narrow slit-like window close to where the kitten was stuck.

"If I can get up inside . . ."

The doorway gaped wide open and beside it was a weatherbeaten notice: THE STONE STEPS IN THIS TOWER ARE DANGEROUS. DO NOT CLIMB.

Actually I knew that several girls from the school, for a dare, had climbed the crumbling stone steps that circle up the inside wall. If I could clamber up, I reckoned I could reach the kitten.

Keeping close to the wall, my knees about as steady as a lemon jelly, I climbed up. There had once been a balustrade along the inner edge of the steps, but much of it had broken away and it was rather like climbing up an eighteen-inch ledge on the face of a cliff.

However, I reached the window — and I even managed to grab the kitten.

And then . . .

Well, I won't tell you what happened then. Instead, I'll describe what had been happening in 5B classroom at Baronscourt a little while before.

It's a ground-floor classroom and Class 5B were having French with Miss Channing. Andrea's desk was by an open window.

Lynne Trevor was sitting next to Andrea and she told me afterwards she noticed the odd tense expression that suddenly came over Andrea's face.

"Miss Channing! I'm sorry, I'll have to go — I'll have to get out to the woods over there —"

"Andrea! Stop!"

Miss Channing might as well have shouted at a shooting star. Andrea streaked over the grass with the whole class watching her, clambered over the boundary wall — and vanished!

Meanwhile, I was feeling just about as scared as I've ever felt in my life. Seconds after I'd grabbed the kitten, about ten of the stone steps below me collapsed with an echoing thud into the base of the tower, leaving a yawning gap. Like a fly on a wall I stood and shivered, clasping the kitten — unable to go down and too scared to climb up. My throat was so dry I couldn't even shout for help.

How long I stayed like that I'll never know, but at last — with a gasp of relief — I realised that someone had entered the base of the tower.

I could hardly believe my eyes.

"Andrea!" I croaked. "It's me, Judy, up here with a kitten. The steps have collapsed!"

"I thought there was trouble . . . Hold on, I may be able to get to you from above."

She did, too. She had already noticed a tree with a spreading branch passing close to the tower-top. She climbed the tree, wrenched up an ancient trap-door in the flat tower roof, and helped me squeeze through with the kitten. Climbing down the tree wasn't too bad after that.

"Splendid!" Andrea beamed.

"Splendid? I should jolly well say it was," I gasped. "You probably saved my life, not to mention the kitten's. But — how did you get here? Weren't you having French with Miss Channing?"

"I was, but I had a sudden urge for the wide open spaces," Andrea said, cuddling the kitten as we started back to school. "Miss C. wasn't too pleased when I hared out through the open window."

"You mean you left the class and made a bee-line for the tower?" I exclaimed. "Then you must have known, somehow, that I needed help! I didn't even call out, I was too darned scared, and yet . . ."

"Let's call it luck, Judy," she said. "It was lucky that I happened to be around."

That was all I could get her to say. Just as on those previous puzzling occasions she wouldn't explain.

Of course there was trouble when we got back. A prefect was posted at the school entrance and Andrea was told to report to the headmistress at once. I went with her, determined to make clear just how brave she had been at the tower.

She didn't get much of a rocket, but I could tell that the Head was worried about her. After all, there had been the previous occasion when she had been found wandering around the grounds after midnight.

"You must try to settle down, my dear," Miss Hamilton told her.

"But of course! It's what I want to do more than anything else, Miss Hamilton," Andrea beamed. "Settle down here at Baronscourt just like a normal everyday schoolgirl."

It must have been a couple of weeks later when I heard staggering news.

As I've said, I'm not the athletic type. I didn't attend the Baronscourt-Redbridge swimming match because I had some special music to practise. It was Lynne Trevor who told me about it.

"I'm afraid that study mate of yours has really blotted her copybook this time," she told me.

"At the match? Didn't she win?"

"She didn't even turn up — at least not till the backstroke race was over," Lynne said. "She had some garbled tale about having had to answer a call for help, but wouldn't explain how or why. Carol was so furious she scratched her from the relay race at the end. I doubt if she'll ever be asked to swim for the school again."

Knowing how thrilled Andrea had been at the prospect of taking part in the match, I was really shaken.

And when I went upstairs to our study . . .

"Andrea!"

She was sitting at the table, her blonde head pillowed on her arms, her shoulders quivering.

"Oh, Andrea, don't cry," I pleaded. "I'm sure you never meant to let the school down. If only you could have explained, Carol and the others would have understood. But you seem to surround yourself with these odd little mysteries . . ."

She shook her head.

"It's no use," she whispered. "I've written to Daddy — he'll understand. I don't think I'll ever do what I wanted to do, settle down here at Baronscourt like everybody else —"

"Of course you will! You were all set to become one of the most popular girls in the school. Andrea, do sit up and take notice!"

But she still kept her head down and her shoulders were still shaking.

It was some time after this that Pietro's Circus paid its annual visit to a site near the school. A party of us had booked to see the show, in charge of Miss Channing. Andrea wasn't with us; she hadn't seemed interested and perhaps she still felt she was under a shadow because of the swimming match incident.

We were in the front row. The first part of the show was over and now they'd erected the big cage for the top-line act: JASON AND HIS JUNGLE LIONS.

A drum was beating and the audience sat in shadow while all the lights were centred on the ring. It's always a thrill when the tawny animals bound up the tunnel into the cage, roving around and snarling while the drums beat louder. One of them, I noticed, was quite the biggest lion I've ever seen.

Outside the cage the ringmaster was introducing the act.

"Ladies and gentlemen! Jason and his lions!"

A thunderous roar came from the big lion as it crouched low, lashing its tail. Two uniformed attendants prepared to slide back the door of the cage so that Jason could enter. The drums rose to a crescendo . . .

"STOP!"

A girl's voice rang out. As Jason prepared to enter the cage, a girl

Before the startled audience Andrea slipped into the cage while attendants rushed up with iron bars.

darted forward.

"Don't go in there — stay out! You'll be in danger!"

We gaped, completely dumbfounded, and Miss Channing half rose to her feet. The girl was Andrea, the spotlights shining on her blonde hair as she seemed to be arguing with the ringmaster.

I suppose Miss Channing felt responsible for the behaviour of a Baronscourt girl, for she actually stepped out into the ring, helping the ringmaster to draw Andrea back into the shadows, close to us.

"Stop him!" Andrea was still pleading. "Don't let him go in with the big lion Simba —"

Miss Channing had caught hold of her arm.

"Calm yourself, Andrea! You're hysterical," I heard her say.

Perhaps the rest of the audience thought it was all part of the show. At any rate, all eyes were fixed on Jason as he stepped into the cage, cracking his whip.

In response to his command the lions, one by one, leapt on to their pedestals — all except Simba.

A woman in the audience screamed. Attendants rushed forward. I felt almost sick with horror, for the huge tawny beast had sprung, throwing Jason to the ground and standing over him, fangs close to his throat.

Somehow Andrea dodged away from those who were holding her. Before the startled audience, she slipped through the entrance into the cage, while attendants rushed up with iron bars.

I could only gaze, spellbound. I saw Andrea raise her arm and utter a strange, piercing cry. Then she walked steadily forward and rested a hand on the lion's mane.

The great beast lifted his head, suddenly calm. The trainer, still unhurt, rolled away and struggled to his feet.

Not a sound broke the silence in the Big Top as the blonde girl stood quietly beside the lion while Jason slipped out from the cage. Andrea bent down, seeming to speak to Simba, and then she too quietly walked out into the ring.

"So that's what it was," Andrea said. "It was the smell of tobacco that upset Simba."

She was holding the trainer's gold and scarlet coat, and she sniffed at it again.

"It's quite strong — and many lions hate tobacco scent." She looked towards Jason who was standing near her. "Surely you've never worn this before?"

"You're right, miss, I never have," he replied. "Earlier in the day someone upset a pot of paint over my own jacket and I borrowed this one. I don't smoke myself and I never gave a thought to the tobacco scent. It's lucky for me you realised Simba was upset, miss."

"But I don't understand!"

It was Miss Channing who spoke.

We were behind the scenes at the circus, after the show — not only our little crowd from Baronscourt, but the ringmaster and some of the circus people, as well as a few lingering members of the audience.

"I don't understand," the mistress repeated, "what brought you to the circus in the first place, Andrea? You seemed to rush in, knowing what was wrong, but — how?"

It was a question most of us were asking and Andrea smiled a trifle wanly.

"Well I suppose I'd better explain," she said. "About six hundred people saw what happened just now, so there's no point in trying to keep it secret.

"And it's really so simple," she went on. "Daddy is warden of a big game reserve in Kenya and I was brought up there. I learnt about animals from Daddy — and from a wise old African who used to take me for trips into the bush when I was just a toddler. Gradually I developed a kind of sixth sense where animals are concerned."

She gave me a flash of her old happy grin.

"I know Judy was puzzled several times," she said. "But when an animal or bird is in distress or pain or danger, it throws out some kind of vibrations which I can pick up . . . That's what brought me to the tower, Judy, because I sensed a kitten in danger. That's what made me late for the swimming match, because I sensed a dog was being ill-treated in a back street. And that's what brought me to the circus tonight. I knew a lion was troubled . . ."

A brilliant flash dazzled our eyes. Then another.

"Back a little, folks, so that I can get a side view of her. Splendid!"

It was Rob Stevens, a local reporter, camera in hand.

"What a story!" he grinned. "This is too good for the local paper — this is going straight to the big dailies. Can't you see the headlines, folks? 'SCHOOLGIRL SPEAKS WITH ANIMALS' — 'BLONDE FIFTH-FORMER SAVES LION-TAMER.' It'll be the scoop of the year!"

In his excitement he grabbed Andrea's hand.

"Honey! Your fortune's made," he exclaimed. "The piece I'll wire to Fleet Street tonight will put you on the map for good and all. You'll have the TV people after you tomorrow, the Sunday papers, the book publishers . . . There'll be film producers queueing to sign you up and — heck, I must rush!"

He went off at the run and Andrea caught my eye.

"When I had a spell at school on the Continent it was just the same," she said. "I didn't try to keep it a secret there and I became a kind of nine days wonder. Daddy understood that here at Baronscourt I wanted to make my way just like any other schoolgirl. Well, I've been here just nine weeks, and if I stay on I'll have people pointing at me in the streets as the girl who speaks to animals, and reporters chasing after me — I'll become a kind of publicity gimmick. Daddy's going back to Africa after a spell of leave the day after tomorrow and he agrees it's best I go back with him, much as I've loved it here."

"Oh, Andrea — no!"

The cry of protest came from me, but in my heart I knew it was no use. Nothing any of us could find to say made Andrea budge from her decision.

There was a big crowd to see her off at the station.

Only a few short weeks ago I'd met her there on that rainy day, bounding towards me, waving her racquet. And now . . .

"A most remarkable girl," a voice said at my side.

Turning my head, I was amazed to see Miss Rapp.

"Quite remarkable," she muttered, as the guard's whistle shrilled out. "Some of us may not have appreciated her as we should, but I think we can say that a rather wonderful person has been at Baronscourt. We are not likely to see anyone like Andrea Landen here again."

Strange to say, I think Miss Rapp was expressing what we were all feeling as we waved and cheered towards that blonde head craning out of the window.

Though I had a lump in my throat, perhaps I was feeling a little different from the others. You see, the previous evening Andrea and her father had invited me to spend a long safari holiday with them next summer — a prospect which thrilled me to the core.

So if it's possible to feel sad and happy at the same time, that's how I felt as the train carried Andrea away from Baronscourt.

THE ASSIGNMENT

by Felice Abbott

Sue's father had her future already mapped out for her. She was to be a school-teacher. But Sue's heart craved for adventure and she longed to be a newspaper reporter.

"I have to go away for a month," her father told her. "Prove to me during that time that you'd make a good journalist and you can go ahead with your plans to become one."

Nothing loath, Sue set to work. But her ambition was to lead her into great peril.

"Oh, Daddy, I would make a rotten teacher! I would much rather be a newspaper reporter," Sue pleaded with her father, who was doing his best to persuade her to apply for entrance to a teacher training college.

"Well, I'll tell you what we'll do," he said. "I have to go away on business for a month. If you can prove to me by the time I get back that you are suited to be a journalist, you can go ahead with your plans to become one."

"Oh, thank you, Dad." Sue hugged him delightedly. "I'm sure I can do it."

"There are a few ideas I would suggest," continued her father, "which will keep you busy for a month."

Sue grimaced. Her father could be a hard task-master at times.

"Firstly," her father went on, "you can try your shorthand out by making a report of a meeting. Then you can interview a celebrity — I don't mind who it is. Next, write a column for women readers, and then find a story for yourself before the newspapers get on to it. I think that will be enough."

Sue set to work with a will. She began by phoning the editor of the local newspaper, asking him if he would give her a few hints. This he good-naturedly did and, after giving him her name and address, Sue ran off, eager to start on her four tasks.

For her report, she went to a meeting about the preservation of the village windmill. Then, luckily for her, a famous pianist who was visiting the town, agreed to give her an interview.

By this time she was well into the third week of her father's absence.

"Now for my women's column!' she decided.

She attended a mannequin parade and made notes on the fashions for the coming season. "And," Sue admitted to her mother, "it was great fun to write up."

It was only when she was ready to tackle her last test that she encountered trouble. Try as she would, she could not find a single story that was not already covered by the local newspaper. What could she do now?

"Oh, dear!" Sue worried. "I simply mustn't fall down on this last test. Daddy will be back some time tomorrow, so I shall have to find a story today!"

It was a Saturday, fortunately, which meant that Sue had more time to look. As she set off early to buy the weekend joint for her mother, she searched her mind once again for a likely place to obtain a story.

After leaving the butcher's, she wandered on to the public library. Perhaps she would come across something there which would give her an idea, she thought vaguely. She went into the reference section first. But to her disappointment, she couldn't find a single item which might be worked into a topical story. Sighing deeply, she replaced the books on the shelf.

She had just finished when the door was flung open and a young woman who had taken out a pile of books came rushing back in again.

"My Tony's disappeared!" she cried. "I left him playing outside with his older brother and sister, but now he's nowhere to be seen! Oh, dear! Wherever can he have gone?"

"What is he wearing?" asked Sue promptly. "I'll help you look for him."

"Oh — er — a red jersey and blue trousers," said the mother distractedly.

"That should be easy to spot," said Sue. "You go that way and I'll look down here."

The woman rushed down the street. Then Sue went in search of the little boy, while the older children made their way home in case he should turn up there. Sue ran quickly until she came to a side street. Glancing down the full length of it, she could just make out a patch of red and blue at the other end.

She raced down the street at full speed, but, almost immediately, the blob of red and blue vanished from sight. Sue ran faster than ever, and soon found herself alongside some tall hoardings which had been erected around a very old building. *Danger! Demolition Work — Keep Out!* read a large notice. Horrified, Sue realised that the toddler must have squeezed through a small gap where some planks had been broken.

"Well, I can't stop to tell anyone because there's nobody in sight. I'll just have to go in after him," she decided, after one glance up the deserted road. Thankful that she was slim and wearing only a thin sweater and jeans, she managed to wriggle her way through the little hole. Then she swiftly straightened up and looked round. For a few seconds, all she could see was a broken-down old building in the midst of a pile of rubble and some machinery, standing idle — but there was no sign of any workmen.

"Oh, of course — it's lunch time! And the men might not be back for another hour! I must find that little boy before he comes to any harm."

Starting to explore gingerly around the buildings, she suddenly saw the boy scrambling like a monkey up a flight of stairs which was open to the outside.

"Tony! Come down, there's a good boy!" she called, trying hard to keep the fear from her voice. "You might fall and get hurt. Besides, your Mummy's looking for you."

The little boy turned at her voice, and as he looked down from the first floor he suddenly lost his urge for adventure. His face crumpled and he burst into tears.

Sue moved forward, carefully picking her way among the bricks.

Sue suddenly saw the boy scrambling like a monkey on the broken-down old building.

58

"Don't cry!" she called. "Just sit still. I'll come and bring you down." She had scarcely finished speaking, though, when a heavy passing lorry caused the ground to shake. The stairs collapsed, leaving the toddler perched like a terrified kitten on the edge of the floor.

Just then a voice boomed behind Sue: "Hey! What's going on? Didn't you see the notice — it's big enough?" And a burly watchman walked round to face Sue.

Swiftly Sue explained. "So now I'll have to go up and get him. We can't risk another heavy lorry passing."

"Leave that part of it to me, young lady."

"Look," said Sue patiently. "It'll be far less dangerous if I go — after all, I'm much lighter than you."

"Um — you may be right. Well, take care, miss."

"I can go up the back stairs and reach him that way if I'm careful," suggested Sue, and the watchman reluctantly agreed.

The stairs were easy enough to climb, but as Sue crawled along the beams her heart was in her mouth — she could so easily slip over the edge. But eventually she reached the child. Then came an even worse ordeal — getting him down safely.

Talking quietly to him all the time, she pulled him, inch by inch, back along the beams and down the stairs. At last they reached the ground, stumbling over the rubble as speedily as possible. Just as they ran the last few steps to safety, another heavy vehicle, completely ignoring the watchman's gesticulations for him to stop, went thundering past and then, with a tremendous noise, the main chimney stack came crashing down.

Fortunately, Tony had spied the now open gate and continued to run towards the burly watchman, but Sue, just behind, was not quick enough. Some falling bricks caught her a glancing blow on her back and she was thrown forward with some force, her arms twisting beneath her as she fell on some broken bricks. Then she blacked out . . .

By the time Sue recovered consciousness, an ambulance was on its way and she was surrounded by people. Standing talking to the watchman was a young man with a pen and notebook in his hand. On seeing Sue move, he approached her and quietly asked her to tell him all that had happened. Then the ambulance arrived.

"Lie quietly, my dear," advised the ambulance man, "and we'll have you in hospital in a jiffy."

Poor Sue! In addition to the pain, she had suddenly had a terrible thought. This could have been the story she was looking for! And now she couldn't write.

Tears of pain and disappointment pricked the back of her eyes but she swiftly turned her head away. Well, she had done her best. The most important thing was that the mother had her little boy back safe and sound . . .

Sue had to remain in hospital overnight, but she was allowed to go home the following day when both her parents came to fetch her.

"Hallo, pet!" he father greeted her. "Your mother tells me that you haven't quite managed to do all the tests I set you. But never mind," he continued hastily, as he saw her lips quiver. "I had a pleasant surprise last night which more than compensates for your missing contribution. As soon as we get home, I will show you something."

Sue sat in a fever of impatience while her father drove her home. Then he came into the lounge where she was sitting, picked up a newspaper, and placed it on Sue's lap. There, staring up at her, was her own photograph and the heading: *Schoolgirl rescues toddler.*

Her eyes wide with amazement, Sue read the report on her rescue mission.

"Although you didn't actually write it," said her father when she had finished, "the way you described it is quite good enough for me. But we have an even bigger surprise for you. The editor rang up late yesterday afternoon to say that he remembered that it was you who has asked him for advice, and now that he has learnt of all your initiative and perseverance, he would very much like to offer you a job when you leave school . . ."

"Oh!" gasped Sue.

"Do you think you will accept the job?" Sue's father asked with a twinkle in his eye.

There was no need for a reply. Sue's shining eyes spoke plainly enough!

PATTI — HAIRDRESSER AT SEA

At two o'clock the ship was crossing the Equator and pretty Jean Ross had been chosen to play the part of Queen Aphrodite, wife to old King Neptune, at the great ceremony.

Then somebody splashed a sticky grey-white lather over Jean's hair. To Patti Swift, the ship's young hairdresser, ran Jean but the lather was proving impossible to remove.

It looked as though someone else would have to step in for Jean.

"Oh, Jean! What have you done to your hair?" With a gasp, Patti Swift whirled.

She had finished her work for the morning as assistant hairstylist aboard the liner *Ocean Star*. She had been taking off her uniform overall, about to go below to lunch, when a girl had come suddenly into the salon.

It was auburn-haired Jean Ross, the ship's prettiest stewardess. Patti had set and styled Jean's hair only yesterday, in readiness for a special role she was to play aboard ship today.

"Jean! Your hair! What's happened?" Patti cried.

For Jean's hair was splashed all over with a thick, grey-white substance that clung to it in wet streaks.

"It got spilt on me from the top of the companionway," Jean explained, with a rueful little grin. "It's the stuff the boys are mixing for today's King Neptune ceremony —"

"The lather, you mean? The lather for the mock shaving?"

"Yes, that's all, but — but — But I just had to come to you, Patti, because I — I can't get it off!" gasped Jean.

Patti plomped her hastily into a chair, swathing a towel round her shoulders, and bent her head over a gleaming bowl.

Today of all days Jean must look faultless, for she was to be a queen!

Today at two o'clock the ship was crossing the Equator, the high spot of the voyage. With gay tradition King Neptune was to be piped aboard — and Jean had been chosen as his Queen Aphrodite!

"What awful luck, when time's so short!" exclaimed Patti, turning on the steaming hot water and pouring a deep-cleansing liquid shampoo over Jean's hair. "Were the boys fooling around?"

"No. I didn't see them and they didn't see me!" said Jean. "The first thing I knew, something splashed me, and this lather stuff was all over my hair. I was jolly worried when I couldn't get it out!"

Patti kept one eye on the clock as she rubbed the shampoo vigorously into Jean's hair. Time was short, but the task ought not to take long. The "lather" that was used in King Neptune's comic ceremony was quite harmless. It would be great fun to see the boys "shaved" with it before they were given their traditional ducking.

The minutes passed as Patti rubbed and rubbed away and at last Jean's voice came a little anxiously through the clouds of steam.

"You're missing your lunch all through me, Patti. And it'll still take some time for my hair to dry!"

But something more was troubling Patti.

Nothing was happening despite all her rinsing and rubbing. That sticky white lather still clung like gum to Jean's hair.

"I'll have to try a different shampoo," she muttered.

But the hand of the clock crept on, and still she tried shampoo after shampoo without success. Patti was only interrupted at last when another stewardess came hurrying in.

It was Jean's cabin-mate, Sandra Blayne.

"Aren't you ready yet, Jean?" she exclaimed. "The crew have already dressed up King Neptune, and it's time you were changing — Oh, goodness, what's happened?"

Sandra gasped, while Jean told her bleakly how her hair had got into this state.

"Those boys are a nuisance!" frowned Sandra. "I guessed something like this would happen when I saw them fooling around with that lather bucket —"

"It was an accident. But even Patti can't get the stuff out now. You'll have to take my place, Sandra!" sighed Jean.

"Me?" Sandra said quickly.

She flushed pink with excitement. She was a much plainer girl than Jean, and could never have hoped to be elected King Neptune's queen.

"My dress and crown and everything are in our cabin. You'll have to wear them in my place, Sandra," Jean went on in a disappointed voice. "We do know the dress fits you."

"Yes, because I tried it on. But — but can't *anything* be done for your hair?" breathed Sandra.

Patti selected another shampoo. She was not going to be beaten. Hadn't she been trained to tackle every kind of hair problem? She saw this as a challenge.

"What time do the crew want Jean?" she asked now.

"Two o'clock sharp," said Sandra.

"Then please tell them she'll be ready. I'll manage it somehow!" vowed Patti.

It was a reckless promise. It seemed to alarm Sandra more than it did Patti, though. She went quite white, warning Patti that the ship's company would never forgive her if King Neptune were piped aboard without his queen!

"Jean'll be there!" repeated Patti.

A last desperate solution had occurred to her. There must be some reason why this lather clung so immovably to Jean's hair. Was it because it was mixed with something else? With *paint*?

Could the lather have been mixed thoughtlessly, in a bucket already stained with paint?

If so, her problem was solved — there was a remedy!

Leaving Jean with her head dripping over the bowl, Patti raced down the companionway to the ship's paint store.

The storekeeper was about to close up and he eyed her curiously when she burst in.

"Quick — it's urgent — can you let me have a bottle of paint remover?" she asked breathlessly. "Something that won't harm hair or skin?"

The storekeeper's eyes narrowed, and he looked at her even more curiously.

"Did you come here before?" he asked. "Are you the one who's been borrowing my paints without permission?"

"No, of course not!" said Patti.

"H'm! Well, someone has!" he muttered.

He handed her a bottle, and Patti went sprinting back up the endless stairways to the hairdressing salon.

"I don't know where you've been, Patti, but you can't do anything now to my hair — there just isn't time!" Jean said to her in panic. "Do tell Sandra to take my place —"

Swiftly Patti uncorked the bottle of paint remover, sprinkling a few drops into the palm of her hand. "We'll do it yet, Jean!" she said.

Then rapidly she got to work, rubbing the cool, pungent-smelling spirit into Jean's hair, watching hopefully to see the result.

Would it solve her problem?

Would she have Queen Aphrodite ready in time to be piped aboard with her august monarch of the deep, King Neptune?

"Hooray — we're crossing now! Crossing the Line! Where's Neptune?"

Cheers of excitement burst from passengers and crew. All were crowded on the sunny deck of the *Ocean Star*, everyone from captain to cabin-boy. The triumphant hour had arrived.

Flags flying and siren hooting, the breakers foaming at her bows, the great liner was crossing the Equator.

As the din died down, another sound rent the air. The shrill whistling of the bo'sun's pipe.

"King Neptune! Here he comes!"

Patti was jammed close against the deck-rail, watching the arrival with delight.

A bluff, bearded King Neptune with crown and trident came striding up the ship's ladder.

One would never have recognised him as Jerry Brent, a junior officer.

Following him up the ladder came an enchanting Queen Aphrodite, robed in a dress of azure blue, a sparkling little crown on her auburn head.

"It's Jean Ross, our little stewardess! Doesn't she look super!" Patti heard the women passengers saying all around her.

And Jean did indeed look super. Patti gazed in pride and knew that all her efforts had been worth it. Jean's lovely hair was faultless once more. She looked a superb young queen.

"Watch out, you lot. Here's the barber!" laughed all the boys on deck, as a third figure followed behind King Neptune.

Wearing a big moustache and a comic ginger wig, the barber was really cabin-boy Tony Briggs. He carried a large wooden "razor" — and a bucket of foaming lather.

"Ouch!" shuddered Patti, and fixed a wary eye on that bucket. It had caused trouble enough!

"Listen to me, you unworthy mortals!" boomed Neptune, as he and his queen mounted to their thrones on deck. "I am the Ruler of the Deep, and none may cross this line without obeying my commands! Every man or boy who has not crossed before must be lathered and shaved and ducked," he commanded. And there were other mysterious fates in store for the women and girls.

"Keeping us guessing, eh?" chuckled Patti, still keeping a wary distance from the barber's bucket.

She roared with laughter now, for one by one the boys were scrambling forward gleefully — to kneel before King Neptune while the barber daubed their faces with mopfuls of that awful lather!

"Don't let it get in your hair!" she gasped, but her words were drowned in the hilarity.

Each boy was "shaved" with the barber's wooden razor, then given a skilful prod with Neptune's trident.

Splosh! And they went toppling into the swimming-pool one after the other.

The fun grew fast and furious, and Patti was dangerously close to that lather bucket when King Neptune commanded, by way of a change, that his girl subjects must now meet their fate.

Patti was the first one seized.

"Hey, Jean —" she gasped, as the barber hauled her up to the throne.

But she needn't have worried. King Neptune only wanted her to pay a forfeit.

"You know this mortal? What can she do?" he asked his queen.

"She's a marvellous hairdresser —" said Jean.

"Anything else?"

"Yes, she's a jolly good dancer."

"Ah, that's it!" And he turned solemnly to Patti. "For your forfeit, I command that you now dance the sailor's hornpipe!"

Patti could hardly obey for laughing — but she had to go through with it.

A space was cleared for her in the middle of the deck. The ship's band struck up, and with an audience of hundreds cheering her, the deck swaying with the roll of the seas, and a tropical sun blazing down, Patti went right through the steps of the hornpipe.

"What does my queen say to that?" asked Neptune amid the applause.

"Passed with honours!" cried Jean.

Out of the corner of her eye Patti saw a stealthy movement. One of the boys had seized the mop from the lather-bucket. He was advancing with it softly towards the unsuspecting barber.

He made a playful thrust.

But the barber spotted him in the nick of time. He ducked. The lathery mop missed its aim —

"Oh!" gasped Patti in dismay.

For Jean was the luckless victim! She sat right in the line of fire — and the whole mopful of lather went flooding over her trim auburn head!

"Jean —" Patti rushed to her.

"Oh — my hair, Patti. After the hours you spent on it. Now it's ruined again!" Jean was almost in tears.

But Patti had stopped dead. She could scarcely believe her eyes. For Jean's hair was changing again to normal in the sunshine. That streaky white lather was vanishing in harmless little bubbles!

"It — it's only ordinary so — soapsuds " she stammered.

"Sure. I mixed 'em myself, so I ought to know," laughed Tony, the barber. "What did you think it was?"

Patti thrust her hand into the bucket — and sure enough it contained only innocent soap-lather. Nor had it ever contained anything more! The inside of the bucket was as clean and fresh as only soap could make it.

"There isn't any paint, Patti? Is my hair all right?" Jean asked in breathless relief.

"Yes, quite all right!" Patti said.

She drifted away. Her relief was as deep as Jean's — but she was puzzled.

How had that paint got into Jean's hair this morning? It was certainly no fault of the boys —

Come to think of it, the storekeeper had hinted that someone had been after his paint. What did it mean?

Someone knew. And someone was missing from the fun this afternoon. Sandra Blayne — Jean's cabin-mate!

An odd thought struck Patti. Leaving the gaiety and excitement, she made her way slowly below decks and pushed open the door of Jean's cabin.

"You —!" came a startled gasp.

Sandra was desperately washing a blue blouse in the washbowl, and she swung round now with a crimson and curiously guilty face.

"Why, Sandra, you're missing all the fun!" said Patti.

Sandra had no time to hide the blouse she was washing. It bore an ominous paint stain.

"Is that paint on your blouse? It's the same paint that I had such a job getting out of Jean's hair, isn't it?" Patti asked levelly.

"You know!" whispered Sandra. "I — I don't know how you found out, but — yes, I was the one who splashed that paint over Jean!"

"On your own friend!"

"I — I took some paint out of the store, then mixed it into some of that soapy lather so that she'd think it was the boys fooling about," faltered Sandra. "I waited until Jean walked under the hatchway — then I splashed it down on her hair!"

"Why?" asked Patti gently.

"Because I —" Sandra's voice choked in her misery — "because I thought it would give me a chance to be queen instead. I know I'm not pretty like Jean. But her dress did fit me, and when I tried it on, and saw myself in the mirror, I thought how wonderful it would be to be queen, and I — I just lost my head. Suddenly I felt I just had to take Jean's place."

Tears of misery and remorse welled into Sandra's eyes.

"I've been punished for it," she gulped. "I hid the paint-tin in my locker afterwards — but the ship's rolling a lot today, and look what happened!"

She opened the door of her locker, and what a sight Patti saw! The paint had spilt, and nearly all Sandra's clothes were badly splashed with it.

"I deserve it," she wept. "The worst thing is, Jean's my best friend, and she'll never forgive me when she knows how I tried to spoil her chance to be queen!"

Patti's heart melted. She could imagine the unhappiness Sandra had been enduring, while all the fun and hilarity was going on above deck.

"You've been punished enough. Jean's not going to know anything about it," she said.

"You mean you're not going to tell her?" gasped Sandra.

"Of course not. Why would I want to break what is really a good friendship? Listen," said Patti, "I've got some paint remover in the salon. I'll lend it to you to take out these stains. Then up you come on deck before the fun's all over."

She dashed out of the cabin before Sandra could find words to choke out her gratitude.

Jean never discovered what had caused her nearly to lose her crown. The situation had been saved, and she knew only that she owed it to Patti. She was the belle of the ball when King Neptune led her into the dance that night.

And no one was more happy at Jean's triumph than Sandra.

DANGEROUS
ENCOUNTER

In the freezing snows of the Canadian North, Marilyn Bathurst yearned to see the bright lights of a big city. But her father loved the tough open-air life and was content. Still, a girl could dream.

Then one day from out of the southland came a mystery helicopter and Marilyn's adventure had begun.

The magazine cover showed a New York street at Christmas time, buildings soaring, lights blazing — the whole scene vivid with life and colour.

"How wonderful to be in a big city like that, Dad." Marilyn Bathurst was wistful.

"I don't go for the bright lights myself," her father answered. "Give me the snow and ice. It's a tough life here in the north, but it's a good one."

"I'm happy, too, Dad," she answered, "but I'd love to see a big city just once."

"Ai, ai! You go city — Oh, no, no!"

The speaker was an Eskimo woman who entered the room — which was both living room and store — from a lean-to kitchen, a saucepan in her hand.

"You stay here — much more better."

Marilyn laughed. Kara was like a mother to her — indeed ever since her mother died the Eskimo woman had looked after her — and Kara's little son, five-year-old Samik, seemed like a brother.

"Don't worry, Kara," the girl smiled. "I'm not likely to go to the big city."

"Maybe you will one day, my dear," Mr. Bathurst told her. "When I can afford it I'll send you on a trip to Toronto."

She was still poring over the magazine when her father got to his feet and began to gather his trapping gear together.

"Nangak and I are heading for the East shore," he told her. "We won't be back till tomorrow night."

It was not the first time she had taken charge when her father and Nangak, Kara's husband, went trapping or hunting. But business would not be brisk so late in the year. Though they kept sledges and teams of dogs for anyone wanting to journey farther north, tourists were few and far between when the vast lake froze over.

Marilyn went outside to see the two men off. The huskies were barking, anxious to get going.

"Mush!" Nangak shouted, and the dogs were off to a good start. Marilyn waved, then went back into the store, and settled down again with her pile of magazines.

After a while she raised her head. The utter silence outside had been broken by a strange, whirring noise that echoed across the lake.

Intrigued by the unusual sound, she went to the door. And then she caught her breath in astonishment.

Kara, a little scared, came out and stood beside the girl.

"What is it?" she whispered in awe.

"It's a helicopter," Marilyn answered.

The machine disappeared from sight heading north across the frozen lake. It seemed to be losing height, then it disappeared below the pine trees bordering the lake.

"I believe it's come down," Marilyn said. "Maybe it's landed on the lake."

Marilyn stood watching the skyline, hoping to see the helicopter again. There was no sign of it, and after a while she and Kara returned to the store.

Darkness was falling when the barking of the huskies in their kennels outside disturbed Marilyn, and she looked up as the door opened.

A tall, thin man carrying a pair of snow shoes entered, followed by a fur-wrapped woman. She looked weary and sulky.

"We're travellers — heading north," the man began. "Can you give us a shakedown for the night and hire us a sledge and dogs in the morning?"

"Er — yes, I guess so," Marilyn said. She didn't care for the looks of these unexpected guests.

"We have a cabin nearby where we lodge travellers," she told them. "But would you like something to eat first?"

"Sure would. Our name's Davis, by the way."

"Do you aim to go far north?" The girl spoke to the woman, but it was the man who answered.

"To the Eskimo settlement on Hudson Bay. My wife and I are writing a book about the Eskimoes and we want to study their ways at first hand."

As soon as they had eaten she took the couple to the warm and comfortable lodging cabin.

"Have the sledge ready by first light, please," the man ordered. "We want to be away real early."

As she returned to the store she wondered about the strangers. How had they got so far north as this on foot? The nearest road fit for a car to travel was twenty miles away. Had they come in the helicopter? She felt sure they had.

Curiosity finally drove Marilyn to put on a windcheater and her parka, with its cosy fur-lined hood, fasten on her snow-shoes and sling her skates over her shoulder.

Then, taking her father's big torch, she set out.

When she reached the lakeside she changed her snow-shoes and began skating over the ice.

At the northern end of the lake, silhouetted in the moonlight, rested the helicopter.

Skating close, she stared at its giant legs straddling the ice. Above it, the arms of the rotor stood outlined against the starlit sky. Between them was the glassed-in cabin.

She drew nearer — then gasped.

There was someone inside the cabin! A contorted little face peered out at her — the face of a badly frightened child!

Marilyn could hardly believe her eyes. Then, realising the child was alone in the helicopter and crying, she hauled herself up and wrenched open the cabin door.

"Don't be frightened, I'm your friend. Won't you tell me your name?" Marilyn asked gently.

"Ruth — Ruth Barlow," answered the child, shivering.

"Who brought you here?" Marilyn asked.

But the little girl — she looked about four years old — was too scared to talk any more.

It was bitterly cold in the cabin and Marilyn saw that Ruth was dressed only in a woollen skirt and jumper, a blue cotton coat and a small cap.

She had obviously been abandoned by whoever had flown the helicopter. Marilyn made a decision. She must take the child back to the store.

Taking off her windcheater and woollen scarf, Marilyn put them on Ruth. Then she slipped out on to the ice, lifting the child down.

At that moment she heard a sound that seemed to freeze her blood to ice. It was a sound dreaded in that part of Canada — the angry growl of a grizzly bear, the most ferocious of all the wild creatures of the Far North.

In the moonlight she could see the huge form of the grizzly lumbering towards them. No time to get back into the helicopter.

Marilyn switched on her torch, shining it into the bear's eyes and momentarily blinding the powerful beast. Holding Ruth tightly, she began skating away — out of reach of the fierce grizzly and towards the safety of home.

Kara waited for no explanation when she saw the white-faced child Marilyn was carrying. She took Ruth into her motherly arms. Comforted by her crooning, Ruth ate some hot gruel and soon fell asleep.

Then Marilyn told Kara how she had found the child, and of her suspicions regarding the man and woman in the lodging cabin.

While she and Kara had supper, Marilyn turned on the radio, imagining the gay scene in some big city where people were dancing to the music.

"This is Toronto," said the voice of the announcer. "A little girl was kidnapped here this morning. Her name is Ruth Barlow, and she is the daughter of Trevor J. Barlow of West Side, Toronto.

"She is four years of age, has fair hair and blue˙eyes. She was wearing a light blue coat when she disappeared while out with her nurse in the park. The kidnappers are believed to be a man and a woman.

"If anyone knows anything of the child's whereabouts will they get in touch with the police immediately!"

Marilyn and Kara stared at each other in horror. So little Ruth had been kidnapped — and the kidnappers were at that very moment in the cabin fifty yards away!

For a few minutes Marilyn was so shocked that she didn't know what to do. Then, as the dance music came over the air again, she leapt for the transmitter radio.

Ten minutes later she was talking to a sergeant at the headquarters of the Canadian Mounted Police.

"I've found Ruth Barlow, the little girl who was kidnapped this morning!" Marilyn gasped. "She's quite safe, but the kidnappers are here, too!"

"I'll send some men at once, but it'll be some hours before they get to you," replied the sergeant. "Can you try to keep the couple there, until we arrive?"

"I — I'll try," Marilyn said doubtfully.

As she put down the headphones Marilyn turned to Kara in dismay.

"We've got to stop them getting away in the morning," she said, "but I don't know how we're going to do it."

Marilyn was up long before dawn. Luckily during the sleepless hours an idea had come to her. Going to Kara's room she outlined her plan.

Ruth woke smiling, and when she asked if "the nasty people" had gone, Marilyn told her not to worry and that it would not be long before she saw her Mummy and Daddy again.

"But right now," she continued, "I'm going to dress you up so that you'll be warm and cosy."

She began dressing the little girl in some of Samik's clothes, and Ruth was delighted. She thought it great fun to wear a woollen jacket, fur-lined trousers and a coat of caribou skin with the fur inside. It was the usual winter costume of the Eskimoes, but it was all new and exciting to Ruth. As Marilyn fastened a pair of sealskin shoes on Ruth's feet, she looked up at Kara.

"Thank goodness she's the same size as Samik. Now for her face.

We'll have to darken it — but how?"

"Ai, ai! Kara knows. See — the ointment used for huskies' harness." Kara held up a jar of brown leather dressing.

"Kara, you're a genius!" Marilyn said delightedly. Then, turning to the little girl, she said: "Ruthie, I want you to let me put this on your face. It isn't going to feel too good, but you won't rub it off, will you?"

"No," Ruth said solemnly.

Soon she was completely transformed. No longer a little Canadian girl, she looked exactly like an Eskimo.

"See, Samik, you have a sister!" Marilyn exclaimed, and the small boy burst into loud laughter.

The distant slamming of a door told Marilyn the kidnappers were astir.

"Those two people are coming in here soon, Ruthie. I won't let them take you away, I promise. But you must stay in here and play quietly with Samik. If the people speak to you, don't answer them."

Then Marilyn went out to greet the couple, who had just entered the store. Kara brought in breakfast, and Marilyn said: "I'm sorry, but you won't be able to leave till later in the day. One of the dogs is ill."

The man scowled. "We can manage without it," he said.

"You can't," Marilyn explained. "It's the leader. The rest of the team won't follow any other dog."

It was plain that the couple were angry, but since there seemed nothing they could do about it they settled down to wait.

Two hours passed — hours of mounting tension for Marilyn. Once or twice she went out to the huskies, pretending to see how the supposedly sick dog was.

Then the thing she had feared happened.

Samik came rushing out of Kara's room, followed by Ruth, laughing excitedly as she tried to catch him. Both children had forgotten Marilyn's instructions.

Ruth stopped when she saw the man and woman, and shrank back. Marilyn spoke quickly to Samik in his own language, telling him to take the little girl back, but suddenly Ruth cried: "Go away, bad man!"

The English words gave her away.

Davis strode towards her.

"It's the kid," he said. "How come she's here?"

Marilyn stood petrified. There was no point in further pretence. For the first time the woman spoke, turning on her husband.

"I knew we'd never get away with it, Bart!" she cried in panic.

"Shut up!" the man snapped. "This girl's not going to snarl up my plans."

He advanced threateningly on Marilyn, but just then the kitchen door opened and Kara appeared. Something flew from her hand — it was a large iron saucepan and it caught Davis on the side of his head.

He staggered and fell. Marilyn reached under the counter for her father's gun. It wasn't loaded, but she hoped that the kidnappers would think it was. The woman cowered back, sobbing hysterically.

And then there came another sound — the noise of a sledge. A moment later the store was full of uniformed figures and Marilyn gasped with relief. The Mounties had come at last!

When all the clamour had died down and the couple were being led away, the sergeant turned to Marilyn.

"You've been great, young lady," he said admiringly. "We'd never have caught up with them once they'd got farther north."

"I don't know what would have happened if Kara hadn't come to the rescue," smiled Marilyn. "But there's something I don't understand," she went on. "Why did they leave the helicopter?"

"It's my guess they'd run out of fuel. They'd already come four hundred miles after leaving the plane they used to make their getaway from Toronto," the sergeant explained. "They didn't dare bring the child here to the trading post in case you'd heard of the kidnapping and became suspicious."

"What did they intend to do?"

"Their plan was to hire a sledge and dog team from you, pick up Ruth from the helicopter and travel north until the hue and cry died down and the ransom had been paid to a confederate in Toronto."

"But Ruth might easily have died of cold in the helicopter during the night!" Marilyn shuddered.

The policeman nodded grimly. Then he said: "About the little girl — will you take care of her until tomorrow, when we'll send another helicopter to take her away?"

"Of course," Marilyn said.

"Good! Then we can fly her back to her parents the same day." The kindly sergeant grinned. "Guess they'll be mighty grateful to you, miss."

★ ★ ★ ★ ★

Grateful was scarcely the word to describe the joy of Mr. and Mrs. Barlow when they knew their little girl was safe.

Messages flew over the radio to the Bathursts and the upshot was that Marilyn received an invitation to take Ruth home and spend a week in Toronto as the Barlows' guests.

She needed no second invitation. To visit Toronto, to see the bright lights of a big city! Wasn't it just what she had longed for?

Two days later, Marilyn found herself in a luxurious car being driven down one of Toronto's main streets. With her on the back seat was pretty Mrs. Barlow, her eyes wet with happy tears, and between them sat little Ruth.

"Don't forget to tell me which is the best toy-shop," Marilyn laughed. "I want to buy a present for Samik. Do you think he'd like a toy motor-car? He's never seen a real one!"

Mrs. Barlow was sure he would, so a motor-car it was.

Marilyn bought presents, too, for Kara, her father and Nangak. Mr. and Mrs. Barlow bought lots of things, too, which Marilyn was to take home as presents for them all.

Mrs. Barlow insisted that Marilyn chose a dance dress for herself. It was pale yellow, and with it went shoes to match and fine nylon tights — so fine that Marilyn had never imagined there could be such lovely things.

Altogether it was the most exciting day Marilyn had ever spent.

And next night, when she went to her very first dance in one of Toronto's smartest hotels, she knew this was the holiday of her life — something she would treasure in her memory when she returned to the trading post in the frozen wastes that was home to her. She knew too, because these kind and grateful friends told her so again and again, that this would not be the last time she would see the bright lights of the city she would always love.

POUND COTTAGE

by Jacqueline Wackrill

Pound Cottage was the kind of place that looked fine on picture postcards or calendars, with its whitewashed walls and thatched roof. Gail was enchanted as she looked at her new home, even if it was somewhat small for the whole family.

But if Pound Cottage was picturesque there was something mysterious about it. Was it haunted, for instance?

Dad said: "Well, even if it is too small, it's the only place we could find and we'll just have to make the best of it."

I rolled over on my back and lay on the grass of the tiny lawn, looking up at our new home. What Mum had been saying was probably right, I decided. Pound Cottage was the kind of home that looked fine on picture postcards, with its whitewashed walls and thatched roof, but with Mum, Dad, young Ken and myself to accommodate, it certainly wasn't going to be too large.

"Maybe if I'd waited a bit —" Dad began.

But Mum shook her head. "Don't be silly, Jack," she told him firmly. "It's not your fault. It's that Mr. Machin I blame. People should keep their word."

I chewed a blade of grass and didn't say anything. Privately, I found myself thinking that perhaps Dad could have waited for a while longer

77

before giving up his job in the Midlands just so that he could live in a pretty West Country village and sell tractors instead of designing them. But then, as a family, we always do things on the spur of the moment. And it certainly wasn't his fault that weedy Mr. Machin, who'd offered us an absolutely super house called White Gates, should suddenly put up his price at the very last minute to some stupid figure that Dad couldn't possibly afford.

So here we were at Pound Cottage, making the best of a bad job.

I said: "You wouldn't think it could be so difficult to find somewhere to live, would you? I mean, back in Bilton there were always thousands of houses up for sale." Then as the thought struck me I added: "I wonder why nobody wanted Pound Cottage."

"Who knows?" Dad said. "I suppose we just came at the right time."

"Why is it called Pound Cottage, anyway?"

Dad sighed. "Gail," he said, "you're a big girl now. Why don't you find out for yourself instead of just asking questions?"

That was Dad's usual reply when he didn't know an answer. Actually it wasn't a bad one, because I'd got quite expert at digging around in libraries for odd bits of information.

"Perhaps it cost a pound when it was built," ten year old Ken suggested hopefully.

"Perhaps," I said. It was a good try but somehow I didn't feel it was likely to be true. In the end I took a book of the district around Little Stoughton to bed with me, and though I went through it pretty carefully before I went to sleep, Pound Cottage wasn't mentioned anywhere.

FUNNY FEELING

I hadn't been asleep very long when something woke me up. I sat up in bed with that funny feeling you get when you wake in a strange room. I could see the oak-beamed walls quite clearly in the moonlight that streamed through the tiny leaded window, and just as I got my bearings I realised what it was that had woken me.

Something was moving about on the flagged stone floor of the kitchen directly below.

Curiosity has always been one of my failings, so I opened my bedroom door, decided that I was the only one awake, and tiptoed downstairs and into the kitchen.

And there was the donkey.

Back in our old home in noisy Bilton, I suppose I just wouldn't have believed it. But here in Little Stoughton it seemed quite natural, somehow.

"Hello," I said, and held out my hand. He blew at it gently, nuzzling it with his whiskery nose. It was quite easy to see how he'd got in. Our kitchen was at one end of Pound Cottage and led straight on to the garden through an old, drop-latch door. Mum must have forgotten to push it quite shut before she went to bed and the donkey, in an exploring mood, had simply nosed it open and come in.

"You'd better have a carrot," I said. There was a big one in the vegetable rack, and I held it out. The donkey accepted it and munched gratefully. Another carrot and an apple went the same way.

"That's the lot," I told him firmly, and gave him a gentle shove. Obediently, he backed out of the kitchen and wandered down the garden path.

Smiling to myself, I went back to bed.

"A donkey in my kitchen!" Mum exclaimed when I told the family about our visitor next morning. "Why on earth should he want to come indoors?"

"Perhaps the people who lived here before us fed him," Ken suggested. Quite sensibly, I thought, although I couldn't imagine anyone feeding a donkey in the middle of the night. I really don't know why I couldn't imagine it, because it wasn't long before I was doing just that. Two or three nights a week Albert — I decided that he looked like an Albert — would drift in. I discovered his secret quite early on — he opened the door by pushing up the latch with a quick upward jerk of his nose. If by chance the door happened to be bolted, he'd stand looking up at my window pathetically until I went down and gave him his carrots.

I'd grown very fond of Albert.

I'd been feeding my new friend for — oh, a couple of weeks I suppose, when I actually met his master. On that occasion I was standing outside the kitchen door and feeding Albert his usual carrot ration when I suddenly became aware that a man was standing in the dark shadows by the gate. He must have seen me look up with a start,

"Hello," I said, and held out my hand.

because he came up the path and said "Good evening" in a broad Irish brogue.

"Good evening," I said back. Though of course it wasn't really evening at all, but the middle of the night.

"My old varmint's been after worrying you again," he said. "Sure and Oi'll have to be takin' better care of him, Oi will." He patted Albert's neck and the little donkey turned and trotted after him as the Irishman went back down the path, raising his hand to me again before setting off down the road.

It was the next day that I decided I really should do as Dad suggested and find out something about our home. I headed for the library, which was a tiny room built on to the village school. On the way I passed White Gates, the house we should have had, just as Mr. Machin was coming out of it. He looked a pretty sneaky sort of man and I think he knew who I was because he'd got a pretty smug look on his face as he went by. I can't say it improved my temper, but I put on my brightest smile as I went into the library and asked the little old lady who ran it if she had anything in stock about Pound Cottage.

She shook her head. "Can't say I have, me dear."

I said hopefully: "But surely someone must know something about it, I mean, why was it empty, for a start? Is it haunted or something?"

Of course I'd only been joking, but the librarian looked suddenly cagey. Then she said: "Well, some say as it is, and that's the truth."

"But — but —" I stared at her blankly, "You mean it really is haunted! What by?"

The old lady said firmly: "I don't know, miss. Best you ask Vicar Turnbull. He's made a study of these parts."

Well, that was all I could get out of her, and so I headed for the vicarage.

Mr. Turnbull turned out to be a frail but friendly old gentleman who led me into a fantastically untidy study and gave me tea while he listened to what I wanted to know.

"Ah, Pound Cottage," he said when I'd finished. "Well, my dear, I can tell you how it got its name easily enough. It's because before it was converted into a cottage it was the old village pound, where stray animals were kept until claimed by their owners. I've even got a picture of it, as a matter of fact."

VILLAGERS JEERED

The Vicar took an old painting down from the wall and laid it on his desk. The village was recognizable enough, and so was our cottage, although what was now the kitchen door had clearly been the entrance to the pound. Locked in the pound was a donkey and its owner, painted as sitting disconsolately on the ground while the villagers jeered at him.

"But that donkey —" I began in a shaking voice.

"Oh, that's Paddy's donkey," Mr. Turnbull laughed. "Paddy was an Irish tinker who travelled around these parts about a hundred and fifty years ago. His donkey was always straying and the village beadle — he was a sort of policeman, you know — used to lock the two of them up quite regularly. He used to encourage the villagers to give poor Paddy a rough time, too. Oddly enough, the beadle's name was Machin, and one of his descendants still lives here today. He lived in Pound Cottage for a short time, as a matter of fact, before he moved to White Gates."

"Do you know if Pound Cottage is haunted?" I asked.

Mr. Turnbull looked at me for a moment. Then he said firmly: "I don't think you should worry your head about that."

But of course I did. All the way home. I mean, was it possible that Albert and his master were really ghosts who still haunted the old Pound. They seemed awfully solid, but then I didn't know enough about ghosts to know if you really see right through them or not.

As luck would have it, Albert turned up again that very night, and as I was feeding him, who should appear but his master.

"Sure an' the old moke is troublin' you again, Miss Machin," he greeted me.

I should have felt scared, but somehow I wasn't. Possibly because I'd had a flash of inspiration.

"I'm not Miss Machin," I said. "Mr. Machin doesn't live here any more. He lives at White Gates. White Gates," I repeated firmly. "Up near the school."

My visitor looked surprised, "Does he now!" he exclaimed. "It's sorry I am to have been troubling you." And knuckling his forehead, he called to Albert and the two of them walked slowly away down the road.

They never came back to Pound Cottage again. But the following week Mr. Machin left Little Stoughton, after writing Dad a letter to say that he could have White Gates at the price he'd asked in the first place.

"I wonder what happened to make him change his mind?" Dad said gleefully. And I wondered too. Perhaps Albert and his owner really were ghosts and they'd driven the descendant of their hated beadle first out of Pound Cottage and then — thanks to me — out of his new home. But I shan't really know until we move into White Gates next week and discover if they're there.

No, I haven't told the family what I've found out. After all, even ghost stories scare Mum stiff.

And besides. I'd miss Albert like anything.

ONE GOOD TURN

The magnificent wild horse had been trapped and brought down from its mountain home to be tamed. For three months, day after day, the beautiful young animal trotted round and round the confining corral.

With endless patience Frances James set out to make friends with the horse. That she had achieved her end she was to discover as she lay helpless before the fangs of a hungry wolf.

The black horse had been a mystery ever since he had been brought down from the mountains. Then as now, he would spend hour upon hour restlessly trotting round the confining corral, his ears pricked and nostrils continually testing the wind which blew from the mountain range, his birth place.

Every day for the last three months, Frances James had quietly approached the corral and gazed at the horse. She had spoken to him in a gentle voice, trying to let him know that the only thing she wanted was to be friends. Gradually, the horse had come to recognize her voice and now, instead of rearing and running away in fright, he would stand with ears pricked, seeming to listen. For the rest of the day, however, he would continue his ceaseless trotting and his yearning glances towards the mountains.

It had been fair-haired Frances, the fifteen-year-old daughter of the Canadian ranch owner, who had found the young horse and it had been Frances who had become his owner. She had soon given him a name, because his coat was as black as the mountain night and it seemed only right that he should be called Midnight.

Today as Frances talked to him, she noticed that the young horse was restless and that, instead of standing still as he usually did when she was talking to him, he was restlessly pawing the ground. The wind which had been rising all day blew through his thick, black mane and long black tail.

Frances suddenly shivered. The day had turned cold and the grey, leaden sky seemed to foretell snow.

"Well, goodbye, Midnight," she said. But the horse did not even prick his ears as he continued to pace the corral.

Frances turned slowly back to the house. If only the horse would settle down and forget his mountain home, she knew that one day they would become real friends. But, she shivered and pulled her jacket tighter round herself, all Midnight really seemed to want was his freedom . . .

Suddenly, a piercing neigh rang out. It was the neigh of a young stallion announcing to the world that he was ready to take his place in it! Frances turned quickly and gazed in amazement. The black horse was cantering with ears pricked towards the high fence which held him prisoner. Frances clenched her fist as she realised that the horse was about to try to jump it.

With a mighty bound Midnight took the fence. For a second he seemed suspended in air and then, with a great effort he was over the top and free. A triumphant whinnying rent the air, then with a thunder of hooves the horse galloped off across the plain to the distant mountains.

Frances knew that her shouts of "Midnight, Midnight!" were useless. She would have to go and bring him back. Quickly she ran to the stable, saddled up the old pony which she sometimes rode, and set off across the plain in pursuit of her horse.

Frances looked round anxiously. Surely she ought to have found some trace of Midnight by now? For three hours she had been searching the mountains and had not even caught a glimpse of him. She brushed off a flake of snow which had fallen on her jacket, but just as she was brushing it off, another fell and then another. The snow which had been threatening all day was now falling thick and fast.

Now, for a moment, Frances was frightened. She remembered her father saying to her that when it was cold the timber wolves were driven down from the higher mountains by hunger to look for food.

Quickly she glanced behind, and almost laughed with relief when she saw nothing resembling a wolf. Still, she had better go home. She could easily come out tomorrow and continue the search. She urged her pony forward, but felt another cold chill of fear creep over her. Which was the way home? Under the ever thickening blanket of snow, all the trees and paths looked the same. But again she felt reassured. Surely she had come up the slope ahead on the way out? With a determined movement, she guided her pony towards it.

Carefully the old pony began to pick his way down the slope made slippery by the falling snow. They were half way when there came a sound which made Frances catch her breath in alarm and urge her pony on. It was the mournful howl of a hungry wolf!

The old pony also had heard the cry and increased his speed. Soon he was finding it harder and harder to keep his foothold on the treacherous slope. Concealed rocks and stones were making him stumble, and the more he slipped the faster he went. A pit covered by the drifting snow caught his foreleg and he fell heavily. Frances was flung from the saddle, felt the cold snow on her face for an instant, then was surrounded by an overpowering darkness and she knew no more.

The black horse, too, had heard the wolf's howl. He knew by instinct that the cry was the call of an enemy and he stamped his foot in defiance. The wind currents brought the smell of the wolf to his nostrils and his ears went back flat to his head. Suddenly his nose caught a different scent — it seemed to be that of the human he had almost come to love. He tossed his head restlessly and took a few steps forward.

Again the hated smell of the wolf came to Midnight's nostrils, this time mingled with the scent of the girl. The horse stopped and remained motionless — a black statue surrounded by falling snow — then, with a flurry of hooves, he turned and was lost in the enveloping white world.

Frances opened her eyes and looked around. What was she doing here? Memory of her pony's fall came back to her and she tried to

"Come on, Midnight," she said, and the horse took a few steps forward.

struggle to her feet. Her body refused to obey, however, and looking down she saw that her right leg lay twisted beneath her. It must be broken, she thought, although it's not hurting. She suddenly felt icy shivers of fear run down her spine. Before her pony had stumbled, she had heard the cry of a wolf. What would happen if a hungry wolf found her unarmed and helpless? Once again, she struggled to stand, but knew it was useless. With despairing eyes, she searched the landscape.

The snow had almost stopped falling, but it was cold, bitterly cold. When would her father come looking for her? she wondered. But when he did, how would he know where she was? Frances forced herself not to think about such a problem and pulled her jacket tighter. Abruptly she stopped moving. Had she been mistaken, or had she seen a grey form among the trees opposite? She strained her eyes, but all seemed still. The next minute however an eerie howl made her skin tingle. She had been right! It had been a wolf among the trees — a wolf who would attack any animal when it was hungry, and certainly something defenceless like herself! With growing horror, she tried to think what to do. She was suddenly conscious of another presence. Slowly, with great self-control, she twisted her body round and almost fainted with relief.

A few feet away Midnight was standing watching her with obvious curiosity. Frances held out her hand. "Come on, Midnight," she said, and the horse took a few steps forward. He was just about to nuzzle the girl's hand when he stopped, his gleaming body taut as a coiled spring.

With sinking heart, Frances turned round. A lean grey timber wolf had come out of the shadows of the trees. It, too, had stopped and with glittering eyes and tense body was watching her.

Instinctively Frances tried to move, to escape from the danger facing her. The spell was broken. Midnight threw up his head and uttered a shrill, challenging neigh. Ears flat, he plunged at the wolf. Gone was the pining young horse he had been in the corral. Now Frances watched, fascinated, as the black horse fought like the mountain stallion he was!

The wolf, with knowledge born of years, lunged at the horse's foreleg, in an attempt to rip a tendon. But Midnight was too quick for him and with a squeal of rage reared up madly. Again the wolf tried, but this time was rewarded by a sickening thud of hooves against his ribs. He was quickly learning that to attack a defenceless animal was easy, but an enraged horse of light movements and flaying hooves was another matter! Once more he tried, but was flung several yards away by the angry horse. With growl of disappointment, he slunk off.

Frances felt limp with relief. She knew all too well what would have happened to her if the horse had been unable to drive the savage killer away. Midnight continued to stare at the place where the wolf had disappeared but when it became obvious that it was not coming back, the mountains rang with the proud neigh of the victorious stallion.

Now that the fight was over, Frances became conscious of the cold spreading through her body. She wondered how long it would be before rescue came, and wearily closed her eyes. She must have been nearly asleep when she was suddenly conscious of somebody nudging her back. "Why can't I be left alone?" she thought. But the nudging continued.

It was Midnight who had been nudging her, and with a shock Frances realised what would have happened if she had fallen asleep in the snow. She had heard many tales of travellers who had dozed in the snow and never woken again.

"That's twice you've saved my life," Frances murmured.

The black horse was neighing and trotting restlessly up and down. From time to time he would stop and with flaring nostrils test the air. Then with piercing calls he would continue his ceaseless trotting. Frances wondered what could be wrong, and hazily thought that the wolf might have returned. But she was now too tired to care. The cold had almost gone from her body and a delicious numbness was creeping over her . . .

She seemed to feel strong arms lifting her out of the snow. With a great effort, she opened her eyes and found herself looking into the worried face of her father. Now she knew why the stallion had been so excited — he had scented her father and called to him.

"Soon have you home, Fran. Have some of this, it will warm you up," she heard her father saying, and Frances felt a bottle being pushed into her mouth. She swallowed some of the liquid and almost choked as it burned her throat. But whatever it was, it spread a pleasant warming glow through her body. Soon she was wrapped in a thick blanket and carried by her father to a waiting horse. One of the other rescuers held her while her father mounted, then she was carefully handed back and felt the horse start to move.

"Just a minute," Frances begged. "I have to say goodbye to someone who saved my life twice."

She looked round the darkening landscape.On the next slope the black stallion was standing motionless with ears pricked.

"Thank you, Midnight," Frances whispered, and as she watched the stallion gave a soft whicker then trotted off into the shadows. His colour merged with the night and he was gone.

"He's paid me back," Frances thought dreamily as her father's horse walked slowly back to the ranch. "I was kind to him when he was captured, and now he's saved my life."

Just before she closed her eyes, she heard a triumphant neigh. The stallion was back in his mountain kingdom!

THE PURPLE DANDELION

by Janice Mitchell

Maggie was practising diligently, hoping to pass her Grade V music exam. But while she was playing Bach on the piano her school chums had tuned in to the pop group that had taken the country by storm. Maggie was despondent. Bach on the piano was no match for the Purple Dandelion on the radio.

Half the trouble was that the Dandelion group used Bach's techniques but when Maggie tried to explain this to her chums, she was met with derision.

Then came the day of the exam and Maggie knew that she was bound to fail.

Maggie sat dismally at the piano in Room 4B and stared blankly at her music. Outside in the hall, the record player was on full volume and the two speakers, unable to cope with the frantic messages being pumped into them, were delivering a blurred, distorted cacophony of pop.

She got up and went to the door. There were thirty or forty girls in the hall, nearly all of them dancing energetically, and in small groups round the outside, some of the boys stood watching. Sylvia was manning the turntable. She was about to play the next disc. When it started, it was the same group whose music had been filling the hall for the past half hour — the group whose latest record had been in the

Outside in the hall, the record player was on full volume.

number one slot for the past six weeks just as their previous record had been, and the one before that. It was The Purple Dandelion.

Maggie moved despondently back to the piano. The jumble of black dots on the music appeared to be dancing too and she knew it was hopeless. Ironically enough The Purple Dandelion used Bach's techniques in their own music — but that didn't mean you could listen to Bach with one ear and to them with the other. For the umpteenth time Maggie launched into the complicated three-part invention that was one of her pieces for her Grade V music exam. As soon as she reached the fifth bar, with that tricky cluster of semi-quavers in the left hand, she came unstuck. It was the same every time she played it — and she knew it would be the same when she played it on a strange piano in front of the strange examiner. Their piano at home was terribly out of tune and school lunch times were Maggie's only chance to practise. But every day The Purple Dandelion lessened her chances of passing the exam.

"Aren't they fantastic?" Sylvia Briggs' shrill voice cut its way across the hall and into Room 4B. Maggie heard the amplified scrape of the needle coming down on to the next record — but then the bell hammered out the beginning of afternoon school and, obediently, Sylvia switched off the record player. Maggie felt her ears slowly relaxing. She folded her music and put it in her bag and then sat down in a desk three rows back. 4B was the music room and the first lesson was music.

The lesson turned out to be quite lively. Miss Fuller was strict, but she also had a sense of humour. These two qualities made her a popular teacher.

"How many people prefer pop music to anything else?"

Sylvia's hand shot into the air followed swiftly by about thirty others. Miss Fuller's eyes roved amongst them. "What about you, Maggie?"

Thirty-odd pairs of eyes swung towards Maggie and stared at her accusingly. She felt awkward and was unsure of how to say what she felt. "Well, I like pop music. I mean, I listen to it on the radio and I've got records and everything. It's — it's just that I like other sorts of music as well — you know, serious music."

"Ugh!"

Miss Fuller smiled. "Well, which composers do you like, Maggie?"

"Bach, mostly, and Mozart . . . and modern composers as well . . ."

Sylvia's hand shot up again.

"Yes, Sylvia?"

"I think serious music is boring. I mean, there's no beat or anything, is there? You can't compare it with pop!"

Maggie interrupted. "You can! The Purple Dandelion base half their music on Bach. I've listened to it on the radio and in the hall at lunch . . ."

"'Course they don't. How could they?"

Sylvia turned appealingly to Miss Fuller.

"Maggie's right, Sylvia. Look, I've brought a record of some Bach with me. Let's listen to it, and then compare it with The Purple Dandelion."

"Have you got a record of The Purple Dandelion, Miss Fuller? Are you going to play it — in the lesson?"

"Certainly, Sylvia. As soon as we've heard the Bach record."

Maggie closed her eyes and enjoyed the music. Unlike most of the other girls and boys, she lived some distance from the city. She couldn't have gone to a discotheque if she'd wanted to because there wasn't one nearby. They hadn't even got a television, but Maggie didn't mind. She'd got her record player and she loved the country. There was a stream running through the village and sometimes Maggie would follow it out to a spot where several willow trees enclosed a small, smooth-grassed hollow. She would sit and read books on her favourite composers — or simply dream of the day she would be able to play all their music on her own piano.

The music stopped and Miss Fuller put on the pop record. Half way through she turned it down. "Now then, Sylvia, you hear the organ?"

"Yes, Miss Fuller, that's Mike Preston, the leader of the group."

"Right. Now imagine it without the beat behind it. Can you hear any similarity between it and the Bach you've just been listening to?"

Sylvia listened intently for a few seconds. "Yes, I suppose so. But it's much better, isn't it? I mean, Bach could never have played music like this, could he?"

The bell for the end of the lesson rang loudly. Miss Fuller packed up the record player and was ready to leave the room. She walked to the door, turned to Sylvia, and said in an American accent: "What you're trying to say, Sylvia, is that Bach is not your scene!"

Sylvia stared after her as she left the room and, in the moment of silence that followed her remark, she muttered to herself in disbelief.

"Well, there goes Miss Fuller surprises!"

"Had a nice day, Maggie?"

Maggie took the cup of tea from her mother, put it on the table in front of her and finished spreading her slice of bread with plum jam.

"Yes, quite nice. Didn't do much playing though with that record player screaming in the next room!"

"Oh, dear! And your exam's on Saturday."

"I can't ask them all to be quiet for me, can I?"

"I suppose not, but it seems such a pity . . ."

There was the rustle of turning pages as Maggie's father thumbed his way through the evening paper.

"H'mmm! Apparently old Horden has sold Hordern Hall. Poor old fellow — must be breaking his heart. It's gone to a fellow called Michael Preston."

"Whoever is he?"

"Some rich businessman, I suppose. The way the paper talks, everyone is supposed to know who he is."

Maggie stared into the distance, racking her brains, Michael Preston . . . Michael Preston. Now where on earth had she heard that name before? She was still trying to place it as she climbed into bed that night, but soon her thoughts gave way to an uneasy sleep. She was worried about her exams.

By the following Friday, Maggie had given up trying to practise altogether. She was now quite certain that she would fail the exam. She wandered into the hall at lunch time and stood watching the girls.

"Going to have a dance, Maggie?"

Maggie jumped slightly as she heard Sylvia's question. "No thanks, Sylvia, I'm not in the mood. I've got my piano exam tomorrow."

They stood together next to the record player, and a sudden thought occurred to Maggie. "Hey, Sylvia, have you ever heard of Michael Preston?"

"What?"

"Michael Preston . . . have you ever heard of him?"

"Are you kidding? He's the leader of The Purple Dandelion!"

Suddenly Maggie remembered that she had heard the name mentioned in her class discussion.

"Why d'you want to know?" Sylvia was shouting at her again.

Maggie thought for a moment before answering. "Oh, no reason."

At exactly eleven o'clock on Saturday morning, Maggie clicked open the door and walked uneasily into the examination room.

"Good morning!" boomed the examiner as he advanced to meet her.

"Good morning, sir," Maggie replied timidly. Then her eyes swung from the examiner to the piano and back again.

"Well, sit down. I want your scales first. Let's start with D minor."

Before she knew where she was, Maggie was sitting at the piano and playing the scale.

Next came the sight-reading. The music he placed in front of her was completely unfamiliar and she had to play it entirely from sight. It appeared to be infinitely more difficult than anything her piano teacher had given her at school. Three sharps. She hated sharps.

"Thank you. Now your pieces," the examiner demanded.

Maggie played the first two pieces reasonably well. Perhaps there was a chance. It all depended on the last piece.

"Now the Bach!" the examiner boomed.

In spite of the situation, Maggie half smiled to herself. His bark is even worse than my Bach, she thought. Her face became serious again and she began to play. Then somehow her left hand seemed to stiffen. She struggled on, but the music was blurred now as tears of disappointment filled her eyes. She fought them back and tried to play from memory — but she didn't know the piece well enough, and again she fumbled and had to stop. At last, hardly knowing what she was doing, she reached the end of the piece.

"Thank you very much," the examiner said.

Without looking at him, Maggie hurried to the door and, a moment later, was gasping in the fresh air and trying to compose herself for the journey home. Maggie knew there was only one place for her that afternoon — underneath the willows by the stream, and by the time she had reached the little hollow, she was feeling better. Somehow her examination didn't seem so important any more. In any case it would be several days before she heard anything, so she might as well try to forget about it.

She was surprised to hear voices as she walked between the trees.

Ever since she had discovered the spot, she had looked upon it as hers. She slowed down. The voices stopped, but then another odd collection of noises came from the clearing. For a moment she couldn't make out what it was, but then suddenly she realized that it was the sound of a radio being tuned. Momentary snatches of a dozen stations resounded through the trees. Maggie moved forward and saw two boys, sitting in the middle of the clearing. They were about eighteen or nineteen, she supposed, and were lying on the grass with a portable radio between them. They were dressed fashionably in bright, exotic clothes.

Maggie was indignant that these two strangers should intrude into her special place, filling the beautiful silence with rowdy pop music, but the next moment she was listening incredulously. The boy fiddling with the radio had found the programme he wanted. It was Bach. And by some odd coincidence, it was the very three-part invention for piano that she herself had played so badly that morning. Maggie stood rooted to the spot.

"Well, what is it, then?" One of the boys' voices came floating across.

A moment later the other replied: "Three-part invention . . . in A minor."

"No, no, it isn't, it's . . ." began the second voice, "it's G minor."

"Wrong!" said the first boy. "It's . . ."

"It is G minor," Maggie interrupted.

Both boys turned in amazement. Maggie was standing, rather nervously, looking down at them. "I — I happen to know it quite well, you see," she said.

Slowly the two boys turned and looked at each other in mock surprise. One of them stood and bowed. "Ah . . . a connoisseur of the musical scene, I presume!"

Maggie wasn't at all sure that she could cope with the situation, but the other boy came to the rescue. "Forgive my friend. He's only a guitarist, but he fancies himself as an actor."

At that moment two more figures broke into the clearing. They, too, were exotically dressed, and one of them carried a guitar. "Right, lads. Let's get on with it. Hello, who's this?"

"Oh, she just turned up to give us some lessons on Bach. She'll probably finish writing the song for us, Mick."

Mick looked at Maggie and said hello. Maggie eyed each of them in turn, and then her curiosity got the better of her. "Are you a pop group, then?" she asked.

Mick turned to her, a surprised look on his face. "We certainly are. A poor struggling pop group trying to make a name for ourselves. We're about to attempt to write a song, and we're determined that we'll have a hit on our hands."

Still grinning, he picked up the guitar and began to strum out a few notes. "Right! I've got a tune vaguely worked out, so we'll try to sort something out from there. We can put it on tape later — unless we forget it by the time we get home, like we did last time!"

"Have you got a piece of paper?" asked Maggie.

"What for?" Mick asked.

"Well, if you like, I can write the tune down as you make it up."

Two hours later they had finished it. Maggie had not only written down the melody but she had also filled in some suggested guitar chords, and a bass guitar part. The boys couldn't wait to get home to try it out.

Mick turned to Maggie as they prepared to leave. "Look, why don't you come back with us, then you can hear how it sounds? After all, you practically wrote it, didn't you?"

"Well, I can't be out long. Do you live far away?"

Mick looked puzzled for a moment. "At the hall. Hordern Hall."

Suddenly Maggie felt very foolish. Everything fitted into place . . . why hadn't she realized? "Then you're The Purple Dandelion!" she yelled.

"Well, yes . . . but I thought you knew," Mick replied.

"And I've been trying to help you to write a song!"

"You were a great help," Mick said, "and I'll make sure you get the credit for it."

Suddenly Maggie started to laugh.

"What's the joke?" Mick asked.

"Oh . . . it's just that there's this girl at school, and . . . oh, it doesn't matter."

When she left Horden Hall two hours later, Maggie was in her seventh heaven. Not only had she met, spoken to, and spent some time with The Purple Dandelion, but she had arranged a song for them which they were delighted with. And there was still more. Another member of the group had written a marvellous lyric to fit the tune. It was about a girl who was as beautiful as the countryside, and they called the song . . . Maggie!

The group said goodbye to her at the door, and Mick put an arm on her shoulder. "Look, Maggie, there must be something we can do for you — you've helped us so much."

Maggie smiled up at him. "No, really, Mick. It's been fantastic meeting you, and helping with the song. Anyway, I'm bound to meet you all again from time to time in the village."

Mick stared after her thoughtfully as she turned to go. "Hey, Maggie! Who was that girl at school you were talking about earlier?"

"Oh, just one of your fans, that's all . . ." she began.

"Come on, tell me about her," Mick demanded.

So Maggie told them everything. When she had finished, Mick turned to the others with a grin on his face. "I think it's about time Maggie's friends realized what a groover she really is . . ."

Just after nine o'clock on the following Monday morning, Sylvia Briggs stood in the playground waiting for the bell to go. It hadn't been a good weekend. She'd spent almost all of Saturday unsuccessfully queueing for tickets to a Purple Dandelion concert at the end of the week.

Still, she reflected, it wasn't as bad as having to take a music exam. She wondered vaguely how Maggie had got on, and looked towards the main gate to view Maggie's arrival. Occasionally, a member of the staff's car would pull in and park down by the side entrance. There was one coming in now, although, in fact, she didn't recognize it. Why wasn't it stopping by the other cars? It was coming straight towards the main playground and it was a Rolls-Royce. A purple Rolls-Royce! As she stared at it in amazement, she was aware that the other girls had stopped to stare at it too. Sylvia got the idea that she ought to know whose car it was. But why? Had she read about it? Seen a picture of it?

As the car circled the playground for the second time, the incredible truth suddenly struck her. Of course she knew who owned a purple Rolls-Royce! Michael Preston! She could see him, sitting at the wheel . . . and looking at her . . . driving towards her . . . stopping right beside her . . . getting out . . . and who was that beside him? Maggie!

Sylvia was too overcome to say anything. She just stared unbelievingly at Michael Preston and the entire Purple Dandelion group, standing with Maggie in front of her.

"Sylvia, I'd like you to meet my very good friends The Purple Dandelion!" said Maggie.

Sylvia was hardly conscious as Michael Preston kissed her firmly on the cheek and pressed something into her hand.

"Delighted to meet you at last, Sylvia. Please accept these tickets for our next concert. Maggie's coming too, so you can keep her company."

For a few delicious moments, Sylvia was in a dream, and when she woke up, she wondered if it had actually happened. It must have — · she was still holding the tickets.

Maggie opened the door of Room 4B, took out her music and sat down at the piano. There had been a letter in the post that morning, telling her that she had failed the exam, but already she'd been to see her teacher and collected the music for the next Grade V sitting. There was another piece by Bach, and this time she was determined to master it.

The record player was already on in the hall and for ten minutes she managed to ignore it. But soon it started to grate on her ears again and she felt the familiar panic rising inside her. Then something happened which shocked everyone.

A face appeared at the door and then a shrill voice soared above the noise of the record player: "Hey! Keep the noise down, will you? Maggie's trying to practise!"

It was Sylvia.

ANYONE CAN SWIM

by Judith Hobson

Jane had had a frightening experience at the age of seven during her first swimming lesson. It was an incident that still lived with her and even today she did not want to learn to swim, even though her Uncle George had sent her for a birthday present a season ticket to the local swimming pool.

But in a moment of peril Jane was to change her mind about the importance of swimming.

Birthday presents from Uncle George usually arrive in exciting-looking parcels, so when, on my last birthday, the only thing the postman brought from him was an envelope, I felt let down.

"But surely," I thought, "Uncle George of all people hasn't run out of ideas and sent me money!"

When I opened the envelope, along with an amusing card depicting a mermaid, was a season ticket to our local swimming pool. It was an odd present to send to me — the only non-swimmer in the family! I can't say I was overjoyed!

I put the ticket on the breakfast table for everybody to see, and immediately there was uproar.

"Lucky you!" cried my elder brother, Pete. "Wish he'd sent me one. Swimming costs a fortune. Tell you what — I'll buy it from you. You'll never use it."

"It's not transferable," I said primly, having had a brief glance at the rules on the back.

"Uncle George must have grown absent-minded. He's obviously confusing you with me," declared my sister Sarah, who's sixteen and the star of the Swimming Club.

"D'you think he'll send me one, too?" This from Simon, whose birthday comes two weeks after mine. Simon's eight, and the baby of the family, but he's been swimming like a fish since he was five.

"No, I don't," said Mother, who had picked up the birthday card and was reading the greeting inside. "He's sent it to Jane for a very special reason. Look!" She passed it across to me.

"'I expect,'" I read aloud, "'to find you swimming like a mermaid when I come down to visit you.'"

Uncle George always spends two weeks with us in September.

After a moment's silence my brothers and sister all burst into uncontrollable giggles. "You mean he really expects Jane to learn to swim?" snorted Pete.

"She'd have more chance of success if she had a go at flying!" put in Sarah. She was obviously in one of her witty moods.

This made Simon giggle even more, but then he caught my eye and must have guessed I was upset. He's a kind little boy really. He stopped giggling and said earnestly: "I'll teach you to swim, Jane. It's easy, honest! Anyone can swim!"

"No," I said quickly. "I don't want to swim, and neither Uncle George, nor anyone else, is going to make me!" I scraped back my chair angrily and stood up.

"We'll talk about it another time," Mother said hastily. "You haven't seen all your presents yet. Look, there are all these."

"Yes, you haven't opened my present yet!" Simon cried, thrusting an untidy package into my hands.

I smiled at his eager little face, and untied the ribbon. Swimming was forgotten for a time.

The first weeks of summer were cold and damp, and no one suggested I should use Uncle George's present, although the other three went regularly to their Swimming Club.

I must admit, here, that at the age of seven I had joined the Swimming Club. It seemed to be the recognised thing in our family. Dad had once swum for the county; Mother had done a bit of exhibition diving in her youth; as for Uncle George, he had surpassed them both by swimming the Channel. Sarah and Pete, then aged eleven and nine, were already vying with each other for a place in the Club team, and I was quite willing to follow in these famous footsteps. So just after my seventh birthday I was taken along to the beginners' class.

All went well until we were told to pretend to be submarines, and sit on the bottom of the pool holding our noses. What the instructor didn't know was that in those days I breathed through my mouth. My submarine surfaced fast, choking and spluttering, scrambled out of the pool, and made a bee-line for the changing rooms. And that — as far as little Jane was concerned — was curtains for the Swimming Club!

My parents aren't the sort who force you to do something you don't want, so from then on I became the odd one out: the Baxter who didn't swim, and now, here was Uncle George expecting me to learn too.

Uncle George is Mother's youngest brother, a bachelor, and my favourite uncle. He's quite old, of course. About thirty, but he's six foot four in his socks, and more handsome than any pop star. Usually I longed all summer for September to come, just to see Uncle George again. Now I found myself dreading it.

Term came to an end, and we had two weeks' holiday in Cornwall. When we came home everyone seemed to be saying: "It won't be long before Uncle George comes . . ."

August was hot. So hot that even I decided the most comfortable place to be was in the water. Sarah and the boys and I nearly lived at the pool, taking our lunch and tea, and only coming home when the sun went down. They swam all the time, of course, but I sunbathed on the edge of the pool, and had a dip in the shallow end now and again.

The others tried to urge me to swim. "Look! It's easy!" shrieked Simon, plunging in off the side of the pool in a straight, effortless crawl.

Watching them only made me less inclined to try myself. They were so good at it. It was like being left at the starting post in a race when everyone else was nearing the winning tape. I hadn't a chance of catching up. Besides . . . I was frightened . . .

Uncle George was due on the third of September. The day before dawned clear and cloudless.

"What would you like in your sandwiches today?" Mother asked.

"I don't want anything," I said. "I'm not going to the pool."

The splash came from further upstream.

Everybody looked surprised.

"Well, there are other things!" I said hotly. "I'm getting bored doing the same thing every day. Besides, it's so noisy there." I really did feel I wanted a little peace, and quiet solitude, to be on my own.

"You can help me get the spare room ready for Uncle George." Mother suggested brightly.

It was better than doing nothing, so I picked some of the brightest dahlias from the garden and arranged them tastefully in a pottery jug, and put them on Uncle George's bedside table. They looked very nice.

We had an early lunch and afterwards, feeling I just had to be alone, I got out my bicycle and cycled down to the river. I walked a long way beside the bank to a secluded spot I knew near a footbridge, and threw myself down on the grass. I tried to read the book I'd brought, but I kept thinking about Uncle George, and how I'd have to admit to him, tomorrow, that I hadn't even tried to learn to swim.

After a bit I was annoyed to hear voices, and two boys came through the trees along the river bank. One was about fourteen, and carried fishing tackle; the other was a toddler of about three.

Our stretch of river is about thirty feet across, rather deep and swift, but full of boulders, so it's unsafe for bathing, but quite good for fishing.

The elder boy took up a position not far from the bridge, and began to bait his hook. The little boy had a toy fishing net, which he thrust in among the reeds. "Don't go too near the edge!" I heard the older boy warn him.

I turned over on my side, shut my eyes, and pretended I was alone. It's funny how sometimes you have a premonition that something's going to happen. I remembered sitting up with a jerk, suddenly alert to danger, a split second before I heard a splash and a shout of terror.

The splash came from further upstream, where the small boy, having wandered off, must have slipped and fallen in the water. The shout came from the elder boy.

He dropped his fishing rod and darted along the bank. I scrambled to my feet and ran after him.

He turned to me, his face white and shocked. "My brother!" he cried. "I can't swim. Can you?"

I was horrified. "No."

"I'm going for help!"

He was about to run off, but I caught his arm. "It'll be too late.

We've got to save him ourselves!''

We stood there, for seconds that seemed like hours, while the current carried the child downstream towards the bridge. He was a good ten feet from the bank, and drifting out into midstream, now below the water, now above, his small arms and legs flailing helplessly. I should like to be able to say that I dived into the water and, miraculously finding I could swim, rescued the boy, but things don't happen like that in real life.

Then I saw a way! "Come on," I yelled to the elder boy, and raced towards the bridge. I picked up his fishing rod, noting that it had a good strong line, and thrust it into his bewildered hands. "Hold on to that. Tight!"

I snatched up the hook, and ran with it on to the footbridge. It's an iron bridge, with supports going down into the river.

If I'd had time to think about what I was going to do I'd never have had the courage, but the seconds were passing, and there was only time to act. When I reached the midstream support, I kicked off my sandals and climbed over the rail, clinging to the support as I slid down into the water.

The coldness of it took my breath away, and for a terrifying moment, as the swift current caught my legs, I thought I was going to be swept under the bridge. I gripped the slippery iron support and found a footing, just managing to keep my head above water.

I was in time! I forced myself to think only of that, and forget the frightful, sickening feel of the water, rushing by my ears and dragging at my legs.

Clinging to the bridge with the hand which also held the hook, I stretched out the other. The child was almost here. Get ready! Now!

I made a grab at his clothing. His arms came up and clung to me, and I pulled him towards me. His legs, thrashing wildly, almost knocked me off balance, but my numbed fingers kept their hold.

It was more difficult than I'd expected to keep the little boy afloat and at the same time fix the hook securely in the back of his sweater. However, I managed it, and, too exhausted to shout, made a signal to the boy on the bank. He understood, and began, gently and steadily, to wind in our precious "catch."

With a sob of relief I let the child go and began to clamber back on to the bridge. When I reached the bank the little boy was lying there, exhausted but conscious. His brother was bending over him.

Anyone can Swim

He looked up. "You saved his life. I'd never have thought of doing what you did. And you can't swim! You must have been scared . . ."

"Scared?" I said, wringing water out of my jeans. "Oh, no! I wasn't scared. Simply petrified!"

He laughed at my feeble joke, and I laughed too. But I had to sit down on the bank suddenly, because my knees had turned to jelly.

The little boy was trying to sit up. "I feel sick," he sobbed.

"I must take him home," said his brother. "But what about you?"

"I'm all right," I said. "I just want to lie here for a bit. The sun will dry my clothes."

After they had gone, I lay for a long time on the bank, re-living the horror of those few minutes in the water. Suppose I had been too late! Suppose I had lost my hold on the bridge, and gone under . . . I shivered, in spite of the heat.

At last, when my clothes were not obviously wet, I cycled home. The family were having tea, so I crept up to my room to change.

"Had a nice afternoon, dear?" Mother asked when I went down.

"Yes, thanks," I said. "Am I too late for tea?"

Uncle George's car drew up at three o'clock next afternoon. "How's my mermaid?" he said to me.

"Uncle George," I said earnestly, "will you teach me to swim?"

"You mean you've been waiting for me?" He raised one eyebrow in a characteristic way he has.

"Sort of. Anyway, I do want to learn — quickly."

"That's my girl!" he grinned. "We'll start tomorrow."

Standing in four feet of calm, clear heated water the next day, surrounded by laughing, friendly people, I wondered how a swimming pool could ever have seemed a frightening place. After the horror of my ordeal in the river, the pool seemed a haven of refuge. With a new confidence and determination, I thrust out my arms, took my feet off the bottom, and swam my first stroke.

By the time Uncle George's stay was over I could manage a length of breast stroke, and float fearlessly on my back, feeling the thrill that comes with achievement.

So take note, all you non-swimmers. Simon was right. Anyone can swim but some people — like me — have to want to awfully badly before they can master it.

For my next birthday, Uncle George has promised to give me another season ticket, and this time I mean to make good use of it.

PAM'S PREDICAMENT

by Amy Moore

The splendour that is Rome! It called to Pam and her elder sister Virginia and neither could resist the magic of its voice. So they decided that they would spend their holidays in that fabulous city.

There was one big snag. Their worldly wealth amounted to ten pounds — which belonged to Virginia!

"We'll buy a second-hand car for ten pounds and drive there," proposed Pam. Virginia winced.

"A second-hand car for ten pounds?" she echoed incredulously.

Pam nodded.

In spite of what most people think, I suppose elder sisters sometimes have their uses. They certainly have their drawbacks — such as being bossy and hogging the bathroom at the expense of everyone else. All the same, there are times when girls have to stick together, and if an elder sister is all you happen to have handy at the time, then you simply have to do the best with what you've got.

Which was what brought about the truce between myself and Virginia.

As a matter of fact, I don't suppose it would ever have come about at all if Andy, out brother, hadn't ganged up with Dad on the dreary subject of cars. This was so normal that it simply wouldn't have mattered if it hadn't been for the fact that, for once, Virginia and I wanted to do the same thing — namely, to spend a fortnight of the summer holidays in Rome.

I'm not absolutely sure what started Virginia off. As she's tall and slim with lots of hair and, I suppose you could say, reasonably good looking, I imagine she suddenly saw herself drifting about the Via Veneto with gorgeous Italians just swooning away on every side. I knew exactly why I wanted to go. You see, my friend Gail Jarvis's father actually works there, which means that Gail spends most of the summer holidays in Italy getting all sun-tanned and cosmopolitan. This year she suggested that I joined her.

"Honestly, Pam, we've got stacks of room. All you've got to find is the price of the fare there and back."

"From what I know of the state of our family finances at the moment," I told her, "I should think it's going to take some finding. But thanks all the same."

Gail nodded sympathetically, one of the nice things about her being that, although her family have oodles of money, she doesn't expect everyone else to be as lucky. "I suppose," she said, "you don't know anyone who's going there by car who might give you a lift. You'd only have to share the price of the petrol then."

Well, it was an idea, and as I'd just learned about Virginia's urge to do the same thing, I thought it was worth trying my luck. As it happened I arrived home at the very moment she had chosen to approach Dad with a view to borrowing the family wagon.

"If you think I'm going to lend my car for you to go launching yourself all over Europe, my girl, you've got another think coming," he was saying.

Virginia sighed, then brightened up as Andy came into the room. My brother has been mad on cars since he was old enough to talk, and his twenty-year-old banger is the pride of his life. I didn't think Virginia was likely to get very far in that direction, and sure enough she didn't.

"You must be joking!" he told her cheerfully. "I wouldn't lend Boadicea to one of my pals, so I'm blowed if I'm going to risk her to a girl!"

"I can drive as well as you!" Virginia protested. Which happened to be quite true.

"In that case," Andy said promptly, "you'd better go out and buy your own car, like I did."

"But that's not fair!" I protested. "You've been working on Boadicea for absolutely ages. You can't expect Virginia to buy an old wreck for next to nothing and rebuild it. She doesn't know how."

"Well, that's just her bad luck."

"You know," Dad said, "I'm inclined to agree with Andy. He wanted a car, so he did something about it. He never asked for anything. But you girls . . ."

"But girls aren't supposed to be mechanics!" wailed Virginia.

Andy smiled smugly: "Well, you're always saying you're just as clever as us. Why don't you go ahead and prove it?"

"It would be almost worth it . . . ," I began.

"Well," said Dad cheerfully, "if you can produce a car with an engineer's report that says it's capable of getting to Italy safely, I'll be delighted to pay for the petrol. I can't say fairer than that."

"Oh, really!" Virginia exploded, and retired with her nose in the air. As I followed her I could hear Dad and Andy hooting with male laughter behind the door.

"Er — I rather want to go to Rome too," I said.

Virginia snorted. "Well, a fat chance you've got, that's all I can say. Have you ever heard anything so childish?"

"Frankly," I said, "no! But supposing you did get a car . . ."

Virginia shook her head. "It's no good. The most I could spare for a car would be ten pounds, and I just don't see myself getting much for that. And heaven knows, I don't know one end of an engine from the other."

"Just suppose," I said cautiously, "that I could get you a car for ten pounds. One that worked, I mean. Would you share the cost of the petrol and the cross-channel fares and give me a lift to Rome so I could spend a fortnight with Gail Jarvis?"

Virginia looked at me narrowly. "I might," she admitted after a while. "But how?"

"I don't know," I confessed. "But it can't be too difficult. And if I could find something that wasn't too awful, there's always that red-haired chap who keeps wanting to take you to the pictures. He works in a garage, doesn't he?"

"Harry Smith. Yes, he does." Virginia brightened up. Then her face fell again. "But repairing a car is one thing. Rebuilding a ten-pound wreck's a bit different."

"I suppose so," I admitted.

"Still, that's your pigeon," my sister pointed out. "If I'm to help you get to Rome, this is strictly a fifty-fifty partnership. I'll drive you there, but it's up to you to get the car."

As I shan't be old enough to have a licence of my own for another year, there wasn't much I could do. "All right," I agreed. "There must be some bargains somewhere."

"Old Mrs. Masters bought a piano for ten pounds the other day," Virginia pointed out. "So a bright girl like you should be able to manage to find a car for a few pounds."

I drifted off down to the village, thinking it over. Now Virginia had reminded me of it, Mrs. Masters had bought a piano jolly cheaply. At an auction somewhere. Could one buy cars at auctions? It didn't seem very likely, but I made my way to the notice board in front of the estate agent's, just to have a look. Apparently the contents of a rambling old house were being sold by auction the following day, and I studied the list of slightly improbable contents . . . the entire contents of the house including carpets, furniture, bed linen, three washing machines, together with a quantity of garden tools, a motor mower and two cars . . .

I read the last line again. Really, I thought, the whole thing was too simple. Everyone always said that house sales were places where you could pick up absolutely amazing bargains for next to nothing.

I don't know if you've ever been to an auction, but I found the whole business fantastic. I turned up in time to look at all the things that were being offered, each with its little numbered ticket and everything looking dusty and pretty awful. I bought a catalogue for 10p and discovered that the cars — not surprisingly, I suppose — were in the garage, so I went there to nose around. Lot 211 was described as: "Touring car. About 1920. Incomplete." That described it pretty well, I suppose. It was a pretty weird wreck of a thing, with four very flat tyres, no radiator — which I suppose accounted for the fact that nobody knew the make — and a large, disused bird's nest on top of the rusty engine. I dismissed Lot 211 immediately, but cheered up at the sight of Lot 212, which was an elderly Austin, very upright and peculiar, but apparently fairly sound. Goodness knows it wasn't anything James Bond would have been seen dead in, but it looked as though it might still work. I fingered Virginia's ten pounds and hoped that nobody else was in desperate need of a car too.

The sale, when it eventually started, was lots of fun. We — which was myself and round about fifty other people who evidently hadn't anything better to do — sat ourselves down in the fusty old dining-room while the auctioneer started to go through the catalogue, and the bidding began.

"Any advance on seven?" I heard the auctioneer ask.

A little man in a checked suit waggled his catalogue and the auctioneer nodded. "Thank you, sir. Eight. Any advance on eight?"

There wasn't any advance on eight and so the man in the checked suit got his cutlery and we went on to the next item. It all took rather a long time, but I was jolly pleased to notice that most things really did seem to be going cheap. Then, now and again, several people got quite excited wagging their catalogues like mad against each other while the price went up and up — usually for some pretty dreary-looking old picture. Mostly people got what they wanted at prices much lower than they'd have had to pay in shops, but after what seemed an age, we got to the cars.

"You've had a chance to inspect the next two Lots, ladies and gentlemen." The auctioneer was getting slightly hoarse. "Lot 211 is — well, to tell the truth I'm not sure what it is. An old car. It must have some value, if only for scrap. Who'll give me a pound?"

Someone at the back of the room said: "Two pounds."

"Three," came from somewhere up the front. I sat tight. It was Lot 212 that interested me, but even as scrap metal, cars were obviously worth something because the price crept up to seven, and it was at this point that I spotted Virginia on the other side of the room. It must have been sheer chance her being there because I hadn't said a word about the auction. Anyway, she seemed to be looking in my direction, so I waved to her.

"Eight pounds," said the auctioneer.

Another voice said "Nine," and this time I really did think I'd caught Virginia's eye so I waved again.

"Ten," said the auctioneer. "Any advance on ten pounds? Going — going — sold to the young lady in the orange blouse."

What young lady in an orange blouse? I wondered. Only, of course, I didn't have to wait long to find out, because one of the first things you must learn not to do at auctions is to wave, or even nod your head, if it comes to that. They're both signs that you're making a bid.

"Name and address please, miss," said the auctioneer's clerk, bustling up. It was only then that the penny dropped. I'd spent Virginia's

Crunch!

money on the wrong car . . .

"Well, honestly!", Virginia said when she found out what had happened. "Of all the . . ."

"I know," I said miserably. We were in the garage, inspecting my purchase at the time, so I could hardly blame her for being furious.

"I've put some air in the tyres for you. You might be able to push her home!" said one of the auctioneer's men, feeling sorry for me. Personally, I just didn't want to look at the mouldering wreck I'd bought, but there the thing was. Solemnly it was wheeled down the drive and into the road. Then we stood around and stared at it, which wasn't surprising really. None of us had ever seen anything quite like it before.

Finally one of the men said: "You'd better get behind the wheel, miss. We'll give you a tow home."

I suppost I must have been still numb with shock. Otherwise I'd have pointed out that I didn't know how to steer a car, and I certainly didn't want the horror taken home for Dad and Andy to gloat over. However, numbed or not, I got behind the wheel. The men went off to find a tow rope.

· Suddenly the old car began to move beneath me.

"Virginia!" I yelled. "Stop me!" Only there wasn't any sign of Virginia. Probably she couldn't bear to look at her ten pounds' worth any more. Anyway, nobody took the slightest notice as I began to roll backwards down the slight hill. Nobody even looked round as I started to gather speed. . . .

I looked desperately over my shoulder, wondering whether to hope for the best or bale out. And it was then that I noticed a car parked about twenty yards behind me — one of those very low, wildly expensive Italian-looking things in an exotic shade of yellow. Andy had been drooling over a picture of one only the day before. "Oh, no!" I yelled. But that was all I had time to do, because the yellow car wasn't twenty yards away any longer.

Crunch!

When I opened my eyes I wasn't moving backwards any more. Which wasn't surprising, considering what was stopping me. I climbed out, thinking how wonderful it would be if only the earth would open and swallow me up. Only it didn't. Dumbly I walked back to inspect the damage. The yellow, crumpled nose of the Italian car bore the name Borani. And even I knew that all Boranis were very

expensive. The two smooth-looking men emerged from the car looking expensive too. Expensive and cross.

"Oh, dear," I said in a small voice. "I'm sorry." I knew it was
hardly adequate, but then what could I say?

The driver of the Borani opened his mouth — to shriek at me, I
think — and then his eyes went past me and he stopped. He said
something in Italian to his companion and in a flash they were past me
and peering at my — or rather Virginia's — ten-pound calamity.
Gabbling away together, they tore open the bonnet and peered in at
the bird's nest and the rust.

"Please," I said, "I . . ."

The older of the two men looked up at me. He had very dark eyes
and his hair was going grey at the sides, like one of the more distinguished film stars. He said in English: "Young lady, is this your car?"

"Well," I said, "yes, sort of."

"I should like to talk to you."

"Yes," I gulped. "I know."

But I didn't know. I didn't know the half of it.

A fortnight later Virginia parked our Borani at the garden gate and
blew the horn till Dad and Andy came out.

"We haven't actually got an engineer's report to say that it'll get to
Rome," I confessed. "But it's brand new." And, of course, they could
see that. It wasn't the five thousand pound super sports Borani,
because Signor Borani — yes, it had been Signor Borani — had said
that something smaller and more manageable would be more suitable
for young ladies. But the bright red, shining coupé was very obviously a highly superior motor car.

Dad and Andy just stared at it.

"Well, you told us to get a car of our own, so we've got one," said
Virginia, rubbing it in. "Now Pam and I will just pop indoors and
make a cup of tea. We've got a lot of planning to do before we set off
for Rome."

With that we went indoors and left them there. I thought we were
jolly dignified about the whole thing. Sooner or later, of course, we'd
have to explain that the old wreck I'd bought by mistake had turned
out to be one of the three earliest Boranis ever made, and that it was

already being flown back to Italy to be restored lovingly for its new life in a museum. And that Virginia and I had graciously accepted a brand new current model as a fair swop.

"You know," Virginia siad, "I think they're rather envious of our little car."

"Yes," I agreed absently. "I think they are." It had just occurred to me that as that gorgeous red coupé had been given to us jointly, I'd have to continue being matey with Virginia. Because, after all, although we were sharing travelling expenses, she was the one who could drive. I was sunk until I was seventeen. Twelve months of being nice to Virginia.

I wonder if it's going to be worth it!

HER PERILOUS
WAR-TIME TASK

It was very unfortunate for Nina Pascal that she should have been on holiday in France when the German hordes stormed across the frontier. Stranded and alone, she was befriended by Madame Madelaine and for four long years Nina had posed as the brave Frenchwoman's niece.

But three weeks ago, Madame Madelaine had been arrested by the Nazis and now Nina was once again alone amongst ruthless enemies.

She had one friend – Thumper, her magnificent Alsatian dog.

A LETTER FROM ENGLAND

"Time to go home, I suppose. It wouldn't do to be out after curfew."

Nina Pascal cast one more longing glance across the sea, then rose from the log on which she had been sitting and looked down at the magnificent brown and white Alsatian which sat at her feet, guarding a piece of wood with a vigilant paw.

"Come along, Thumper," she said.

But Thumper knew nothing of the curfew that the Germans had recently imposed on the French. He couldn't see any reason why he and his beloved mistress should leave their secluded spot between the wood and the beach. He gave a bark of protest, and gripping the piece of wood in his strong teeth, thrust it into Nina's right hand.

"So you want to play some more?" Nina said. "Well, I'll throw it once more and then we really must be going."

Thumper gave an expectant bark as she raised the stick above her head and hurled it deep into the woods. Eagerly the dog went in search of it. Left alone, Nina's gaze went back to the sea, and a wistful sigh escaped her lips as she looked towards the distant horizon.

Somewhere over there lay England — the England she had not seen for over four years. Although the Germans believed her to be the French niece of Madame Madelaine, who lived in the Rue de la Fontaine — Nina was in fact, English.

She had been holiday-making with an uncle when war had broken out and in the hurried flight to reach a Channel port, she and her uncle had become separated. Later she had learnt that he had been killed in a bombing raid. She, not yet twelve at that time, had wandered into the little fishing port of Griselle, and there she had been befriended by Madame Madelaine, with whom she had since lived.

She had posed as Madame's niece for four long years, living in the little stone cottage in the Rue de la Fontaine. But for the last three weeks she had lived alone, except for Thumper, her Alsatian pet, for Madame Madelaine had been taken by the Nazis, suspected of secretly helping the underground movement that daily fought the oppressors.

"If only the Invasion that the Maquis speak of would begin," she murmured to herself as she stood there, her gaze riveted on the distant horizon. "It would be wonderful to see an English face again — to hear an English voice — and to see the Nazis running for their lives."

She gulped, hardly able to restrain her emotion, and then her heart leapt.

What was that?

The crack of rifles! There it was again — coming from the depths of the wood. Instantly she feared for Thumper's safety, and running to the edge of the trees she called anxiously:

"Thumper! Thumper! Never mind that stick! Come here at once!"

There came an answering bark, and to her relief, the Alsatian came running, unhurt, out of the wood.

"Oh, thank goodness!" she exclaimed, rushing to meet him. "For a moment I thought —"

She again broke off, for suddenly she realised that Thumper was gripping something in his mouth. It was not the piece of wood that she had thrown, but a round piece of green material.

"Why, whatever have you got there?" she asked.

As if he had understood every word she had said, Thumper thrust the material into her hand and he watched excitedly as she examined it.

"A small parachute!" she whispered. "A parachute they use for sending messages!"

Her heart leapt and her hands trembled as they fingered the fabric. The parachute had obviously been dropped by a British plane, but it looked as if the Maquis had been unable to find it. But for Thumper, it might have remained in the woods for weeks.

"Where did you find it, Thumper?" she asked the Alsatian. "And was that why the Germans were firing? Did they see you with this? I wonder," she added thoughtfully if somewhat fearfully.

The Alsatian's bushy tail wagged and he gave a low whine as he struggled to try to tell her what she wanted to know. Nina's gaze again fell on the parachute, then with sudden decision, she opened the little pocket stitched inside. A letter lay hidden there. Excitedly she drew it out, to catch in her breath as she saw the three words typed on the envelope:

'URGENT — FOR ANTON'

"Anton," she whispered. "It is for M'sieur Anton! Then — then it must be of tremendous importance — perhaps secret instructions from England!"

For a moment or two she surveyed the sealed letter with awe-stricken eyes. Anton was the nick-name given to the leader of the Maquis in this part of France. His feats against the enemy were legendary and for years the Germans had hunted him. But though everyone in Griselle knew M'sieur Anton's real name; knew that he had his headquarters in the nearby town of Caen — not for all the money in the world would they have betrayed him.

The letter clutched in one quivering hand, Nina gazed down at her pet.

"Thank goodness it was you and not the Nazis who found this, Thumper," she whispered. "It wouldn't do for them to see it, and I think it will be safer on you than on me," she added, bending over Thumper.

Fitted in the dog's collar was a tiny pocket, and, as if understanding what was in her mind, the dog sat like a statue while she hid the letter. But suddenly he growled a warning and his black nose turned towards the wood.

Realising that the Germans must still be searching, Nina made for

the cobbled road that ran close to the sea-wall. She had reached a point where the trees ran alongside the path when there came another warning growl from Thumper and he stopped, tugging at the hem of her frock.

"What is it?" she whispered.

Thumper made no attempt to try to tell his mistress. There was no need, for she could now clearly hear the sounds of feet crashing through the dense undergrowth and the angry mutter of voices.

"Shoot, the moment you see the brute!" The order came in gutteral German. "The dog must be stopped before it can hand that letter over to its owner."

Nina's heart gave a startled beat.

So the Nazis knew what had been secreted in the parachute!

Her gaze went across to the sea-wall. Below came the splash and gurgle of water on the shingle, for it was nearly high tide.

Impulsively Nina took a step forward.

"There's a chance for you, Thumper — you and the papers," she breathed. "I'll have to stay behind but you must swim home."

Thumper whined softly, as if in protest, and suddenly the thought came to Nina that she might never see him again. Impulsively she bent and hugged him, then resolutely she seized him by the collar, half-leading, half-dragging him to the edge of the sea-wall.

"Jump!" she ordered. "Jump!"

One last look the Alsatian gave her, then with another plaintive whine he obeyed. With a resounding splash he hit the water and began to paddle around, his gaze never leaving that slim, urgent figure above.

Frantically Nina waved towards the tiny harbour along the coast.

"Swim for home!" she commanded. "Never mind me. Make for the harbour and home!"

But it seemed that the dog, knowing the peril, hated to desert her, for to her dismay he continued to paddle aimlessly around. Urgently she gestured again, but before she could see whether or not her pet had obeyed, there came a harsh shout, followed by the thud of heavy boots on the cobbled road.

Hurriedly Nina turned away from the sea, and icy fingers seemed to squeeze her heart as she saw a burly German officer, followed by half a dozen grey-clad soldiers, emerge from the wood.

It was obvious that they had seen her, and, her one thought was to

The Nazi officer grasped her roughly by the arm.

prevent them from suspecting the presence of the swimming Alsatian, as she walked to meet them.

A moment later, the Nazi officer grasped her roughly by the arm and a pair of grim, gleaming eyes bored into hers.

"Where is he? Where is that dog?" the man asked. "Answer, Fraulein. We have no time to waste."

And the muzzle of a Luger revolver glinted threateningly in the fading light.

UNDER SUSPICION

Frightened though Nina was, it was not of herself she was thinking.

Had her pet started to obey her? Was he now swimming towards the harbour — and home? The thought that he might still be paddling around filled her with alarm.

"Have you lost your tongue, girl?" The Luger prodded her in the ribs. "Answer! Where is that dog?"

"Dog? M'sieur? I do not understand," she stammered. "What dog is it you seek?"

"The brute that stole the letter that the 'plane dropped yesterday — the letter we have been searching for all day. You must have seen him, for the dog was heading this way."

"I am sorry, M'sieur, but I was not looking. You see, it was the sea that held my attention, not the wood."

"The sea!" He regarded her sharply. "What was there to attract your attention?"

"Nothing, M'sieur. It is only that — that —"

"Bah! Don't lie. You are like all the French. You await the invasion. That is why you are so fond of gaping out to sea. You expect to see the British ships, but you find you wait in vain for them. The Englanders will never dare to cross the Channel."

The officer laughed scornfully, and then he scowled again. "But that may account for the dog's disappearance," he muttered. "The brute may have leapt into the water."

He beckoned to his men, shouting a quick command in his own tongue, and Nina again knew an icy fear as she saw the soldiers go running forward.

She stood there in an agony of suspense. Every second seemed a year. If Thumper should be seen —

She gulped, and then tried hurriedly to hide her agitation as she realised that the officer's eyes were still fixed suspiciously on her.

A minute dragged by . . . another . . . and then a plump, helmeted under-officer came running back to the road. He saluted stiffly.

"The sea is empty, Herr Captain," he reported. "There is no sign of any dog."

The relief for Nina was so overwhelming that she nearly collapsed. Thumper had made his escape — the precious letter was safe!

Her captor gave an irate grunt.

"Ach, but the brute can't be far off . . . search for him!" he ordered. "He must not be allowed to get away. Our Secret Service say that letter is of supreme importance. Unless we secure it —" Breaking off, he glared down at Nina. "For your sake, I hope you know nothing of this business," he began.

"But, M'sieur, what should I know?" she bluffed. "I am just a girl, out for a stroll before curfew."

"Maybe, maybe not," he muttered. "Anyway, get off home. It is nearly time for curfew. If we need you we can easily find you again. And remember — the Gestapo gives short shrift to treachery."

He made a gesture of dismissal and thankfully, Nina turned and went hurrying off along the road. She could hardly believe that she had escaped so easily, but gradually a wonderful feeling of exultation gripped her.

"Thanks to Thumper, the letter is safe," she murmured and her heart leapt as she remembered what the Nazi officer had said. "So it is of supreme importance, is it?" she repeated to herself. "I thought as much. Well, the Gestapo shall never set eyes on it. First thing tomorrow, we'll go to Caen — and take it to M'sieur Anton."

Overjoyed that she had been able to play some small part in outwitting the Germans, she walked on. At last the cobbled streets and white-washed houses of the little fishing port loomed ahead. At the top of Rue de la Fontaine stood a German sentry, but he made no comment as she hurried by.

Anxiously her gaze went to the tiny detached cottage across the road and she knew a terrible anxiety as she saw that the doorstep was empty. There was no dog waiting admittance there.

Oh, goodness, had Thumper failed after all to get home?

Agitatedly she opened the front door, but the moment she entered the tiny parlour her fear disappeared and a joyful gasp escaped her lips. For standing in front of the fire, his soaked fur steaming, was the Alsatian and a wet pawmark on the sill below the half-open window showed how Thumper had got in.

"Oh, you clever boy! Clever old Thumper!" Nina exclaimed and running forward, she flung her arms around the dog.

Thumper wriggled in ecstasy and it was obvious that he was as delighted to see her as she was him.

Snatching up a towel she dried him, then gave him his supper, and as he ate she examined his collar, satisfying herself that the precious letter was still secreted there.

"Tomorrow morning, we're going on a trip," she told him. "To Caen. We've got to seek out M'sieur Anton —"

She broke off suddenly, for Thumper had raised his head from his dish and his whole body had stiffened.

"What is it?" she whispered.

The dog cocked his head, remained listening for a moment, then, running forward, he reared up on his hind legs before the window which overlooked the street and pushed his nose between the curtains. As he peered out, a low growl escaped him. In alarm Nina ran to his side and very cautiously, she also peeped between the curtains. What she saw drained the blood from her cheeks.

A military car had drawn up outside the cottage, a blonde-haired, tough-looking woman in uniform was at the wheel, and from it was descending an all-too-familiar officer, followed by several helmeted soldiers.

"The captain who questioned me!" Nina whispered in dismay. "But surely he can't have learnt the truth. Surely —"

Breaking off, she agitatedly clutched at Thumper's collar.

"They mustn't see you," she gulped. "You must hide. But where? Where?"

Frantically she looked around, but there was no possible hiding-place for such a large dog as Thumper in the parlour. Into the back kitchen she rushed, and even as she reached it there came a thunderous knock on the front door.

For a moment a sense of panic overwhelmed her and then, as she saw the large copper, filled to the brim with the week's half-completed washing, a desperate idea seized her.

"It's our only chance, Thumper," she breathed and went rushing forward, the wondering Alsatian trotting beside her.

There came another angry tattoo, a short pause, and then the door swung open and heavy feet thudded on the parlour floor.

"Where are you, Fraulein? And where is that dog? You cannot bluff us again. The sentry saw the brute heading this way!"

As the angry shout rang out, the kitchen door crashed open and the burly officer peered through.

He saw a slim figure at the sink, engaged in rinsing a tablecloth. But there was no sign of the Alsatian.

"Why did you not answer our knock?" he roared. "Himmel, but there is no limit to the insolence of you French!"

Nina swung round. Her eyes were wide and innocent, but her heart was pounding.

"I am sorry, M'sieur, but as you can see I am doing my washing, and it is perhaps that I am a little hard of hearing. But what is amiss M'sieur? Have you not found the runaway dog?"

His hand closed furiously around her arm and he dragged her away from the sink.

"You know that I have not," he roared. "The brute came straight here. He belongs to you. You are not as innocent as you pretend."

"But, M'sieur —"

"Cease your lies. The sentry at the top of the street saw the dog . . . saw him jumping over your garden wall. Where is he? Where have you hidden him?"

"But I do not understand, M'sieur. There is no dog here. If you do not believe me, please look for yourself."

The Nazi gave a harsh laugh.

"Don't worry, fraulein, that is what I mean to do . . . and search for that letter, too."

He barked an order to the men who had followed him in and instantly they began to explore the tiny cottage from top to bottom, opening cupboards, peering under beds, ransacking with a thoroughness born of great experience.

Nina, still in the grip of the officer, waited with increased dread. Slowly but surely the search was drawning nearer and nearer the back kitchen.

Involuntarily her frightened gaze went to the copper that stood beside the sink, covered with a wooden lid. If they thought of looking in there the mystery of Thumper's disappearance would be solved!

One by one the soldiers came to report and the Nazi captain's scowl became more and more savage as he listened. At last, only the kitchen was left. The soldiers peered around and Nina's heart leapt wildly as one of them crossed to the copper. Anxiously she watched his hand reach for the wooden lid. He raised it, peered down at the pile of wet washing it appeared to contain, then dropped the lid with a clatter.

"Nothing here, Herr Kapitan, except dirty clothes," he said.

A wave of tumultuous joy swept over Nina, but it was short-lived, for from the parlour came an excited shout. Dragging Nina with him, the officer hurried through the doorway. The fat under-officer was standing by the open window which overlooked the yard, and was pointing at the sill.

"Yes, Herr Kapitan, a paw mark!" he exclaimed.

The captain's eyes gleamed with triumph as he peered down at the wet smudge.

"Then that sentry was not mistaken. That dog *has* been here!"

"Ja, ja, but the brute is not here any longer, my captain." The N.C.O. shook his head, saying: "It is clear what happened. When the fraulein heard us knock, she opened the window and pushed the dog through. Now he will be far away."

Slowly the officer nodded. It was obvious that he found the fat N.C.O's theory plausible. He swung round until his cold, glittering gaze was once more centred on Nina.

"The dog does not matter now. It is the letter that is important. Where is it?" His hand tightened cruelly on Nina's arm. "Answer, fraulein, where is the letter? Hand it over."

"But I haven't got it!"

"Nonsense, you must have."

"But I haven't. Honestly, M'sieur, I have no letter."

"Ach, but it is lies you tell, but no matter. We shall find it, then you shall pay for this obstinacy. Hans!"

"Ja, ja, Herr Kapitan."

"Tell your men to search again . . . but for a letter this time. And instruct the fraulein driver I wish to see her."

The fat under-officer hurried away and pale and apprehensive, Nina waited. Hardly had the second search begun than the blonde-haired woman driver appeared inquiringly at the threshold of the parlour. The Nazi officer pushed Nina roughly towards her.

Search her. I believe she has a letter hidden on her," he barked.

Nina was hustled into the cold back kitchen and there she was forced to undress. The woman driver keenly inspected every garment as it was handed to her, but of course, she failed to find the missing letter. Silently she gestured to Nina to dress again, and hardly had she done so, than the Nazi captain came striding unceremoniously into the kitchen. Obvious it was, from the black, baffled look on his face, that his soldiers had fared no better.

"You little trickster. You think you are clever, don't you?" he cried. "But do not think you can fool us for long. We know you have hidden that letter and we mean to get it."

The woman driver looked across at him.

"The Gestapo Headquarters?" she suggested. "Shall I take the fraulein there? They will loosen her tongue."

The officer hesitated, then to Nina's relief, shook his head.

"Nein. First we will try other means," he said. "Perhaps if the fraulein is given time she may realise the folly of her obstinacy. Besides it occurs to me that she may be speaking the truth."

"You mean about not having the letter, Herr Kapitan?" asked the woman.

"Ja, ja. What if she gave it to that dog? Perhaps hid it in his collar?" Nina could not repress a start of alarm, and the officer's eyes lit up. "So! That's it! Your dog has got the letter!" he cried. "Good! Then now I know what to do."

Followed by the woman driver and the soldiers, he strode across to the front door. Then he paused looking back at Nina.

"Well, we will leave you to your thoughts, fraulein," he said. "But do not think you are to escape. Tomorrow the Gestapo will teach you that it does not pay to defy the Nazis."

The door banged behind him and Nina, trembling and shaken was alone. For a minute or two she did not dare move, then on tip-toes she stole across to the copper and lifted the lid. Pushing aside the wet clothes she looked down at Thumper who had been curled up underneath them!

At the sight of her he sat up and gave a bark of relief. Instantly Nina's fingers closed around his mouth.

"Sh! Not a sound," she whispered, adding, "The Nazis think you have run away."

From outside came a harsh order, followed by the sound of marching feet and the thud of rifles. Creeping across to the yard window, Nina peeped through and saw three armed soldiers taking up their positions at the end of the garden. She took a cautious look through the opposite window. More sentries had been posted there, and her heart sank as she realised that the cottage was surrounded.

Obviously, the Nazi officer believed that sooner or later the Alsatian would return, and the sentries had orders to shoot the moment he appeared.

"Of course, their plan would fail, because Thumper was already inside — not outside the house but — Oh, goodness! What about the letter?" Nina gulped. "With the cottage surrounded, how will I be able to smuggle it over to M'sieur Anton tomorrow?"

NINA COLLECTS THE NAZIS' WASHING

"Ach, but it is cold!"

The grey-clad sentry in the alleyway beyond the garden laid aside his rifle and rubbed his hands together. It was only six o'clock and the early morning sun could barely be glimpsed through the vapoury clouds.

Near where the German soldiers stood was a ramshackle old shed, and he stiffened and reached for his rifle as he heard the double doors being pushed open.

"Halt! Who goes there?" he challenged.

The doors swung right open and into sight appeared a slim girl pushing an empty hand-cart. It was Nina, and she looked across at the sentry with an expression of impatience.

"Kindly let me pass, M'sieur," she said. "I have my business to attend to."

"But it is forbidden," he declared. "No one is to enter or leave. Those were the Herr Kapitan's orders."

Nina, showing no sign of her real thoughts, shook her head.

"Don't be absurd. It is a dog the Herr Kapitan ordered you to watch for, not me," she declared. "I have to collect the washing."

"Washing, fraulein?"

"But of course. My friends and I do the washing for the military headquarters up on the hill. Are your comrades to go without clean sheets just because of your stupidity? Let me pass."

But the sentry did not budge. Stolidly he stood there.

Nina's heart missed a beat.

All night she had lain upstairs in the dark, racking her brains for some way of outwitting the enemy, but it looked as if the plan she had thought of was doomed to failure.

She began to argue, and the fat under-officer in charge, emerged from a nearby garage on hearing the noise.

"What is the matter?" he demanded.

Forcing herself to look indignant, Nina explained. To her dismay the N.C.O. also began to shake his head. Concealing her alarm she stamped the ground with an impatient foot.

"But the headquarters must have its laundry. It should have been delivered yesterday as it is. I'm only going to my neighbours to collect the washing they've done. I shall not run away, and you can send one of your men to keep an eye on me if you like. I warn you, the Herr Kommandant will be angry if he does not receive his clean linen."

The under-officer rubbed his fat chin doubtfully and then to Nina's relief he nodded.

"Very well," he said, "you shall deliver the laundry, but a sentry shall escort you there and back, so no tricks, mind."

Nina could hardly conceal her delight. Her daring plan was working after all!

With a tall, watchful soldier marching beside her, she trundled the hand-cart up the cobbled street, calling at first one house, and then another. And never before had she blessed the fact that the women of the Rue de la Fontaine had been bullied and threatened into undertaking the nearby military headquarters' laundry. At last, the hand-cart was piled high with large wickerwork baskets of washing, but instead of proceeding up the hill Nina swung the hand-cart round. The sentry regarded her suspiciously.

"Ach, what means this?" he demanded. "Our headquarters is not this way but over there."

He waved towards the hilltop and Nina nodded.

"I know that, but I've forgotten my receipt book. The Herr Kommandant always insists on a receipt. Without my book I shall not be paid. I must return home for it."

And calmly she set off back for the garden gate of Madame

Madelaine's cottage. When the under-officer heard the reason for her return, he prodded the baskets suspiciously then grunted —

"Very well, get your book, but hurry!"

Nina's heart pounded furiously for now came the most daring part of her plan! In apparent concern she looked up at the sky and exclaimed: "Ma foi, I hope it doesn't rain. I would hate all this clean laundry to get wet. I'll just wheel the cart under-cover, just in case!"

Before the Germans realised what she was doing, Nina had trundled the hand-cart into the dark shed at the bottom of the garden. Frowningly, they waited until she emerged from the other side and walked up the garden into the house. A few moments later she reappeared, gaily waving a tattered note-book.

"Voila, here it is!" she cried. "And it didn't rain after all, thank goodness."

She entered the shed once more and after a slight pause when she seemed to be having difficulty in turning the hand-cart round, she finally pushed it into sight. The N.C.O. suspiciously counted the number of wickerwork baskets — which were the same number as before — then growled:

"Off you go then."

With the same soldier at her side, Nina set off down the cobbled street once more. At the end, she turned to the right which caused the soldier to exclaim:

"The entrance is straight on."

"But the laundry is not delivered at the front entrance," said Nina. "We have to take it round to the side door."

Before he could make any further comment, Nina set off down a narrow, deserted side-street. The soldier became more and more suspicious as the street led into little more than a lane that appeared to be leading out of the village into open country.

"Stop! What trickery is this?" he shouted. Striding forward he gripped Nina's shoulder so roughly that she gave an involuntary cry of pain.

At once, the snowy white linen in one of the baskets began to shake loose and suddenly, up rose the brown and white Alsatian dog.

Thumper!

The soldier's eyes bulged and as if in a dream, he stared at the dog that had so magically appeared.

"Ach, but it is the Alsatian!" he gasped. "How did he get here? I saw Hans prod and check each linen basket."

Nina laughed. "But not the one Thumper was hidden in. That one was in the shed and I switched it over when I wheeled the cart in while I went indoors for my receipt-book."

For a moment, the soldier continued to gape at the dog, and then, as he realised how he had been tricked, he snatched the rifle from his shoulder.

"Himmel! But I'll soon deal with him!" — but he did not get the chance, for Thumper sprang.

From the hand-cart he launched himself onto the sentry like a ton of bricks. The man lost his grip on the rifle and struck his head as he fell.

One quick glance from Nina satisfied her that the soldier was temporarily stunned and then she turned her attention to her dog.

"Good for you, Thumper!" she cried. "Now's our chance to get to the railway station before he comes round and gives the alarm. The sooner we get a train to Caen, the better."

Leaving the laundry cart where it was, Nina and Thumper made a dash for the station.

★ ★ ★ ★ ★

"You block-head!" Did I not give orders that no one was to enter or leave that cottage?"

Apologetically the under-officer faced his irate superior, but the captain was in no mood to listen to his excuses. His keen wit already detected trickery on Nina's part and when, after a phone call to H.Q. he heard that neither she, the guard nor the laundry had arrived, his worst fears were confirmed.

The Gestapo were notified and later came the information that a girl and Alsatian dog had been seen at the railway station. A talk with the booking clerk told the officer all he needed to know. Revolver in hand, he went charging along the booking-hall and onto the platform from which the Caen-express was about to leave.

As the train moved forward, the captain made a dash to get aboard — but too late — it was gathering too much speed. For a few seconds the outwitted Nazi stood watching it disappear, his expression as black as thunder, then he gave a harsh, grim laugh.

"She cannot escape," he reminded himself. "I will drive to Caen by car and will be there to welcome her, for the train will take longer than I will."

THANKS TO THUMPER

"Another five minutes and we will be there," Nina whispered to Thumper as she gazed through the carriage window at the factory chimneys on the outskirts of the busy manufacturing town and saw the broad river that wound its way to the inland port.

In the dock area, M'sieur Anton had his secret headquarters. He would have been warned to expect an urgent letter from England and Nina could imagine how worried he must be because it had not yet reached him.

Bending down, she reached for Thumper's collar and with trembling fingers pulled out the crumpled envelope.

What did it contain? Again she asked herself that question. Impossible to guess its contents, but obviously it was of supreme importance. No matter what happened, it must not fall into the Nazis' hands. And yet, how could she prevent that happening for when the train reached Caen, she knew she would be caught and hustled off to Gestapo headquarters, for she realised that they must have found out where she was going by now.

She shuddered at the prospect and buried her face in Thumper's soft fur as she held him close.

"Oh, Thumper!" she gulped. "It's such a shame that you should be made to suffer, too."

The Alsatian blinked in surprise as he felt her warm tears drop on to his long nose. Sensing her distress, he reared up and placed his front paws on her shoulders and with a low whine, he gently licked her face.

It was all he could do to show her that he loved her and knew her to be unhappy — although why, he certainly did not know.

The train was running alongside the river now. Ahead, the line curved and crossed a bridge into the station. Already Nina could see the domed glass roof and again she clutched the letter and whispered.

"Less than a mile to go and the Nazis will be waiting for us . . . guarding every exit. There can be no hope when —"

Breaking off she suddenly got a tremendous idea. She hurriedly put the letter in her pocket and gasped: "Oh, Thumper, I believe there is a chance for us after all!"

Thumper watched her as she crossed to the door of the railway carriage — and waited. As the train neared the bridge, it began to slow down. Nina waited a second or two and then she pulled the communication cord. Almost instantly there came a screech of brakes and, bracing herself as the train gave a violent lurch, she quickly opened the carriage door and leapt on to the track, urgently calling Thumper to follow!

Alarmed heads were thrust out of the windows all along the train, many of them helmeted, and the sight of the girl and the Alsatian aroused cries of suspicion.

Frantically Nina raced for the end of the bridge and looking at the river below, she pointed at Thumper and shouted "Jump! Jump, boy! Jump!" At the same time, she herself made ready to leap but in that instant, bullets began to whistle around her and there were hoarse shouts and the sound of running feet. A bullet bit deep into her arm and Nina slipped, banged her head on an iron girder and fell into the river in a half-dazed condition.

Thumper paddled around the spot where Nina fell and gratefully she was able to hang on to him as he swam for the far shore. Nina realised she would never be able to make it all the way and whispered to Thumper: "Make for the barges in the middle of the river where we will be out of sight."

Somehow, Thumper *knew* — he just *knew* what she said and he gallantly swam towards the boats.

Just how long they were in the river, Nina didn't know, for she lost consciousness but when she did regain her senses, she found that Thumper had almost carried her to the opposite bank!

Vaguely she saw, crouched in the arched entrance to one of the old warehouses, two men were waiting and as Thumper reached the river bank, they raced forward and helped Nina out of the water.

A wave of faintness swept over her and she lost consciousness again. When she came round she found herself lying on a bed of straw in an underground room lit by a solitary lamp. Bending over her, with a steaming mug of coffee in his hand, was M'sieur Anton!

She realised this must be his secret headquarters and at once, she struggled to sit up, saying:

"I have a message for you — a letter — from England!"

With a cry of surprise, the leader of the Underground Movement took it and quickly read it. Then he looked down at her with shining eyes.

"But this is splendid news, ma petite," he declared. "News about the forthcoming invasion. The Nazis would give their eyes to read this letter — but thanks to you, it is safe."

Nina's gaze went to Thumper, who lay curled up at her feet. "No, not thanks to me," she replied. "Thanks to Thumper!"

One dark, misty night, a few days later a rowing boat set out from the river-mouth, heading for where a fast motor-launch lay waiting.

At the oars were M'sieur Anton and one of his trusted guerillas, while in the bows sat two silent figures, their eager gaze concentrated on the horizon.

Nina and Thumper!

Their work done, they were being smuggled out of France — were being sent back to England — Nina to be reunited with her family and Thumper to go into quarantine for a short while.

It was a happy moment for Nina, marred only by the forthcoming separation from Thumper — although but temporary . . .

It was an even happier moment, six months later, when she and Thumper stood on the English cliffs watching wave after wave of fighter planes go hurtling across the Channel, to mark the beginning of the Invasion and the end of Nazi tyranny.

THE GALES OF GLENTOR

by Lynette Murray

One day a letter arrived from the council to tell the Gale family that the house they were living in was to be knocked down because of subsidence.

Where could they go? They were helped out of their predicament by a wealthy American client of Lindy's father. He offered them a home in Scotland — but he didn't tell them what sort of home!

There are five of us in our family. Mum, Dad, my eighteen-year-old sister Gillian, Mike my kid brother and, of course, me — Lindy Gale.

But on the day I'm telling you about it was our bad luck day. You see, Dad had a kind of shop in the front rooms of our house, for his business, which was selling old gramophone records, and he was teaching me the business.

Anyway, a letter had arrived from the council which said that . . . the ground under our road was sinking, and that our house was one of several that would have to be knocked down.

"It's all very well saying that they're going to have to knock our house down," Dad said despairingly. "But where are we all going to go?"

At that moment there was a knock on the door. Dad went to answer it. Standing on the step was a short, tubby, middle-aged man holding a brief-case in one hand. He said his name was Mr. Bronstein, that he was an American, and his car had broken down.

"Oh, I'm sorry to hear that," said Dad. "You'd better come in, and I'll see if I can get a garage on the phone."

"Say, that's real kind of you," smiled Mr. Bronstein, "and I'd be mighty grateful if you could tell me where I can locate a guy called Gale. He sells phonograph records — you know him, maybe?"

"But I'm Bill Gale!" Dad exclaimed. "You don't mean to say you're Sam I. Bronstein of Idaho?"

Mr. Bronstein grinned. "Correct," he chuckled.

Dad turned to us and explained: "Mr. Bronstein's one of my oldest customers."

Mum brought tea in then, and we all went into the shop to drink it because Dad wanted to show his old customer some special records. Mr. Bronstein looked at them reverently.

"Mr. Gale," he said, "I don't mind telling you that this is the high spot of my whole trip."

"It's as well you came when you did, because the chances are we won't be here next week," Dad told him.

"What goes on? You closing down?" asked Mr. Bronstein.

"It isn't that I want to close down." Dad explained about the letter he'd received that morning, and added: "So I'm not very sure where I'll be by the time you get back home."

"That's kind of tough." Mr. Bronstien looked thoughtful. "Just how important is it that you have a shop?"

"As a matter of fact, a shop doesn't matter much," Dad replied. "I do most of my business by post these days. I suppose I could work from almost anywhere."

"Yep. That's what I thought." Mr. Bronstein said thoughtfully.

Well, Dad arranged for the car to be repaired, and after lunch Mr. Bronstein said goodbye. By then, he and Dad were like a pair of old friends. Just how friendly we didn't realize until the letter arrived the next day.

"Dear Mr. Gale" (it said),

"I'm sorry this must be a short note, but I am due to catch the boat train in half an hour. It was a real pleasure to meet you and your family.

"You remember the little problem you were telling me about? I've got a place in Scotland I don't reckon I'll have time to visit for the next couple of years. It's kind of old, but if you'd care to move in till something better turns up you'll be doing me a favour. It does a place good to be lived in.

"Your sincere friend,

"Samuel Bronstein.

"P.S. My place is called Glentor. Same as the village. My Scottish geography isn't so hot, but you should find it okay on a map."

Dad read the letter out loud. When he finished we just stared at him. It was Mum who spoke first. And all she said was: "Scotland!"

"Scotland's not the other end of the world, Mary." Dad was looking quite excited. He dug in a bookshelf and unearthed an old road map. "Glentor. I wonder where the dickens it is?"

It took us five minutes of hard looking before young Mike spotted it in tiny letters in the Western Highlands.

Dad had a far-away look in his eyes. He said slowly: "If there's a village, there must be a post office."

"And if there's a post office," Mum butted in, "you could always post your old records off from there."

I knew then that the whole thing was as good as settled. And the very next week, we loaded up Dad's old car and off we went — bound for Scotland.

It's a funny thing, but there don't seem to be many towns once you get past the border — just little grey stone villages every now and again, and great towering mountains that seem to go on and on. We followed winding roads by the side of lochs for miles without meeting a soul.

"Look!" I suddenly yelled as we came to a signpost. "Glentor. One mile!"

We reached the brow of a hill. Below us lay the blue waters of an inland loch, and we could also see the big square tower of a castle, complete with moat and drawbridge.

Dad stopped the car so that we could see it better. Gillian was staring at the castle in a dreamy sort of way.

"That's quite something," I heard her say. "I wonder who lives there?"

But Mum's a more practical sort of person.

141

"It's where we're living that worries me," she reminded Gillian.
Dad sighed, because I think he does a bit of day-dreaming, too.
"We'd better look round," he said. "All I know is that we're
looking for a house called Glentor. Same as the village."

Well, apart from the castle there didn't seem to be another building
in sight. But at that moment an old man came through a gap in the
stone wall that ran alongside the road.

"I suppose we could always ask," I said, and jumped out of the car.
"Excuse me, do you happen to know of a house near here called
Glentor?"

"Aye." The man with the dogs waved his stick in the general
direction of the castle. "Ye can see it there. Just a wee bit ahead."

Dad smiled and shook his head. "Not the castle. It's a house I'm
looking for. It belongs to an American — a Mr. Bronstein."

"Och, I ken Mr. Bronstein well." The old man went on pointing
with his stick. "He's away just noo. But when he's here, he lives down
there at Glentor."

I gulped and said: "But Mr. Bronstein's house is called Glentor.
Isn't that — well — Glentor Castle?"

The old man nodded cheerfully. "Right enough, lassie. But it's
Glentor we're calling it around here. It's the only castle in these parts,
so we'll not be makin' a mistake."

Dad started the car again with an air of determination. Down the
road we roared, across the drawbridge, and drew up in a cobbled
courtyard.

The main part of the castle was right in front of us, full of square
windows and little slits that people used to shoot arrows through in
olden days. There was a big, nail-studded door, and a bell on the end
of a chain. Dad pulled it.

There was a sound of footsteps, and then the door swung open.
There stood a real-life butler.

Dad said: "I — we — er —"

"Yes, sir. You would be Mr. Gale. Mr. Bronstein informed me of
the situation." He had a lovely, plummy voice, and he added: "My
name is Hitchen, sir."

"Well, thank you, Hitchen." It doesn't take Dad long to get abreast
of things. Then to Mum: "Come along, Mary. We'd better go in."

"And welcome, madam," said Hitchen, "to your new home."
Then before we had a chance to say anything: "Perhaps I might

have the pleasure of showing you round so that you have — er — the lie of the land, so to speak."

So we started on a tour. It was absolutely fabulous. All stone corridors and galleries, and suits of armour and pictures. We were shown the library, the Long Corridor, and four different drawing rooms.

It was in the last of these that Mum sat down and announced that her feet hurt. Hitchen went off to get some tea.

"Think of keeping it warm in winter!" Mum said in her down-to-earth way. "It must cost a fortune!"

"That's a point, Mary." Dad looked a bit worried for the first time. "I mean, it's one thing to live here if that's what Mr. Bronstein wants. But one can hardly ask him to pay the coal bills. Or the servants' wages."

"I bet you never thought you'd be living in a Stately Home!" Gillian giggled.

"I suppose we are." I stared around the lovely room. And then, right out of the blue, came The Idea. "Of course!" I cried.

Dad looked at me. "Of course what?"

"Well, this is a stately home," I pointed out. "So why don't we do the same as everybody else who's got one? We can write to Mr. Bronstein and if he agrees we can open Glentor to the tourists each day. Charge fifteen or twenty pence for looking round!"

Mum said: "Don't be silly, Lindy."

But Dad was looking at me thoughtfully.

"I don't know," he said. "If you ask me, Lindy's had a bright idea."

"But, Bill," Mum objected to Dad, "how am I going to keep the place clean?"

"Oh, I don't think you'll have to worry about that, Mary," Dad replied. "Sam Bronstein must have a staff here."

Just then Hitchen returned with a tea-laden trolley.

"Ah, Hitchen," said Dad, "just how many servants are there here? We were wondering about opening Glentor to visitors!"

"Well, sir —" Hitchen paused and stared thoughtfully at the ceiling, "there's cook, two maids, two women from the village to clean, the head gardener, his assistants, and the chauffeur."

In the end Dad wrote to Mr. Bronstein.

Living at Glentor turned out well for us all, for the first fortnight.

Then we had a letter from Mr. Bronstein agreeing to our opening the house to the public and trouble started.

"It's a pity there isn't a ghost we can tell the visitors about," sighed Gillian over lunch.

"There is reputed to be a ghost, Miss," replied Hitchen, rather stifly, as he pointed to a picture high on the wall over the fireplace.

It was a painting of a small boy wearing a tartan and beating a drum. In the background there seemed to be battlements, as though he were walking along the top of a castle wall.

"That is a painting of Wee Willie," Hitchen said. "I understand that his correct name was William McBryle. His father was head of the Clan McBryle, and the family occupied this castle for more than three hundred years."

It sounded jolly interesting, so I asked: "What was special about Wee Willie that he should haunt the castle now?"

"I understand, Miss, that this castle was besieged by a rival clan in the year 1612," Hitchen replied. "Wee Willie's father was about to surrender, when the boy beat on his drum to draw attention to the arrival of a friendly army. Unfortunately the young man was killed shortly afterwards, and his ghost is said to walk along the wall above the main gate."

"Golly!" Mike exclaimed. "That sounds absolutely super! Have you ever seen him?"

"I regret to say I have not. In fact, I should say that the whole story is just a legend." Hitchen coughed. "The — er — good people in these parts are rather simple."

"By which I gather you're not from these parts yourself," Dad grinned.

"Indeed not, sir." Hitchen looked quite shocked. "I was engaged by Mr. Bronstein in London, sir."

Well, of course, that explained why the butler didn't take the Ghost of Glentor very seriously.

After tea I found Mike staring at the picture.

"If you ask me," he said, "Hitchen's a silly old fossil. How does he know the ghost is a fake?"

"I don't suppose he does," Dad told him. "But he doesn't know it's true either."

But Mum was thinking of something else.

"We could give tourists a special Glentor tea!" Mum broke in.

"I'll have to have a word with Hitchen," decided Dad.

As it turned out, it was the butler who came to see Dad.

Hitchen tapped at the door of the drawing-room — the Yellow Drawing-Room — about five o'clock. As soon as he came in I noticed that his face had lost its wonderful calm look.

"May I have a word with you, sir?" he asked Dad.

"Of course," Dad said. "What's the trouble?"

"It's the staff, sir," Hitchen said with an unmistakable gulp. "They've gone! They say they don't wish to work here any more."

"Oh!" As usual, Dad cottoned on pretty fast. "I suppose it's something to do with our idea for opening the castle to the public?"

"Yes, sir." Hitchen looked relieved at not having to break the bad news himself.

"But that's ridiculous!" Gilian looked indignant. "All sorts of earls and dukes have done the same sort of thing."

"I quite agree, Miss," nodded Hitchen. "Unfortunately, Cook and the others don't look at it that way. If you were part of the — ahem — Scottish nobility, they would have no objection. But I fear they class anyone from England as foreigners. Mr. Bronstein was acceptable because he never stayed here for more than a few days. But in your case —"

"All right, Hitchen. And thanks for letting us know." Dad knocked out his pipe and sighed. "We'll have to talk this over."

We talked it over all that evening, after Mum had gone down to the kitchen and produced us a scratch meal of bacon and eggs. But the more we talked about the situation, the more impossible it seemed.

"Let's all go to bed and get a good night's rest," Dad said at last. "Maybe things will look better in the morning."

Well, I went to bed, but I can't say I slept very well. I was dozing, when suddenly something made me sit bold upright in bed, wide awake.

It was the sound of a drum!

I sat listening to it for what seemed ages and ages — a measured tapping from the direction of the main gate. And, of course, there was only one thing a drum tapping from that direction could mean. It just had to be Wee Willie, the ghost of Glentor Castle!

Although I was scared stiff, curiosity finally got the better of me and I hopped out of bed and had a look. There, sure enough, was the figure

"Come down, you ass!" I hissed. *"Stop playing the goat!"*

of a boy in a kilt, slowly pacing his way back and forth across the battlements while he tapped the drum slung round his neck in front of him.

I must admit I felt jolly queer as I watched him. There was a bright moon, and it threw the figure up in sharp relief against the sky. And then —

"I wonder —" I said aloud. I wasn't sure but there seemed something very familiar about that figure. Almost before I knew what I was doing, I was hurrying next door to Mike's room. Well, I suppose I should have guessed the answer right away. Mike's bed was empty.

Ghostly Wee Willie was my wretched young brother!

I pulled on a sweater and a pair of slacks, and hurried out into the courtyard. There was a flight of stone steps that led up to the wall, and as I approached a man's figure fairly scuttled down. He shouted: "It's Wee Willie!" at the top of his voice, and as he crossed a patch of moonlight I recognized our dignified butler, Hitchen!

I was giggling so much I could hardly climb the steps after that. When I did I was just in time to come face to face with Mike.

"Come down, you ass!" I hissed. "Stop playing the goat! And where did you get that kilt and drum?"

"I found them hanging up in a cupboard," Mike grinned. He looked jolly pleased with himself. "Did you see old Hitchen scuttling away? I wanted to give him a scare! This will make the silly old buffer believe in the castle ghost!"

Now the really funny part of the whole business was breakfast next morning. Hitchen was there, looking his old self again as we sat down.

"Hello!" Dad sniffed the gorgeous scent of grilled bacon. "Who prepared the breakfast?"

"Cook, sir," replied Hitchen.

"You mean she's back?" I exclaimed.

"Yes, Miss. In fact all the staff is back. I think I may say that we shall have no more trouble in that direction."

Dad asked blankly: "But why?"

Hitchen poured the coffee. "There is a legend, sir, that Wee Willie only appears when he feels the castle is in safe hands. Some of the staff had returned last night to collect their belongings. When their attention was drawn to the ghost they concluded that if Wee Willie — er — approved of the castle's new tenants, then they couldn't very well object themselves."

"Well, I must say that Wee Willie certainly turned up at the opportune moment," Dad concluded as he finished up the last of his bacon. "It was almost as if he knew we were in trouble."

But I still had a sneaky suspicion that there was more in the ghost story than had come out.

"It was jolly lucky somebody told the cook about Wee Willie," I said. "It would have been a shame if she'd missed him."

"It would indeed, Miss."

At which point Mike couldn't resist saying: "Well, anyway, Mr. Hitchen — you've seen the ghost of Glentor Castle yourself now."

Hitchen handed him a plate of bacon and eggs.

"That is exactly what I said to Cook, Master Michael." Then he paused and added: "If I might be so bold as to suggest it, the castle walls are dangerous to walk along after dark."

Mike stared at him.

"Why," he began accusingly, "you knew all the time!"

"One has to do what one can to help." Hitchen retreated discreetly towards the door. "After all, we're all — er — foreigners together, so to speak."

And even Mike hadn't an answer to that!

SANDIE IN SWITZERLAND

by June Baxter

Sandie Foster was enjoying her new job as Assistant Winter Sports Instructress at the Alpine Hotel. There was only one drawback — Carol Barr, the spoilt daughter of a wealthy father. Carol's arrogant and supercilious ways were continually annoying Sandie and the situation reached crisis point when Sandie unaccountably failed to turn up for a skating lesson. Her pupil seized the opportunity to get Sandie sacked.

"That's the new Assistant Instructress."

"She's very young for such a job."

"She's also very efficient. You couldn't wish for a more patient and expert teacher."

Sandie Foster couldn't help but feel thrilled as she crossed the wide entrance hall of the Alpine Hotel in the Swiss town of Carosi. A group of guests, all of them in colourful ski-ing outfits, were standing in the hotel entrance. They didn't realize that their whispered comments had reached Sandie's ears. She had been appointed Assistant Winter Sports Instructress at the hotel only recently, and was naturally pleased to hear herself being praised in this way.

Sandie entered the tiny office occupied by Miss Mallory, the Chief

Instructress, and herself. On this particular morning, Miss Mallory was out of the hotel so Sandie was in charge. Her first task was to consult the Engagement Book.

"I'm rather sorry it's my half day off," Sandie told herself with a smile. "I shall feel quite lost having no one to teach."

She settled down to do some routine office work. A little while later the door was flung open and a fair-haired girl burst in.

"Can you tell me if my skating lesson is booked for eleven or twelve o'clock this morning?" she demanded.

There was something very supercilious about Carol Barr. She was the only daughter of a wealthy man and she was thoroughly spoilt. Her overbearing manner prevented her making friends, and Sandie sensed that she was really a lonely girl, in spite of so many people of her own age around.

"You're down for eleven o'clock, Carol," Sandie answered.

The girl gave an impatient exclamation.

"What a nuisance!" she burst out. "I was sure it was twelve. Can it be changed to twelve o'clock?"

"Sorry!" Sandie shook her head. "I have to take another pupil at twelve."

Carol Barr stared at her almost as though she doubted Sandie's statement.

"All right," she said ungraciously. "I suppose I'll have to try to turn up but you might see to it that my skates are properly sharpened this time. If they hadn't been so blunt, I wouldn't have made such a hash of things yesterday."

Sandie knew perfectly well that there had been nothing wrong with Carol Barr's skates the day before. Carol was a beginner, and skating didn't come at all easily to her. Also, she lacked the patience to practise really hard.

"I'd better make sure she's no cause to complain this morning," Sandie told herself then.

She made her way round to the large equipment room at the back of the hotel and there she found Old Fritz, the odd job man, already engaged upon the task of sharpening skates. From a shelf Sandie took down a pair of very expensive white doeskin boots — a small size, for Carol Barr had neat small feet.

"Make an extra good job of these would you please, Fritz," Sandie said with a smile.

The old man looked at the boots.

"I made a good job of them yesterday," he grumbled. "Some people are never satisfied. But leave it to me, Miss Sandie."

Just before eleven o'clock, Sandie, wearing her own skates, set off along the side of the frozen lake which fronted the hotel. She was making for the quiet back-water where all the first lessons in skating were given. Beginners always did much better if they knew there was no one looking on to see their mistakes.

At eleven o'clock Carol Barr had not turned up. Sandie was not surprised, for Carol was a girl who never worried about keeping appointments on time. When a quarter of an hour had gone by, Sandie felt something must be done. She decided to look in at the equipment room to see if Carol had collected her skates. A wooden walk led from the ice to the door of the equipment room so that it was easy to walk the path on skates.

Sandie had almost reached the door when she heard the sound of movements inside. She entered, expecting to see Old Fritz still at work.

"Fritz!" she called. "Are you here?"

When there was no reply Sandie frowned. She had been so sure there was someone inside the room. She crossed the room to the shelves where all the skating boots were stacked. One look was sufficient to show her that Carol Barr's expensive doeskin boots were missing.

"So Carol has taken her boots. I must have missed her . . ."

That was when Sandie heard the sound again. She spun round and was just in time to see a small girl hobble quickly through the door-way. A small girl who was wearing Carol Barr's expensive doeskin skating boots!

By the time Sandie reached the open door, the child was already on the ice, skating away at a speed that amazed her. She must go after her, Sandie decided. Perhaps Carol had lent the boots to her. Though, knowing Carol Barr, that didn't seem likely.

The girl was almost at the other side of the lake before Sandie succeeded in catching up with her. She appeared to be a local child, poorly yet neatly dressed. The moment Sandie skated alongside her, the girl burst into a flood of tears.

Gerda changed into her own shoes and Sandie took the white skating boots.

"I'm not a thief!" she burst out, before Sandie could say a word. "I didn't mean to steal the boots. I only wanted to borrow them."

Gently Sandie piloted her to the lakeside. She used her own handkerchief to wipe away the child's tears.

"Of course you're not a thief," she said gently. "Now, don't you think you'd better tell me all about it?"

In a flash the little girl seemed to lose her fear of Sandie.

"I only wanted to borrow the boots for the competition this afternoon," she explained tearfully. "My own skating boots are old, and now they're too small for me. I've never worn white skating boots before, and I thought that perhaps the judges would take more notice of me if I wore real skating boots."

It was a pathetic story Sandie heard then. The girl explained that her name was Gerda Schroeder, and that she lived in a small house on the outskirts of Carosi. She had learned to skate almost as soon as she had learned to walk and her ambition was to be a famous skater. It was one of the reasons she wanted so much to win the competition that afternoon but the chief reason was because her mother was seriously ill.

"You see, the competition is only for children under twelve. If I do well, I'd be given a job. I could be one of the juvenile skating troupe in the ice carnival," Gerda said. "Then I'll be able to give money every week to Mummy," she added.

Sandie looked down at the wistful little face, and she smiled.

"We'll have to return the skating boots, Gerda," she said quietly, "but I have a free afternoon today, so I'll come and see you skate. And I'll bring you a pair of skating boots that will fit you almost as well as these. How's that?"

Next moment Gerda's arms were round Sandie's neck.

"You're like the godmother out of the fairy tale!" she cried.

It was decided that Sandie would be down at the far end of the lake well before three o'clock that afternoon. Gerda changed into her own shoes that had been looped round her neck by the laces, and Sandie took the white skating boots.

It was only when she had parted from Gerda and was skating back to the hotel that Sandie remembered Carol Barr's lesson. A very angry Carol was awaiting her outside the hotel.

"If this isn't the limit!" Carol flared at once. "I went to all sorts of trouble to get to my skating lesson, only to find that you weren't there."

"I'm sorry, Carol," Sandie apologized. "I waited a quarter of an hour for you, and then I came back to the hotel to look for you."

Angrily Carol stamped her foot.

"I've paid for a lesson," she rapped. "It's your duty to wait for me, even if I don't turn up at all and because you had my skating boots with you, I couldn't even practise on my own. What have you been doing with them?" she added, snatching the boots away from Sandie.

Sandie was about to explain, and then stopped. There was no knowing what Carol might do if she learned that little Gerda Schroeder had dared to wear her expensive boots without permission.

"You may not know it," Carol went on, "but my father has just started to take an interest in half a dozen ice shows. That's why he's so anxious for me to learn. He's arriving here tomorrow, and I wanted to show him the progress I'd made. I must have at least one lesson before tomorrow."

"I'm sorry but I've another pupil waiting for me now," Sandie began, "and this afternoon I'm off duty."

"I can't help that," Carol said. "You owe me a lesson. I shall come down from the slopes at half-past two, and I shall expect to find you waiting for me on the ice with my skating boots. If you're not there, I shall complain to Miss Mallory."

Just for the moment Sandie was at a loss. She couldn't give Carol Barr a lesson that afternoon. She had promised little Gerda Schroeder that she would take skating boots to her at the far side of the lake. No matter what happened Gerda must not be disappointed but if Carol did complain to Miss Mallory, it might all come out about Gerda's visit to the equipment room. Then Sandie thought of a solution to the problem.

"Very well, Carol," she said quietly. "You'll find me waiting for you on the ice at two-thirty this afternoon."

At the end of her next lesson Sandie went back to the equipment room, and there she sorted out a pair of skating boots that were practically the same size as Carol's. She paid for their hire herself. Making them up into a parcel, she gave it to Old Fritz, who was going into the town early that afternoon. She asked him to deliver the parcel at the address Gerda had given her. She wouldn't be on the spot to see Gerda skate, but at least the little girl wouldn't be disappointed over the boots.

Half-past two that afternoon found Sandie on the ice, waiting for Carol with the skating boots. The minutes ticked by, but she saw no sign of her.

"She's probably keeping me waiting deliberately," Sandie told herself.

A moment or two later there was a hail from the bank, and she turned to see Old Fritz beckoning to her.

"I'm sorry, Miss Sandie," the odd job man said, "but when I called at that house early this afternoon I found it shut up. I was told that Frau Schroeder was hurried away to hospital just before I arrived. I couldn't deliver your parcel so I've brought it back."

"But what of Frau Schroeder's little daughter?" Sandie asked. "Wasn't she at the house?"

"They told me she was being looked after by some friends in the town," he answered. "That's all I could discover."

"Poor Gerda," Sandie said in dismay. "Now that her mother is in hospital, she'll be even more anxious to do well in the contest."

Old Fritz turned away, and Sandie was left holding the pair of skating boots that Gerda needed so desperately. She looked about her, and there was still no sign of Carol Barr. What was she to do?

"I just can't let Gerda down," Sandie convinced herself. "I must get to her as quickly as I can and then rush back here."

As she skated away Sandie saw one of the permanent guests at the hotel — a girl named Rosemary Dawn.

"Oh, Rosemary," she said, "if Carol Barr should show up will you tell her that I've had to go to the far end of the lake, and that I'll be back as soon as I possibly can."

Sandie was scarcely out of sight before Carol appeared at the lake-side. Quickly, Rosemary skated towards her and explained. Carol made no attempt to hide her anger.

"This is the second time she's let me down," she burst out. "It'll take her half an hour at least to go the length of the lake and back again, and I have a tea appointment for four o'clock."

"But Sandie must have had some very good reason," Rosemary pointed out. "And it looked as if she'd been waiting some time for you —"

"She's not going to treat me like this and get away with it," Carol flared. "I'll fetch my skates and go after her. I'll tell Sandie Foster what I think of her! Then I'm going to complain to Miss Mallory and the hotel manager! I'll see she gets the sack!"

Sandie had no difficulty in finding the place where the Juvenile Skating Competition was being held. As soon as she came in sight of the end of the lake she saw a large crowd of spectators grouped around a wide circle.

"It's almost three o'clock," Sandie gasped. "Gerda must be wondering what's happened to me."

Sandie was still some distance away from the circle of spectators when a small excited figure came running towards her at top speed. Never had Sandie seen such delight on a child's face.

"I knew you'd be here," Gerda cried as she raced up. "I knew. Fairy godmothers always keep their promises."

Gerda's faith in her made Sandie more glad than ever she had come — and at the moment she didn't care how upset Carol Barr might be.

"I'm sorry I'm late, Gerda," she said. "You see, I sent a messenger along to your home early this afternoon. He told me about your mother going to hospital."

The child still smiled.

"I've been to see Mummy in hospital," she said. "The doctor said he's going to make her really well. More than ever now I want to win the competition. It'll be such a wonderful surprise for Mummy and —"

She broke off with another cry of delight.

"Oh!" she gasped. "You've brought me the wonderful white skating-boots after all!"

Only then did Sandie realize she had Carol Barr's white skating-boots slung over her arm. And before she could do anything about it, Gerda had taken the boots. At the same moment there was a shout from the nearest line of spectators.

"Gerda Schroeder! Gerda Schroeder!"

Instantly Gerda dashed off. For a moment Sandie thought of calling her back but she realized it was too late. By the time she had done that and explained, the further delay might cause the child to lose her chance of appearing in the competition.

"I may as well face it," Sandie told herself. "I'm glad now that Gerda took those boots. She's so sure they'll bring her luck that she's bound to skate better because of them. As for Carol Barr — well, I'll just have to face the consequences."

She edged herself into the front rank of the spectators, and she was just in time to see Gerda skate into the centre of the circle. The child was called upon to perform a few simple figures, and she carried them out to perfection. Sandie felt as pleased as if Gerda had been her own pupil.

Other competitors followed Gerda and most of them skated very well indeed. At the end of the first test Sandie was sure Gerda must be leading on points.

The little girl came on to the ice a second time, and now she was called upon to execute a few more difficult figures. Again she carried them out well. This second test eliminated most of the other competitors but one rather older girl did particularly well.

"That's Gerda's closest rival," Sandie told herself. "But I still think Gerda is leading."

Free skating followed, with only half a dozen competitors taking part in this test. The older girl appeared before Gerda. She made no mistake, and she was well applauded at the end.

Gerda appeared next, and soon Sandie's eyes were shining with excitement. The little girl was doing splendidly.

"She'll be a star when she's older," Sandie murmured. "I'm sure she's still leading that other girl —"

Suddenly Sandie caught her breath — she wanted to shout a warning to Gerda that she was swinging towards a patch of ice that had been badly roughed up by some of the less expert competitors. If Gerda attempted anything at all intricate upon that particular patch it might be her undoing.

And then it happened! A groan of dismay went up as Gerda suddenly stumbled and fell. She was up in a flash, and carrying on, but several points had been lost.

It was nerve-racking waiting for the result. Sandie bit her lip in disappointment. The older girl had won by a very narrow margin — Gerda had been placed second. That unlucky fall had cost her the competition. She had lost her chance of skating with the juvenile troupe, and so helping her mother.

Bitterly disappointed, Sandie made her way out of the crowd.

Almost at once Gerda came walking towards her, and Sandie's heart was touched when she saw how bravely the child was trying to smile.

"It was bad luck, Gerda," Sandie told her. "If the rough ice hadn't tripped you up, you'd have won."

"I didn't deserve to succeed," Gerda answered. "It's my punishment for borrowing these skates this morning —"

That was when a familiar voice broke in.

"What's all this about borrowing my skates?" it demanded abruptly.

Sandie turned quickly to find herself facing Carol Barr. Her heart sank.

"There is rather a lot to explain, Carol," she said at once.

There and then Sandie told the full story. Carol listened quietly, and long before she had finished Sandie realized there was something different about Carol's manner.

Carol spoke then, and she told of her meeting with Rosemary Dawn, and how she set out after Sandie on hired skates.

"I saw you among the crowd," she went on. "Then I saw this little girl skating. She was so good that I just had to watch her, even after I noticed she was wearing my skating-boots. I was dreadfully sorry when I saw her fall."

Sandie couldn't help showing her surprise at such a remark from Carol.

"What you've told me, Sandie, makes me thoroughly ashamed of myself," Carol went on. "You knew I'd complain if I didn't find you waiting for me, yet because you made a promise you were prepared to face that trouble. That was wonderful of you, Sandie."

Then she was smiling at Gerda.

"Don't give another thought to the boots," she said. "They're yours from now on. And you'll also be interested to know that this juvenile troupe you want to join belongs to the ice show my father is financing. He's coming to the hotel tomorrow, Gerda, and if you come and see him I'm sure he'll have a surprise for you." With these intriguing words Carol Barr skated off across the lake towards the hotel, leaving behind her a surprised and happy Gerda.

The following morning was bright and clear as Gerda made her way to the hotel. There she was greeted by Sandie, in the entrance.

"Mr. Barr is waiting for you in his room," Sandie said, as she ushered Gerda towards the stairs.

"Oh, Miss Foster, I'm feeling so nervous. I wonder why he wants to see me?"

"You'll soon know," answered Sandie. "There's Carol waiting for us at the door of his suite."

As they were shown in by Carol, Mr. Barr came forward to greet them.

"Hello, my dear. Carol has told me all about you and how you'd like a part in one of my ice shows."

"Oh, yes please," answered Gerda, her eyes shining with excitement. "I would like it more than anything else in the world."

"Well, my dear," continued Mr. Barr, "it so happens there is a part you could fill very well, and on Carol's advice I'm offering it to you."

Gerda was almost speechless with surprise and could only murmur "Thank you, Mr. Barr. I'll do my very best."

Later, when all the details had been sorted out with Mr. Barr, Gerda and Sandie held a celebration party in a nearby café.

"Oh, Sandie, I'm so happy," bubbled Gerda. "Now when Mummy comes out of hospital I'll be able to afford to take her away on holiday."

Before Sandie could answer, Carol came in and sat with them.

"I've been looking everywhere for you, Gerda. I just wanted to say how happy I am for you and hope that we can be friends."

Gerda threw her arms round Carol. "There's nothing I'd like better," she answered.

A few weeks later when Gerda made her first appearance with the troupe, both Sandie and Carol were there to applaud her.

HEROINE IN THE DESERT

Jim Stephens was dazzled by the thought of the gold waiting in those distant mountains for some lucky prospector. But his wife was dreaming of a different kind of gold — the gold they could grow themselves on their small ranch.

Then the rattlesnake struck and the little world of the Stephens family exploded.

Young Mrs. Stephens stood in her doorway, looking out over the desert that shimmered with heat under a blazing Californian sun. As it rose higher, the shadows of tall cacti shrank and the cicadas' shrilling in the sage-brush drowsed into silence. No life stirred except where, against the sky, buzzards planed and glided on motionless wings.

Yet Mrs. Stephens found nothing dull in the vast open space with its silent shifting of shadows and colour, and hoped never to return to the noisy bustle of city life. Nor was she lonely, for she had her children, her seven-year-old Timmy, and little Anne, two years younger, and over there, where mountains showed blue through the desert's veil of heat, was Jim.

She smiled as she thought of her husband, for he was one of those Californians who, even in 1910, with the days of the gold-rush long past, could still not see distant mountains without saying, "There may be gold in those hills!"

So there might be, but Mrs. Stephens cared only that there was water under their bit of desert, far down at the bottom of the deep well. She dreamed not of gold mines but of a little homestead with rows of tall Indian corn; squat tomato-plants, and trailing melon vines. A dream that would come true, as soon as Jim bought the modern pump for the water.

Yet he had worked hard to instal his little family in their new home, and now deserved to follow his own dream for a time, his pot of gold at the rainbow's end.

She turned back into the house and, crossing the kitchen with its great iron cooking-stove that never quite went out, called from the open window.

"Timmy, Anne!"

"Yes, Mom," they answered, and came out of the open stable, where the four-wheeled buggy stood, and where only the goat was tethered, since the horse had gone with Jim, carrying his flour and bacon, and his prospector's tools.

"I'm going to see if I can find any prickly pears for supper tonight," she told them. Timmy, dark-haired like herself, hopped on one foot and cried, "Oh, goody, goody!" Anne, who had her father's ruddy curls, thrust out her lower lip and protested, "I'd rather have an orange!"

"Well, we'll see," her mother said and turning away, she went out to the desert.

With the sun's heat prickling through the calico of her dress, she walked on past the cacti that, like huge candelabras, raised elbow-jointed arms towards the sky, to the other cacti, whose branches were made of flat, oval disks, strung together like great beads, and at whose tips grew the pink, egg-shaped pears.

These she knocked off with a stick, then rolled them in the sand, to rid them of their hair-thin spines, that could stick so painfully in mouth and throat. Then, gathering them in her basket, she turned homewards.

As she passed the candelabra cacti, she heard the sudden, harsh warning of a rattlesnake, that sounded more like the hiss of escaping steam than a rattle. She had never seen a "rattler" before, but there was no mistaking that grey, black, diamond-patterned body, coiled like a thick rope, and the rattles at its tail's end vibrating over the coils.

It was about ten feet away, but it could leap farther than that, by launching itself from the powerful spring of its coiled body. Paralysed

Paralysed with horror, she stared at the rattler as it sprang.

with horror, she stared at it as it sprang. At first she felt nothing but the blow of its head, like a stone throw against her ankle, and she stood motionless, unable to think.

Then as the pain began, like the touch of a red-hot poker, her mind cried out, "In a few hours, I shall be dead!"

The horse was gone, the nearest neighbour five miles away, and she dared not try to walk so far for help, lest she fall on the way, and the children be left alone. The children!

Desperately she hurried home, while the pain rose like a flame up her leg. She must prepare food for them, enough to last until Jim came back. In the kitchen she stood, half dazed wondering where to begin. Then she opened the blowers of the stove, put on more fuel, and went down to the underground store-room.

In trip after trip, each more painful than the last, she carried up supplies. Soon, in iron kettles on the stove, bacon was boiling, while from the oven she took out batch after batch of corn bread. On the marble slab in the pantry she set out butter, cheese and preserves.

Her leg felt like hot iron now, rigid, and almost too heavy to drag about. Yet her head seemed light, and empty of everything but an echoing voice that said, "Sleep! Let me sleep!" It went on, "Nothing else matters, only that. Sleep!" But her heart found the answer. "No. It's the children that matter. Nothing but them. Nothing." And love, stronger than mind or body, drove her on.

She set the tin bath-tub on the floor, then went out to the old deep well with its wooden bucket on a chain, and the iron wheel to wind it up. She carried bucket after heavy bucket to empty into the tub. Once she stumbled and fell, so that the water was lost, and her mind cried, "You see, you can't do it! Why try?" But she struggled up again. She could do it, she would, for the children must live, they *must!*

When it was done, and the tub full, she stood leaning against the wall, not daring to sit, lest she could not get up again. About her the air looked dim and seemed to waver, as though she stood under deep water. She wondered if anything remained to be done. Then, pushing herself away from the wall, she went to the door and called, "Timmy, Anne! Come to supper."

She had set out buttered bread and goat's milk for them, and as they ate, she stood looking at Timmy's dark, tousled hair and Anne's copper-red curls, thinking, "I shall never see them again — not ever again." But she forced her lips to smile as she said:

"My darlings, I have to — to go away tonight."

"Why?" demanded Anne, while Timmy said firmly, "You can't. Dad's got the horse, and you can't get into town, to the station, without it."

"Somebody is — coming to fetch me," she answered. "Now listen, my darlings. There is food in the larder. Eat what you want, but don't waste anything — not a thing. Do you understand? There's water in the tub, but use it only for drinking, not for washing."

Timmy nodded, but Anne, who was a dainty little girl, wrinkled up her nose and asked, "Not even my hands, Mommy?"

"No, dear," she answered and said to the little boy, "Timmy, you've seen me milk the goat. Do you think you can do it, too?"

"Course I can," he said, nodding again.

"Then remember to do it, dear," she warned him. "And, both of you, you're to stay near the house, and not go outside the wire fence Daddy put up. Timmy, promise to take care of Anne, and never let her out of your sight. Remember, you're the man of the house until Daddy comes, and you, Anne, promise to do as Timmy tells you. Promise, both of you!"

"I promise," said Timmy solemnly, but Anne complained, "He's not my Daddy, only my brother. Oh, all right, I promise."

"It's going to be fun, isn't it?" cried Mrs. Stephens, hearing herself laugh as though from a long way away. "You two, playing at house-keeping, all by yourselves! Now, come along to bed."

With numb fingers she fumbled Anne's buttons undone, and when they were both in bed she kissed them, not daring to clutch them to her lest she frighten them.

She did not feel as though she had a body at all, now, only a sort of heavy, dark cloud about her, dragging her down and down. But there was still one more thing she must do.

The pencil in her hand felt as heavy as an iron bar as she lifted it and high up, on the outside of her bedroom door where Timmy couldn't read it, wrote in sprawling letters:

"Jim, my dearest, break open the door but don't let the children come in. Stung by a rattler."

Then, clinging to the doorknob she went in, pushing the bolt to behind her. Now she could surrender, lie down, and let the soothing darkness sweep over her. Soon she was asleep.

It was very comfortable to be dead, she thought — whatever it was that she lay on, it was so nice and soft. It was pleasant, too, that there should be the cheerful shrilling of the cicadas in the place she had come to. That, and the sound of children's voices. Children's voices — a little boy's voice saying:

"Mom *told* you not to wash in the water!" And a little girl's shrill treble answering, "Oh, all *right!* I only dipped my finger in, anyway!"

Children. Timmy and Anne! Mrs. Stephens opened her eyes and saw that she was in her own room, with the morning sun streaming in at the window. She moved, and found that she could sit up. She could stand and walk too though her head swam a little, and her leg was stiff and sore but she was alive — alive!

As she opened the door the children ran to her with shrieks of joy, and she wasn't afraid now to hug them to her and to kiss them again and again.

She told them wasn't it lucky that she had not had to go away the night before. Just how lucky, how incredibly lucky, she did not dare to dwell on too much, and certainly not to talk about to the children. What miracle had brought about this most wonderful moment of a life so nearly lost she did not know then.

She was still very tired but she thought smiling, there was no cooking to do. Only one thing must be done, wipe off the pencilled words from the bedroom door before her husband returned.

Young Mrs. Stephens became a heroine, with her name in the papers. For on ranches and homesteads that were far from help, the only hope for a victim of a rattlesnake's bite was to force himself to walk up and down, hour after hour, and do everything possible to keep awake.

But that lone woman had found the strength of will to keep her going, to keep on her feet with no one to help her. She only smiled, knowing that it was not strength of will, but love and devotion that had worked the miracle.

Her thankful husband whispered to her:

"Sweetheart, if those hills were made of solid gold, I would never again leave you for a single day to go after it."

"No," she answered softly, "we'll be content now with the gold that we can grow ourselves, the corn and the golden melons!"

DANGEROUS VOYAGE!

The four friends – Anne, Philip, Audrey and Tommy – had built their own sailing dinghy and now the great day of their maiden voyage had arrived. They were sailing across the calm waters inside the Great Barrier Reef bound for an off-shore island. All was well and set fair.

But suddenly a squall struck them and before Philip could lower the sail, the mast was gone, broken like a rotten carrot.

Now they were in deadly peril for they were adrift in a frenzied storm on one of the most dangerous seas in the world.

There were four of them in the trim little sailing dinghy which had set out that morning from Mallory, a small seaside village a few miles north of Cairns, in Queensland — four happy-go-lucky Australian youngsters who, like most Australians could swim like fishes, and were as much at home on the water as they were on dry land.

It had been the idea of Philip Arden, the oldest of the group, that they should build their very own sailing dinghy, and now the great project was finished, and they were sailing across the calm waters inside the Great Barrier Reef bound for one of the many offshore islands.

They had a whole week-end ahead of them, and their idea was to pitch camp on the island and spend a crusoe-like existence there until they had to return on Sunday evening.

Besides Philip, there was his younger sister, Anne, and Tommy and Audrey Baynes. Tommy, the youngest of the group, was at the tiller, while his sister, Audrey, looked after the main sail. Philip and Anne stretched themselves out in the sunshine.

"This is certainly the life," said Philip. "Don't mind me if I take things easy."

"Go right ahead and relax, Philip," said Audrey. "We know you got up early to put the finishing touches to the dinghy. You certainly deserve a rest."

The gentle rocking of the boat as it breasted the slight swell that was running from the northward, together with the comforting warmth of the strong sunshine, lulled Philip into a doze.

It was a slight spatter of raindrops on his face that eventually made him sit up and look anxiously at the sky. A cloud was hovering over them, borne onward by a breeze which had suddenly sprung up.

"Rain before the wind, topsails you must mind," he quoted, remembering an old sailor's saying. "Look out for the sail, Audrey."

"I can manage," said Audrey. "Nothing to worry about, Philip."

It was just then that the squall hit them! It came suddenly — a blast of wind that caused the dinghy to heel over sickeningly. Philip sprang to lower the sail — but he was just too late!

There was a crack like the sound of a whip as the full force of the squall caught the sail, making it billow out and sending a disconcerting shiver through the little boat. Then the boom swung over with violent force, barely missing Philip's head as he ducked.

A second later there was a splintering of wood.

"The mast!" gasped Philip. "It's going!"

The mast had never been intended to stand against such a tremendous blast. It broke off like a rotten carrot and the dinghy heeled over almost on its beam ends as the mast crashed sideways.

"Cut it loose — quickly!" yelled Philip, and shot forward, his sheath knife slashing at the fastenings of the sail, while Anne and Audrey bent to unravel the twisted halliards and sheets.

Tommy let the tiller go, snatched up an axe, and began hacking away at the remains of the mast.

The dinghy had now keeled over to a perilous angle, and was in imminent danger of capsizing. It had drifted broadside on to the swell which was now beginning to assume gigantic proportions.

Waves pounded against the side of the boat, sweeping over it. It was half-full of water before the combined efforts of the four succeeded in cutting free the mast. As it flopped overboard, the dinghy righted itself. But the damage had been done! Without a mast they were now at the complete mercy of the waves, for they realised that the squall was by no means a passing one but the fore-runner of a storm which had sprung up with all the suddenness of such things in the tropics.

Darkness was closing in upon them as heavy clouds came lower in the skies. The wind was howling like a thousand furies, and the waves were being lashed into a turmoil of frenzied water.

"The paddles!" shouted Philip. "Grab one, Tommy! Our only hope is to get into the lee of the island!"

Together he and Tommy snatched up the paddles which they had brought with them as a precaution, and began to paddle frantically, heading for the island which they could barely see now through the gathering darkness.

While the boys paddled, the girls bent to the task of baling out the water which had poured in.

For hours, it seemed, they laboured, then a momentary flash of lightning allowed Philip a glimpse of the island. Something like a groan escaped his lips. It seemed further away than ever. He realised then what had happened.

Dismasted, almost half-submerged, they had been caught in the grip of a current that was sweeping them past one of the many islands which formed the Barrier Reef. They were being carried out to the open sea beyond!

In the open sea they faced the full fury of the gale-swept ocean. It was almost pitch dark now, for the heavy clouds gave them no glimpse of the sky. The thunder was deafening, and the momentary flashes of vivid lightning showed them only a mass of heaving sea surrounding them.

"Keep her head-on to the waves, Tommy!" yelled Philip. "We've got to try to ride out the storm."

He knew that was going to be difficult. So long as their strength held out they might be able to do so, but they couldn't keep it up for ever.

It was then that Anne gave a sudden cry!

"A sail!" she yelled. "Over on the starboard bow!"

As the others looked in that direction, the dinghy rose to the crest of

"A sail!" she yelled. "Over on the starboard bow!".

the next wave — and they all saw what Anne had seen. There was a trim-looking two-master heaving and rolling as she headed into the waves. Only a tiny rag of sail was keeping her head-on to the sea, and there was no one on deck or at the wheel in her tiny cockpit.

The two boys bent to their paddles, and, guided by the lightning, edged towards her, coming up under her lee.

"She looks as though she's been abandoned," said Philip grimly. "Take the painter, Audrey, and get ready to jump as soon as we're near enough."

Soon they were within a few feet. Audrey jumped. She grabbed the gunwale and scrambled aboard, just as the boat gave a violent heave. The painter slipped through her numbed fingers, and the dinghy slipped away.

But Anne and the boys had also scrambled on board and Philip cast a rueful glance at the dinghy as it slipped away.

"That looks like the last we'll see of it," he groaned. He glanced around. "Hello," he went on. "Someone's rigged a sea-anchor — that's why she's heading into the waves. But there can't be anyone aboard or —"

A cry from Audrey who had jumped down into the cockpit interrupted him.

"There's a man here!" she called, "and he's badly hurt!"

The others hurried to the spot. The man lay inert on the floor of the cockpit. Audrey knelt down alongside him, and felt his pulse.

"He's alive," she reported. "But he's had a crack on the side of his head. We'd better get him below."

The little cabin opened out from the cockpit. Soon they had the man stretched out on a bunk. Audrey bent over him.

"I reckon he was caught unprepared by the squall," she said. "He was probably hit by the boom as it swung over."

There was a small calor gas stove in the cabin, and before long the two girls had cleaned and bound up the man's head wound."

"He could be suffering from concussion," said Audrey. "We must get him ashore as soon as possible."

"And we may be able to do that sooner than I thought." The girls turned. Philip had come into the saloon.

"This looks a marvellous sea-boat," he reported. "I believe we can bring her round and head for a gap in the reef, but we'll need all hands on deck."

There was nothing else that could be done for the unconscious man at that moment, so all hands scrambled on deck. Anne took the wheel and Audrey went to the sail, while Philip and Tommy began to heave in the sea-anchor, inch by inch, and then foot be foot.

Anne waited until Philip should give the word to go about. Then —

"Hard over to starboard!" yelled Philip as the sea-anchor came aboard.

The bows swung round, then with a shuddering lurch the vessel slid into the trough of the waves. Now was the testing time! They all held their breath. If the heavy seas caught them broadside on before they were properly underway they would be finished.

But the manoeuvre succeeded. The vessel had come about on a course that would take them back towards the gap in the reef.

Philip gazed anxiously ahead. Time passed slowly before he could see the long line of breakers which showed the position of the Barrier Reef, and the stretch of comparatively calmer water that marked the gap.

"Once we're in the lee of the reef, I think we can set more sail," he announced. "We can relax a little now."

Anne slipped below. She was feeling chilled and soaked to the skin, but her first thought was for the injured man.

He was still lying on the bunk, still breathing heavily and stirring uneasily. As she boiled a kettle and prepared mugs of tea, she kept shooting glances at the man. Suddenly she started. He had opened his eyes. Instantly she was alongside him, a mug of hot tea in her hand which she raised to his lips.

"Are you all right?" she gasped. "Here, try to drink this."

He made no reply. His eyes were glassy as he looked at her wonderingly. She had almost to force the hot liquid down his throat. Then he closed his eyes again.

She took tea up to the others in the cockpit and told them what had happened.

Time passed. All of them went below occasionally, taking turns to warm their chilled limbs and refresh themselves with strong, hot tea. Then a cry from Philip brought them all up on deck.

"All hands to set sail," shouted Philip. "We can risk more sail now. We're inside the reef."

His words lent them new energy. More sail was set, and then all four gazed eagerly ahead. Sea and wind were still strong, but they no longer faced the full fury of the gale.

"Where are we heading, Philip?" asked Audrey.

"We'll have to make for Cairns," Philip told her. "We can anchor her there — and get that fellow ashore for medical treatment. I'm going down below for a while. There's bound to be some charts somewhere."

Audrey went down in the cabin with him. She crossed immediately to her "patient" who, half-conscious now, was tossing about uneasily.

"He'll be all right," Audrey said with relief.

Philip looked up from the chart which he had been examining.

"With a bit of luck, we should be in the harbour at Cairns, by dawn," he said. "We can get him to hospital there, and —"

He broke off. Above the chart table was a book-shelf, and one of the books had caught his eye. It bore the simple word "Log" on the spine. He opened it, read for a while, then gave a low whistle.

"Do you know who he is?" he gasped. "It's Peter Derwent! You remember — the fellow who set out from Cairns nearly a year ago, saying he was going to sail single-handed around the world. And he's done it!"

"Gosh!" gasped Audrey. "Of all the bad luck!"

"Bad luck? What do you mean?"

"We've jinxed him, Philip! We've spoiled his record! And yet there was nothing else we *could* do! We've got to get him ashore — and so we've pipped him on the post! Don't you see — he *hasn't* sailed single-handed around the world!"

It took only a moment for the grim truth to sink in to Philip's understanding.

"You're right," he said glumly. "He started from Cairns, so to have sailed round the world alone, he must get back to Cairns — alone! But we came aboard outside the reef — oh gosh! Of all the bad luck!"

"It can't be helped. He *must* have medical attention."

They sat down on the little bench in the cabin, and gazed at each other. To think that the lone-hand sailor should have been robbed of his triumph on the last day of his long voyage was heart-breaking.

Suddenly Audrey leapt to her feet.

"I've just thought of something," she said excitedly. "Listen! He's in a state of coma. He won't remember anything of what happened to him after the boom caught him that crack on the head. He'll never know — and, *if* we four keep our mouths shut —"

A light of understanding dawned in Philip's eyes.

"You mean, that if we sneak into the anchorage at Cairns just before dawn, drop anchor, and then clear off, when he recovers he'll think he must have brought the boat in himself, although he doesn't — or won't — remember anything about it? But —"

"We can put through an anonymous 'phone call to the hospital," Audrey explained.

"They'll send a boat out — and find him here, but not us. We can slip over the side and swim ashore. And say we had a bit of trouble with our own boat and had to swim for it."

The plan worked! Everything went without a hitch. They had arrived in the harbour at Cairns before dawn where they dropped anchor and hoisted an Australian flag upside down as a distress signal. Then they slipped over the side silently and swam ashore.

Just to be on the safe side, Audrey rang the hospital, reported that a man was ill and needed urgent treatment, and then hung up before any awkward questions were asked. Afterwards, they set off on the long walk home.

When they reached their homes they merely said they had lost their dinghy in the storm, and had swum ashore. The loss of the dinghy was the only thing that worried them, but, as Philip pointed out, they would have lost that anyway, and might even have lost their lives if it hadn't been for their encounter with Peter Derwent's craft.

Derwent had, in a way, saved their lives. They owed him their silence for that if nothing else.

Next day the papers were full of the story of Derwent's arrival. As he had been taken straight to hospital still in a state of coma no one had been able to interview him, and the newspapers had taken it for granted that he must have navigated his vessel into the harbour before he lost consciousness.

It had been several days before he recovered sufficiently to report that he knew nothing of what had happened after he had taken in sail and put out the sea-anchor. Once he recovered consciousness he made a rapid recovery, and soon it was announced that he would lecture on his experiences at a local theatre.

"We'll be there," said Philip when he met the others.

"We certainly will," nodded Audrey, flourishing four cards in front of them all.

"These came by post addressed to me this morning. There was no covering letter with them."

They looked at the cards. They were marked "complimentary", and were for admission to the very front row of the lecture.

"Maybe they're from my uncle in Cairns," said Audrey. "He knows how keen we four are on sailing."

"It's going to be interesting to hear what Derwent's going to say about how he reached the anchorage," Philip chuckled. "I guess he must be just as puzzled as the newspapers were."

The night of the lecture was the first time they had seen Peter Derwent since they had left him unconscious. He looked perfectly fit as he came on to the stage and began his lecture. It was an interesting one, but naturally, the four were on tenterhooks until, near the end, he reached the incident of the storm off the Great Barrier Reef. He explained how he had taken in the sails, and rigged the sea-anchor, then how he must have been hit by the boom and knocked unconscious.

"What happened after that, I really don't know," he confessed. "I woke up to find myself in hospital, and it wasn't until I was really fit again that I started to make enquiries to solve the riddle." He paused to . let his words sink in, then went on:

"Now I'm going to ask someone else to finish the story," he said, and advanced to the footlights.

He gave a signal to the ushers in the stalls. The next moment, to their surprise, Philip and the others were motioned forward by the ushers.

"You're wanted on the stage, all four of you," they were told.

"But look here —" began Philip.

"Up you go! You can do all the talking when you get up there."

As though in a dream they found themselves pushed up a flight of steps and on to the stage. Peter Derwent came forward, hand extended to greet them.

"So, you're the four gallant youngsters to whom I owe my life," he said. "Now, don't protest. Just get on with it and tell us what happened."

"Then you know?" gasped Philip. "You — you knew all the time?"

"I didn't know until I was fit enough to piece things together. Then I began to remember . . . I seemed to have dreamed that there were other people aboard that boat — four of them. I might still have though it was only a dream, if one of the harbour officials hadn't mentioned that four youngsters had been seen having a swim in the harbour fully dressed early the morning of my arrival, and the hospital people told me of a mysterious 'phone call. It happened that the harbour official knew the four of you and the fact that you had set sail the previous day in your dinghy."

Things happened rapidly after that. Briefly Philip told the truth.

"But why on earth didn't you wait until the harbour officials came aboard, and tell them?" Peter Derwent asked.

"We didn't want to rob you of the credit of sailing single-handed round the world," said Audrey. "You see, you hadn't finished up in Cairns single-handed."

A roar of laughter came from Derwent.

"But I *had!*" he explained. "If you'd read the beginning of my log, you'd have seen that I didn't log my point of departure on the trip until I'd passed through the reef. At the time you picked me up, I'd reached that spot, and my round-the-world-voyage had been completed. Most probably, I would never have lived to know if it hadn't been for you four bringing my boat and me into harbour! You lost your own boat and risked your own lives to save me, and you'll learn that I am grateful."

Peter Derwent was more than grateful. Philip, Audrey, Anne and Tommy soon possessed what was to them the finest boat on the whole Australian coast. True, it was second-hand but it was named *Lone Voyager* — the boat in which Peter Derwent made his record-breaking round-the-world-voyage!

THAT DREADFUL HOLIDAY

by Sally Cade

Beth Valiant was a nurse in charge of the two little sons of the President of Santa Rica and she was taking them to a famous holiday resort for two weeks of sun, swimming and picnics.

But unknown to Beth, plague was raging in the resort. Even so, Beth maintained a cool control . . . until one of the little boys disappeared!

The private aircraft of the President of Santa Rica had circled low over the treetops, giving Beth and the children their first view of the lakeside village. The two boys were excited.

"Tell us again, Nurse Val, 'bout all the things we're going to do," Mel urged Nurse Beth Valiant.

Beth grinned. She had been as thrilled as the children when the President had suggested she should take them for a holiday to this famous beauty spot. They were to have two weeks of fun, away from the routine of the palace.

"There will be boating," she told them, "and swimming and picnics."

There was a slight bump as the aircraft landed and then they were taxiing across the grass.

Beth looked out of the window and was surprised there was no sign of the car that should be waiting to meet them.

Rodriguez, the pilot came to help them all out of the plane and said anxiously, "The car should be here by now, Nurse Val. If anything, we're a little behind schedule. I don't like leaving you here unescorted, but I have to get back to the capital. The plane is wanted by the President this afternoon."

"You must go," Beth told him. "We'll just have to start walking, that's all. There's been a mix-up somewhere but don't worry. You take off."

But Rodriguez was worried although there was nothing he could do about it for he was under orders to return. First, he unloaded their luggage and then took off on the return trip.

When the plane was little more than a speck in the sky and the boys had stopped waving, Beth took each of them by the hand and began to walk towards the village.

How still it was — and how silent, except for the sleepy call of wood pigeons and the chirp of crickets in the undergrowth — and not a human being in sight.

They hadn't gone far when Juan looked back and cried, "Look! A mule train!"

Beth pulled the children to the side of the road to let the mules pass and found herself staring at the man who sat astride the leader. He was covered in dust but there was something about that lean, lithe figure that swayed so easily to the mule's motion. And then she was looking into a pair of familiar piercing blue eyes. . . .

"Beth Valiant! Nurse Val!" exclaimed the man.

"Well, Dario! Dr. Dario Matrice! What on earth are you doing here?"

Dario leapt off the mule and took Beth's hands in his — much to the surprise of the two little boys. Beth and Dario were old friends. Once, in a time of crisis for Santa Rica, that tiny Caribbean republic, she had helped him nurse the peasants while bandits terrorized the country-side.

But right now, Dario did not seem too pleased to see her.

"You shouldn't be here, Beth," he began but she interrupted him with a laugh —

"We've just arrived on holiday, but our car —"

"Holiday!" repeated Dario with an expression of horror on his face.

"Then you don't know about the plague?"

Dario took her arm and walked a few steps along the dusty road.

"Better not frighten the boys," he said and Beth agreed, although she was frightened for them!

Quickly Dario explained that the plague had broken out unknown, until yesterday, when it was too late to check it. Panic had swept the region. All holidaymakers had been evacuated and the peasants had shut themselves indoors. Dario had come on the scene bringing mules laden with medicine and hospital equipment.

He stood scowling at the beautiful castle ahead of them, set on a hilltop.

"I blame that old miser," he said bitterly, nodding his head towards the castle. "He's the local landlord and rolling in money. I went to see him last week, begging him to build a hospital here for the peasants, who are his responsibility. But he was too mean!"

Beth shared his bitter despair for she knew how much Dario cared about the sick and the poor of his country. She wondered how he would cope with the plague without hospital or staff?

Dario turned back to sweep the two little boys on to the mule's backs. They grinned at him shyly, glad of the rest. Then Dario went back to Beth.

He handed her a small bundle.

"Here are three phials and a syringe. You must innoculate yourself and the children at once."

Beth took them gratefully. At least the children would have some defence against the plague.

They had now arrived at the village and were standing outside the hotel, which to Beth's dismay, was shuttered.

Dario hammered on the door until the Manager appeared. When he saw Beth and the children he was appalled.

"I sent a cable to the President —" he began.

Beth shook her head for no cable cancellation had been received at the Palace.

"It's been chaos here," said Dario. "No doubt much of the work at the post office was left undone." Turning to the manager he said "See that they get comfortable rooms and look after them as best you can."

To Beth he said, wryly, "It won't be much of a holiday, I'm afraid. Keep the boys indoors, away from possible infection. I'm setting up Headquarters in the next village and I must press on. I'll do my best to get a message through to the President for you."

Beth hurried the children upstairs behind the Manager. Once he had seen them safely unstalled, he set off with a cart to collect their luggage at the airfield.

The children listened quietly while Beth explained that she was going to give them an injection —

"Just a little prick — like this —" she told them as she quickly and efficiently innoculated them both in a trice before either of the boys realized that it had been done, for they both remained looking very baffled but brave, still waiting!

The third phial she knew Dario had intended she should use herself. But what if the injection didn't take on one of the boys? No, she would keep it in reserve.

The day dragged slowly by while Beth did her best to keep the children amused and their minds off the exciting things they wanted to do outside in the sun.

She devised and played games with them. She read to them, "The Sleeping Beauty" from cover to cover and then again. And at Juan's insistence, she read it yet again!

"Right through to the end, Nurse Val!" he had begged finally when she had at long last put the children to bed.

So, for the fourth time that day she read aloud.

"The Prince strode along the echoing corridors and up the gloomy staircases. And there at last, in a great chamber hung with velvet, he found the beautiful princess who had been asleep for a hundred years . . ."

"A hundred years!" breathed Juan, his eyes wide with wonder staring out of the window, across the lake where the fairy-tale castle on the hill above the village, shimmered in the moonlight.

By the time Beth had finished the story, both children were fast asleep. Then she stood at the window for a while admiring the view of the beautiful lake; the forest that hugged its shores and the lovely castle whose miserly owner refused to build a hospital for his peasants.

She sighed and turned away. It had been a long and strange day. She could scarcely believe that it was only the same morning when she and the President's two sons had left Santa Rica's capital, all set to enjoy a wonderful holiday!

On the second day, both Juan and Mel became bored at having to stay indoors again. Mel was plaintive and the corners of his mouth were turned down in a sulky fashion.

Juan was sitting on the floor, turning over the pages of "The Sleeping Beauty", gazing at the pictures of which he never tired. But, before Beth had given him his precious book, he, too, had been cross and restless.

Beth was worried on their account for they were used to plenty of fresh air and exercise. And on top of her normal concern for their daily welfare, she was now worried about the food situation.

That morning, with many apologies, the manager had only been able to give them bread for breakfast. Just bread alone! With an empty hotel and everyone staying in their own homes, there had been no baking done and no replenishment of food-stock. Beth knew she could not keep the children healthy on just bread. They needed fruit and other things if they were to resist the plague germs.

"There must be fruit trees somewhere," she thought to herself. "I'll just have to go out and see what I can find."

She called the boys to listen to her carefully.

"I have to go out for a while," she said. "Now you must promise not to go outside. Do you understand?"

The boys nodded and Beth gave them each a kiss and hurried downstairs.

All the shops in the village were shuttered and after walking for ten minutes, she still had not met a single person. As she came out on the far side of the village she saw what she was searching for — an orchard, the trees weighed with fruit.

She picked as many peaches, oranges and apples as she could carry and hurried back with them to the hotel.

This, she knew, would give the children pleasure for they both adored fresh fruit and in particular, Juan liked nothing better than a peach.

"Juan!" she cried as she flung open the door. "Look —" and then the words died on her lips, for Juan was not there. Only Mel sat playing with a toy car and as she went to him she saw his face was streaked with tears.

"Mel, where's Juan?"

"Gone."

"Gone!" Beth's heart felt as though it missed a beat. Quickly she picked up the child and sat him on her knee, holding him close.

"What's the matter, little one? What's been happening? Where has Juan gone?"

Mel flung his arms around her neck and burst into tears.

"He said I was too little," he sobbed.

"Too little for what?" asked Beth.

"To be a Prince and rescue the Sleeping Beauty!"

Beth was mystified for a second as she stared over the boy's head at the lake and the castle that so strangely resembled the picture in Juan' story book. Then, in a flash, she knew where Juan had gone. He had gone to the castle across the lake in search of the Sleeping Beauty!

Leaving Mel in the care of the hotel manager, Beth had set out for the castle, half running and half walking in her anxiety for Juan. He must have travelled very fast for her not to have caught up with him by now — if he was ahead of her. Her breath caught in her throat. There were a hundred things that could happen to a little boy: he could fall in the lake; run across wild animals, lose his way and be lost for days on end in the forest!

At last she came within a stone's throw of the castle. It towered above her, silent and unreal with a mossy track winding ahead uphill.

In her imagination she could see Juan striding up the track to the castle, feeling strong and tall and brave as a fairy Prince. There was nothing for her to do but to go on.

So Beth came to the door of the great castle itself. It was as if she were expected, for the great door stood wide open. She hesitated, then entered, looking for a servant to ask if Juan had been seen. But there were no servants. The great castle was deserted! She could almost believe that the castle had been asleep for one hundred years!

"Don't be so silly," she told herself. "All the servants must have deserted because of the plague."

A door on her left was open and Beth could see an old woman sitting in front of a spinning wheel. Only she wasn't sitting, she was slumped forward, her white head resting on her hands, fast asleep. Didn't the Sleeping Beauty have an old nurse. Beth found herself asking?

At the far end of the room a door stood ajar in a slant of sunlight and from the way her heart was beating, Beth knew that beyond that door lay the end of her quest.

She went forward and found the Sleeping Beauty!

Lying on a great bed hung with velvet lay a little girl of six or seven just as lovely as a fairy-tale princess. Her long golden hair was spread out over the pillow and her lashes lay long and dark on her pale cheeks.

Juan was leaning over her, his face flushed with excitement. As Beth entered, he turned to her with shining eyes, so wrapped up in his adventure that he wasn't even surprised to see her.

"I've found her, Nurse Val!" he cried. "She's been asleep for a hundred years but she's going to wake up now! Watch!"

His young voice rang shrill, clear and eager through the chamber, chasing away the mystery and the shadows — and as they fled, Juan bent down and kissed his sleeping beauty.

★ ★ ★ ★ ★

The little girl's eyelids fluttered and then opened. The blue eyes were hazy and far away and as Beth gazed at her she shuddered. This little girl, this sleeping beauty — had the plague!

"AAAAAAAgh!" came a groan from the doorway. Beth spun round and saw a grey-haired man with ashen face and sunken cheeks staring at them in horror.

"You kissed her. I saw you. Now you will get the plague, and die like my darling will die. We are lost — all lost — and it's all my fault!"

He sank into a chair and rocked backwards and forwards, sobbing with remorse and grief. Suddenly, Beth snapped back to life. She was first and foremost a nurse and now all her training came to the fore.

"Stop it!" she admonished. "There's no time for such self-indulgence. We must get to work immediately!"

The man stared at her blankly. "He came to me, the young doctor, asking for money to build a hospital. I turned him away. Now we have no hospital, no doctor, no nurse. . . ."

"Fortunately we have," said Beth grimly, feeling in her pocket for the third phial that Dario had given her. What a miracle that she had not used it on herself but had saved it until now!

Was it too late? Or, was there still time to save the little girl! At all events, one injection would not be enough, thought Beth as she pricked the girl's arm to inject her.

Lying on a great bed hung with velvet lay a little girl just as lovely as a fairy-tale princess

Beth had by now more or less got the picture from the old man. He was a widower and this was his only child, whom he adored. The child's old nurse had stayed on when all the other servants had deserted and she had faithfully looked after the child until the previous night when she, too, had fallen asleep as Beth had seen for herself.

"You will have to fetch the doctor," Beth told the man. "We need more medicines, urgently. I will tell you where to find him and you must ask him to come back with you at all speed."

The man nodded, glad to be of use. Briefly he laid his hand upon his daughter's brow — and then left. A few minutes later Beth heard the thunder of horse's hooves going down the hill.

And now her long vigil started; a vigil that lasted through sunset and moonrise. Juan slept soundly but the little girl shivered and burned with fever alternately. Beth had to draw on all her experience and courage, but even so, her hope began to fade.

Then came the pink flush of dawn over the tree tops and a burst of birdsong. The little girl opened her eyes and looking straight at Beth, asked:

"Water . . . water, please?"

In that same moment she heard the clatter of feet pounding up the stairs. Then the room began to reel around her, faster and faster. She felt herself falling and then Dario caught her. The last words she heard was the old man's tense whisper: "She has the plague!"

When Beth opened her eyes, it was bright and sunny and Dario was grinning down at her.

"Don't worry, old girl," he told her. "You haven't got the plague. Although why you haven't I just don't know. Disobeying doctor's orders and not innoculating yourself!" He meant to sound a bully, but Beth noticed the warmth of admiration in his voice as he added, "You passed out from exhaustion and worry."

"How's the little girl?" asked Beth.

"Fine, thanks to you. So, too, are both the boys. The best thing I can recommend for you all, is to get back to the capital for a good holiday!"

Dairo made contact with the capital that afternoon and the President's aircraft arrived later with the President himself on board.

Having embraced his sons and congratulated Beth and Dario he allowed himself to be taken to see "The Sleeping Beauty" . . . "Juan's own discovery," Beth told him.

Permission was given by the girl's father for her to stay with the President and his sons until she was fully recovered.

Once they were all safely aboard the plane, Dario had a quiet word with Beth.

"Juan really started something," he said exultantly. "His Sleeping Beauty's father is turning the castle into a hospital and nursing home — plus financing the whole project!"

Beth looked at his shining eyes and then at little Juan who was tucking the rug around his princess and beaming at her fondly and with pride.

"So this tale is ending as all fairy tales should," said Beth softly. "They all lived happily ever after!"

THE MYSTERY OF THE LAKE

Two girls swam down towards a drowned village and found themselves in an exciting new world. A silent world where the sun's rays slanted gently down through a kind of pale, watery fog but gave light enough for the girls to see around them for a radius of two hundred feet or more.

It was as Sally was swimming through the eerie rooms of the Glendower Inn that she saw a vague shadow. It was too big and much too oddly shaped to be a fish. As it moved, panic seized her!

It was a perfect summer day, with not a cloud in the sky, and the heat haze shimmered on the distant hills as Sally Dryden and Judy Morgan took the footpath through the woods.

"This weather is just perfect for underwater exploration," Judy said. "With no wind to ruffle the surface of the lake, we ought to get a perfect view of the drowned village."

The two girls were spending a holiday in North Wales, staying at the Bronwen Hotel, which was managed by Judy's Aunt Dilys. They had arrived the previous day and now they were on their way to a big reservoir which supplied water to a large industrial town many miles away. An artificial lake had been created by flooding the whole valley, and several farms and an entire village had been sacrificed in the process.

Sally and Judy had learned underwater swimming with an aqualung the previous summer, and now they planned to explore the drowned village.

Soon, the girls saw the bright gleam of water ahead, and they came out to the edge of the lake. Not a ripple broke its glassy, smooth surface.

"This must be the dinghy Aunt Dilys told us we could use," Judy said, and pointed to a small sailing-dinghy which was tied up to a wooden landing-stage. Sally read the name BRONWEN on its bows as they went out on to the landing-stage.

They had to go some distance to get to the drowned village, but at last Judy leaned over the gunwale and pointed down into the water.

"There it is!" she cried excitedly. "We are right above it."

Sally cupped her hands over her eyes to shade them from the dazzling sunlight, and peered down into the clear, pale green water. Below their keel she could see the grey, shadowy outlines of buildings, all a little distorted by the refraction of the water.

It gave one a rather odd feeling to look down upon the dead village, for many of the front doors stood open, and it was easy to imagine someone stepping out of a cottage into the street at any moment. And there were still raspberry canes and currant bushes in the gardens, although they were all dead, of course; whilst here and there the leafless branches of an old fruit tree seemed to stir in a faint breeze — although that was an illusion created by the water. There was even a small inn, "THE GLENDOWER", with its signboard swinging slowly in a slight current.

"Golly! It looks a bit spooky, doesn't it?" Judy said in a rather awed voice.

Aunt Dilys had said that some of the local people believed the place was haunted. "All nonsense, of course!" thought Judy, trying hard to be practical. "Whoever heard of underwater spooks?"

Sally was already slipping out of her tartan slacks and jumper, beneath which she was wearing a swim-suit, and underwater breathing sets, which consisted of two cylinders of compressed air, strapped to the back, a harness to hold them, and two breathing-tubes made of gas-mask piping. And, of course, there were goggles, and foot flippers to help them swim under water.

Sally took a last feel at the harness to make sure it was secure, and looked at the pressure gauge to see that the cylinders were full.

"Ready?" she asked. Judy nodded, and pulled the goggles down over her face. Sally did the same, and the girls lowered themselves over the side of the boat and slid gently into the water.

As they swam down towards the drowned village they were in an exciting new world. A silent world where the sun's rays slanted gently down through a kind of pale, watery fog, but gave light enough for the girls to see around them for a radius of two hundred feet or more.

Half paddling, half walking, Sally and Judy moved about the village with the slow, deliberate movements of actors in a slow-motion picture, using their hands when they wanted to change direction.

Moving up and down the village street, they peeped through gaping, paneless windows or wide-open doors. Many of the cottages were in good condition still, but others were fast tumbling into ruins.

Presently, Sally reached the village inn and paddled up to the open front door.

On an impulse, she swam in and began to explore the ground floor. All the furniture and fittings had been removed, and only the shell of the building remained. Sally peeped into the rooms which opened out of the hall, and was just paddling towards the stairs when she had a sudden, oddly uncomfortable feeling that she was no longer alone.

She turned quickly, and something vague and insubstantial as a shadow moved at the far end of the hall. Then it was swallowed by the green darkness.

But in the split second before it was gone, it seemed to Sally that what she saw was too big and much too oddly shaped for a fish, and a sudden panic seized her. She turned and swam out through one of the gaping empty windows, just as Judy came up to the entrance.

Speech was impossible, of course, but Sally pointed overhead to show that she wanted to return to the surface. Then she shot upwards with powerful kicks of the foot flippers, beckoning urgently to Judy to follow her.

When Sally reached the surface of the lake, she blinked for a moment or two in the bright sunshine. The dinghy was not twenty yards away, and Sally swam to it and heaved herself over the gunwale; a few moments later Judy scrambled up after her.

"Is anything wrong?" she asked anxiously as they removed their goggles and breathing sets.

"I don't really know," Sally answered. Trying to sound as matter-of-fact as possible, she related what had happened.

"Golly!" Judy said, saucer-eyed with wonderment. "It must have

As they swam down towards the drowned village they were in an exciting new world.

been a big fish you saw."

"Are there any fish five or six feet long in the lake?" Sally said quietly.

Judy shook her head. "No, of course not," she answered. "The lake was stocked with trout some years ago, and there are tench and bream in it, but nothing bigger — no pike, for instance. And anyhow, I don't think pike grow to five or six feet. Are you sure you saw a fish that size? I mean, underwater shadows can play queer tricks sometimes."

Sally nodded. "Yes," she said. "But I really saw something — it wasn't just a shadow or my imagination."

"Well," said Judy, after they had discussed the mysterious incident without being able to think of any really satisfactory explanation. "I suppose we ought to be getting back for lunch."

As they entered the hotel grounds they saw old Mr. Peacock sunning himself in a deck-chair. Mr. Peacock had been staying at the Bronwen for some days when the girls arrived, and he spent most of his time sitting about in the grounds or taking walks through the woods.

He was an amusing and charming old gentleman, who never grumbled, as so many guests did, and he had a neat, silver beard which, Aunt Dilys said, made him look distinguished. "Like a famous artist or a diplomat," she added rather vaguely. But no one knew much about him beyond the fact that his home was in London — and that he had plenty of money.

When he saw the two girls, the old gentleman took off the dark glasses which he had to wear almost continuously because he had weak eyes. He beamed good-naturedly at Sally and Judy.

"I trust you have spent a profitable and amusing morning," he said.

Mr. Peacock had this rather pedantic way of talking which made Aunt Dilys wonder if he were a writer — though Judy thought he sounded much more like a schoolmaster.

Judy had told him at breakfast that morning that she and Sally were going to explore the drowned village with their aqualungs. Mr. Peacock had sighed faintly, and wished that he were a few years younger so that he might take up underwater swimming.

"We certainly had an exciting time," said Judy, who was bursting to tell someone about Sally's queer encounter.

"Indeed," said Mr. Peacock, and listened attentively whilst Judy told him all that had happened.

"Bless me!" he said, when she had finished. "What a really remarkable occurrence. And you have no idea what it was that startled you?"

Sally shook her head.

"No," she replied. "I only caught a glimpse of whatever it was that was hiding in the old inn."

Mr. Peacock replaced his dark glasses and stroked his beard.

"Mmmm!" he said. "There are no freshwater fish or amphibians native to this country which grow to such a size. This is most puzzling. Perhaps you imagined it, my dear?"

Sally shook her head.

"It wasn't imagination," she answered quietly. "There was something there."

"Dear me!" the old gentleman said. He seemed to be looking very hard at Sally from behind his dark glasses. "Can there be any truth in the strange story your aunt told me?"

"That — that the drowned village is haunted?" Judy asked. "Oh, bosh!"

"There are more things in heaven and earth, Horatio, than are dreamt of in your philosophy," Mr. Peacock said solemnly. "A quotation which sounds somewhat trite because of over-use, but one which expresses a profound truth."

"Well, nothing is going to make me believe in spooks," Judy said stoutly. "Especially one that lives at the bottom of an artificial lake!"

"When I was in the Far East . . ." old Mr. Peacock said, and began to talk of some queer adventures which had befallen him in the Burmese jungle and other outlandish places. He was still talking when the gong sounded for lunch.

"We shall have to dash," Judy said, and they hurried off, leaving Mr. Peacock to make his more leisurely way to the dining room.

"Even Mr. Peacock isn't going to make me believe you saw a spook in the lake this morning," Judy said as they went upstairs to their rooms. Sally nodded in agreement.

"All the same," she answered soberly, "I can't imagine what it was I saw."

When the girls told Aunt Dilys about Sally's adventure, she was alarmed.

"You'd better keep away from the lake in future," she said. "You know I don't feel at all happy when you go swimming under water with those aqualungs. If anything happened to you, I should feel responsible."

"You are an old worry, Auntie," Judy laughed. "You surely don't think there's some sort of Loch Ness Monster hiding in the lake?"

Aunt Dilys was not amused.

"Of course not," she said, a trifle tartly, "but I think it's unsafe for you to go exploring the drowned village. The old houses must be in a very dangerous condition by now."

"Very well, Mrs. Morgan," Sally said — for she could see that Judy's aunt was really worried — "we'll do as you say. In any case, we've seen all there is to see down there."

"You've taken a great weight off my mind, Sally," Aunt Dilys said in a relieved voice, and bustled away to give some orders to the cook.

"Aunt Dilys is a dear," Judy sighed, "but she will fuss so. I almost wish we hadn't told her what happened — she'll go on worrying about it for days. It was only a big fish you saw — it couldn't have been anything else."

"No, I suppose not," Sally answered.

Judy noticed the hesitant tone in her friend's voice.

"You surely don't think that old Mr. Peacock is right, and that what you saw was an underwater spook?" she joked.

"Of course not," Sally said — rather too quickly, almost as though she had been wondering something like that.

The girls spent the afternoon tramping across the hills to an old border castle. They got a wonderful view from the top of the keep, but they didn't stay too long because there was a curious stillness in the air, and an occasional far-off muttering of thunder, as though a storm were brewing.

When they got back to the Bronwen Hotel, the girls went straight up to their rooms. Sally was just wondering whether to change into a dress for the evening, when Judy burst in upon her.

"Sally" she gasped, hardly able to speak for indignation. "Our aqualungs — they've been damaged! I went into the bathroom just now and . . . but come and see for yourself."

She rushed Sally to the bathroom at the end of the corridor, where they had dumped the wet diving-gear when they had returned from the lake that morning.

Sally examined the aqualungs, and was suddenly as indignant as Judy — for the breathing-tubes had been cut through so that they were

193

absolutely useless.

"The damage is quite deliberate," said Judy, almost in tears. "Someone must have slashed them with a sharp knife."

"But who would want to do such a mean, senseless thing?" Sally asked.

Judy shook her head. "I can't imagine," she said. "But we can't use them again, that's certain."

"It might be worse," Sally remarked, after she had made a thorough inspection of the aqualungs. "Only the breathing-tubes have been damaged, and we can replace them when we get back to London."

"I suppose so," Judy agreed gloomily, "but it means the end of our under-water swimming while we're staying here."

Sally nodded slowly and frowned. "Yes," she said. "It could be that someone wants to make sure we don't explore the lake again, or return to the drowned village."

"You may be right!" Judy cried. "But why should anyone want to do that? And who can it be?"

Then another thought struck her. "That big fish, or whatever it was that scared you," she said, "can that be why someone wants to make sure we don't pay a second visit to the drowned village?"

"I suppose it could be," Sally answered. "But I think we ought to tell your aunt about this."

They went back downstairs and found Aunt Dilys wrestling with some accounts in her little office.

She was just as startled as the girls had been when she heard the news.

"I can't imagine who would have done such a thing," she said in a shocked voice. "It's so — senseless and spiteful."

"We were wondering whether someone wanted to stop us paying a second visit to the drowned village," Sally put in quietly.

"Because of the enormous fish Sally saw," Kky added.

"Dear me! Yes, it might be that," Aunt Dilys said, looking more and more worried. "You were talking about it at lunch to the other guests, and you may be sure the maids overheard you and have been gossiping with the tradesmen. By now everyone in the village will have heard about your adventure — and some of the local people certainly dislike us using the lake for boating and swimming."

"Well, I think we ought to tell the police," Judy said. "They'll be able to find out who did the damage. I mean, there must be fingerprints and things."

"I don't know about that," Sally answered, a little ruefully. "We've both handled the aqualungs since we discovered the damage, and I dare say we've messed up any fingerprints there may have been."

"Oh dear!" Aunt Dilys said. "I . . . I don't really want to call in the police. If the other guests learn what has happened it will alarm them — and give the hotel a very bad name."

"Well then, is the person who did the damage to go scot free?" Judy asked indignantly.

"The police wouldn't have much to go on even if we did call them in," Sally said. "If we say nothing, but keep our eyes and ears open, we may find out who did it ourselves."

"I hadn't thought about it being bad publicity for the hotel," Judy admitted. "Righto, Auntie, have it your own way."

And they left it at that.

That night the storm, which had been threatening for most of the day, rumbled nearer. Sally woke to hear the faint muttering of thunder in the distance, and the night was so hot and oppressive that she found it quite impossible to get to sleep again. Glancing at her wristwatch, she saw that it was nearly one o'clock. She slipped out of bed, and went across to the window.

The honey-coloured moon was coming up behind the woods, and in the distance the hills were black against the sky, except for the occasional far-away growl of thunder.

Just as she was thinking of going back to bed, she heard a faint sound such as the cautious opening of a window might make. Sally supposed it was one of the guests trying to get a little more air into a bedroom, but when she peeped over the sill, she was astonished to see a man scrambling out of a ground-floor window.

For a moment she was so startled she could hardly believe her own eyes. Then, as the shadowy figure dropped silently to the ground, she drew back quickly so she was hidden by the curtains.

The man looked up at the house, and the pale yellow moonlight fell upon his face, so that Sally saw it clearly. It was Mr. Peacock — although for once he wasn't wearing his glasses.

He stood for a moment and seemed to listen. Then he turned and ran silently across the lawn, with long swift strides quite unlike the rather short, feeble steps with which he usually moved. Before he was swallowed by the shrubberies at the end of the garden, Sally saw that he was carrying a humped pack on his shoulders which might have been a rucksack.

Sally was flabbergasted! The alarming thought occurred to her that perhaps Mr. Peacock had robbed the hotel and was now making off with his plunder. But somehow that didn't seem very likely and, for an instant, she wondered if she had imagined the whole fantastic incident.

But Sally knew she wasn't dreaming — she had never been more awake in her life — even if it was a strangely rejuvenated Mr. Peacock.

Hastily, Sally went next door to Judy's bedroom, woke her friend and gave her a brief account of what she had just seen.

"Heavens!" Judy said, sitting up in bed, round eyed with wonder. "Are you sure you saw Mr. Peacock climb out of his window — you didn't dream it?"

"Of course not!" Sally answered, rather impatiently. "I was wide awake and saw him clearly. What shall we do?"

"Follow him, of course," replied Judy, "and find out what he's up to."

Sally wasn't sure they were behaving wisely, but she didn't argue. "I'll get dressed," she answered, and hurried back to her own room, where she slipped into tartan slacks and a sweater, and put on some rubber-soled sandals.

The two girls stole downstairs. No one else seemed to have been disturbed, and the hotel was so silent that the faint squeaking of the lock when Judy unbolted the back door seemed loud enough to wake an army. But it didn't rouse anyone, and the two girls slipped out into the back garden and gently closed the door behind them.

"Come on!" Judy said in a ghostly whisper, and they ran across the lawn into the shrubberies. They stopped to listen and look about them — but there was no sign of the mysterious Mr. Peacock.

"Perhaps he left the grounds by the door into the woods," Judy whispered, and Sally nodded.

They stole to the door which the guests used as a short cut into the woods. It was usually kept bolted, but now it stood ajar.

They hurried silently along the woodland path. There was just enough moonlight for them to see where they were going, but under the trees it was pitch dark and a little misty, and it was easy to imagine that every bush or clump of undergrowth was some lurking enemy.

Then the path turned, and they saw the lake ahead, smooth as polished black marble except for a ghostly shimmer of moonlight on the distant shore.

The girls halted on the edge of the woods, and felt loath to go out into the open where they might so easily be seen by the man they were seeking. Everything was so silent and still — as though the woods were holding their breath and listening.

And then Judy clutched at Sally's arm and pointed with her other hand at the lake.

"Look! Look at that!" she said in a quaking voice.

Sally followed Judy's pointing finger, and gasped at what she saw. Some distance from where they stood, the lake stirred faintly in a series of rippling circles, and a queer green glow had appeared under the water.

The strange glowing radiance was moving away from the shore, and growing weaker all the while, and presently the girls lost sight of it completely. For a little while longer, however, they could still hear the faint whisper of water as the ripples spread across the lake and reached the shore. Then everything was silent.

"Wasn't it spooky?" Judy said. "I — I wonder whether there is some sort of Monster that lives at the bottom of the lake? Like those queer phosphorescent fish that lurk in deep water in tropical seas?"

"How can there be?" Sally said in her practical way. "This lake is artificial and was only made a few years ago. It isn't very deep, and this isn't the tropics."

"Well, we saw something just now, and what about the spooky thing you saw in the drowned village this morning?" Judy asked. "Oh golly! I'm so scared I feel as though caterpillars with cold feet are walking up and down my back."

Then she thought of something else.

"And old Mr. Peacock? What was he doing down by the lake in the middle of the night?" she said. "And where is he?"

"Just what I was wondering," Sally answered, and they looked up and down the lakeside, without seeing anything of the mysterious Mr. Peacock.

"Do you think he came down here hoping to see the Monster — or whatever it was?" Judy asked. "He seemed awfully interested in it. when we told him about your adventure this morning."

"Well, if so, he's certainly chosen an odd time to go investigating,"

Sally replied "and an odd way of leaving the hotel — climbing out of his window."

"Perhaps he didn't want to risk waking anyone by unbolting the back door," Judy suggested. "And perhaps he thought he would come to the lakeside when it was certain to be deserted. And golly!" she gasped. "Our aqualungs — could he have damaged them?"

"Well, it isn't much use standing here just wondering," Sally said. "We might think of a hundred and one explanations without hitting on the right one."

"I suppose we ought to report this to the police," Judy said.

"Yes," Sally agreed, "although they'll probably say we imagined it all. That is why I should like to have a shot at solving the mystery ourselves, before we go back to the hotel."

"But how?" Judy asked in an alarmed voice. "I don't see how we can solve it."

"Well," said Sally, "at least we could take the hotel dinghy and try to find out what that light was."

"Do you think we ought to?" Judy asked hesitantly.

"Well, that is the only way we can find out the meaning of the mysterious light in the water," Sally answered quietly. Common sense told her that there must be an explanation for what they had seen.

Then she saw how scared Judy was. "Never mind. If you don't want to risk it, we . . ." she began.

But Judy couldn't let herself be dared like this, especially as she had been the one to suggest following Mr. Peacock in the first place.

"Come on," she said recklessly, and ran out of the woods and down to the little landing-stage where the boat was tied up.

Sally followed her and, jumping into the dinghy, the girls untied the painter and pushed off. Then they hoisted the little red sail, and Judy took the tiller.

There was a faint whisper of wind out on the lake — just enough to keep them moving, and Sally crouched in the bows and scanned the dark water ahead, while Judy steered.

"Th-there it is," she whispered.

But it was only the reflection of moonlight she saw.

By this time the moon was well up above the woods, and had changed from a blotchy honey-coloured ball to a pale yellow disc which made everything look unreal.

Then Sally looked back over her shoulder, and beckoned to Judy. "What do you make of that?" she whispered, and pointed to where the water was rippling into tiny wavelets.

Judy left the dinghy to steer itself, and crept forward and joined Sally in the bows.

"There must be something swimming about in the water," she said in a whisper.

"I can't see anything," Sally whispered back, and the two girls watched the glittering ripples, whilst the boat drifted silently through the water.

"It's gone," Sally said presently. The lake lay glassy smooth again.

"There certainly is something in the lake," Sally said. "I suppose it could have been a fish that made those ripples, but if so, it must be an awfully big one."

"Don't you think we ought to turn back?" Judy asked in a scared voice.

"Yes, perhaps we had better go back," Sally agreed.

But even as she spoke, a sudden gust of wind stirred the distant treetops and sent a little shiver of water across the lake. Then it filled the boat's sail, and the dinghy seemed to shake herself, and glided more swiftly through the water.

"Listen," Sally said impulsively, "with this wind it won't take more than a few minutes to reach the other end of the lake where the drowned village is. Suppose we sail over it before we turn back?"

"All right," Judy answered, and went back to the tiller, and steered in the direction of the drowned village.

"We must be right over it now," she said presently. "I can judge where we are by that dead tree over there."

And she nodded to the wooden shore where an old elm tree, which had been struck by lightning some years ago, raised its bare, bleached branches to the sky.

Sally made no answer, but scanned the water as Judy put the tiller hard over, and brought the dinghy round.

At that precise moment the breeze dropped, the little red sail went limp, and the dinghy almost stopped moving again.

"We shall have to use the paddles to get back," said Judy, who didn't at all relish being becalmed out in the middle of the lake with goodness knows what monster swimming around. But Sally wasn't listening to her. She was staring down into the water beneath their bows.

"Judy," she said in a thrilled whisper. "Come here."

"Wh — what is it?" Judy quaked as she crept for'ard to join Sally again.

"Look!" the latter hissed. "There's the light again."

Down below in the water they could see a misty green radiance, which appeared to be moving about. Sometimes it was quite brilliant, but then it would almost die out, and presently the girls realised that it was shining out through the open door and windows of the Glendower Inn.

For a few moments the whole building seemed to glow faintly with diffused light, as though it were burning up inside with green fire. Then the ghostly light streamed out through the open doorway, and picked out the empty shells of the ruined cottages across the village street. The effect was beautiful, but rather eerie, and the two girls stared, spellbound, whilst the light grew brighter.

Then the beam flashed up towards the surface of the lake. Sally and Judy were momentarily blinded by it.

But the beam of light sank again, and shone directly down the village street.

And then the beam of light swept round again, in a great circle, and seemed to fumble about the upper storey of the old inn, until it found one of the unglazed windows set high beneath the gabled roof. There it seemed to be sucked in through the broken window and dwindled to a faint glow inside the building. But as it vanished the girls had a glimpse of a creature with goggle eyes and a hump.

And suddenly the mystery was solved! Judy's Monster was a diver, wearing an aqualung and carrying an electric torch made for underwater work.

The same thought occurred to Sally and Judy simultaneously.

"It must be Mr. Peacock swimming about down there," Sally whispered.

"And he must have been here this morning when he scared you," Judy whispered. "But what can he be up to?"

"I don't know," Sally answered. "But it must be frightfully important for him to come out here in the middle of the night. And I should have thought he was much too old to go diving with an aqualung."

Leaning over the side of the boat they continued to peer down into the water. They could see the torchlight flickering about inside the old inn.

"Do you think he is searching for something inside there?" Judy asked presently.

She was too excited now to be scared any longer. Mr. Peacock was altogether a different proposition from a Monster.

"I think he must be . . ." Sally began, but she never completed the sentence, because at that moment the old inn started to collapse.

"Oh, gosh! I wonder what happened?" Judy asked in a scared voice, as they peered down into the murky water and tried to catch a glimpse of the man they had seen swimming around in an aqualung. A faint gleam of light was still visible in the muddy water, but it was impossible to see anything of the drowned village.

"Your Aunt Dilys was right," Sally said soberly, "the old buildings down there are in a very rickety condition. Mr. Peacock must have disturbed the rotted beams which supported the roof, and caused them to collapse."

"I wonder what we ought to do?" Judy said. "He may be badly hurt, or trapped down there among the ruins. Shall we go back to the hotel for help?"

"Wait," Sally replied. "The water seems to be clearing. Perhaps he escaped."

The mud was beginning to settle, and presently the shadowy outline of buildings began to emerge, quivering in the beam of light which streamed athwart the street.

Now Sally and Judy saw that one end of the old inn had collapsed and was a jumbled mass of bricks and rubble.

Then they saw something else. Mr. Peacock (if that was who he was, for the breathing-mask and goggles concealed most of the man's face) lay pinned down among the ruins, with a great slab of masonry lying across his body. The powerful electric torch lay beside him, and the girls could see that he was making no attempt to free himself.

Judy turned a white, frightened face to Sally. "He must be badly hurt," she said shakily. "What are we going to do? Even if his compressed air cylinders were full when he started, the supply of air won't last for more than another half an hour, and then he'll be drowned."

Sally, who had already thought of that, made a quick, practical decision.

"I'm going to dive down to him, and see what I can do." As Sally spoke she was slipping off her shoes.

"I'll go with you," Judy said, "but I do wish we had aqualungs."

"We'll have to do the best we can without them," Sally answered, and stood up in the dinghy's bows. She dived into the lake and swam down to the trapped man.

Judy followed suit, and together they tried to shift the slab of masonry which pinned him down. But it was too heavy for them, and the man made no attempt to help himself. He seemed to be unconscious, although he was still breathing.

The girls were forced to return to the surface to breathe.

"I don't think we shall manage it," Judy said rather hopelessly.

"The thing to do is to clear away those smaller pieces of rubble which are holding down the end of the big slab?" Sally answered.

So, filling their lungs with air, they swam down to the trapped man again.

They set to work clearing away some smaller lumps of brick and rubble. The powerful electric lamp gave them enough light, and training with their aqualungs had accustomed the girls to moving about and working under water. Before they were forced to surface again they had got the end of the slab of masonry clear.

They shot to the surface, and clung to the dinghy, breathing deeply. Then they dived again, and seized the big slab of masonry. This time they really were successful. With their lungs almost bursting, they surfaced again.

Almost immediately, however, Sally and Judy dived once more.

Sally held the man under his armpits, Judy grabbed his ankles, and together they kicked their way back to the surface and got the injured man into the dinghy — although it wasn't easy doing that.

Sally removed the man's goggles and breathing-tubes so that they were able to see his face.

"Why," Judy said breathlessly, "it isn't Mr. Peacock after all."

For the man they had just rescued was young and clean-shaven.

"I don't know," Sally said shrewdly. "He seems familiar to me. The beard could have been false, and he wouldn't wear it to go swimming. Anyway, I think we had better get him to the hotel as quickly as possible. He seems to be in a bad way, and there's nothing we can do for him."

"Righto!" Judy agreed. "But half a tick."

She dived into the lake again, and was back almost at once, clutching a black japanned deed-box in her hands.

"I spotted this," she said, "just as we got that lump of masonry off him. It may be what he was looking for."

Sally took the box from her and put it in the bows, whilst Judy heaved herself up over the side.

"Better not waste time trying to find out what's in the box," Sally said. "It's locked — and this chap badly needs a doctor. Let's get back to the hotel."

"Okay!" said Judy. "But I'd love to know what's inside."

"Whatever the box contains, it must be very valuable for him to have gone to so much trouble to get it," Judy remarked.

"This is Mr. Peacock," Sally said emphatically. "But why did he come to the Bronwen Hotel wearing a disguise? And how did he know that old deed-box was hidden in the Glendower Inn?"

They were still trying to think of an answer to these questions when the dinghy slipped alongside the landing-stage.

The girls decided against trying to get the injured man back to the hotel.

"I doubt whether we could carry him to the hotel," Sally said. "And if he's badly hurt, perhaps we ought not to move him."

So they left him lying in the dinghy, after tying up at the landing stage, and ran back to the hotel. Judy took the black box with her.

When they got to the hotel and woke Judy's aunt, she could hardly believe what they told her.

"I can't understand it," she kept saying, in a dazed voice. "Mr. Peacock of all men — such a charming old gentleman, and much too old to go swimming."

"But, Aunt Dilys, darling," Judy said, "don't you understand? The beard and the dark glasses were a disguise."

"Well, that only makes it all the more puzzling," Aunt Dilys said helplessly.

"We ought to get a doctor to him, Mrs. Morgan," Sally managed to break in.

"Oh, yes!" Aunt Dilys said. "I'll 'phone for Dr. Roberts."

Luckily, Dr. Roberts lived in the village, and by the time Aunt Dilys had got dressed, they heard his car drive up to the house.

"Now, where is the patient?" he demanded, when they went to meet him.

"In the hotel dinghy," Judy answered.

"I think you ought to come and see him immediately, doctor," Sally added. "We can explain what happened on our way to the lake."

Dr. Roberts shook his head and frowned as though he thought they were all a little mad, but he went with them to the lake. On the way, the girls gave him an account of their adventures.

But when they reached the landing-stage, he wasted no time on questions, but examined the injured man, and presently announced that he was suffering from two broken ribs and severe shock.

"We must get him to the hotel, where I can attend to him properly," he said.

So Judy dashed back to the Bronwen, roused the hotel porter and his assistant, and between them they carried the injured man up to the hotel and into one of the bedrooms. Then, while Dr. Roberts was attending to him, the girls had a chance to examine the black japanned deed-box.

"Do you think we ought to open it?" Judy asked.

"I don't see why not," Sally answered.

So Judy found a hammer and a big screwdriver, and they didn't have much difficulty in prising open the lid, for the lock was old and half eaten away by rust.

Then they gasped, for the box was crammed with jewellery!

"Oh gosh!" Judy said in a squeaky voice. "There must be a fortune here. What are we going to do about it?"

"Inform the police," Sally said firmly.

And even Aunt Dilys no longer objected to calling in the police when she saw that the little black box contained a small fortune in jewels.

There isn't much more to tell.

The police were summoned and took a long statement from the two girls. They also arranged for the injured man to be removed in an ambulance to the nearest hospital. Then they took charge of the jewellery and drove off, leaving Sally and Judy just as puzzled as ever by all the mysterious happenings in which they had been involved.

However, the following day, a Detective Inspector of the County Criminal Investigation Department arrived at the Bronwen and explained everything.

"Peacock will recover all right," he said, "but he realises that the game is up and so he has told us everything."

Then the Inspector went on to explain that Peacock was a criminal who had recently been released from Prison after serving a term. In prison he had been in contact with another convict, Bilby.

The year before the valley had been flooded to make the artificial lake, Bilby had stayed at the Glendower Inn, and had posed as an artist. Using this as a cover, he had carried out several daring burglaries, and among his plunder were the jewels. But then he made a blunder, and realised that he stood little chance of breaking through the police net which was closing in upon him. So he concealed the jewels among the rafters of the Inn.

Bilby was caught soon afterwards, but the police never found out what became of the jewellery.

Bilby told Peacock about this, shortly before the latter was discharged from prison. Bilby still had several more years of his sentence to serve, and he struck a bargain with the other crook. Peacock was to recover the jewels, half were to be his, but he was to use the other half to fix things so that Bilby could make a break from prison.

But when Peacock got out of prison he learned that the Glendower Inn was at the bottom of the lake. So he took lessons in aqualung diving, and came disguised to the Bronwen while he laid his plans to recover the jewels.

The underwater search proved more difficult than he had anticipated, however, and he made several visits to the old inn without finding them. It was he, of course, who Sally had seen lurking in the Glendower, and later he had damaged the girl's aqualungs so that they could not make a second visit to the drowned village.

Finally, he decided to go there by night, and he slipped out of his bedroom by the bedroom window, hoping to leave the inn that way without disturbing anyone. The rucksack which Sally thought he was carrying was really his diving equipment. He had changed in the woods, and was swimming out to the drowned village when the girls reached the lakeside and saw the light of his underwater torch.

Peacock had found the metal box, but in rummaging among the half-rotted rafters of the attic he had caused part of the roof to collapse, and he would have been drowned but for the girls' timely arrival.

As for Sally and Judy, they received a substantial reward for the recovery of the stolen jewellery, and they are never likely to forget the exciting holiday they spent at the Bronwen Hotel.

JUST JACKIE

Perhaps the fact that Jackie was a farmer's daughter was the reason why she was generally late for school. There were always some last-minute chores to be carried out before she left for school each morning.

Jackie's headmistress was Miss Slatterley who claimed to be an expert in Road Safety and driving vintage cars. The fun started when Miss Slatterley borrowed an ancient car from Jackie's cousin Alex and offered to get Jackie to school on time just for once. You see, Miss Slatterley had her own ideas on how to handle a vintage automobile!

It's quite an extraordinary thing, but whenever I have some very special reason for not being late for school, I generally am. Of course, the fact that I am a farmer's daughter is often the cause. There are sometimes last-minute jobs to do — such as closing a gate that shouldn't be left open — and it is usually one some two hundred yards away.

The other afternoon it was most important that I should be at school bang on time, because Miss Slatterley, our Headmistress, was giving us a lecture on the Highway Code, Road Safety, and all that.

My cousin Alex was staying with us for a few days, and I said I'd take notes of the lecture, and pass them on to him, although he was rather contemptuous of the whole idea. He owns an old "banger" of a car, and considers himself an expert, quite capable of winning a Grand Prix, if someone would lend him a racing car, and if he had the right licence, enough money — and a lot of other "ifs".

Some trusting friend had actually lent him a vintage car, and Alex was doing something to it just as I was leaving for school.

"Jackie," he called from inside the bonnet where his head was. It sounded pretty urgent, so I rested my bike against the wall, and rushed to his aid.

"Hold this rod!" he said, pulling something up.

Simple-minded as ever, I held it while he fiddled.

"Hang on!" he said, sharply, rushed to the driving compartment, and pressed the starter. The engine fired; there was a cloud of oily smoke, and also a generous spray of oil — right in my face.

"It fired!" he said in triumph, as I drew back from the bonnet, my right hand greasy, my face smeared with oil.

"Oh! I say, you're oily, Jackie!" he exclaimed in surprised concern. "Sorry about this; but here's some cotton waste. That'll get it off."

He tossed me an oily chunk of stuff, but luckily I didn't smear it on my face. In horror I went to his rear-view mirror, and peered into it, moaning at what I saw. Having oily hands and face meant nothing to Alex, but when I saw the mess I was in I could have boxed his ears.

"Why, you goop!" I gasped. "I'm due at school. Now I'll have to go and take this off. I'll be late!"

Alex takes every disaster in his stride.

"Think nothing of it," he said. "I'll give you a lift. Get you there in half the time. In fact, you could have a bath, and still be on time, Jackie. Not to worry — hark!" He started the engine, and there was a shattering roar. "Running sweet as silk."

There was no time to argue. I rushed into the house, and washed with the special stuff Alex uses. It didn't take long, and the oil came off quite easily. But minutes mattered, and easy and swift job though it seemed, it was obvious by the time I had finished, that I couldn't cycle to school in time. I had to accept his offer.

"If you can drive me there, I'd be glad," I said.

"O.K. We'll bung this old bike in the back," he decided. It was a four-seater car, and the state of the upholstery was such that the bike flung on to it could do no damage anyone could notice. Actually, it was rather a thrill driving in that old car, when it kept going, and anyway I'd be at school on time.

We set off at speed, just as if we were in a road race. Alex revved it well up on every gear, and the din was shattering. But it really went, and in a short time we were bashing along at sixty miles an hour. I say 'bashing along', because the springs were hard, and I was being banged up and down in the seat.

All being well, I reckoned I'd be at school with time to spare; but all was not well. When we rounded a bend with a shrill whistle of tyres, I saw a small, ancient saloon car on ahead, pulled in at the roadside, with a woman of middle age standing alongside it.

"She's got a puncture!" yelled Alex. "Tough luck!"

"It's the Head, Miss Slatterley! Stop!" I howled above the din. "She needs help!"

The exhaust blared as Alex "dipped into third"; and made an ear-splitting din as he went down into second gear. The brakes were on, and we made a spectacular stop about ten yards beyond the small car. It was probably a pretty nerve-shattering sight, for the Head seeing that vintage car roar up; in fact, it must have been, for she let go of the spare wheel she was trundling, and leaped at her car, half way up the roof, and clung on.

Alex and I scrambled out, and went back, just as the Head dropped back on to the road; and I saw at once that something displeased her.

"Jacqueline!" she exclaimed. "You! I was scared out of my wits! What a way to drive —" she added fiercely to Alex.

"I thought you might like me to change the wheel for you, ma'am," he said with his most charming smile. "A dirty business, you know."

The Head seemed about to carry on with her caustic comments, but that softening speech changed her mind. As Alex said, it was a dirty business changing a wheel, and she didn't seem too sure what she was doing.

"That would be most kind of you," she said, when I had introduced Alex. "There is a special reason why I should not be late, although I'm afraid I shall be. From experience I know that it takes about twenty minutes to do the job. The jack is a nuisance and it slips."

I didn't mind being late, of course — not as I was with the Head, and I agreed it would be a long job, even with three of us at it. But Miss Slatterley is not a woman easily daunted, and the glint in her eye told me that she had an idea.

"I suppose you couldn't let me drive your car to the school?" she asked Alex. "I could take Jacqueline with me. But perhaps it is asking too much — leaving you to tackle the puncture alone?"

I nudged Alex warningly. I just couldn't imagine the Head driving that old car; and what's more, I wasn't keen on being her passenger, especially when there was a chance of loitering by the roadside.

"Well, er — certainly," said Alex, taken off guard. "But, — er — it's an old timer — crash gear changes — no synchromesh."

The Head smiled at his naïvety.

"My dear boy," she said. "I was driving cars before you were born. My father had an ancient car with crash gear-box which I learned to drive on. There will be no difficulty — if you are agreeable. It will certainly enable me to be on time. And as a school governor is attending my lecture, it really is important —"

Alex did not argue, but he showed the Head the controls and offered her some advice, which she listened to with scant attention. She likes telling, but hates to be told!

"Well, come on, Jacqueline," she said briskly, settling at the wheel, and dabbing at the throttle.

I climbed in beside her, and we set off. In fact we set off so suddenly, I was tipped back in my seat, and had to cling on. I gave a hurried look back, and saw Alex in the middle of the road, like a statue, until suddenly he waved his arms, flapping them up and down, although why, I didn't know. Later, I learned that the Head was "flogging" the engine.

Suddenly, when we were doing about thirty in bottom gear with the old car throbbing, and the engine shrieking, she tugged the gear lever, bringing a scraping clanging crashing sound, as though the insides would soon burst asunder.

With grim expression, lips set, eyes glinting, she kept dabbing the throttle pedal, and without warning, she suddenly got the gear engaged. We shot forward. The next gear change was better but took about a quarter of a mile. Then she really did get up steam.

"Not far now," I yelled, as she managed to engage top.

The Head stood on the brakes, and I hit the windscreen. But she got going again, and presently we were nearing the school entrance.

"Never have I known such a shocking car," she gasped. "Much too fast. And the steering —"

She swung it towards the gates, and then swung it back and accelerated. So on we went past the school.

"Aren't we going in, Miss Slatterley?" I asked, amazed.

She was red-faced, and grim.

"I shall turn round farther along the road," she said curtly.

"The next turning is about a mile along," I reminded her.

"I am aware of that, Jacqueline," she retorted. "But I happened to notice the police-inspector's car just inside the gates, and I did not wish to drive this monstrosity in."

I suddenly realized that the reason why she didn't want to drive in was for fear of making shocking scraping noises with the gears, stalling the engine, and putting up just the kind of exhibition that would be out of place as a prelude to a lecture on Road Safety.

We bowled along at a rumbling forty miles an hour, and all seemed well until, of its own accord, the car slowed down. The engine had packed up.

We coasted to a halt, and the Head in seething fury looked at me.

"Really, Jacqueline, you must have known what a wreck it is and you should not have let me drive the thing," she said quite irritably. "Now what do we do? Leave it here, and walk nearly a mile back?"

We sat in silence, thinking. There were pleasant fields on either side, and peace reigned. At school, the girls were doubtless assembling, ready for the lecture; the school governor, and the police-inspector would be twittering with eager excitement, counting time.

Then an idea clicked in my mind. I remembered that the same thing had happened when Alex was driving. And he had shown me the trouble.

"The petrol tap has shaken down — that's all," I said, and hopped out. I opened the bonnet, found the tap, fixed it open, tied the string back in place — and sure enough, when the Head pressed the starter, bedlam was let loose again. What's more, I had noticed a farm gate at the side of the road behind us leading into Mr. Warwick's field.

"You can reverse into the field, Miss Slatterley," I said. "I'll open the gate."

Actually, the Head wasn't mad keen on the idea, but when she saw me with the gate held open invitingly, she had a hunt for reverse. A wild screeching sound proved she had found it, and suddenly the car shot back into the field.

It seemed to me that the Head was going rather far back if all she wanted to do was to drive out again the other way. Fascinated, I watched. About five yards from a rick, she stopped, and wrestled with the gear lever. In triumph, she suddenly sat up and grabbed the wheel. The engine howled, and before my very eyes she shot back at the rick — right into it.

The thud was a dull one, of course, but the back of the car went

The engine howled, and before my very eyes she shot back at the rick.

halfway into the rick; the Head tipped back in her seat, and the top of the rick collapsed.

A moment later, only the radiator and bonnet of the car was in sight; the rest was hay. With wonderful presence of mind the Head turned off the engine and the only sound was her muffled yells.

Naturally, I rushed to the rescue at top speed, and hauled away hay until her face showed through — glowing red.

"Jacqueline, I — I apparently selected the wrong gear," she gasped, "or reverse did not disengage! Oh, dear, oh, dear. Just look at this rick —"

But I was looking across the field to a running figure, a man who was waving his arms and shouting something — although just what, the distance prevented my hearing.

"Here comes the farmer, Mr. Warwick," I told her.

Miss Slatterley looked at him, and gave a heavy sigh that was almost a moan; for it was pretty obvious that there would be a prolonged conversation.

"My lecture is doomed," she groaned, "and I have no means of telephoning, and explaining why —" Then she added more to herself than to me, "and a most embarrassing explanation in the circumstances —"

However even the trickiest problem may have a far simpler solution than seems first probable, and my bike, poking through the hay gave me the answer.

"Miss Slatterley — all is not lost," I said, rushing to my bike. "You can cycle to school on this . . . won't take long. And I can stay and explain to Mr. Warwick. He's a friend of Dad's, anyway. Then, if Alex is at the school with your car . . . he can cycle the bike back to me here, and collect his car. I don't suppose the old thing's damaged much —"

Miss Slatterley's face brightened; but then her eyes clouded.

"The responsibility is mine," she demurred.

"But I can give your name and address if Mr. Warwick wants it, although I don't think any real harm has been done," I said, and held out the bike temptingly. Mr. Warwick was still a good hundred yards away, striding fiercely to the scene.

"Oh, very well. Perhaps it will be the best plan. Mr. Warwick can call at the school to see me if he is not satisfied," she said; and with that she mounted the bike, and cycled back to the road.

A less satisfied man than Mr. Warwick would have been hard to find when he first arrived, although recognizing me eased him a little. From a distance, he said, it had seemed as if the driver had deliberately rammed the haystack with malice aforethought. Naturally, his opinion soon changed when I explained that she was a woman motorist who had borrowed a car because she was in a hurry.

"Dad can lend you a man to put the rick right," I said, "and the car belongs to my Cousin Alex. Awfully sorry, you know —"

Mr. Warwick calmed right down, and started to examine the car which he had been staring at with interest. And when Alex came up some ten minutes or so later, there the farmer was kneeling down and peering underneath the engine.

"That's a genuine nineteen-twenty-six sump," he told Alex.

"Yes, it is," agreed Alex, "and a B-type box."

What they meant I didn't know, but they got quite excited, going around the car, opening the bonnet, peering underneath and all around.

To get a full view, we had it out from the rick.

"While you two are patting it, and clucking your tongues over it, I ought to be getting back to school. I'll miss the lecture," I said.

But Alex insisted on driving me back, he said he wanted to assure "the old girl" that she had done no damage. So off we went, and Mr. Warwick, still unaware of Miss Slatterley's identity, asked me to tell "the old girl" not to worry — but to forget the whole thing. In fact, I got the impression that he felt his rick had been honoured by being crashed into by an old-type car with a nineteen-twenty-six sump, whatever that might be, and a B-type box. It doesn't happen to every rick.

Naturally the lecture was over when Alex and I showed up at school. It was my loss, and I bore it well. The Head made no comment at all on my absence, when I reported to her, but she was enormously relieved to hear that the car was undamaged.

"Mr. Warwick says to forget the whole thing," I told her. "You won't be hearing from him, though, because I forgot to mention your name, Miss Slatterley, or who you are. Sorry!"

A look of tremendous relief came on to her face as she realized I didn't mean to spread the word round the school. She even thanked Alex warmly for the loan of his car, but insisted on sending him a typescript of her lecture! I haven't seen it, and still remain in ignorance of the Head's theories on Road Safety — except, of course, what I have managed to pick up from practical experience.

THE BLUE HANDBAG MYSTERY

Little did Doreen dream when the blue handbag in Maison Roberta's caught her eye that she was on the threshold of the most exciting adventure of her young life.

Was there a link between the handbag and the jewel robbery that had taken place at Mitcham's the jewellers earlier that day? Doreen's quick wits were to bring about a surprise ending to the adventure.

Yes, there it was — the blue handbag of her dreams! Exquisite in design, and just the right shade to match her new suit.

It was with a number of white ones arranged attractively at the bottom of the window; but surely it couldn't be as cheap as the price-ticket indicated? Not at Maison Roberta's, a noted gown shop also specializing in accessories. Doreen pointed it out to her friends. She was trying to decide how she should spend her birthday present from Uncle Jeremy, and Olive and Sybil were helping her.

"It does say they are a special offer," remarked Sybil.

Doreen took a quick step sideways in order to get a better view of it and accidentally bumped into a young woman standing close by.

"I'm very sorry!" Doreen said, smiling apologetically.

She received no answering smile — only an unfriendly glare. Doreen raised her eyebrows in surprise, then renewed her inspection of the handbag.

"Oh go away!" snapped the young woman, edging closer and nudging Doreen with her shoulder. "You three don't want to stay around here any longer. You've spent ages looking at everything — let someone else have a turn."

Doreen felt tempted to ask on whose authority the young woman attempted to interfere with window shoppers at Maison Roberta's, but it seemed hardly worth while. She'd made up her mind now.

After waiting a few moments longer as a protest at the other's attitude, Doreen led her friends into the shop. There she asked to be shown the blue handbag of her choice.

"It is with the white ones showing as a special line in the side window," she explained to the young assistant.

The assistant slowly shook her head.

"I'm afraid there are no coloured handbags at that price," she said. "The special offer is for white ones only."

"But, excuse me, there is a blue one with the white ones in the window," interposed Olive. "At the back and near to some gloves and an open umbrella."

Doreen and Sybil nodded in support.

The assistant directed a puzzled look towards the manageress hovering near them. This austere-looking woman gave a very emphatic shake of her head.

"Those white handbags in the window are the only ones selling so cheaply, and we have plenty of them to choose from in the shop. If there is a blue one, then it must be part of the whole window display and we couldn't possibly take it out for you."

Doreen tried not to show her disappointment, and she was about to suggest that it was misleading to show a handbag which wasn't for sale, when a door marked "Office" jerked open, and a quietly-dressed pleasant-looking woman emerged, closely followed by an undersized man who showed every sign of annoyance.

The woman had large, intelligent eyes and seemed to find the situation faintly amusing. She certainly took no notice of the man's ill humour, and gave the girls a keen glance as she walked by them and out into the street. The little man watched her go, muttering to himself angrily.

"And now that the — the inquisition is over, Mrs. Bates," he barked at the manageress, "we can, perhaps, return to our normal routine. Please come into the office. There are several business matters

I wish to discuss with you."

The manageress went with him, and Doreen and her friends turned to go.

"And who might that Very Important Person be?" Doreen laughingly asked the assistant.

"He's Mr. Sprigglethwaite, the managing director," replied the assistant, speaking in awe, and glancing nervously in the direction of the office. "He doesn't often come here, but it's lucky he did this morning." She seemed flustered and anxious to talk.

"Has something gone badly wrong?" asked Sybil.

"Why, yes, I'm afraid it has," the assistant — a girl not much older than themselves — replied. She automatically picked up a nylon scarf — one of the many unpacked, in vain, for a previous customer — and deftly folded it. "There was a robbery farther up the road first thing this morning. At Mitchams, the jewellers. A woman walked in there just as the shop opened and asked to see some expensive rings. While the young man was serving her, she took a small bottle out of her handbag and threw something horrible into his face. It made him absolutely helpless. Then the woman made off with the rings."

The three friends looked mystified.

"But what has that to do with this shop?" asked Olive.

"Well, you see, the police think the thief might have been a woman who came in here immediately afterwards — to throw people off the scent."

Doreen smiled and nodded.

"But why do the police think that? I mean, did anyone see her come in?"

"In a way, yes. A policewoman, or lady detective, or whatever she's called. The one you saw go out just now. She happened to be walking along on the other side of the road and she remembers seeing a woman hurry out from the jeweller's and turn this way. But that was before the alarm was given, so she couldn't really have noticed, could she? I mean, there's an awful lot of traffic and people about at that time. A real rush it is usually. Anyway, the manager of Mitcham's heard his assistant screaming and came down from his flat over the shop, discovered what had happened, and rushed to the door shouting for assistance; and the lady detective called the ambulance and the police."

"But the police weren't able to find any clues here?"

"No — well, we'd hardly had anyone in the place then. The police soon went, but the lady detective just hung on and on. She questioned everybody again — even Mr. Sprigglethwaite; and I'm afraid she's made him awfully angry, which won't make the day any easier for us."

Having folded all the nylon scarves to her satisfaction, the assistant placed them in a drawer. "I'm sorry about that blue handbag you said you wanted," she remarked in friendly fashion to Doreen.

"Oh, do stop gossiping, Miss Skinner!" shrilled the manageress's voice from across the shop as she reappeared; and the young assistant instantly turned her back upon the girls and started to re-arrange a show-case.

Feeling the manageress's eyes uncomfortably upon them, Doreen, Olive and Sybil left the shop and strolled away discussing the robbery among themselves. Not unnaturally they stopped outside Mitchams, temporarily closed, and looked at the glittering display of jewellery.

"Just a little too expensive for me!" said Doreen laughing. They moved away, and Doreen glanced back down the road in time to see the young woman who had been so unpleasant walk rapidly away from Maison Roberta's entrance. Hardly the one to complain about others spending a long time looking in shop windows, thought Doreen, noting the young woman's smart suit and her blue handbag.

Blue handbag! Doreen felt instantly certain that she hadn't carried any blue handbag during the unpleasant episode earlier. The fair-haired young woman — "Blondie", Doreen automatically christened her — hadn't been carrying any sort of handbag.

The shape and size of the one Blondie had now were familiar too; and if Doreen required any confirmation, there, when she dashed back to look, was an empty space in the side window where the blue bag had been. So, after all they had told her in Maison Roberta's, they'd sold the blue handbag to someone else the moment she left the shop. It was really too bad of them — all three girls were agreed on that.

Doreen looked in through the open door. There was no sign of the friendly assistant, but Mrs. Bates, the manageress, mounted guard over that counter instead. She, then, was the one to blame!

Mrs. Bates caught Doreen's quizzical look and returned it with one of such malice that the girl almost jumped. Why, she thought, should this woman show her such marked antagonism? Then, suddenly a possible reason came to her. Perhaps the blue handbag was linked up with the robbery — and Mrs. Bates knew all about it!

As if she read Doreen's thoughts, the manageress moved aggressively towards the door — and Doreen called to her friends who had wandered away.

"Quickly!" she told them. "We must catch that blonde girl going towards the bus stop."

"The one who was rude to us?" asked Olive.

Doreen nodded. "That's right — hurry!"

Off they raced as hard as they could go, Olive and Sybil feeling quite bewildered. Then Doreen looked back over her shoulder and saw that Mrs. Bates had come out of the shop and was running too — but in the opposite direction!

"Bother!" cried Doreen, and all the girls came to a standstill. "You two had better follow the manageress," she went on. "Try to find out where she is going, and if you can get a policeman to help you, so much the better."

"Oh, all right!" said Olive resignedly. "But I wish I knew what it was all about."

"You will soon — if you keep tags on Mrs. Bates," Doreen assured her. Then they separated.

Blondie with the blue handbag suddenly realized she was being followed. As a bus started to draw away from the nearby stop, she chased after it and just managed to get on as it gathered speed. Doreen was left behind.

She could have cried in vexation as she stood there undecided what to do next.

"Can I help you?" enquired a brisk, feminine voice. There, walking quickly up to her was the lady detective.

Doreen blurted out a few words of explanation; and in a matter of minutes, in answer to an urgent message from a call box nearby, a police patrol car drew up alongside them.

A police officer alighted and hurried towards Maison Roberta's; Doreen took his place.

"This observant young lady will identify the suspect," said the lady detective to the sergeant in charge of the patrol car.

The bus was intercepted at a road junction not far away, and Blondie removed from it. Her blue handbag was found to contain a number of diamond rings of great value. There was also a letter which showed her to be Mrs. Bates's sister-in-law.

She chased after the bus and just managed to get on as it gathered speed.

And after Olive had waited anxiously outside, and Sybil had followed into the booking hall, Mrs. Bates herself was arrested as she entered a tube train.

"You two girls did very well," they were told by the police. "Following her to see where she went, saved us a lot of trouble!"

"What a series of misfortunes it was for Mrs. Bates and her sister-in-law, that morning!" remarked the lady detective, when, some time later, she was telling Doreen, Olive and Sybil the whole story. "Firstly, Mr. Sprigglethwaite took it into his head to visit the shop unexpectedly; secondly, I happened to be in the district on a routine enquiry; and thirdly, you girls chose that particular time to do some window shopping."

Her listeners nodded eagerly.

"But I still don't see how they hoped to work things," Doreen confessed; and Sybil and Olive said they didn't either.

"It was quite neat and simple, or should have been!" continued the lady detective. "Blondie carried out the actual robbery. She put the stolen jewellery into her handbag and then, in case anyone had noticed her coming out of the jewellers, she handed over the bag to her sister-in-law in the handbag shop. Then, if Blondie was stopped and questioned by the police, she wouldn't have the jewellery on her."

"Yes, I can see the point of that," said Doreen. "But why did Mrs. Bates put the handbag in the shop window? That seems such a silly thing to do. If she'd just kept the bag in the shop and put it under the counter, we should never have seen it and then they might not have been found out nearly as quickly as they were."

"True enough," said the lady detective. "Of course, that's just what she intended to do. The original idea was that Mrs. Bates should just keep the bag out of sight for a while, until the hue and cry died down.

"But things went wrong. Mr. Sprigglethwaite arrived to make a surprise stock check. Mrs. Bates did not want him to see the bag because there was none of that particular shade of blue in stock. So she waited until he had checked the window, then put the bag there, thinking it would be safe. Meanwhile Blondie was hanging around, waiting until she felt sure she was not suspected of the robbery, so that she could get the bag back and go off in safety. When she saw you three taking such an interest in it, she got into a real panic and tried to scare you off."

"And what a silly thing that was," said Olive. "If she hadn't been so jolly unpleasant she might still have got away with it. Why, I don't suppose we should have looked at her twice if she'd just smiled pleasantly when we apologized for bumping into her. It was only because she was so horrid that we remembered her when we saw her again later."

"That's true enough," said Doreen. "But try to put yourself in her place. She'd seen the handbag in the window and didn't know why it was there — though she probably guessed that something had gone wrong with the original plan. She didn't dare go away until she found out what was happening. And there we were, taking much too much interest in the bag for her liking. After all, she couldn't be sure that if we went in and asked for it, the assistant wouldn't sell it to us — and if the assistant took it out of the window for us — and then where would she be? In any case, if the assistant took it out of the window for us, she'd probably find out about the jewels inside it when she opened it to show us the lining of the bag."

"She must have felt even worse when you went into the shop," said the lady detective. "Especially when the assistant was talking to you. Of course she didn't dare to go away until she found out what was going on, although it was dangerous to stay around the area of the jeweller's shop.

"When you really went at last, she popped into the shop and took the handbag in case somebody else came along and insisted on buying it. Even then she might easily have got away with it, but for Doreen's sharp eyes and quick wits. Now is there anything else you'd like to know?"

"Only where we can get another handbag just that shade," laughed Doreen.

"Oh, Superintendent MacKensie has already found that out for you," said the lady detective, "and the bag has been bought. You'd better come along with me to the police station and collect it — I believe there's something for Olive and Sybil, too!"

And there was! A little later three very happy girls left the police station — Doreen with her blue handbag and Olive and Sybil with pretty new headscarves.

ALL FOR FATHER

by Sarah Flower

Jane and Gwen wanted new dresses for a party to which they'd both been invited. But their father was worried because, as he pointed out, money was scarce.

Then an apple fell on Gwen's head and this gave Jane an idea. They would set about making more money on their own.

But making money isn't easy as the two girls were to find out in this amusing story.

"Wouldn't you like me to look pretty, daddy?" wheedled Gwen. She put her head on one side and smiled up at him under her lashes.

"Dad gave up hoping for that years ago," I hissed, giving her a nudge, "when you were born!" Gwen trod on my foot.

Dad didn't seem to hear either of us. He was running his hands through his hair, and as the sun streamed through his study window, I noticed it looked pretty thin — poor Dad. There were piles of papers on the desk in front of him and he sighed, then he looked up at us very solemnly.

"My dear girls," he said, "it's no good you running in here every alternate weekend asking for new party dresses. You've got to realise money doesn't grow on trees!" He gestured out of the window and Gwen and I looked — almost as if we expected to see pound notes dangling in ripe bunches from the orchard trees.

"Have you two girls ever thought," asked Dad, "how much I have to pay out each week? There's my fares up to the City each day, constant repairs on this house, Mrs. Briggs' wages . . ."

"You can cut down on those," Gwen and I both suggested quickly. Mrs. Briggs is a woman from the village who has come in to "do" for us ever since Mother died, and that was years and years ago. But we don't like Mrs. Briggs any more now than we did at the beginning. She's always complaining and moaning and grumbling. She never smiles — not at me and Gwen, anyhow.

"And have you cooking the meals? No, thanks," said Dad wryly. "Mrs. Briggs may not be ideal — but at least the house keeps running, after a fashion. And I don't want my daughters running any more wild than they are at the moment."

When we got outside the study, Gwen puffed out her cheeks and said: "Men! Can't Dad see we couldn't possibly go to Nellie's party in those old things!"

Perhaps because I'm nearly fourteen, three years older than Gwen, I wasn't thinking about our dresses any more — I was really concerned about Dad.

"Can't you see poor Dad's worried stiff?" I told her. "He just doesn't know how to pay for anything. Maybe he hasn't got any money any more. Let's go to the den and discuss what to do."

The den is right at the bottom of the garden — where Mrs. Briggs never comes — and it's made where two old apple trees have got all twisted up together. In spring it's the prettiest thing you've ever seen with blossom all over it.

"But what can we do?" said Gwen, when we were settled. "We're not old enough to go out to work."

I didn't say anything because I just didn't know what we could do — all I knew was that we'd got to do something. This was a time when poor old Dad really needed his daughters. We both thought as hard as anything and Gwen was the first one to break the silence when she said "Ow!"

"An apple fell on me," she said, rubbing her head. "Want it?"

Then she stopped rubbing and stared at me. "Jane, whatever's the matter?"

"Money doesn't grow on trees," I said slowly and very importantly. "But apples do! Perhaps we could sell apples to the greengrocer."

"AND mustard and cress!" said Gwen.

"And spinach and potatoes and all sorts of things," I said.

We spent all the rest of that morning excitedly discussing our plans. It all seemed so obvious now that we wondered why we hadn't thought of it in the beginning. We would make the garden earn money for us!

Everything we grew — we'd sell.

"And what about that goat?" hissed Gwen, excitedly.

For days we'd been wandering along to say "hello" to the white goat that was tethered in the field at the bottom of the road. Over her head was a notice board that read "FOR SALE". The poor old thing had been waiting to be bought for days and no one seemed to care.

"Nobody would know," said Gwen. "We could keep her in the orchard. I mean — a cow would be too big but you get milk and butter and cheese from a goat just the same, don't you?"

We stared at each other excitedly.

There was so much to do we hardly knew where to start. We collected every penny of pocket money we had and Gwen went dashing down to the village to buy seeds and things. I started to pick apples and lay them tenderly in a box I'd lined with tissue paper. When Gwen came back she looked rather crestfallen. She began reading instructions off the backs of the packets to me:

"Plant in the spring . . ." "Produces a fine crop in three months . . ." "Plant in February, harvest in July." "But we can't wait that long!"

I could see Gwen was near to tears with disappointment. So I said quickly: "There is still the apples and the goat. Let's go and sell some apples quickly so we've got enough money to buy her."

So we began with Mrs. Vincent who lives next door to us. She's very nice though she talks an awful lot. I rang the bell and we waited tensely. After a minute Mrs. Vincent flung open the door and beamed down at us, her eyes fastened on the box of our best apples.

"My dears, how perfectly sweet of you both," cried Mrs. Vincent. "It was quite charming of you to bring me some of your lovely apples. But as a matter of fact, my dears — I was just going to bring you some of mine! As you can see, I have so many this year."

As fast as we could Gwen and I muttered polite things and hurried off. When we got into the road again Gwen said "Look!" in a quivering voice and pointed down the road.

*For days we'd been wandering along to say "hello" to the white goat tethered
in the field.*

Every house as far as we could see had apple trees. And every apple tree was loaded down under its weight of apples.

There was just one hope left, the goat! Tomorrow was Monday and I determined I would slip off on my own in the morning, without telling Gwen.

★ ★ ★ ★ ★

The man seemed only too pleased to let me have the goat. He didn't seem to bother about the money, when I explained my plan about pocket money instalments.

A little nervously I untied the rope that tethered the goat to a stake in the field.

"I am going to take you home," I said firmly.

Just the same, it was the goat that took me home.

We went tearing along the streets at about fifty miles an hour. Somehow or other I just managed to tug her round the right corners. Everything passed me by in a blur of speed. The goat had her head right down and was going as if her life depended on it.

I don't know what would have happened if Gwen hadn't been hanging over our front gate wondering where I'd got to and saw us coming. She flung open the front gate — the goat saw it and dived in.

When she got to the bottom of the garden she saw the apples and stopped to munch one. Quick as a flash Gwen and I had her tied up to one of the trees. Then I sat on the grass and panted while Gwen burbled with excitement.

After a bit, Gwen said: "We'll have to milk her. I'll go and get a milk bottle." She was gone ages, so I was sitting up and feeling human again when she returned.

"Mrs. Briggs is on the warpath," she said. "She's doing the washing and says she doesn't want us anywhere around. I had to creep past her to get the milk bottle."

I took the milk bottle Gwen held out and looked at it rather dubiously. "What do I do now?" I asked.

"That's easy," said Gwen. "You just milk her."

The goat had stopped grazing and was watching me, her yellow eyes rolling. I thought I began to understand why the man had let me have her so easily.

"Come on, goatie. Good goatie," I coaxed and squatted down beside her.

That was as far as I got!

The goat put her head down and charged, not at me this time but away. With the sudden yank our knot that had tied her to the apple tree slid undone — and she went charging off up the garden.

"Catch her!" I shrieked. We set off in hopeless pursuit — and almost before we started the disaster happened.

At the top of the garden, just outside the house, Mrs. Briggs had been hanging out the washing. Large sheets billowed from the line in the summer breeze. Into one of these the goat rushed headlong. The sheet came off the line and wrapped itself neatly around her.

At that very moment Mrs. Briggs came out of the house and met the full impact of some ghostly-white careering object.

I should think her screams must have been heard all over the neighbourhood.

"That is that!" she said. "Never again, do you 'ear me? Never again will I set foot in this 'ere mad house!"

She really meant it! Within five minutes Mrs. Briggs had departed and we never saw her there again. Normally this would have delighted us — but what about poor Dad? Then I thought of something.

"Gwen," I said slowly, "do you remember seeing that place advertised in the local paper — employment exchange?"

"Do — do you think they could find us someone?" Gwen breathed. "But they'd never listen to a child!"

"I can sound grown-up when I want to," I said with dignity. And I went off there and then and grabbed the telephone — making my voice as business-like as possible.

When I'd rung off and told her the news, Gwen gave a whoop of delight.

"They've got someone there now and they're sending her along right away! Oh, Jane, we're being lucky at last!"

"Quick! Quick!" I begged her. "There's no time to dance about. What am I going to wear?" Because, of course, if I'd got to interview a new housekeeper I'd have to be grown-up, just as I was on the phone.

Luckily, Mrs. Briggs had left behind one of her overalls — and there was a pair of high-heeled shoes she'd chucked out ages ago. Then

Gwen found an enormous straw sun-hat with ribbons on that she'd used for dressing-up when she was little — and a lipstick.

I thought the overall and the hat looked a bit funny — but Gwen said they were stunning together. And just then there was a knock at the door . . .

Gwen rush to open it and left me all alone — feeling awful.

"This way, please," I heard her say. "The lady of the house is at home."

I came down the stairs to meet them with as much dignity as I could manage. I'd just caught sight of a pleasant face with a wide smile peering over Gwen's shoulder — when I caught my heel. Bonk! Bonk! . . .

I came tumbling down the last few steps and sat up in a spin. At first I couldn't see where I was — then I realised the hat must have fallen over my eyes. When I pushed it back there was Gwen, splitting her sides with laughter.

I tried to glare — but suddenly I saw the woman laughing too, and she had such gay, catching laughter that I began to laugh too. In a minute all three of us were rolling about helplessly.

"Oh dear," said Mary at last (her name was Mary, as you'll see in a moment), wiping her eyes. "What a shame, and you looked such a picture coming down those stairs. Can I help you up — madam? I presume you are the lady of the house?"

Mary suggested that, as she was coming to be our house-keeper (she seemed quite sure of that), we should tell her everything. She said she sensed we were in some sort of trouble or something.

So Mary made a cup of tea and we sat in the kitchen (which we haven't done for years and years because of Mrs. B.) and told her everything. All about Dad's worries over money and the goat and Mrs. Briggs.

Then Mary seemed to bustle about like magic and by the time Dad came home the house was clean and tidy, supper was cooked — and she'd even milked the goat!

Of course, we couldn't wait to see what Dad was going to say about her. I mean, he'd probably be cross because Mrs. Briggs had left to start with.

But when he saw Mary his eyes popped.

"Mary!" he exclaimed.

"Hello, George," she said calmly, because she'd already seen him and got used to the surprise.

You can imagine how our eyes were popping! We just couldn't imagine what the grown-ups were talking about — they seemed to know each other.

And so they did. When they were quite young they used to live in the same road. Then Dad moved away and married mother and Mary stayed there to look after her invalid mother. But her mother had died a few years ago and Mary was looking for a job as housekeeper — luckily for us. So they hadn't met for ages, but they had always liked each other very much. After a bit Gwen and I went to bed and left them to talk.

Next morning we woke up to a delicious smell of bacon — we never had anything but lumpy porridge with Mrs. B. We raced down to the kitchen and there was Mary.

"Girls," she said. "I thought we might buy some material today so I can make your new party dresses. What do you say?"

Gwen said: "Yippee!"

I said: "Marvellous, Mary. But — I'm afraid Dad can't afford it."

"Oh, I had a little talk with your father," said Mary. "I'm afraid he gave you rather the wrong impression. He's actually not too desperately broke."

"I'm not broke at all," said Dad, who breezed in just then, looking jolly for eight in the morning. "But I haven't enough money to be extravagant, so I didn't want you girls to grow up thinking that money grew on trees."

"You mean you don't really need money so badly after all!" I said accusingly. "Oh, Dad, how could you? We did all those things for nothing!"

"Nothing?" said Dad, laughing. "Do you call Mary nothing? I reckon you two girls achieved a great deal when you set out to help me yesterday. Even if things didn't turn out the way you had meant them to."

"What your father means," said Mary, "is that if you have good intentions in the beginning, things will work out right for you somehow." Then she held up a frothing white jug.

"Anybody care for goat milk in their tea?" she asked.

SECOND SIGHT

by John Montgomery

Wendy's father had been blinded in the war. Since then Judy, his big guide dog, had served him in place of his eyes and led him everywhere. Dog and man were devoted to each other.

But Judy was getting old and proving rather unreliable. For how much longer could Judy serve her master? It was a question that was causing Wendy considerable anxiety.

Miracles don't usually happen in our own home town, and anyway many people don't believe in them. But I'd like to tell you a strange story about a man and a dog and a little girl. And it happened right next door, just over the fence from where I live. I like to think that it was a modern miracle, if you believe in such things. Personally, I do — after what happened to the Shaws.

I remember the day Wendy Shaw was born, and I've seen here grow from a chubby little infant into an attractive youngster of nearly ten. The Shaws were lucky to have such a daughter, she was a real little beauty, with her long fair hair and blue eyes. But then the whole family was attractive, and if it hadn't been for Mr. Shaw's blindness they wouldn't have had any problems.

Mr. Shaw had been blinded in the war, and that was why they kept the big dog named Judy, and were so devoted to her. She was Mr.

Everyone they passed on their daily journeys knew the tall, distinguished man and his handsome dog.

Shaw's faithful guide dog. And what a wonderful creature she was. Every morning, when Wendy's mother was clearing away the breakfast things, Judy would go bounding into the room, swishing her big tail, delighted at the prospect of taking her master to work. Wendy would fetch the harness, and then they would guide Mr. Shaw out to the pavement and along towards the bus stop.

I don't think Judy ever put a foot wrong. She could be trusted to take him safely on and off buses and across the road, no matter how dangerous the crossing. She never took risks. And everyone they passed on their daily journeys knew the tall, distinguished man and his handsome dog. Bus conductors, policemen, folk hurrying into their offices, the girl in the cigarette shop on the corner — we all had a cheerful greeting for them.

"Good morning, Mr. Shaw," we would say, and some of us would add, "Good morning, Judy."

I suppose I knew Mr. Shaw better than most people, because although I have retired from business, I am still a director of the big engineering works at the end of the town, and there hadn't been too much difficulty in finding him a job as a telephone operator. It was about the only job we could give him, because of his blindness, but we looked after him well. All the staff knew that during the day, Judy lay on a blanket underneath the switchboard, only moving during the winter to stretch out near the hot radiator. Sometimes, when people asked Mr. Shaw for a number, they would add the enquiry — "How's Judy?" Mr. Shaw liked to be asked.

Mrs. Harper, our canteen manageress, would often take the dog a bar of chocolate or some biscuits on the morning tea trolley, and always there was milk. I don't think it's too much to say that we really cared for that dog. And that made what happened seem very serious indeed.

Wendy didn't see her father all day until he returned home at six, but the family had every week-end together, and if the weather was fine, I would see them setting out for long rambles over the heath, or pass them on their way to the woods. The countryside around our town is very beautiful. In spring there are primroses to be gathered along the banks of the old dried-up canal, and there is a hill covered with bluebells where I have seen Judy scampering more like a puppy than a sedate eleven-year-old. I have never seen such an active dog. Once she knew her master was in good hands there was no stopping her; she would race away among the brambles and bracken, searching for rabbits that never appeared, and not return until she was almost exhausted.

There was no doubt that she was a dog in a million. But I sometimes wondered what would happen when she grew too old to guide Mr. Shaw. Really, that was a very serious problem. For Judy was now eleven, and the difficulty would soon have to be faced.

★ ★ ★ ★ ★

I think it was just after Wendy's tenth birthday that the accident happened. She had been away, staying with an aunt in Cornwall, and she returned with a wonderful colour looking even prettier than ever. From over the fence, I saw her coming down their garden path.

"Hullo," I said, "you look healthy enough."

"I've been swimming every day," she said. "We had super weather. And I played tennis every evening."

"And ate lots of Cornish cream?" I added.

"Masses," she said. "How's everyone?"

"Oh, fine," I said, "just fine."

"Is Daddy back yet?" she asked.

"No, I haven't seen him. He's late this evening."

I watched her go indoors and a few minutes later Mr. Shaw came down the path, with Judy leading him.

"Young Wendy's back," I announced.

"Oh, good," he replied. "You know — I've had a rather frightening experience."

"Yes?" I said, and I noticed for the first time that his suit was dusty and his hair was untidy, which was unusual for him. He was always so smart.

"It's Judy," he said. "I don't know what's come over her. She's always so reliable. But guess what she did this evening. You'll hardly believe it."

"What did she do?"

"She suddenly led me right out into the middle of Market Street, just where the traffic was thickest. If there hadn't been a policeman there I daren't think what might have happened."

"But she's never done anything like that before, has she?" I asked, surprised.

"Not Judy," said Mr. Shaw, "I just don't understand it. I feel quite shaken up."

"You'd better go indoors," I said. And when he had gone inside I turned back towards my own front door, wondering. I felt anxious for Mr. Shaw and his dog, but I found it hard to believe that she had made a mistake, she was so well trained. Was she losing her ability in her old age? It was a dreadful thought. But it wasn't until the next evening that I knew the truth. I was weeding one of my rose beds when I looked up and saw Wendy coming in their gate.

"Evening, Wendy," I said, noticing how serious she looked. Not at all like the girl who had smiled so happily the previous day.

"Hullo," she said.

"How's Judy?" I asked.

"Oh, do you know about her? Isn't it dreadful?"

"Why, what's the matter?" I asked.

"Poor Judy — we had the vet in this morning, and he said she's going blind. You can see it if you look closely in her eyes. Don't you think it's dreadful? I don't know what we're going to do."

For a moment, I didn't know what to say, I was so taken aback. Then I asked: "Does your Daddy know?"

"Yes," she said, "he's terribly upset. When he heard the news he just sat there in his chair with his hand on Judy's head. What on earth are we going to do?"

"Well," I replied, "Judy's bound to get older. That's the tragedy, that dogs and cats don't live long enough. I don't think you can do very much except perhaps keep smiling, and hope for the best, and say a little prayer."

"Do you think that would help?" she asked.

"Why not? It usually does. Try it."

She smiled, a rather thin watery smile. "All right," she said. "And thanks for helping."

Next day was Saturday and it rained all day, so I didn't see the Shaws, but on Sunday afternoon, just as we were having a cup of tea, there suddenly came a violent knocking on the front door, and when I opened it there was Wendy, looking very upset and excited.

It really was a dreadful situation. They had all gone out for a Sunday morning walk over the heath, but just as they reached the stores at the corner of the wood a car had come tearing round the bend in front of them. And then the most extraordinary thing had happened. Instead of stopping, as Judy should have done, she walked straight on. Mr. Shaw had been slightly in front and there was no time to do anything but shout a warning. Within a second he was down and underneath the car. They rushed him to hospital and bandaged his head.

"Is he badly hurt?" I asked.

Wendy said: "No, it isn't that. He's just bruised on the head, that's all, and he hurt his wrist a bit. But it isn't that. He just sat up in bed, and looked around, and told us he could see again. Isn't it fantastic?"

"He can see? Are you sure?" I could hardly believe it.

"Yes," she said, "the doctors said it was probably the shock of the accident. He can't see very well yet — only dimly, but he knew the colour of my hair, and he could see Mummy sitting by the bed. They say his eyes may get quite well again."

"Goodness," I said, without really thinking what I was saying — "It sounds like a miracle." And when Wendy had gone, and I went back to the kitchen for my cup of tea, it occurred to me that I had probably hit on the truth. Whether Wendy had taken my advice or not, I cannot say. After all, you can't very well ask a little girl if she remembered to say her prayers.

Wendy is nearly eleven now, and she is captain of the junior hockey team and top of her class. Mr. Shaw's eyesight is almost perfect now, and I have managed to find him a more responsible job with the firm. We've got a new telephone operator from St. Dunstan's.

And Judy? She is still a very important member of the family. They take her everywhere they go, and although she is now totally blind, they never leave her alone. Neither do they forget that she has given them the best years of her life, and that but for her, Mr. Shaw might not have been able to see. And everyone in the town — bus conductors, policemen, passers-by, the girl in the cigarette shop — we all continue to greet them, just as we used to do.

Well, there you are. Maybe you don't believe in such things. But I like to think what happened right next door was a miracle.

THE HAUNTED CHALET

by James Edgar

White Lady Chalet once belonged to a rich American and his beautiful young wife. Then something tragic happened and they never came back again. For years it lay empty and many people whispered that it was haunted.

Then one night Julie and Dirk watched a mysterious man who had entered the house, searching for something. For what?

"Oh, Timothy! No wonder you keep falling down! You shouldn't cross your skis!"

Julie Cairns was speaking to her nine-year-old brother as he lay on his back in the snow, struggling to disentangle his crossed skis. They were on the nursery slopes of St. Auspice in the Swiss Alps, and despite the instructor's patient coaching, Timothy had made no progress.

"I can't help it, Julie," Timothy protested. "I did everything the way Toni said, didn't I?"

Julie and Timothy were staying with their mother in a little pension in the village. Their father was working in India, and since Mrs. Cairns disliked spending Christmas alone in their London flat, she had decided to take the children to Switzerland for a short stay.

Julie helped Timothy to his feet and began to disentangle the skis.

"Can I help?" a voice broke in quietly.

Julie looked up, startled, to see a fair-haired boy of about her own age. He was watching her with a faint gleam of amusement. She recognised him at once as the boy she had seen coursing down the snow-slopes with such admirable skill.

"It's my brother," she explained. "He doesn't seem to get the hang of this. We've been practising for three whole days and he's no better than when we started."

"Let me have a try," suggested the stranger. "By the way, I'm Dirk Neilson and I'm staying next door to you in the village."

As he spoke Dirk made an adjustment to Timothy's skis and then he began to coach him with a fluent ease that amazed Julie. Soon Timothy was moving down the slopes, a little hesitantly at first, but with a rapidly-growing confidence.

"I think your brother can look after himself now," said Dirk. "Come on, I'll take you for a run on the Lunewald slope where all the experts go."

Soon Julie had forgotten her nervousness and she and Dirk were like old friends. Later, as they returned to the village, he gave her a challenging smile.

"I say, you're not so bad for a girl. There'll be a full moon tonight. Supposing I call for you at eight o'clock and take you to see the White Lady Chalet."

"White Lady Chalet," Julie breathed. "It sounds lovely and . . . mysterious. All right, Dirk, we'll go. Eight o'clock tonight."

That night while her mother was putting Timothy to bed, Julie joined Dirk, and they began the climb up the snow-covered mountain side. It was bright moonlight, and spread below they saw the myriad lights of the hotels spilling across the frozen lake.

"Oh, it's beautiful!" Julie gasped.

"I like it too," Dirk nodded. "But we've quite a way to go yet."

At last they rounded a coppice and there, seeming to float in the moonlight, Julie saw a chalet. It was unlike any chalet she had ever seen. It was built of gleaming white birchwood, with a wide verandah and huge windows. A soft wind moaned eerily round its eaves.

"So that's the White Lady Chalet," whispered Julie. "How did it get that name? Doesn't she live in it any more?"

"They say it belonged to a rich American and his beautiful young wife," Dirk explained. "They used to come up here every year. Then something happened and they never came back again. It's been lying empty for years. Some people say it's haunted — but I don't believe that.''

As he spoke, Julie's eyes opened wide in astonishment. For at one of the windows she saw the reflection of the light — mellow, as if it came from a candle or an oil-lamp. She clutched Dirk's arm and pointed. "Look, Dirk," she said tensely. "There must be someone inside."

"It could be a burglar. Let's go nearer and have a look inside."

They tiptoed along the verandah and peered in at the lighted window.

"Gosh!" Julie whispered. "It is a thief! Look, there's a man going through the drawers in that bureau. Maybe we ought to tell the police."

"Keep quiet," Dirk muttered. "Let's see what goes on first."

In the glow of a candle set on the table, Julie saw a tall, slender man in a ski-ing uniform. He was investigating the contents of a bureau against the wall — not hurriedly but with a slow, patient deliberation. At last he seemed to give up the search. He shrugged his shoulders wearily, took a last, lingering look about the room then blew out the candle.

"Look out," Dirk whispered. "He's coming out again. Keep low."

As they ducked below the window-sill, holding their breath in suspense, they heard the mysterious stranger close the door behind him, lock it and walk slowly past them. Something fell from his hand to the verandah-floor with a metallic tinkle.

While Julie waited, expecting discovery at any moment, the stranger felt along the floor with his hand then rose abruptly and went on down the slope.

"Gosh, I thought he'd found us out," Julie breathed. "I wonder what he dropped."

"The key!" said Dirk triumphantly. "And I've got it. It fell right against my foot. Julie, we're going inside!"

As he spoke, he moved towards the door and Julie followed him nervously. Dirk fumbled for the candle, lit it and started to look about him. In the candle-glow Julie studied the luxurious furnishings of the room, the deep, exquisite square of carpet which almost covered the floor, the valuable pictures ranging the walls and the obviously expensive furniture.

Dirk examined a rack of books by the fireplace then turned to Julie in bewilderment. "I don't understand," he said. "What was he after?

In the glow of a candle set on a table a tall man was investigating the contents of a bureau against the wall.

All these valuable things, but he took nothing. He couldn't be a thief. What the dickens did he want?"

Julie's eyes lit up purposefully. "I've got it, Dirk!" she explained. "Somebody left a will that couldn't be found! They hid it somewhere in here — and he knows that! If he finds it, he'll inherit an enormous lot of money."

"Rot!" said Dirk shortly. "That sort of thing only happens in story-books."

A little downcast by Dirk's lack of enthusiasm, Julie started to finger a china dog on the mantelshelf. It was a trumpery thing, utterly out of keeping with the rest of the furnishings. A small bunch of withered violets draped limply from an aperture in the head of the dog.

Somehow Julie's fingers slipped on the porcelain surface of the china dog. The next moment it fell into the stone hearth!

"Oh dear!" she cried in dismay. "I've broken it! Aren't I the clumsiest idiot! Let's get out of here, Dirk, before . . ."

"Just a minute, Julie," Dirk interrupted. He stooped to the hearth. "Something fell out of it. Look, it's a gold locket — and it's valuable. Real diamonds and rubies!"

Wonderingly, Julie followed him to the table and they began to examine the locket. In the soft candle-light the inset rubies and diamonds glittered with a rich lustre. Carefully Dirk opened the locket to reveal the tiny miniature of a woman. She wore a sad, thoughtful expression.

"Why, she's beautiful," Julie breathed. "Maybe she was the woman who used to live here."

"Could be," muttered Dirk. "The inscription on the back says — 'To Martin — from Mary. À JAMAIS.' That's French for 'forever'." Thoughtfully he slid it into his pocket.

"We'd better hand it in to the police in the village," Julie suggested.

"No, Julie," said Dirk resolutely. "I've a better idea. I think maybe that man was looking for this. We'll come back here tomorrow night and take him by surprise."

The following evening Julie's mother had a headache, and Julie was left to put Timothy to bed. For some perverse reason, he refused to go off to sleep and Julie waited impatiently until at last he closed his eyes. Then, she slid into her ski-suit, tiptoed out of the room and snatched her skis from the rack in the hall. Dirk was waiting for her outside.

Moving towards them from the darkness was a tall man in a ski-suit.

But Timothy had deceived Julie. From the window he watched Julie and Dirk moving out towards the mountain slope. Five minutes later he was trudging in their tracks.

Clouds were gathering about the moon and a cold wind funnelled along the valley. In spite of her warm woollen clothing, Julie shivered. When at last they reached the chalet, the moon had disappeared and all they could see was the faintly-glimmering outline of the chalet.

But although they waited, nothing happened. At last Dirk spoke, his teeth chattering with cold. "It's no good, Julie. He won't be coming tonight. We'd better get down to the village. It's no joke being caught up here with a blizzard blowing up."

It seemed an endless journey down the slope, and but for Dirk's experience Julie might easily have lost her way, for flurries of snow had completely obliterated the lights in the valley.

Julie said goodnight to Dirk and ran into the pension — to find her mother anxiously waiting. "Julie! Thank heavens you got back. Timothy must be perished with cold. Where is he . . .?" Her voice faltered. "Surely he went with you! Julie!"

Julie's heart tightened with dismay. "No, Mummy! He was asleep when I left him!"

"Then he must have followed you!" cried Mrs. Cairns.

Papa Herriot and his wife, who ran the pension, stood beside Mrs. Cairns, their faces grim with anxiety. "Ma foi! A child up there on the mountain in a blizzard!" growled the old man. "Alors vite, Marie! We must form a search-party. Vitement!"

In a stupor of mounting panic Julie watched the search-party form up in the village street, their resin torches spluttering in the wind-driven snow; Dirk had joined her.

"Don't worry, Julie," he said gravely. "We'll find him. He's probably taken shelter in a hollow and fallen asleep."

Suddenly someone raised a shout. Moving towards them from the darkness was a tall man in a ski-suit. Timothy lay asleep in his arms.

"It's all right, folks!" he called out cheerfully. "I found him below the funicular. Poor little chap. All he needs is a glass of hot milk and then bed, I guess."

As Julie's mother whisked Timothy away, Julie turned to the stranger gratefully. There was something familiar about his appearance. But Dirk had noticed it, too.

"Excuse me, sir," he challenged. "Weren't you in the White Lady Chalet last night?"

"That's right, son," replied the stranger. "It belongs to me. I come back each year from America just to look it over."

"But the White Lady!" Julie broke in excitedly. "She would be your wife. Did she come with you this time. I'd love to see her."

"Why no, miss," said the American with a slow, sad smile. "You see, she died a long time ago. But she loved this place so much I felt I had to come back to it now and again."

As he spoke of his wife Julie saw his eyes cloud over with the memory of an old sorrow.

"We saw you looking inside that bureau, and we thought you were a burglar," Dirk went on.

"You saw me, did you? Well, I can explain that, son. I was looking for something that belonged to my wife. I'll probably never find it again — but I have to keep trying."

Julie looked at Dirk as the same thought occurred to both of them. Suddenly Dirk delved into his pocket and produced the locket. He held it up before the American.

Julie watched the American take the locket from Dirk, his hands shaking with emotion. When he spoke again his voice was husky.

"I guess this is it, son. How did you come across it?"

When Julie explained the accident the American gave her a grateful smile.

"Thank you, Julie," he said softly. "This means more to me than you'll ever know. I think that the chalet needs some youth and laughter. Tomorrow, we'll go up there together, shall we? I'll have some supplies sent up and we'll have tea there. What do you say, kids?"

Dirk and Julie eyed each other rapturously. "Gosh! We'd love to go!" they gasped. "Thank you."

And not long after, the owner of the White Lady turned the chalet into a holiday home for children so that its ghostly silence was broken for ever and it became a place of fun and happiness.

PATSY'S PRINCESS

by Joyce Sanderson

The Heron *was an old lightship that, having seen better days, had been converted into a Maritime Museum.*

Patsy's father, chairman of the committee that had planned the conversion, was worried because the bank that had advanced the necessary money was asking for the loan to be repaid at an early date.

Patsy had come to regard the museum exhibits as friends – in particular the charming figure-head from an old sailing ship. What could Patsy do to help her father?

It was a great day for the little fishing village of Ballymacken when the old lightship *Heron* instead of being broken up, was towed into the harbour and moored by the quay. Now, you would hardly know her, the way she was painted up, with her row of gaily coloured flags flying overhead, and a notice at the quayside which read —

MARITIME MUSEUM
OPEN DAILY 10 A.M. TO 6 P.M.
ADMISSION 10p, CHILDREN 5p

Patsy Power glanced at the church clock as she hurried down Main Street to the harbour. There was hardly anyone about yet but there

245

There stood the Princess, a charming wooden figure-head from an old sailing ship.

would be plenty to do before Ned, the retired lightshipman, arrived later in the morning. Patsy sang to herself as she unlocked the cabin door and arranged the postcards on the counter. Visitors from the bigger nearby seaside resort had already heard of the *Heron* and yesterday had seen the biggest takings since the museum was opened a couple of months ago. Trade in the village was growing, too, thanks to the committee of twelve men who had put up some money for the ship and obtained a loan. Now Michael Power, Patsy's father and chairman of the committee had gone up to Dublin to discuss financial matters with the original owners, leaving Patsy to help Ned.

A frown creased Patsy's brow as she descended the ladder and began to dust the exhibits. Her father was worried lately she knew. There was something about the loan on part of the purchase price having to be paid back sooner than expected. They couldn't carry on he said, unless the money to pay it off came in soon, and where could it come from? That was the problem.

Close the *Heron*! They just couldn't do it. Patsy gently touched the beautifully carved model of a sailing ship and looked at the faded hand-writing of a letter home from a local sailor on a voyage to New Zealand with Captain Cook. Nearly all the exhibits had come from people living in the district, they just couldn't be handed back now. Patsy had come to know them as friends, especially the Princess, as she had decided to call her. There she stood, in the upper cabin, a charming wooden figure-head from an old sailing ship, her long golden hair flowing around her shoulders and a blue cloak wrapped about her, gazing out through the porthole as if thinking of the days she cut a path through the breakers or glided elegantly amongst Pacific islands.

"If only you could talk!" Patsy muttered. "You could tell even better stories than Ned himself." And that was something, because Ned was known as the best storyteller in the parish.

She was jerked back to reality by the sound of footsteps overhead and hurried back up the ladder to welcome the first visitor. A man was coming up the gangway, a stranger, holding a small parcel under his arm. His tall figure stooped as he came on board. He paid his money and glanced curiously around, his dark eyes darting from side to side.

"Good day to ye!" He bowed slightly to Patsy. "I'd like to see the museum."

"You're very welcome," Patsy assured him, thinking that although he sounded like a local, she had never seen him before. The man spent some time looking at the exhibits before halting by the Princess.

"A fine specimen, too," he said, almost to himself.

"'Twas given by old Captain Collins," Patsy told him, "up at the big house. He was a queer sort of a man, lived by himself and never spoke to anyone. He died a few weeks ago and he didn't have any relations at all so the place was sold. He collected things from ships and Dad and the others bought the figure-head for the museum. Nobody knew where he got her, they say she's 300 years old."

"Is that so?" The man turned to Patsy. "What I really came for was to make the museum a present of this. 'Tisn't anything to do with the sea but 'tis very interesting, maybe 'twill bring good fortune." He unwrapped the parcel to reveal a smooth round stone, with a slight hollow on top. He lowered his voice.

"It's a stone from a fairy ring, some say these stones were used by the druids of old as holders for a light of some sort at their burial places, but I wouldn't like to say. But 'tis a stone to be reckoned with to be sure. 'Tisn't every day a fairy ring stone is found so look after it well." He winked at Patsy, placed the stone on the counter and was gone before she could reply.

Patsy handled the stone curiously. It was very smooth and pleasant to touch. Then she laughed. Though some people said fairy ring stones were unlucky, she'd place it where everyone could see it and people could decide for themselves. The English visitors would be sure to love it, it would be the next best thing to having a leprechaun on board!

She reached for a white card and carefully printed the words "STONE FROM FAIRY RING FOUND —" she thought for a moment and then wrote "IN A FIELD BY THE SEA."

It was time to fill the kettle. Ned always liked a cup of tea as soon as he came on board. There he was. She could see him ambling slowly along the quay, hands in pockets.

"Good morning, girleen, and how are things today?" he inquired as he came up the gangway.

"The kettle is on, and I've got a new exhibit." But Ned had already seen the stone. His face paled; then he went closer and looked at the stone, hands behind his back.

"Heave it overboard," he ordered. "That's terrible bad luck, terrible." Ned sounded frightened, then he turned to Patsy. "No, don't touch it, that's even worse bad luck."

"But sure I have touched it," Patsy protested. "I don't believe all the stories about —" but Ned interrupted.

"I've lived a long time, Patsy alanna, and I'm tellin' ye, I know these things aren't for the likes of us to interfere with. If I'd known the boyo who left it — tell me, what was he like?"

"A tall dark fellow, very polite, I never saw him before."

"One of the tinkers, maybe."

Another visitor was coming up the gangway of the *Heron*. It was Mrs. Cullen, proptietress of the grocery shop in Market Street. Her round rosy face beamed at Patsy and Ned.

"I've been that busy in the shop I haven't had a chance to come in and see the ship till now," she broke off. "For goodness sake, would you look at that!" Mrs. Cullen took the fairy stone in her hand. "I've never seen one of these before."

"It's bad luck, ma'am," warned Ned, but Mrs. Cullen only laughed and went on to look at the other exhibits. "Well, if any bad luck comes to me ye won't be long hearing of it. News travels quickly in Ballymacken!" She was still laughing heartily as she left the lightship.

Paddy and Johnny Murphy, two small boys, came on board a few minutes later.

Paddy drew a sharp breath.

"A fairy stone! I've heard about them, they're bad luck!"

"They're not!" retorted his brother, picking up the stone.

"They are so," contradicted Paddy. "I'm not going to touch it." He put his hands in his pockets.

"That's right, lad, that's right," Ned told him. "I wouldn't have anything to do with those things meself."

Patsy leant over the counter.

"Johnny, if any bad luck comes to you, will you tell us?" she asked.

Johnny nodded, chuckling.

"I will, to be sure."

Ned took the card from behind the stone and added something in his clear handwriting — "HANDLED AT YOUR OWN RISK." Then he sat back, puffing at his pipe; the matter, he felt, was now out of his hands.

Business was good on the *Heron* next day and by the time Ned arrived at mid morning, Patsy had already taken several pounds. But Ned wasn't his usual cheerful self Patsy noticed.

"Your Dad has been on the 'phone to one of the committee members I've heard, and the news isn't good. It seems the bank wants the loan repaid within a month, and not a thing he can say will make any difference."

"But more and more visitors are coming," protested Patsy.

"I know," nodded Ned, "but 'tisn't enough, girl, not if we had a thousand visitors a day."

Patsy determined not to be downhearted.

"I won't believe it," she said to herself. "It just can't happen."

Next morning Patsy bought a copy of the local paper on her way to the lightship. She opened it and stared. A large headline topped one page.

"Local grocer's shop damaged by stray cow! While Mrs. Cullen, proprietress of Cullen's Grocery Shop, was absent from the shop last Thursday morning, a stray cow wandered into the street and became frightened and smashed the window. The cow then entered the shop and ran wild, damaging a large part of the stock before being captured by Mr. Denis Owen of Market Street. Mrs. Cullen returned to find —" Patsy read no further. When she reached the lightship she folded the paper and stuffed it into a locker. Thursday morning! The time Mrs. Cullen had visited the *Heron*! At least she could hide the news from Ned in case he hadn't yet seen the paper.

A few minutes after the door of the cabin had been opened, Patsy heard a small voice from outside. It was young Paddy Murphy and he looked scared.

"Come on in, Paddy," Patsy encouraged, but Paddy backed away.

"I can't, I'm not allowed, Johnny has got the measles." He was gone, running like a rabbit.

Patsy forced a smile and straightened the card behind the fairy ring stone. But a strange uneasy feeling had come over her as she descended the ladder and took a duster out of a locker. She crossed to the model of the sailing ship *Santa Maria* and began to dust it. As she did so the fragile mast came away in her hand. Patsy replaced the model on the shelf, her hand was shaking. Dad would be really cross. He knew she was extra careful with the exhibits, that was why he allowed her to take over in his absence in the first place. Maybe Ned would mend it, Ned was great with his hands, but he might say it was a job for the experts. She climbed the ladder thoughtfully and went to look at the Princess, still smiling with that faraway look.

It proved to be one of the busiest days aboard the lightship and Ned and Patsy had no chance to talk until almost closing time, which was just as well, as one of the visitors dropped his camera overboard and it was only just rescued by a fisherman before it sank.

Next morning Patsy stood and stared at the stone. What if Ned had been right after all? What if it was her fault for keeping it? She just couldn't take any more risks, the stone would have to go.

Patsy reached for the stone but at that moment she heard footsteps on the gangway and two teenage boys entered followed by a large Alsatian dog. The dog was young and playful, leaping up and barking as one of the boys tried to take a ball he held from his mouth.

"Be careful, please." Patsy looked worried as she watched the dog follow the boys into the upper cabin where the Princess stood. "You had better leave the dog outside." But the boys, talking and laughing, paid no attention and Patsy held her breath as she could hear the boys pushing each other and the dog becoming more excited. A moment later there was a crash, Patsy dashed into the cabin, too late. The Princess lay on her side, the excited dog barking loudly while the two boys vainly tried to catch it.

"Oh, no!" Patsy dropped to her knees beside the fallen figurehead and tried to raise it. The boys, now looking thoroughly ashamed and frightened, at last managed to capture the dog and quieten it. The paint was chipped where the Princess had fallen, and Patsy felt tears prick her eyes as she lifted her up and ran her hand over the shoulder and arm. The paint could easily be repaired but something else was wrong, too; the Princess couldn't stand erect, the base looked as if it was damaged. While one of the boys held the figurehead, Patsy looked at the flat base on which the Princess stood. It was loose and had moved. Suddenly it came away in her hand revealing a cavity with an opening several inches wide.

For a moment Patsy stared, then thrust her fingers into the opening and drew out a small bundle enclosed in an elastic band. They were £5 notes, dozens of them! At the back of the cavity was another bundle, and another!

"What's going on here at all?"

Patsy's father stood in the doorway with Ned behind him. Patsy held up the bundles of notes without speaking, but one of the boys gave a stumbling explanation of what had happened. Mr. Power and Ned were down on their knees examining the opening. Ned nodded wisely.

"Sure we might have known the old Captain had his money hidden away somewhere, the way he never trusted a soul, not even the banks. Bedad, wasn't it a perfect job the way he did it?"

The only thing was to close the museum for the morning while the police were informed and the money counted, and, of course, it wasn't long before a reporter from the paper called and insisted on having the whole story.

"A great piece of publicity, Patsy girleen. Couldn't be better," Michael Power slipped his arm around his daughter's shoulder. "You've done a fine job while I was away. Ned told me there had been a few bits of bad luck, but if I'm any judge, there'll be some of the best luck ever out of this, and not before 'twas needed, too."

Michael Power was right. As there was nobody else to claim the money, it went to the ship's owners, and there was more than enough to pay off the debt. Ned touched up the Princess's paintwork and mended the base. There she stood, looking happier than ever now that her secret had been discovered.

From that day on there was no more bad luck aboard the *Heron*. The man who had given the fairy ring stone never turned up again. It still lay in its place on the counter, its fame now widespread. But Ned still refused to touch it. After all, one never knows!

PHILLIDA TO THE RESCUE

by Hilda Parry

Next door to Mrs. Susan Larter's boarding school for young ladies stood a house of mystery. Its former owner – one of the men guilty of bringing about the execution of the martyred king Charles I – had fled the country when the son of the dead monarch returned to claim the throne.

Then one evening Phillida, one of Mrs. Larter's young pupils, saw a light gleaming in an upper window of the derelict house. Who could the new tenant be?

Phillida had a wonderful way of discovering things without looking for them, and it was Phillida who first saw the light in the empty house next door.

"Good! Oh, good!" she cried. "We have neighbours at last!" and the girls in her room crowded to the curtain to see for themselves.

Only a pale yellow glow, the gleam of a candle across one of the upper windows, but faint though it was, it somehow seemed to make the mansion alive, after remaining tenantless and deserted as long as any of them could remember.

It had always been a house of mystery, standing in the neglected garden behind the high red wall; and even from the road all one could see of it was the roof, beyond the wrought iron gates which were always locked, a tangle of over-grown shrubs hiding the front of the building.

From the big apple trees in the school orchard, it was possible to look over the wall into the garden whose walks were covered with tawny, withered grass, that had not known a scythe since the Lord Protector died; and what with the neglected arbours where the roses rioted, and a general sense of decay about the whole place, it well deserved the name of "The Wilderness" which the girls had given it.

Of course, being forbidden ground, they were dying to explore it, but even Phillida hesitated. It would be easy enough to get into the place, but getting out again was the difficulty.

Its former owner, one of the Regicides, had wisely escaped to France when the Restoration came about, but several of those curious pairs of eyes wondered whether he had ventured back, and said so aloud, as they watched the light descending the staircase until the top of the wall hid it altogether.

"Whoever it will be, we will find out tomorrow," said Phillida, dropping the curtain into its place; with which, those seven unhappy little ladies, condemned to spend their holiday at school because the dreadful Plague was raging in London, undressed and said their prayers, and fell asleep, there being nothing else to do.

In the days of King Charles II, the then pleasant village of Hackney was quite a fashionable district for boarding schools, and Mrs. Susan Larter's establishment for young ladies overlooked the windings of the river Lea.

In that long-fronted, white house the inmates were taught to use the needle, and to strum on the spinet.

Also, there was a little French, of sorts, with less arithmetic, and a great deal of dancing and deportment thrown in. To which might be added the raising of a piecrust, with other useful things, all accomplished under the watchful eye of Mrs. Larter, who had three front teeth, and could read Latin through them — at least, so it was said.

"Peg," whispered Phillida after breakfast, "let us go into the orchard and look over the wall."

The two friends wandered demurely away from the others until they were out of sight beyond the kitchen garden, and then ran to their favourite spot among the gnarled apple trees.

They loved that corner because, firstly, the orchard was forbidden, and secondly, it was the farthest possible place they could get from the school house; and swinging themselves up on to a crooked branch, they climbed higher and higher until their noses were on a level with the wall top.

For once curiosity was more than satisfied, and they gasped and gaped.

A stout, pompous looking elderly gentleman in a plum-coloured suit, with beautiful lace ruffles covering his fat hands, was walking in "The Wilderness" garden, where they had never seen a living soul before, and beside him tripped a dainty girl, so graceful and so surprisingly lovely, that they had eyes for nothing else.

Ringlets of spun gold framed a sweet face clouded by an expression of trouble, as she listened with downcast eyes to the gentleman's conversation; and though they were too far away for the watchers to catch more than the sound of his voice, they rightly guessed that he was laying down the law somehow, from the way he flourished his walking staff.

"Did you ever see the like, Peg?" murmured Phillida. "She wants but wings to make her the fairy queen! Who can she be?"

Margaret shook her own rebellious red locks, lost for an answer, and the strangers passed out of sight behind a neglected arbour, followed by a lean, yellow mastiff snuffing suspiciously in the rank herbage.

"Persons of quality, my dear," said Phillida with a wise nod. "How I should love to have speech with her. She cannot be older than ourselves. And what wonderous pearls about her throat."

Before Peg Mallow could reply, a bell rang somewhere in the distance, and the mastiff tore off to the front of the house where he joined with two other hounds in a chorus of savage barking.

"How I hate those fierce creatures," whispered Phillida. "Who are these folk that need a pack of such brutes to protect them?"

"Maybe fugitives from the Plague, like ourselves," said Peg. "Perhaps we shall see her again if she walks in the garden. But the girls are calling us for our promenade with Madame!" and with a little grimace they clambered down.

"Do not say what we have seen. Why should Madame have to

know everything?" said Phillida, pouting. "The old cat watches us as if we were so many mice, as it is."

"Girls," said Mrs. Susan Larter severely when they were all mustered in the hall, each with their hat and gloves, "there is no reason why we should depart from our daily custom just because it is holiday time. We will now take the air, and you, Margaret and Phillida, will walk with me."

It was just as well that the brim of Phillida's hat was large enough to hide the grimace she made, but her reward was not long in coming.

Sedately bringing up the rear of the little procession as it left the gate of Mrs. Larter's garden — as trim as that of "The Wilderness" was unkempt and neglected — Phillida and the grim lady had scarce made a dozen paces when a very strange thing happened.

Cantering his bay nag across the road towards them, a young gentleman in brown velvet, who seemed to have come from nowhere, reined up so close as to bar their further progress, and doffing his plumed hat, bowed almost out of the saddle.

If the girl on the other side of the wall had seemed like a fairy, surely this was Prince Charming himself, thought Phillida, who had never seen anyone so handsome in all the seventeen years of her short life.

To Mrs. Larter, he said: "I crave a thousand pardons, Madame, for the liberty I take, but seeing you come forth from your gate, I make bold to ask who lives next door?"

Susan Larter, frightened of horses to begin with and finding the rider far too handsome for her liking, bridled stonily and snapped her three teeth together like a rat-trap.

"Nobody lives there. The house is empty, sir; you can see that for yourself!" she made severe answer, ruffling her feathers out as an old hen might when a hawk draws too close to her brood.

Phillida saw the young gentleman's face change, and knowing that her own cheeks had grown crimson, she wondered whether he had seen the start she had given as she checked the sudden desire to contradict Mrs. Larter.

"Again I crave your pardon, Madame," he said with an odd smile. "I thought where there were dogs loose in a garden there might be also some that would feed them; but maybe the hounds of Hackney live on air!"

Although he spoke laughingly as he again bowed low, Phillida marked the keen expression of disappointment as he turned his horse away. Somehow she thought he would have had speech with her had they been alone.

She hated herself now for not saying openly what she and Peg had seen — but there again her tongue was tied, for the orchard was out of bounds.

So, with Mrs. Susan Larter in a white heat of indignation at the young man's impudence as she deemed it and Phillida dying to speak to Peg about it and the rest of the girls homesick and unhappy, the morning walk did not promise to be a success.

Nor was it, until, at the end of half an hour, when Mrs. Larter stopped at Blind Betty's cottage on the way back, that the two girls managed to exchange whispers.

The cottage was on the river bank, where a lane came down to the ferry under the willows.

"Do not wander from sight of the door. I shall be inside only a few moments," said the school-mistress as she gathered up her rustling skirts and entered.

"Peg!" began Phillida, and got no farther, for round the corner of the hovel appeared the head and withers of a bay horse; also the face of "Prince Charming," who, after a quick glance at the little group of waiting girls, laid a warning finger to his lips, and beckoned Phillida to him.

"Mademoiselle, I read in your eyes that you had something to tell me," he said rapidly, as she ran to his stirrup with her best curtsey. "Do you know the name of your neighbours in the Mansion of the Mastiffs? I am but newly returned from France, and seek one, very dear to me, who has been spirited away by a villain."

"Oh, sir, since they came only last night their names I have not; but Peg and I saw a young lady walking in the garden with a gentleman, less than an hour ago," replied Phillida.

"Ha! What is she like, this young lady?" and the question came with an eagerness there was no mistaking.

She told him, but he checked her almost before she had begun, backing his horse out of sight round the corner of the cottage.

"Odds life! My informant was right!" he cried. "It is Dorinda — and you, my unknown friend, will you help me to save my sweet sister from a foul plot to rob her of her fortune? Can you get speech with her?"

Phillida had never looked prettier than she did just then, gazing up at the speaker with parted lips, and great eyes filled with wonder.

"Indeed, sir, it shall not be for want of trying! And if I succeed, what would you have me say?"

"That brother Jasper sends this message — on no account must she set her name to any document Sir Gregory puts before her, or she will lose everything — can you remember those words? Sir Gregory is her guardian, and one who shall face my sword ere many days have passed."

"Trust me, sir. Peg and I will never rest until she has your warning; but how may we let you know when it is done?"

"I shall not be far away — and Peg is —?"

"Here! — to bid you fly, sir, before Mistress Susan sees us!" said Peg as she reached Phillida's side, anxiously half-looking back at the cottage.

"Prince Charming" waved his embroidered glove without a word and took the hedge at a bound, vanishing completely before Mrs. Larter came round the corner of the lane.

"Now girls, we will return," she said, "and tomorrow, Phillida, you and Margaret shall take a basket of comforts to the poor blind creature."

At which, Phillida Merrydew, all of a tremble at the nearness of her escape, felt mighty thankful that old Betty was not the only blind creature in the world just then!

"Mistress Dorinda, would you like an apple?" The girl with the spun-gold hair looked up as the voice came from the sky, to see a wealth of black ringlets escaping from the snowy cap of that other girl on the top of the red wall.

"You are wondrous kind, but how come you to know my name?" she asked in surprise.

"This will tell you," replied Phillida from the overhanging boughs. "Hold out your dress!" Phillida let fall a great rosy-cheeked pippin, which parted in halves, revealing the folded paper that had lain between them.

The ripple of amused laughter, that had passed across the girl's face, left it as she read the message and there was anguish in her eyes as she looked up again at her brother's go-between.

"It is too late," she moaned in a stricken whisper. "I signed Sir Gregory's authority this morning!"

"Authority for what?" demanded Phillida.

"To withdraw my fortune from the bank at Temple Bar. My Guardian has even now gone to London and will bring the chest hither ·in his coach before nightfall!"

She continued to look up, open-mouthed now, for Phillida had suddenly dropped out of sight, warned by the faithful Margaret that Mrs. Larter was walking abroad.

"Oh, Peg, the mischief is done!" cried Phillida as the two con-spirators slipped, just in time, from the orchard into the kitchen garden, where they were allowed to wander at will — onions being considered safer than apples in the hands of Mrs Later's precious charges. "We must tell him at once!"

"But how?"

"Let us remind her of the basket for old Betty — it is our only chance," said Phillida. To their great joy, and no small surprise, the usually watchful Mistress Susan took the bait there and then.

But not until she had carefully reconnoitred the high road in search of young gentlemen with plumed beavers, and found none, did she open the gate, and her last words were: "If you do not return within the hour I shall come in search of you!"

★ ★ ★ ★ ★

Very prim and demure looked those two dainty maidens, tripping on their errand of mercy with the basket between them; at any rate, until they had passed out of sight of the school house, when they quickened their pace almost to a run.

But the high road was empty, as was also the lane leading to the ferry, and their faces grew wondrous long and mightily troubled.

It was a perfect morning, with the bright glint of swishing water among the pollard willows, and they had been hoping that so much might have happened in that short hour of freedom; yet, a lad herding cattle on the marsh, and a solitary angler on the opposite bank, were the only living things that rewarded their anxious eyes.

"I fear we are too early, Peg," said Phillida dolefully. "He said he would not be far away, but maybe he is a late-riser, not thinking us up and .about at this hour."

"Welcome and well met, my little unknown friend!" he cried.

"Tis a thousand pities he did not tell you where he housed — but listen!" cried.Peg, shaking her mop of red locks, and tilting her nose in the air. "I'll warrant me 'tis at the 'Three Feathers' so let us first make haste to old Betty's and once rid of our burden, we can speed back the other way past the inn, where he will surely see us as we go by."

"You are an angel, Peg," nodded Phillida. "I only wish we had better news for him, poor gentleman."

Peg smiled to herself, and glanced sideways at her bosom friend. At the bottom of the hill she stopped.

"Wait here — in case!" she said. "I will scarce be gone before I am back," and taking the basket she went into the cottage, leaving Phillida to seat herself under the willows, hoping against hope.

She made a pretty picture in her blue gown with its wide sleeves, and the great hat perched above the little lace cap.

But the winding lane up which she gazed remained provokingly empty and poor Phillida's dark eyes were dimming with tears of disappointment when the thud of cantering hooves on the soft grass behind her, made her turn with a glad cry.

If "Prince Charming" had seemed handsome yesterday, surely he was doubly so this morning, as he pulled up beside her, the sunshine sparkling on the gold guarding of his brown velvet suit.

"Oh, welcome and well met, my little unknown friend!" he cried. "I saw you both leave the abode of that Gorgon woman with the terrible teeth, but judged it wiser to meet you here. Dare I hope for news so soon?"

"Indeed, yes, sir, even though the news could not be worse, I fear!" and she told him all she had learned.

For a moment the sun seemed to have passed behind a cloud, so dark was the frown that blotted out his smile; and then he laughed, oddly, but with a gaiety that surprised her.

"Mistress, you have done more than well," he said, very serious on a sudden. "Do but tell me your name, that I may know to whom Dorinda and I owe a gratitude we can never repay?"

"I am Phillida Merrydew — and you?" she faltered shyly.

"I am Jasper, Earl of Eglantine, and eternally at your service, Mistress Phillida," he replied. "Think me not churlish if I leave you on the instant, for there is much to be accomplished before nightfall, and after I have settled accounts with Sir Gregory Biggleswade, my next task will be to rescue my sister from his servants and the fierce hounds that keep her prisoner behind those high walls. For the life of me I do not yet see how it is to be done, since the scoundrel schemes to wed her to his whelp of a son, and has more friends at Court than I."

He was gone once more, with a sweep of his feathered beaver, and Peg, coming out of the cottage just then, saw Phillida apparently curtseying to thin air.

Mrs. Susan Larter awoke with a start from her afternoon doze, disturbed by the rumble of wheels and the gallop of horses being furiously driven, which brought her to the window in some haste, in time to see a coach pull up so suddenly that it almost over-turned, in front of the empty house next door.

"What is going on?" she murmured with a snap of those terrible teeth. "And where are the girls?"

Smoothing her dress and very angry because the clock told her that she had overslept, she went downstairs.

Silence reigned in the old panelled rooms, and the garden seemed deserted. Had the Plague itself visited the place, it could hardly have left it quieter or more empty.

"They can never have gone forth into the village without my permission," she gasped, "unless, indeed, Phillida has led them astray, the baggage!" She listened for a moment, with a great fear upon her, then she caught the sound of voices from the orchard — strictly forbidden to them all.

Gathering up her skirts in each hand, lest they should rustle, she sailed majestically across the trim lawn, so filled with rising wrath that she was all unaware of the approach of a gallant figure in brown and gold that had dismounted at the school gate and coming round the corner of the building, paused a moment at sight of her, before he followed with a smile of mischief in his eyes.

"If ever I saw an old tabby cat stalking sparrows I see it now," he said under his breath. "And the sparrows are doubtless twittering from the wall-top to my Dorinda, with whom I must have speech, no matter what the cost!"

So Mrs. Susan Larter tiptoed through her spacious kitchen garden, and my lord tiptoed in her wake, treading so softly that the spurs on his riding boots made no sound.

And well might the good dame stop and start, aghast, as she came to the orchard and saw what was happening.

Under the high red wall, five of her young lady boarders were standing in a group holding on like grim death to the new well-rope in which someone had dared to tie knots! Stretched full length along the coping above them, lay Phillida Merrydew and the inseparable Margaret, both leaning over into the adjoining garden with the end of the rope beween them.

"Pull!" cried Phillida on a sudden, and they pulled.

"Alas! Oh, my goodness gracious!" murmured Mrs. Susan Larter from the shelter of the nearest tree. "Disgraceful and most unseemly behaviour!"

"Pull!" repeated Phillida from the top of the wall as she and her companion stretched their arms downwards. The next moment, a golden head showed above the moss-grown coping while Phillida and Peg grasped a pair of tiny hands, and after a second's pause for breath, the trio scrambled down the fruit-laiden apple tree boughs with a low cry of triumph.

"And what is the meaning of this?" came the indignantly, angry voice of Mrs. Larter, that brought a sudden hush to the jubilant girls among the trees.

The answer came from a very unexpected quarter. "It means, Madame, that Mistress Merrydew and her friends have rescued my sister from a very dire peril while I have been busy elsewhere!"

The voice brought Mrs. Larter round with a jump, to find the same young gentleman of the day before, standing behind her.

"If there be any fault, Madame, then the fault is with me," he continued quickly, as the girl with the hair of spun gold ran into his arms. "I am the Earl of Eglantine and this is my sister, Dorinda. I will plead these young ladies' pardon on bended knee, if you so desire it."

Mrs. Larter's own knees knocked together so much from all she had seen, and so agitated was she at the unexpected announcement of the young gentleman's name and station, that she bungled her curtsey, and nearly sat down!

"Nay, indeed, my lord, 'tis I should plead," stammered the poor woman, overwhelmed as she recalled how she had answered him at their last meeting.

"But will you not come indoors, and if there be peril the constable shall be summoned."

"You are very gracious, Madame, but I fear 'tis no matter for the constable since I have already taken the law into my own hands," laughed the young nobleman. "But stay — what is this? — someone tries the climb the rope, and I am eager to see who it be!"

Catching it as it began to slip over the coping towards the adjoining garden, he took a turn of the well-rope round the nearest bough, and holding it taut in one hand, whipped out his rapier with the other, while the girls fall back in a frightened bunch.

In a moment or so, fingers grasped the top of the wall, and a head came into view; the head of a young man with a thin, evil face under his tousled wig, who stared blankly at the figure below him, greatly startled at what he saw.

"Come along, Master Biggleswade, provided only that you bring your sword with you!" said the Earl sternly. "I have a great wish to meet you, foot to foot, and what better spot than the grass of this orchard?"

He made his rapier flash in the mellowing light as he spoke, with the result that the face blenched ghastly white and vanished on the instant.

"Better so, perhaps, little sister," said my lord, slipping the blade back into its velvet scabbard. "We have foiled them both — father and son — without bloodshed, and all their schemes have come to naught."

"But Jasper, I signed that fatal paper, ere I had word from you," cried Dorinda, clinging to his arm.

"And, thanks to Mistress Phillida, I learned of it in time to gather half a dozen gay sparks of my own regiment who made a frolic of it," laughed her brother as they followed Mrs. Larter into the house. "Our faces hid behind a yard of black crêpe, we turned highwaymen for a while, and stopping Sir Gregory's coach in the land that leads from Dalston hither, in broad daylight, rescued the chest that held your fortune, and trounced the old rogue so soundly that he will neither sit nor lie in comfort under a week, I warrant me!" The recollection tickled him so much that he laughed for a full minute before he could continue.

"But come, little mouse, we must indeed ask pardon of this good dame for all unwittingly causing such a flutter in her dove-cot," said the young Earl, "and then, perched behind me on the croup of my brave 'Brown Eyes', I will carry you home, whither the chest has already preceded us under willing escort, out of reach of the Biggleswades and the Plague — and, in truth, I know not which of them be the worst!"

During a recent visit to a fine old hall in northern Essex, two pictures in the gallery interested me greatly. One was "Prince Charming," and a handsomer fellow surely never smiled proudly from a painter's canvas. The other, hanging beside it, showed a lovely lady with black ringlets all a-curl round a sweet face.

On the frame was the inscription, "Phillida, Countess of Eglantine" — and it set me thinking!

Also, I wondered whether Mrs. Susan Larter ever really forgave her precocious pupil? — but that we shall never know!

THE GREAT PENTREVEN PLOT

by Samantha O'Brien

The times were perilous. England in the days of Queen Elizabeth I stood at bay, confronted by the armed might of Spain, always ready to launch another Armada, a new invasion.

To the Cornish home of Sir Walter Pentreven come two strangers seeking word with Sir Walter. But the knight is in London with his wife. It falls to his daughter Elizabeth and her friend Catherine Kerewen to entertain the new-comers, and so begins a stirring adventure of danger and intrigue.

With excited whoops and shrieks the three youngest Pentreven children dived in pursuit of a tennis ball round the beech hedge screening the archery lawn. Overhead the sun blazed down from a blue sky faintly dappled with flimsy white clouds. There seldom had been a more glorious summer than this of 1595.

They were a handful at the best of times, these Pentreven youngsters — young Walt a strapping ten, Ann a tomboy seven, and little Mary a tumbling, rosy-cheeked four — and now, with their parents away in London and their governess gone unexpectedly to a sick kinswoman, they took some keeping in order.

Watching them from a mullioned window in the Big Room of

Pentreven Hall, their eldest sister Elizabeth exclaimed: "Honestly, Cathy, I don't know what I would have done without you!"

Catherine Kerewen laughed, a bubbling little explosion of a laugh that went with her plumpish figure, bright brown eyes and boundless energy. "You would have managed — you always do!"

Elizabeth was as slender as her friend was plump, and the sun's rays streaming in at the taffeta-draped window made a shimmering halo of her fair hair. "This is one time I couldn't have managed," she said. "The children know me too well — I'm their sister! You're not, so you can keep them in check."

"Well, partly in check anyway. Which reminds me, it's time I fetched them in for their meal."

With Catherine the thought was the deed, so gathering up the rich fabric of her russet-coloured gown she marched purposefully across the panelled room to the door. For some moments after she had gone, Elizabeth remained at the window, gazing across the lawns to distant conifers and elms. The only sound now was the mewing of gulls as they wheeled ceaselessly over the cliffs. She was unaware of the familiar sound. Her thoughts were in London. Had her father succeeded in gaining an audience with the Queen? And if so, had Her Majesty heard his plea?

The tiniest of frowns puckered Elizabeth's brow. Being a girl, she knew little of the intricacies involved in her father's fight to regain those estates lost two years ago in dispute with a second cousin; only that new evidence which recently had come to light had raised hopes of reversing the court's original decision — and that everything now depended upon the Queen. Either their full lands — and their fortunes — would be restored or they must leave the Hall.

Elizabeth plucked absently at the threads of her girdle. The very thought of leaving Pentreven filled her with dismay. She had been born and bred here. For as long as she could remember her entire world had revolved about this house. She knew every copse and stream, every field and track. There had always been the golden-gorsed cliffs in summer and the sea sweeping gently into Pentreven Cove to form a turquoise pool. In winter, of course, it was different. Then great Atlantic rollers, surging over jagged rocks, boomed against the cliffs, and high winds buffeted the Hall. But — summer or winter — Elizabeth loved Pentreven.

Scampering footsteps and shrill shouts jerked Elizabeth from her day-dreaming. Catherine had succeeded in rounding up the children. Elizabeth had turned from the window and was smiling when her brother and sisters came charging boisterously into the room.

Elizabeth was in the herb garden two evenings later when a maid-servant brought word that two gentlemen had called to see Sir Walter. Wondering who the callers could be, Elizabeth passed over the basket of herbs she had gathered and started for the house. As she stepped through an arched gate in the garden wall she met John Carew leading a pair of horses to the stables.

Carew halted. A short, sturdy man with a chest that seemed on the point of bursting the seams of his buff jerkin, he had served at Pentreven man and boy. The thatch of rough hair topping his rugged face, together with bushy brows over piercing blue eyes, gave him a somewhat fierce appearance, but in truth there were few men more gentle than John Carew. And no servant Sir Walter Pentreven trusted more.

"Aye," he said now, interpreting Elizabeth's glance at the weary horses. "The gentlemen have ridden far. I showed 'em into the house."

"Did you tell them Sir Walter was away?" she asked.

"I told them."

Elizabeth thanked him, continued to the house and climbed broad steps to the lofty main hall which at this hour, with the sun in the west, was cool and in partial gloom. At first she saw only the tall bearded man who advanced to meet her, then she made out a second figure half hidden by the deeper shadows.

The tall man bowed. Even the film of white dust from dry roads and tracks couldn't disguise the quality of his doublet and hose, nor dim the sparkle of the beringed hand resting lightly upon the hilt of his sword.

"Richard Venning, m'lady." The deep-set eyes in his lean face were jet black, as was his neatly trimmed pointed beard. His quick smile showed strong, large teeth, but the smile vanished as he added: "I have travelled far to meet your father. Perhaps you have heard him mention my name for we are old friends. But I understand Sir Walter is not at home. It's a pity because I have urgent and important business with him."

"He is in London with my mother," Elizabeth said. Then she shook her head. "No — I do not recall his ever mentioning your name."

Richard Venning frowned; then, seeming to remember his companion, he turned and beckoned to him. In response this man stepped softly forward. He was sombrely dressed and without sword, and his narrow shoulders sloped away from a long neck. His bow was awkward. Almost colourless eyes in his pasty clean-shaven face glided vaguely over Elizabeth before lowering.

"Henry Morton, my secretary." Richard Venning's brow was still furrowed. "Have you any idea when your father may return? It is imperative that we meet and talk as soon as possible."

Elizabeth shook her head. "I'm afraid not. It could be tomorrow, the day after — or next week even." She remembered suddenly that in her parents' absence she was mistress of Pentreven. "Forgive me, you must be tired and hungry."

"Both. Our journey has been long and tedious."

Elizabeth led them into the Big Room. "It is growing late. Will you stay overnight?" she offered.

Richard Venning hesitated before accepting. "Just for tonight then. Thank you."

Elizabeth made arrangements for a meal to be prepared for her unexpected guests and had them shown to rooms on the first floor. In their absence Catherine returned from a walk with young Walt and Ann, and learned of their arrival. When she had seen her young charges to bed — little Mary was already asleep in the nursery — Catherine met the pair.

"Kerewen." Richard Venning mulled over the name when she was introduced. "Would you be related to Charles Kerewen of Fowey — a deputy lieutenant of the county?"

"My father," Catherine told him. "Though just now he is inspecting the sea defences around Falmouth."

Richard Venning arched an eyebrow. "Surely there aren't still fears of a further invasion by the Spanish?" he asked.

Elizabeth answered the question. "Hardly a year has passed since Spanish troops landed at Mousehole and seized Penzance. If you had seen the ruin they left in their wake you would understand why Cornishmen remain wary — and prepared."

"We saw a great pile of brushwood and timber along the cliffs as we rode in. Are they for firing in the event of an emergency?"

"Let one soldier from Spain set foot upon our soil," Elizabeth assured him, "and these cliffs will become a string of blazing beacons."

"But here — along the north coast?" Richard Venning sounded incredulous. "I should hardly have thought. . . ."

He shrugged off the rest of the sentence in a manner that somehow belittled Cornwall's fears and prompted Elizabeth to counter: "The cat doesn't always pounce twice in the same spot."

Venning inclined his head as if conceding the point.

The meal was served — shoulder of veal well larded, and salted beef, roasted pears, malmsey wine and sweetmeats — and afterwards Venning announced that he and Morton would retire as they were anxious to be away early next morning.

"Did Richard Venning say what his business was with your father?" Catherine asked when the two girls were alone.

"No, but it seems to be important — and urgent — from the way he talks. What he plans is to continue on to Newlyn where he has other business and when that is settled to return here in the hope that Father will have returned by then."

Catherine toyed with a stray black curl and said: "He seems quite nice — Venning, I mean. But Morton rather gives me the shivers the way he sits there never looking directly at you but taking all in and saying nothing."

To which Elizabeth replied charitably: "That's the way with scholars. They listen and learn."

Elizabeth was up early next morning to attend to the needs of her departing guests. But a surprise awaited her. Overnight Richard Venning had changed his plans. Morton had reminded him that when passing through St. Ives he had left instructions for a letter he was expecting to be sent on to him at Pentreven. He could, of course, have this letter re-despatched to him at Newlyn, but would prefer to be in possession of it before proceeding. There was also the chance that during that time Sir Walter might return.

"Our remaining won't inconvenience you?" he asked.

Elizabeth assured him it would not.

Certainly the pair were no trouble. Venning spent almost the whole day at the archery butts with young Walt, while Henry Morton used the sunlit hours poring over books and maps in Sir Walter's library. Only once did he venture forth, when he wandered down to the cove, and then he didn't stay overlong. Within half an hour Elizabeth spotted his black-clad, long-necked figure climbing back up the track.

Young Walt returned from the butts full of excited praise for Venning's skill with the bow.

"He overrates me somewhat," the man said modestly.

The expected letter had not arrived by evening.

"Perhaps tomorrow," Elizabeth thought as she settled down to sleep that night. Perhaps tomorrow, too, her parents would return. Already half asleep, she smiled at the prospect.

It was close on midnight when she was awakened abruptly by a hand shaking her by the shoulder. She stirred, blinking. Clouds had blanketed the earlier moonlight but she recognized Ann.

"It's Mary, she's had a nightmare!" The words came bubbling from Ann's lips. "She's frightened and won't stop crying. I thought —"

But Elizabeth was already out of bed and running along the passage to the nursery. By the spluttering light of a tallow candle she found little Mary sobbing her heart out. Gently Elizabeth lifted her from the cot and gradually the tears subsided. When the last one had trickled down a chubby cheek Elizabeth said brightly: "I have an idea! You can spend the rest of the night in my bed. Would you like that?" As Mary nodded, Elizabeth glanced enquiringly at Ann. "You'll be all right alone?"

Ann looked outraged at the very suggestion that she would be anything else. "I'm seven!" And to prove it she snuffed out the candle.

Back in her own room Elizabeth settled Mary in her own bed where almost at once she fell soundly asleep. After watching her for a moment or so Elizabeth drifted to the window. It was a warm night, the air smelled fresh and sweet. Resting elbows on the sill, she stared out across the lawn. From close at hand came the soothing murmur of the sea.

Then suddenly Elizabeth's heart gave a jester's tumble. Someone had moved in the garden below. Over by the herb garden wall. "Who's there?" she called sharply. "Who is it?"

Silence, then a figure stepped forward. The upturned face belonged to Richard Venning. "It is I. Is something wrong?"

Elizabeth breathed a sigh of relief. "No. No — but you startled me."

"I'm sorry." Venning sketched a bow. "I'm taking a short stroll before retiring for the night. A walk usually prepares me for sleep."

"Oh . . . I see." Elizabeth returned his smile. "Well, I hope it does the trick. Good night."

As Venning bowed again, moonlight filtered through the clouds. Only fleetingly, but by the gossamer rays Elizabeth gained an impression of a second figure pressed against the hedge. Was she imagining things? She must be. Leaving Venning still smiling up at her, she returned to bed and snuggled up against little Mary. But on the verge of sleep she gained a fresh, sharper impression of the second figure she had imagined by the hedge. This time it bore a strong resemblance to Henry Morton. Which, of course, was moonshine. . . .

Sir Walter Pentreven had always made a habit of calling regularly upon his tenants, and during his absence Elizabeth had taken over this duty. The next day, therefore, she had Carew saddle horses for Catherine and herself, and as he helped them mount she reminded him: "If a messenger arrives for Mr. Venning you'll let him know at once, won't you?"

"Aye." Entirely out of character, John Carew sounded a trifle churlish. "Will them two be staying long, Miss Beth?"

"Until Mr. Venning receives the letter he's waiting for." Elizabeth regarded him closely. "Don't you like our guests, John?"

"Tain't my place to like nor dislike, but since you ask I'll answer straight. The gentleman, he's fair enough, save there are times he speaks over-sharp to the likes o' me. The other, he's too still-tongued, too watchful like a fox at a hen run."

Elizabeth laughed. "It's simply his manner. Most scholars are the same — interested only in books."

"Not only in books, this one." Clearly Carew had no liking for the sombre secretary. "Several times I've seen him in the cove, gaping at the house like it had cast a spell on him. Then gaping seaward in the same way."

"I'll wager he writes verses!" exclaimed Catherine. "He'll be seeking inspiration."

Carew's grunt said such fanciful notions were beyond him. . . .

The rest of the morning and afternoon were taken up with visiting the tenants. At every house and farm there was a warm welcome, for the Pentrevens had always been good landlords. However, Elizabeth also sensed uncertainty about the future. The tenants knew why Sir Walter had gone to London, knew that their own fortunes were linked with his and were naturally concerned about the outcome of his journey. Whenever such fears were hinted at, Elizabeth did her best to dispel them.

The final call at last made, the girls rode back by way of the cliffs and were in sight of the Hall when they spotted Richard Venning down in the cove. He was using a spy-glass, training it upon the house, then sweeping it in a broad arc across the cliff face. Curious, the girls reined in.

The spy-glass swung past them, hovered, then jerked back to bring them into focus. Abruptly it was lowered. Venning stared, then with a wave clambered quickly up to where they sat.

"The more I think about it, the more I'm convinced Sir Walter should build a harbour here."

"Is it because of this that Henry Morton has shown such interest in our cove?"

Elizabeth's direct question plainly took Venning aback, but he recovered quickly: "None other. I sought his opinion," he said.

Catherine sighed. "And I had imagined him writing poetry!"

Venning laughed, but the laughter wasn't reflected in his eyes, which remained fixed intently on Elizabeth.

He chatted amiably enough when he walked alongside them as they continued to the Hall. They were following a bramble-hedged lane when they came unexpectedly upon Carew and young Walt bending over a man collapsed on a wayside bank. Bearded and unkempt, this man was obviously exhausted. A lute and knapsack had fallen nearby.

Carew glanced up. "He's in a bad way, Miss Beth."

"You know him?" Elizabeth asked.

"A stranger — a minstrel, I'd say. Aye, he's in a bad way." Carew's tone and unwavering gaze were a reminder of what her father would have done; an unnecessary reminder.

"Take him in," Elizabeth told him. "Give him food and shelter till he has recovered."

Carew heaved the man to his feet while young Walt gathered up his meagre possessions.

As they did so Venning said: "It's your own affair, of course, but I would be very careful about who you let into the Hall."

Carew glowered and Elizabeth interceded hastily: "Pentreven has a reputation for helping those in need, and I hope always will have."

Carew continued with the exhausted man. Venning said nothing more, but his set expression told Elizabeth that beneath his outward charm he was a man as hard as the steel of his sheathed sword; a man she wouldn't like to have for an enemy.

At the first opportunity Elizabeth hastened to the kitchens to enquire after the stranger. She found him at a trestle table talking to Carew. They at once got to their feet. The stranger looked decidedly more healthy now. His cheeks held colour, his blond hair and beard had been combed and he was much younger than Elizabeth had supposed; no more than in his middle twenties.

Carew announced proudly, "He feels better already, Miss Beth."

"Much better m'lady," the man confirmed. "My name is Harrington — Robert Harrington."

As Carew moved away, Elizabeth frowned: "You must have neglected yourself to grow so weak."

Robert Harrington had a pleasing smile. "I'm a wandering minstrel," he said, as if that explained everything.

Elizabeth dropped to a stool, indicating that he, too, should be seated. This stranger intrigued her. "You sound like a gentleman. Is the role of strolling minstrel the best a gentleman can do?"

"If it's the role he desires, what better?" he replied.

Elizabeth found herself returning his smile. "Have you come far?"

"From Sussex." Robert Harrington fondled the head of one of the house spaniels that had padded across the rush-strewn floor to where he sat. "Carew tells me you are mistress of Pentreven during your parents' absence and that it is you I must thank for taking me in. Which places me in your debt — one I can repay only by doing some service."

"You owe me nothing."

"Except possibly my life." He regarded Elizabeth seriously. "I like to repay my debts."

Robert Harrington was sprawled on the floor. Preparing to run him through with a short sword was Henry Morton.

"There's no need, but if you insist then Carew will no doubt find some light task when you are strong enough." Elizabeth rose. "Meanwhile you are welcome to rest here."

Venning broached the subject of Robert Harrington over dinner that evening. "At the risk of seeming to interfere," he said somewhat tartly, "I feel bound to repeat my warning against admitting strangers. What do you know of this man?"

"You also were a stranger when you arrived," Elizabeth reminded him softly. "And this man comes of gentle stock."

"All the more reason then for watching him." Venning almost snapped it. "No one willingly surrenders a gentleman's life for the hardships of a wandering minstrel's."

There was a strained silence which Henry Morton, speaking for the first time during the meal, broke with: "There is logic enough in my master's reasoning, Miss Elizabeth."

Elizabeth gave him a long, steady look under which he shuffled uncomfortably and lowered his heavy-lidded eyes. No further reference was made to the stranger.

Robert Harrington was employed next day on various light duties and Carew declared himself well satisfied.

Throughout the day Venning kept to himself and spoke hardly at all. Catherine believed this was due to his growing impatience to receive the letter he was expecting, but Elizabeth had other ideas. She was convinced that Venning's mood was due to her refusal to heed his warnings against Robert Harrington. As for Morton, as usual he closeted himself in the library.

It was early evening and Elizabeth was in the nursery with her sisters and Catherine when the peace of the house was shattered by a sudden angry shout. Almost immediately it was followed by a scuffling and the thud of toppling furniture which sent Elizabeth racing into the passage.

The door of Richard Venning's room was open and it was from within that the commotion was coming. She entered. Stunned by the scene which confronted her she jerked to a halt.

Behind an overturned leather-studded chair Robert Harrington was sprawled on the floor. In the act of preparing to run him through with a short sword was Henry Morton. At Elizabeth's sharp cry he wheeled, eyes ablaze with fury. Simultaneously Venning pushed past Elizabeth into the room.

"What goes on?" he damanded.

The fury in Morton's eyes died. Slowly he lowered his sword. "This man is a thief! I found him searching through your possessions!"

Venning took a pace forward, remembered Elizabeth and whirled to face her. His deep set eyes were as cold and hard as black diamonds. "What did I tell you?"

Elizabeth's cheeks burned hotly. Harrington had struggled to his feet but refused to meet her shocked gaze. When she demanded: "What are you doing in this room?" he made no reply, but remained silent.

As Carew, attracted by the disturbance, clumped in, she told Harrington: "Unless you can explain your presence we can only assume you were here to steal."

When again he made no reply Elizabeth ordered Carew: "Take him below. Lock him up till we decide what to do."

When Carew remained standing dumbfounded, Venning rasped: "You heard, man! Take this scoundrel below, keep him under lock and key — and guard him well if you value your own liberty."

Carew had no need to lay hands upon Robert Harrington. He went of his own accord.

Robert Harrington's betrayal of her trust left Elizabeth hurt, angry and disappointed. When Carew reported him locked up in a room below the kitchens she dismissed him without further comment.

Surprisingly Venning made no attempt to crow that events had proved him right. Indeed he made no reference to the affair. At least, not until the following morning when he said bluntly: "I think Harrington should be taken to Penzance and charged there. I will deliver him myself." Seeing Elizabeth's indecision he pressed: "A dungeon is the proper place for him. Escape from here isn't impossible — and I can't say I entirely trust your man Carew."

He couldn't have said anything more calculated to set Elizabeth against his advice. Springing to John Carew's defence she said coldly: "Carew is entirely trustworthy. Harrington will remain here until my father's return."

"You've had word from Sir Walter?" The question was put sharply.

"None. But his return can't be delayed much longer."

"Of course not." Venning stroked his trim beard, eyeing her meditatively. "Then I can't persuade you Harrington should be removed to Penzance?" he asked.

Elizabeth returned his stare levelly. "I would trust John Carew with my life," she replied flatly.

Venning shrugged, but his pretended indifference couldn't disguise the fact that he was galled at not getting his own way.

Towards evening Carew brought word that Robert Harrington wished to speak with Elizabeth. "He claims it's urgent, Miss Beth."

"I don't wish to see him. He's getting food and drink?"

"Both." Carew squinted at Elizabeth from under bushy eyebrows. "I'm no scholar, Miss Beth, but I reckon I'm a middling judge o' character and I'm thinking there's more afoot than meets the eye."

"Does that mean you think I should see him?" And when Carew nodded, Elizabeth agreed. "Very well, but only for a few minutes."

Narrow steps descended steeply from the kitchens to a damp passage where Carew unlocked a heavy oak door and stood aside.

The room Elizabeth stepped into was tiny. The only daylight seeped in through a slotted window high in one wall and Harrington was standing beneath this. There was a straw mattress in one corner. Elizabeth hadn't realized it was as miserable as this. As Carew closed the door upon them she said: "You wished words with me?"

Harrington nodded: "Words which I would ask you to listen to carefully. I am no thief. Neither — in honesty — am I a minstrel. My business at Pentreven Hall is of a much graver nature." He paused, but when a puzzled Elizabeth remained silent, he continued: "Briefly, my business is to learn what brings Venning and Morton to your home. Neither man is to be trusted, they have abused your hospitality for reasons which can only bode ill for England."

Elizabeth's blue eyes widened.

Harrington went on: "Venning is known to have been at the Spanish court in Madrid as recently as eight weeks ago. Morton, we suspect, was with him."

"Agents of Spain!"

"Yes."

"But here — at Pentreven? Why?"

"If I knew that, I would know all."

Elizabeth shivered. Perhaps it was the damp, cold room; perhaps the shock of what she was hearing. "Why were you in Venning's room?" she demanded suddenly.

"Searching for evidence to explain his presence here."

Elizabeth's mind was in a whirl but she forced herself to think clearly. "Why should I believe your story? Have you any proof to support it?"

"No proof. But you have nothing to lose by doing as I ask — which is that you send word to Sir Philip Dunne the magistrate in Falmouth. Tell him the minstrel urges him to come with all speed to Pentreven Hall. He will know what to do."

Elizabeth considered this. "If I believed your story, wouldn't it be easier just to set you free?"

"And arouse Venning's suspicions?" Harrington shook his head. "Putting him on guard might drive him to desperate measures. We can't — daren't — risk that. But you will get word to Sir Philip?"

Elizabeth was remembering many things. The unexpected arrival of Venning and Morton; their decision to delay their departure — ostensibly to await a letter which had never arrived; Venning prowling the grounds at midnight in company — she was suddenly sure of this — with Morton. There was the interest of both men in the cove, explained away by Venning's talk of building a harbour; their disquiet at a stranger being admitted to the Hall. And two other factors: the certainty that Morton would have used his sword on Harrington but for her intervention, and Venning's eagerness to have him transferred to Penzance.

She frowned. "Venning was anxious to take you to Penzance."

"I doubt I would have got there alive." Harrington spoke with dry finality. "Well — will you send word to Falmouth?"

Elizabeth's mind was made up. "Tonight — by Carew."

Relief flooded Robert Harrington's face. "Thank you. But take care. One false move and Venning will know he is under suspicion."

Carew locked the door and slammed home the bolts as Elizabeth emerged and they were half way up the steps when she became aware of Venning at their head.

"So," he sneered, "the thief pleads for mercy?"

"And wastes his time." Elizabeth continued her ascent. "It is for Sir Walter to decide what shall be done."

Venning made way, fell into step beside her. "Upon what did he base his plea?"

"The usual ground — that he fell victim to temptation."

"Nothing else?"

Elizabeth pretended puzzlement. "Could there be anything else?"

To which Venning replied casually: "Scoundrels have smooth tongues. I never cease to marvel at their inventive powers when it comes to saving their own necks!"

Was it her imagination, Elizabeth wondered, or was Venning suspicious? The message to Sir Philip Dunne had been written behind locked doors, Carew had ridden out with it overnight, the key to Harrington's prison was safe in the pocket of her gown, and she had tried to behave naturally. Yet she felt uneasy whenever Venning's gaze settled thoughtfully on her.

She was relieved, therefore, at seeing little of either Venning or Morton the following morning. In the afternoon she watched them ride out together, heading west, and they had not returned by evening when the younger ones were put to bed. When darkness fell and there was still no sign of them she became uneasy and decided upon further words with Robert Harrington.

"I'll come with you," insisted Catherine, to whom Elizabeth had told all that was afoot.

However, they did not get beyond the main hall, for as they crossed it the front door was suddenly hurled open and Venning strode in, sword unsheathed. In his wake clumped all of a dozen breast-plated, helmeted soldiers bearing arms that glinted in the candlelight. Then alarmed shouts came from the kitchens, followed by the sharp explosion of a musket. More heavy boots clattered and Henry Morton marched in from the rear with more soldiers. He had cast aside his scholarly role like a discarded cloak. He was armed, his eyes gleamed fanatically. In prompt response to orders barked by him in a foreign tongue the soldiers took up positions about the hall.

All this had occupied only the space of minutes and as the awful truth struck Elizabeth she whirled upon Richard Venning. "What does this mean? These soldiers —"

"Soldiers of Spain!" Venning cut in harshly. "A new invasion is under way. An armada of Spanish ships lies off this coast. Already men are landing by the score. Come dawn hundreds — thousands will be ashore, driving south and east. Cornwall will be subded within hours. Then — Plymouth, Exeter, Bristol! And this time they have come to stay." He bowed mockingly. "You were right, young lady, the cat does not always pounce twice in the same spot!"

"Traitors!" Elizabeth flung the word contemptuously. "But you are too late! Word has already gone out to warn —"

"And has been intercepted." With a triumphant flourish Venning produced a sheet of paper. Elizabeth's heart sank as she recognized it. "Exactly," gloated Venning. "Your letter to Sir Philip Dunne sent on the advice of Robert Harrington. Did you really imagine you could outwit Richard Venning?"

"Carew!" breathed Elizabeth.

"He lives — for the moment. But we talk too much. You will be confined to your rooms. And remember, you have a brother and sisters whose safety depends upon you."

Resistance was out of the question. The two girls were ushered up the stairs by Venning and four soldiers. It was the door of Catherine's room that Venning threw open. "In here!"

Elizabeth halted defiantly. "My brother and sisters must be with me."

"Very well, then," Venning agreed impatiently. "But hurry!"

Little Mary was plucked, still sleeping, from her cot by Catherine and they were followed by a querulous half-asleep Ann. Elizabeth roused young Walt who stared in astonishment and awe at the soldiers. When they were all in Catherine's room Venning warned: "Make trouble and I shall not be responsible for the consequences."

The door slammed shut on them, the key grated in the lock. In Catherine's bed now, little Mary thankfully still slept, but Ann and young Walt were wide awake, clamouring to know what was happening.

"It's nothing," Elizabeth told them. "For the moment though we must stay here. That's all."

"But those were Spanish soldiers!" Walt protested indignantly. "Here — at Pentreven!"

Elizabeth crossed to the window. It overlooked the cove and in the darkness she saw it had become a hive of activity. Soldiers were leaping from flyboats, clambering up from the beach, and out at sea were others — thousands Venning had boasted — waiting eagerly to set foot on English soil. She could have wept. Her beloved Pentreven was being used as the base for treacherous invasion of England, and she was powerless to prevent it.

Or was she? From the sill of the room to the left of this one a lantern was hung, and similarly another was suspended from the sill of the room to the right. They were undoubtedly navigation lights which, together with others in the cove, would enable the captains of the Spanish ships to steer their craft safely through the dangerous rocks further offshore.

Elizabeth stared at the lanterns, then at the ornamental ledge linking the window sills. Not very wide, but wide enough. She beckoned Catherine to her side and outlined her plan.

Catherine shuddered. "But if you should slip. . . ."

"I mustn't slip. Snuff out the candles," Elizabeth commanded.

Seconds later Elizabeth was climbing barefoot on to the sill and from it to the ledge, praying that none of the scurrying figures would chance to glance up from below. Slowly, cheek pressed close to the stonework, she inched along the ledge. At one point it seemed the lantern was moving away from her, but at last she reached it. Extra caution was needed now, for the lantern had to be moved carefully; any quick movement of the light would attract attention and bring her plan to a swift and inglorious end.

Now, grasping the lantern, progress was even more difficult and fraught with danger. One false step and she would plunge from the ledge. She cast aside the terrifying thought, concentrated on her task, and after a seemingly endless time was re-hanging the lantern all of fifteen feet from its original position.

A brief pause to regain control of ragged nerves, then she was edging back. Passing Catherine's room to the lantern beyond, she was aware of hazy faces at the open window. Momentarily she was attacked by dizziness but it passed and she resumed her inching. Finally she reached the second lamp, transferred it to the sill further along, and started back to the window.

Then it was that her legs turned to water, her head swam and invisible hands tried to drag her backwards, but she retained her precarious balance until miraculously she was dropping white-faced and trembling into Catherine's room.

Catherine helped her to a chair on to which she sank with a strained smile. How long it would be before the changing of the lights was discovered, or what it would achieve she had no idea, but if it caused the wrecking of only one Spanish ship it would have been worth while.

Ann had relit one of the candles when from over at the window young Walt suddenly cried: "The beacons! They're blazing!"

The girls ran to the window. It was true. Eastwards and westwards along the rugged coastline the beacons were ablaze, alerting sleeping Cornwall to the peril which threatened. The invaders had been seen.

Then all of a sudden the house, which until then had been wrapped in stillness, exploded with frantic shouts and the pounding of heavy boots. Elizabeth's jubilation ebbed. These sounds of near-panic close at hand served as a sharp reminder that now a new danger faced them. She recalled vividly the pillaging and plunder at Mousehole a year ago. Once thwarted, the invaders would show no mercy.

Then Elizabeth remembered the loophole in the corner of this room; the secret door that gave access to a hiding place no larger than a cupboard but where they could hide till immediate danger had passed.

She ran to the far wall, fingers tracing swiftly over the carved oak panelling. Nothing happened. Where, oh where was the spring which operated the mechanism? She tried again. This time the secret door swung open. Catherine, who had snatched up little Mary, went in first. Ann and young Walt followed, then Elizabeth. As she re-closed the door they were plunged into inky blackness.

Hardly had the door clicked shut than through the spyhole Elizabeth saw Venning burst into the room with soldiers at his heels. Disbelievingly he jerked to a halt on finding his prisoners gone. Then with a snarl of rage he told them to search the walls.

Catherine hushed little Mary who had begun to whimper. The others held their breath as the soldiers, carrying out a methodical search, drew ever closer. The nearest could have been only inches from the secret spring when the sound of violent fighting broke out within the house itself. Abandoning the search, the soldiers rushed from the room to do battle. Venning hesitated, then vanished after them.

"They're gone," Elizabeth told the others. "But we had best remain here a while."

So they waited. Waited until the fighting within the house died down, although outside it continued unabated. Waited an eternity it seemed, until through the spyhole Elizabeth saw a familiar sturdy figure stride into the room. John Carew! With his name on her lips

Elizabeth swung open the secret door.

At the sight of them Carew almost wept tears of relief. "Praise be you're all safe! And we're driving them back — back into the sea!"

"But the beacons?" demanded Elizabeth. "Who lit them?"

"'Twas Robert Harrington's doing, Miss Beth. Aye, Harrington's. I saw him only minutes ago." Carew chuckled deeply. "A prowling Spanish soldier broke into his cell. He handled the man, got clear and fired the first beacon. Before you could say Land's End the rest were ablaze and the men of Cornwall came running fast, and as luck would have it a troop of regular soldiers was moving overland to join ships at Penzance."

"I'm so glad you came to no harm!" breathed Elizabeth.

Carew looked suddenly crestfallen.

"Reckon I let you down there, Miss Beth. Venning nabbed me before I'd rode two miles and locked me in the old windmill. Time I'd broke free of my bonds and out of the place, near a whole day had passed. I got back just a bit since." The broad smile returned to John Carew's face as he echoed: "Praises be the lot of you are safe!"

Sir Walter Pentreven and his wife arrived home two days after the invasion had been repulsed. The Hall still bore the scars of the recent battle and off the coast could be seen the wrecks of once proud Spanish galleons, at least one sent to its doom by Elizabeth's action in changing the navigation lights. Reports were still coming in that many more ships had gone down when Raleigh's fleet had engaged the fleeing armada off the Scillies.

Hundreds of prisoners had been taken, and Richard Venning and Henry Morton were already on their way to the Tower to meet their treacherous deserts. Robert Harrington was in Falmouth but had promised to return as soon as he was able.

"We were at Bodmin on our way home when the news reached us," Elizabeth's father told her. "We came on as quickly as possible. It seems you have done well."

Elizabeth nodded. "But the Queen?" she asked eagerly. "Did she decide in your favour?"

"The Queen did indeed! She reversed the court's decision and all the Pentreven lands are to be restored to me and my heirs for all time."

For all time. . . .

Elizabeth glanced to where, from beyond the beech hedge, came the happy shouts and shrill laughter of young Walt, Ann and little Mary at play with Catherine.

Following her gaze Sir Walter understood the sheer joy that shone in his daughter's blue eyes. For he, too, loved Pentreven.

THEIR GUIDE IN PARIS

by Christine Landon

Patsy and her three cousins were in Paris on a two-day holiday and looking forward on this, their first day, to a grand tour of that fabulous city.

Then Patsy noticed that Odile, their charming girl courier, who was scheduled to guide them, was close to tears.

On learning the cause of Odile's distress, Patsy offered to help – with unexpected results!

"Well, this is Paris! And in ten minutes' time the girl from the travel agency will be here to take us on a grand tour of the city. What do you think of that?"

Fair curls dancing as she turned her head, Patsy Haverland gazed eagerly at the girl and the two boys standing with her in the sun lounge of one of the largest hotels in Paris. Sue and Basil Elland, and Noel Martin were her cousins and she was going to spend two exciting days in Paris with them before going on to Nice to join her parents.

And Patsy, because she knew Paris, had been allowed to choose this hotel herself, and book it through a travel agency, which would look after the chums during their stay.

From here, the highest room in the building, could be seen the glittering Seine and at least three of its famous bridges. There, too, was the tree-lined Champs Elysées, and dominating everything was the slim, elegant height of the Eiffel Tower.

"I must say I'm looking forward to this trip!" grinned Noel. "I only hope the guide speaks English though. That's the trouble with France — everyone speaks French and — H'm!"

He stopped with a cough and, looking past him, Patsy saw they were no longer alone. Stepping across the sun lounge towards them was a dark-haired girl a year or so older than themselves.

She wore a cool green linen uniform, with an attractive peaked hat.

"Which one of you is Mam'selle Haverland, please?" she asked; and when Patsy stepped forward: "Mam'selle, I am this hotel's representative of the travel agency, through which you booked —"

"How do you do?" Patsy said promptly, and held out her hand. "Have you come to tell us about the tour of Paris?"

To her surprise, the girl's pretty face seemed to tauten.

"Y — yes, Mam'selle," she said in a low and oddly reluctant tone. "The — the coach is ready waiting and we leave as soon as you wish. I — I am to guide you —"

She stopped. Patsy had the impression that the last thing she wanted to do was to go on this trip. So did Basil. He stared.

"Why, what's the matter?" he asked bluntly. "Why are you looking so miserable about it?"

To their surprise, the French girl burst into tears.

"Oh, Basil! Really! You are a tactless idiot!" Patsy flew to the girl's side. Impulsively she flung an arm about her shoulders. "I say, we're so sorry —"

"No — no! It — it is not you!" With an effort the girl tried to capture her tears in a tiny, lace-edged handkerchief. "If —"

Then, as if she could not stop herself, it all came out. The girl, whose name was Odile Ducharne, had a friend, Philippe, who was an officer in the French Foreign Legion. That evening he was to leave for a tour abroad, and he had asked her to meet him to say good-bye.

"But it means going, this afternoon, to the Café des Fleurs!" sobbed Odile. "That I cannot do because of the Paris tour. I dare not refuse to guide the tour, or I lose my job."

Patsy pressed her shoulder in silent sympathy. She had taken an instinctive liking to Odile. She could guess there was more behind the story than that. If only they could help her!

Had she and her chums alone been going on the tour, they could have backed out. Patsy herself could have shown them round Paris.

She had lived here for seven years and knew and loved every street and boulevard. This trip was like a homecoming, but she could not guide the other guests Odile said were going.

Or could she?

"Oh, goodness! Yes!" she cried. "That's it! Odile, I've lived here, and I — I think — with a bit of luck —"

"Patsy could take the tour. That's what you're trying to say, isn't it, Patsy?" breathed Sue. "And, Odile, I'm sure she could."

Odile stared at them. She could hardly grasp it at the moment, but she was given no chance even to think about it.

Calmly Basil took the small, winged agency badge from Odile's lapel and fixed it on the lapel of Patsy's smart suit. Then he put Odile's peaked hat on her head.

"There! That's settled," he decided. "This tour starts as soon as possible, you said, Odile? I suppose the driver knows where to go? O.K. Lead on, Patsy."

Patsy led on. The look in Odile's eyes was reward enough for her as she hurried her chums towards the door. It quite made her forget the fantastic nature of the task she had taken on.

Not until they tumbled down the stairs into the foyer, with its rows of palms from the South of France, did she realise. Then, as she saw the group of people, obviously waiting to join the tour, her heart sank.

They were all very much older than herself and her chums — most of them middle-aged. True enough, most of them looked kindly, but out of the corner of her eyes she saw the manager emerge from his office with a plump, severe-looking Frenchman.

Oh dear! He wasn't going on the trip, too?

Summoning up all her courage, she approached the group.

"Are — are you the party for the tour of Paris?" she asked, and gave a shaky little smile. "I — I'm deputising for the — the real courier, the real guide. Will you step this way please?"

Before anyone could ask questions about Odile, she hurried across to the swing doors, leading out into the busy Parisian square outside. An open-roofed blue coach was standing there.

Her pulse racing, Patsy waited on the kerb for the party to climb aboard. What had she done? Of all the strange, madcap ideas to get on her first day in Paris!

"Mam'selle!"

Patsy turned. Standing on the pavement behind her was the Frenchman she had seen earlier. With him was the manager, and neither looked too pleased.

"Mam'selle, what is this I hear?" the stern-faced Frenchman questioned sharply now. "You are taking this tour round Paris?"

"Well, yes, m'sieur!" gulped Patsy. "You see —"

"I do see!" The words were almost barked out. "I see some glaring neglect here, mam'selle. I am an inspector of the travel agency; it is my task to see our clients are satisfied. I know you should not be leading this tour. Where is Odile Ducharne?"

"Well — well — you see —" Patsy fought for words, and then got an inspiration. "You see, sir, I took her place because she — she was too indisposed to come!" she jerked out.

That was true. "Indisposed to come" could mean that Odile did not want to come. But this time the manager intervened.

"You mean she is ill?" he exclaimed. "Why, I passed her on the stairs ten minutes ago and she looked all right!"

"We will go and enquire into this," declared the inspector, turning. "Which room has Odile Ducharne?"

"Number Fifty-two. Fourth floor, M'sieur Robert."

They moved into the hotel, and Patsy stared after them helplessly. If they visited Odile they would find her well and happy — getting ready to meet Philippe! She would lose her job and might not be able to see Philippe after all. Oh, what —

Then her eyes fell on the little box beside the driver's seat in the coach, marked with a Red Cross. She thought of first aid lessons at school — and had an idea.

"Basil! Noel!" she called out softly; and as the two boys came tumbling out of the coach: "Oh, boys — get after them, please! Try and delay them. I've an idea, but I must have time."

The boys didn't ask any questions. They went charging into the foyer of the hotel and, after a second, Patsy caught up the first aid box and started after them.

Patsy dashed back into the foyer — where M'sieur Robert, the manager, Basil and Noel had all crowded into the hotel lift. For some inexplicable reason, that lift was refusing to rise. Patsy had the impression it was because Noel had a hidden thumb conveniently pressed against the "Stop" button. Drawing a deep breath she sped up the stairs to Room 52 and threw open the door.

Odile, her face flushed, was tidying her hair in the mirror. She turned round with a startled face as Patsy ran in.

"What —"

"Time's too short to explain!" panted Patsy, and pushed her willy-nilly into the blue brocade French armchair by the window. "Off with your shoe — good! It's a sandal and you've no tights on."

Another moment and she had pulled off Odile's left sandal and began to wind a bandage round the French girl's ankle.

"You've hurt your ankle, you understand?" she said. "It's only just been done —"

She finished binding Odile's ankle and tied it in a knot. Seizing the first aid box, she went sliding under the bed. The blue cover dropped down, hiding her.

At the same moment she heard the room door open.

"Mam'selle Ducharne —" came M'sieur Robert's voice, then he stopped. "Ah, mam'selle," he went on, in changed tones. "I wondered what had happened to you. I heard you were indisposed, and now —"

Odile, whose face had paled again, realised now just the reasons for Patsy's amazing actions. But she played up magnificently.

"As you see m'sieur, it is my ankle. Mam'selle Haverland, who is one of our clients, kindly took my place."

"So I understand!" M'sieur Robert said gravely. "But I will say, mam'selle, I am most displeased. As you are indisposed, you should at least have found an authorised guide to take your place. It is kind of Mam'selle Haverland, but what guarantee have I that she — who is supposed to be in your care — will uphold our fine record?"

"I — I believe she has lived here, m'sieur," gulped Odile. "And — and there was not time to find another guide —".

"Nevertheless," the inspector frowned, "I do not like strangers working under the badge of our agency. I think I will go with Mam'selle Haverland, to see this task you have appointed her to is not too much for her. Should I find you have delegated your job to someone incompetent, you will hear more from me. Good-day to you, mam'selle."

He turned on his heel and was gone. Patsy could only hope Basil and Noel would delay him again as he went down. She scrambled from

"I will say, Mam'selle, I am most displeased!" said M'sieur Robert gravely.

beneath the bed, her breath coming fast.

"Can't stop! Good luck, Odile! And wish me luck too — Gosh! I'll need it if M'sieur Robert is coming on this trip to inspect my work!"

She went down the stairs two at a time and reached the foyer. To her relief, when she rejoined the coach, Basil and Noel and the agency inspector had not yet put in an appearance.

They arrived a minute later, M'sieur Robert again looking rather ruffled. Apparently this time Basil had jammed the lift half-way by pressing the button on the fourth floor and holding it there.

As M'sieur Robert climbed in the coach and sat himself down he announced: "We are ready to start, and I am coming too!"

They pulled away into the streams of traffic.

If only, thought Patsy, I can keep the group interested and M'sieur Robert happy. But she must — for Odile!

She did. All through the afternoon the tour went on. They did not stop, of course, but they looked at each place of interest and each time Patsy had to find something to tell them.

Now and again she glanced apprehensively at the inspector, but not once did he fault her — not once did he interrupt.

They turned into a quiet street off the Rue de la Paix. It was getting on for four o'clock, Patsy noticed by a clock ahead — and then, with a start, she saw the name over the clock.

"Café des Fleurs."

Café des Fleurs! That was where Odile was going to meet her Philippe. It had, Patsy remembered, a famous roof garden on top, and she gazed through the open roof of the coach up towards it.

She could clearly see tables and chairs on the roof, bright with gay umbrellas. She could also see people there — and one couple, sitting together at a table near the side, she recognised.

At least, she recognised the girl. The man, in the blue uniform of a French officer, she had not seen before, but the girl whose hand he clasped over the table — was Odile.

"I hope no one else sees them!" she thought. "If the inspector did, the game would be up!"

Then her heart seemed to stop beating. The inspector was gesturing to the driver. The coach slowed up, to come to a stop outside the Café des Fleurs.

"We will stop here for tea!" M'sieur Robert announced. "Most days we stop at the Café des Oiseaux, but today is so fine, I am sure you would like to visit the famous roof gardens."

They were stopping here — for tea! Patsy sat as if stunned. Stopping here, and if they went up on the roof garden, Odile would be discovered without a doubt!

"Well, mam'selle. You have done well, and you have earned your tea. I shall tell Mam'selle Ducharne I approve of her choice of you as our guide."

The others were climbing out of the coach when M'sieur Robert stopped to have a word with Patsy. He was smiling, he was pleased, and at any other time Patsy would have been too.

Now Odile's job was in more danger than ever!

Dully she rose to follow the others out of the coach. If only there was some way she could warn Odile. Warn her that they were here; warn her to make good her escape.

"Oh!" she gasped. The driver, moving out of his seat, had collided with her. Her handbag went spinning to the ground beside the driving seat.

"Mam'selle — I am sorry!" he exclaimed. "Permit me —"

"Oh, don't worry. I'll get it."

Patsy bent over his seat to retrieve her bag, but she hardly knew what she was doing. Inspiration. A way to save Odile!

As she stooped to lift the bag her arm brushed the steering wheel of the coach, and, of course, as on most modern vehicles, the horn button was on the steering wheel.

Patsy stared at it, and her heart thudded. Dare she?

Yes! She straightened up, bag in hand — and jabbed her elbow firmly against the horn, as if by accident. Patsy had fortunately remembered that part of a campaign to cut noise in Paris was to prohibit the sounding of hooters.

The resultant blast of sound startled even her, and she jumped and fell sprawling across the seat. As she straightened up she glanced through the open roof of the coach and saw a crowd of people at the railings of the roof garden above staring down.

Odile and Philippe were among them. As she had hoped, the sound of a motor-horn was so unusual in Paris today, everyone wanted to see why it had been sounded.

Then Patsy saw Odile start and grasp her companion's arm. A moment later they vanished from her view.

"Patsy! What happened?" Basil was at her side. "Are you all right?"

"Odile's up there!" whispered Patsy, and while he gasped, she turned to apologise shakily to the inspector.

"Gave us all a shock, you did," said Noel thoughtfully. "Good job no gendarmes are about."

In that moment Patsy could not have cared less. Her eyes were fixed anxiously on the door of the café. There was no sign of Odile. Had she recognised the agency coach, or had Patsy been mistaken?

They moved into the café and into the lift. Patsy shepherded her little party, but her mind was far away. Would they arrive on the roof garden and find Odile there?

The lift whizzed upwards and stopped with a jerk — not being checked by the boys. Patsy's heart seemed to stop with it. The gate clanged open, they climbed out and she gazed around.

"Oh, thank goodness!" she breathed.

There was no sign of Odile on the roof garden. Another flight of stairs, leading outside the building to the boulevard at the back, showed the way they had probably taken.

M'sieur Robert was striding across the restaurant — to the table Odile and Philippe had just vacated. Nearby were some other tables, also empty at the moment.

"Come on! Come on!" he said, genial now. "We'll take our seats here. Mam'selle Haverland, perhaps you can order the meal for our English guests who do not speak French well?"

"Why, of course, m'sieur," breathed Patsy, hurrying forward. "I'll be glad to."

Fortunately for Patsy, the remainder of the afternoon passed without incident — much to her relief.

"Oh, my friends, how can I thank you?"

It was later that evening. Patsy & Co. were seated in Odile's room round a table filled with luscious gateaux and with bottles of soft drinks. This was Odile's treat for them.

"I think you've thanked us enough," said Sue. "Anyway, it's Patsy who was the brain behind it all."

"Patsy, indeed!" And Odile laid a slender hand on Patsy's arm. "You are — what you say? — super!"

But Patsy was gazing down at the hand on her arm. It was Odile's left hand — and on the third finger sparkled and shone three points of fire.

"Odile, an engagement ring! You're engaged!" she breathed happily. "So that's why you wanted so much to meet Philippe?"

"Yes, indeed!" Odile blushed. "And if I had not met him, perhaps he may have thought I did not wish to see him. As it is — we shall be married as soon as he returns from abroad. Meantime, I have my job and can save for our home —"

"Unless," murmured Noel, "our celebrated inspector, M'sieur Robert, gives the job to Patsy. Seemed quite taken with her!"

"I don't think so!" laughed Patsy. "Besides, I wouldn't take it. I'm here on holiday. From this time on it's fun, not hard work for us. What do you say?"

LOOKING AFTER JOHNNY

by Josephine Squires

Mrs. Gates had doubts as to how well Nicola would look after little Johnny while she and her farmer husband went out for the evening.

"It's the unexpected one has to worry about," said Mrs. Gates as she left the farm. "If anything serious should happen I'm not at all sure a teenager could cope."

Well, the unexpected did happen. Now it was up to Nicola to prove whether she could cope or not.

For the third time, Mrs. Gates said: "I think that's everything, Nicola. Are you sure you'll be all right?"

"Honestly, Mrs. Gates, everything's fine. I'm sure Johnny won't be any trouble at all."

The farmer's wife sighed. "I do hope not."

"Even if he is, I'm sure I can manage. I've two young brothers, you know." Nicola West found herself thinking that anyone would have thought she had never spent an evening baby-sitting before. She picked up Mrs. Gates' handbag and gave it to her. "I'm sure I heard Mr. Gates with the car outside. If you don't hurry you'll be late."

"I suppose so." Mrs. Gates opened the farmhouse door reluctantly.

Then she added: "I know you think I'm worrying unnecessarily, but it's the unexpected one has to worry about. If anything serious should happen I'm not at all sure a teenager could cope."

"Well I'll do my best," Nicola said soothingly. She quite liked Mrs. Gates, but there was no doubt at all that she fussed. She watched her get into her husband's car and waved goodbye with relief. After all, Nicola thought, they were only going to have dinner with friends and they had promised to be back by eleven. Nothing really awful could happen in three hours.

Nicola shut the door and went upstairs to Johnny's room. A quick peep showed that the three year old was sleeping peacefully, his curly head buried in a pillow and a teddy bear hugged firmly by a small, brown arm. Nicola smiled and tiptoed downstairs again. There was a roaring fire in the big stone-flagged kitchen. For a moment Nicola hesitated. The television set was in the next room, but that meant sitting in front of a cheerless electric fire. And anyway there was some homework that really should be done. She pulled a chair nearer and switched on the radio.

" — Charles Machin. Machin, who is thirty-five years old, is wanted by the police in connection with a robbery at a jeweller's shop in Torrington early this evening. This man, who is believed to have stolen a car from a cinema car park about an hour ago, is wearing a tweed jacket and grey slacks. He has red hair and is probably short sighted, as eye witnesses state that he wore thick-lensed glasses. Anyone seeing —"

The announcer's voice stopped abruptly as Nicola tuned in to the first station broadcasting pop music. She had already heard about the robbery in nearby Torrington, and she didn't particularly want to listen to the news all over again. She opened her book and stared without enthusiasm at the chapter devoted to the adverbial clause.

Someone knocked on the door.

Nicola got up and opened it. The last time she had looked after Johnny, one of the farm hands had cycled in from the village with a message about the next day's milking, and Nicola took it for granted that the same thing was happening again. But it was not one of the farm hands standing at the open door.

It was a red-haired man, wearing thick-lensed glasses and a tweed sports coat.

"Good evening. Is your father in?" He had an ordinary face. Certainly he didn't look like a man on the run. Only his rather thin lips would have marked him out in a crowd.

"Not just now." There was no point in lying, Nicola thought. Machin had almost certainly seen the Gates' car leave. If she admitted to being the baby-sitter it would be obvious that nobody was due back for some hours. Hoping that her voice sounded steadier than it felt, she added: "He'll be back soon."

"Ah." Somehow, Nicola felt, he didn't believe her. Then "Well, it's a cold night, so might I come in?"

He walked through the door and into the kitchen with the easy assurance of a man who knew that there wasn't really any way of stopping him. After a quick, wary look around, he dropped into a chair.

"I wonder if you could help me, young lady. I'm in a bit of a jam." The man's eyes had not left Nicola since he came in, and they were cold and calculating, even though his mouth smiled.

Nicola swallowed. "Yes?" She must appear natural, she thought. If once he suspected that she knew . . .

The stranger said: "Yes. My car's just a little way down the lane. Like a fool I didn't check the thing before coming out and I've run out of petrol. I suppose your father doesn't keep a spare can?"

"I'm afraid not." Nicola tried to sound regretful. In fact she hadn't any idea if Farmer Gates did or not. She went on: "He gets all his petrol from the garage in the village."

The smile vanished from Machin's face. Obviously the car he had stolen had run out of petrol, and he wouldn't want to go round the village on foot. He said sharply: "Doesn't he have a tractor?"

"Oh yes, but it's diesel." It was amazing how quickly one could think when one had to. Nicola managed to look regretful. "You know — it works on a different sort of fuel."

"Oh." The man was silent for a moment as he worked out what to do next. As if he had made up his mind he said: "What's the name of the nearest garage?"

A germ of a plan was forming at the back of Nicola's mind. It was a risk, but . . . "West's," she said.

Machin lit a cigarette. Almost as if talking to himself he muttered: "I'd better give them a ring. Tell them to bring some petrol along." Obviously he didn't like running the risk but couldn't think what else to do.

Nicola went over to the telephone, feeling the intruder watching her every move.

Nicola drew a deep breath and said casually: "They'll be shutting about now, and Mr. West isn't awfully obliging unless you're an old customer. Would you like me to ask him?"

The red-haired man nodded eagerly. "Good idea, young lady."

"I'm glad to help." Nicola went over to the telephone in the corner of the kitchen and spun the dial, feeling the intruder watching her every move. She said clearly: "May I speak to Mr. West, please? Oh, Mr. West, it's Nicola at Hathways Farm speaking. I've a gentleman here who's run out of petrol. I wonder if you'd do me a personal favour and send someone out here as quickly as possible? He's — er — very anxious to be on his way."

"Well?" Machin eyed Nicola as she put the phone down.

"He's sending a car right away," Nicola told him. She added: "He said he'd hate to lose a customer."

"Good." Nicola's unwelcome guest stretched his legs, smiling with satisfaction. "How long do you reckon he'll be?"

"Oh, only about ten minutes. You'll hear the car when it arrives."

As it happened it was only seven minutes before they heard a car.

"Quick work." The red-haired man stood up and opened the door. "Here, what . . ."

"All right, Machin. Don't let's have any trouble." The three policemen closed in smoothly. There was a flash of metal and handcuffs clicked. A fourth blue-uniformed figure, wearing a sergeant's stripes, strode quickly through the door.

"You all right, Nicola?"

"I think so." Nicola sat down. "My legs are a bit wobbly."

From the doorway, Machin said resignedly: "O.K. I'll come quietly. But I'd still like to know how, when you rang the garage . . ."

Nicola said sweetly: "But I didn't ring the garage. I rang the police station." Then as the robber still stared at her in bewilderment: "Oh, the garage isn't owned by Mr. West. But this is Sergeant West."

"I must be going daft," Machin said. "I heard what you said. You asked for petrol."

"I asked for someone to come out here as quickly as possible," Nicola reminded him. "And, you see, Sergeant West happens to be my father."

There was a moment's silence. Then Sergeant West said briskly:

"All right, lads. Take him away."

When Mr. and Mrs. Gates got back, Nicola had a pot of tea waiting.
"Oh that is kind of you, Nicola dear." Mrs. Gates took off her coat.
Nicola said truthfully: "Johnny didn't wake up once."
"Oh, I'm so glad." The farmer's wife poured herself a cup of tea
gratefully. "I know you young people think I fuss, but one never
knows what might happen if —"
Farmer Gates winked at Nicola. "If an escaped criminal came
knocking at the door?" he suggested.
Nicola smiled back. "If one did," she said, "I expect I'd cope."

THE HAUNTED VALLEY

by Sue Downham

Exmoor — dark and mysterious — land of legend, reputed haunt of many ghosts. This is the setting of this strange story of two girls and the eerie adventures that befall them on the wild moor.

"Notice how cold it is," says Janet. "It's a kind of iciness, that sends shivers up my spine."

"Are you sure this is the right road, Sue?"

Janet Wilson glanced anxiously at her friend as they free-wheeled down a narrow Exmoor lane.

Susan Perry shook back her long fair hair. "That old boy back there said to take the right fork past the fallen oak, didn't he?"

"I know, but he also said climb the hill — and we're going down-hill!"

She laughed carelessly. "Why worry? We've gone wrong again. So what? This lane must lead to the other side of the moor eventually and we've got all the time in the world. By the way, Janet, what is the time? My watch stopped at half-past two, but it must be later than that now."

Janet took her left hand from the handlebar and peered at her wristwatch. The dust had filmed her horn-rims and it wasn't easy to see the tiny numbers.

"Queer," she said. "Mine seems to have stopped, too —"

"Hey, look out, you idiot!" Sue yelled frantically. "Keep your eyes on the road! You'll —"

The warning came too late. Janet wobbled and then collided with Sue. Locked together, the two cycles leapt the low grass verge and crashed into the far bank of the overgrown ditch. The girls somersaulted over the handlebars into the hedge.

Janet was vaguely aware of hurtling through the hedge, of thorny twigs scratching her face, tugging at her dark hair. Then she was falling . . . falling. . . .

The awful sensation seemed to go on for an age. Then she landed with a bump that jarred every fibre of her body, and something seemed to explode in her head like a bomb. She knew nothing more.

Janet blinked open her eyes and stared numbly up at a ribbon of cloud-flecked blue sky above her. Then gradually her mind cleared and memory came flooding back.

She pushed herself up on one elbow. Her glasses were unbroken, lying in a patch of dust, and automatically she picked them up, rubbed them clean, and put them on. Everything kept in focus then, and she saw she was lying in what looked like a ravine, about twenty feet wide and twice as deep. Its steep sides were overgrown with stunted scrub, but here and there she could see bare reddish rock showing through.

"Wow!" she gasped. "Did I fall all that way? No wonder my head hurts."

"Lucky we didn't break our necks!"

She looked round to see Sue struggling into a sitting position, rubbing her temple, on which a nasty bruise was darkening.

"You okay, Sue?" she asked anxiously.

"Guess so. Can't find anything broken, except my watch. It's smashed to pieces." She flashed a wry grin. "Serve me right for bawling you out like that, I suppose. If I hadn't shouted and made you panic, maybe we wouldn't have finished up here." She got stiffly to her feet. "Better try and climb out, I suppose."

But nowhere could they find a place which was climbable. They tried shouting to attract attention, but then gave up.

"Might call all day and not be heard," Sue said. "Not many people live in this part of the moor, and still less come this way in the late autumn."

Janet looked at her friend with a sense of helplessness. Sue was usually the practical one, the one with ideas, who rarely let any situation get her down, but now, Janet thought, she sounded a little despondent. Maybe that crack on the temple was making her feel a bit groggy.

"But we can't just stand here!" Janet protested. "If we can't climb out perhaps we can walk out?"

Sue glanced at her. "That makes sense. The ravine's too choked for us to go up it, so we'll have to go down. Let's get cracking. We may have a long trek and it'll begin to get dark in three hours or so."

"Three hours?" Janet regarded her friend anxiously as they set off. "Hope it doesn't take us that long to get out of here, Sue!"

"Not to worry, Janet. Odds are this ravine will run into a coomb before long and we'll find a snug old farmhouse where we can have tea while a kindly farmer fetches our bikes on his tractor."

"I'm keeping my fingers crossed," Janet said.

She tried to smile as she said it, but smiling didn't come easily. She was conscious of a strange feeling, almost of unreality, as if somehow they were having a dream.

"Sue!" she said suddenly. "Notice how cold it is?"

"Figures," Sue said carelessly. "Don't suppose much sun gets down here, and it is the end of October."

"I know, but — well, it's not that sort of cold — it's more a kind of — of iciness, if you get what I mean? It sends shivers up my spine!"

Sue stopped dead and stared at her. "You mean spooky?" she challenged.

"Well, yes! I've felt it in old abbeys and ruins and places like that. I know you think I'm daft."

"No, Janet. I don't think that. I've always felt you were a bit too sensitive about things like that, but — well, I don't mind admitting, I feel a bit that way myself right now."

"You do?" Janet forced a grin. "Well, that's a relief. Let's hurry. The sooner we're out of here the better both of us are going to like it, I think."

They hurried on. The going wasn't easy, for there was no definite track in the bottom of the ravine, and in many places the scrub was so thick that it almost blocked the way.

Presently, to their relief, the ravine began to widen and the light grew better, but the strange chill remained.

Janet, finding an easier way through at one place, had gone ahead of Sue. Suddenly she stopped, staring ahead at a spot where the scrub, growing thickly against the base of the ravine wall, was speckled with yellow gorse bloom.

"What's wrong?" Janet asked, stopping behind her.

"I — I thought I saw something among those bushes — something that moved."

"A rabbit — or a hare." But Janet thought her friend didn't sound too confident.

They stood there, reluctant to go on. Then Sue laughed and pushed past Janet.

"We're letting this get us down," she said. "If there was anything, it's a sign of life, isn't it — and goodness knows we want to see some. Come on!"

Feeling a little sheepish, Janet went after her, but she was conscious of a niggling little feeling that something was — well, not exactly right. Then suddenly she stopped again.

"Sue!" she called softly. "I — I'm sure we're being watched!"

Sue stopped and looked back at her with a smile.

"Gosh, you've really got 'em, haven't you? Maybe it's the little people — the pixies?"

"Don't, Sue! I'm serious. I'm positive there's someone in those bushes," and she called, "Come on out, whoever you are!"

For a long time nothing happened. Then there was a faint crackling of undergrowth and from the bushes, a dozen paces from them, appeared a dark-haired girl about their own age.

Janet's first reaction was one of relief, and she uttered a shaky little laugh. Then it froze on her lips, for there was something weird about the girl.

The girl was dressed in old-fashioned clothes. With her ankle-length, wide-bottomed dress, she reminded Janet of illustrations of Little Nell in the "Old Curiosity Shop".

"Hi!" Sue greeted her cheerfully. "Why were you snooping on us?"

"Snooping? I don't understand." The girl's voice was gentle, and held a hint of nervousness.

"Spying — watching us!" Sue added. "Why?"

They had reached her by then. She was pretty with hair in ringlets down to her shoulders where it escaped from her shawl, but strangely pale with an almost translucent skin.

"I'm sorry if I offend you," she said. "But I was afraid. You — you look so strange. You are girls — yet you wear men's clothes."

Janet and Sue exchanged puzzled glances. Hadn't this girl ever seen girls in jeans before?

"Where are you from?" the girl went on curiously.

"Janet comes from London," Sue said. "She's staying with me for half-term, over at Dulverton. I'm Susan."

"London? I have heard of it. It is a long way away. I am Sophia. I live in the coomb. We have a farm. If you would care to be our guests?"

"Thanks," Sue said. "To be honest we could do with a strong cuppa. You see we had a spill on our bikes back there and fell into the ravine and —"

She broke off, for the girl was staring at her in amazement.

"Cuppa? Bikes?" she said curiously. "How strangely you talk! What are these things?"

Again Sue flung a puzzled look at Janet, then said patiently, "Cuppa — cup of tea! Bikes — bicycles."

"Ah, yes. Tea! That I know. We have a little. My brother brings it when he comes home. It is very dear to buy. But these bicycles?" For the first time a faint smile appeared on the girl's pale pretty face. "I still do not understand. But come! I will make you some tea."

"I can't wait!" Sue said cheerfully. But as the girl turned to lead the way down the ravine, she hung back and whispered to Janet. "This is crazy. Either she's having us on or — or —"

"She doesn't really exist — she's a ghost!" Janet said quietly.

"Eh?" Sue's blue eyes widened. "You must be joking!"

"I wish I were. But she's so obviously out of the past. And that icy feeling I spoke about. It's still with me, Sue."

"Come!"

Janet realized the girl had stopped some yards down the ravine and was smiling and beckoning to them.

Sue had gone a little pale, but she set her jaw determinedly. "I can't believe it — I won't! There's one way to test it, anyway."

Sue hurried towards the waiting girl. A step or so from her, Sue seemed to stumble and fell forward against her, catching hold of her as if to keep balance.

"I'm sorry!" she gasped. "Slipped! Always was clumsy."

"It is nothing," the girl smiled. "Lucky I was here to catch you or you might have hurt yourself."

She went on, and Sue followed more slowly, allowing Janet to catch up with her.

"She — she's as solid as you or me," she whispered. "So much for your ghost theory. There's only one thing for it."

"What's that?"

"She's having us on. She must be from a film unit on location."

The farmhouse stood in the bottom of the deep coomb, beyond a stream that burbled off into the gloom of the distance.

"So much for your film unit," Janet said with a wry smile.

"Silly idea, anyway," Sue muttered. "Queer! Dusk is creeping up, and yet when we took that tumble into the ravine —"

"You reckoned it would be three hours to dark."

"This gets crazier every minute."

They followed the girl who called herself Sophia across a wooden footbridge into the farmyard.

A woman had come out on to the porch and was staring at them in astonishment. She was pleasant looking, with ruddy cheeks, and greying hair escaping from under a frilled white cap.

"Strangers, mother," the girl said. "They've lost their way. One comes all the way from London."

"Aye? If that be the latest fashion them wearing, I don't think much to 'un."

"They were trying to get back to Dulverton —"

"'Tis late for that. Moor's a bad place after dark. You'd best stay the night, young ladies."

"But —"

Janet's protest died as the woman turned away into the house.

Sue whispered. "Whatever's happening to us, there's nothing we can do, and she's right about the moor. Besides I'm starving!"

They followed Sophia into the house. In the big kitchen, hams hung from the ceiling beams. A log fire blazed cheerfully in an open stone hearth, where a black cat sat on a hob, washing itself unconcernedly. An oil lantern was already lit, and a big scrubbed wooden table was laid for three.

"Your father's late back from the market, Sophia," the woman said. "We'll wait a while to eat. Maybe the young ladies would like to wash first. Take them up to Jeremy's room."

The girl lit a candle and beckoned to them to follow up a twisting creaking staircase. On a cold gloomy landing she opened a door and led them into a room with bare plaster walls and oak beams. A rush mat scantily covered the bare boards beside a big four-poster bed. A frail washstand with pitcher and basin, a heavy wardrobe, and a massive brass-bound sea chest completed the furniture.

"That's Jeremy's," the girl said, indicating the chest. "He's at sea. We're not expecting him for a while, but we keep the sheets aired in readiness." She lit a lantern from the candle, then picked up the pitcher. "I will bring the hot water."

As the door closed on her, Sue said, "Kick me on the shin — hard, Jan! This must be a dream — and I'd like to wake up."

Janet laughed uncertainly. "Could we both have the same dream — together, I mean?"

"Guess not. But if we're not dreaming and these people and the animals aren't ghosts, then —?"

She broke off helplessly and went to the window, which looked down the coomb.

"It's almost dark now," she said. "Maybe I was wrong about not taking our chance on the moor. Maybe we ought to get out of here while —"

She stopped and leaned across the deep stone sill, peering out into the gloom.

"What's the matter?" Janet asked, going to her side.

"I can hear hoofbeats."

"Sophia's father coming home from market, perhaps."

"At a gallop? It's not a horse and cart, anyway. Look, Jan! Here it comes!"

A rider galloped into the yard. As he reined in the horse, Sophia dashed from the house, just in time to steady him as he half fell from the saddle.

"Jeremy!" The girl's voice, shrill with fear, reached them clearly. "You — you're hurt — bleeding!"

"Sophia! Thank heaven —"

The rider's voice trailed off and the girls heard no more. They saw Sophia help him into the house and the door closed.

"Must be her brother — the one she said was at sea," Sue said. "He's all in — wounded! What's going on?"

The girl dashed from the house again, seized the horse's bridle and led it into the barn. Then she came out, barred the doors and ran back into the house.

"I'm going to see what this is all about," Sue said. "Come on, Jan!"

They'd almost reached the head of the stairs when they saw Sophia coming up, holding a lighted candle in one hand, helping a young man in sea-faring clothes with the other. His right sleeve had been cut away to reveal a blood-stained bandage about his upper arm. His rugged face was unmistakably like the girl's, but pale in spite of its tan and drawn with pain.

Sophia looked up with a start as she realized the girls were on the landing.

"I — hoped you would not see. My brother is hurt. I was going to put him in my room."

"Might as well put him in his own," Sue said. "We'll give you a hand."

Between them they got him into the bedroom. He was weak from loss of blood, dazed, scarcely knowing what was happening to him.

"Thank you," the girl whispered. "Now, if you will leave us I will attend to him. My mother —"

She broke off, her glance going fearfully to the window. Clearly on the evening air came the sound of galloping horses.

"They — they have come already!" she gasped. "The Revenue men — they are after Jeremy." She looked at Sue and Janet with desperate appeal in her dark eyes. "They think he is one of a gang of smugglers, but Jeremy just happened to be in the inn when it was raided. He is innocent, and when he ran away they shot him. He thought he would be safe here. We must save him!"

"We?" Sue asked.

Sophia clutched at her arm. "You must help me! Oh, please! He's innocent, but if they find him they will — will hang him!"

The riders clattered into the dark yard and the girl's fingers dug into Sue's arm. "They will search. If they come up here —"

Sue shot a glance at Janet, who said impulsively "Okay, we'll help, but how?"

"There is no safe place to hide in the house, but that ravine where I saw you — on the left there is a cave where he can hide. Get him there while mother and I try to delay them. There is a hidden stairway to the back yard. Quick, help him to his feet!"

Raising her brother's head and shoulders, she forced brandy between his lips from a small bottle she took from her apron. Colour seeped back into his face and his eyes flickered open.

There was a thundering on the front door and a voice shouted, "Open in the King's name!"

The shout did more to revive Jeremy than the brandy and he forced himself off the bed.

"I — I must get away, Sophia!" he said, wincing with pain. "If they find me here they will arrest you and mother for harbouring me."

"Take it easy," Sue said, helping him to stand up. "We'll get you away."

He stared at her. "Who — who are you?"

"Don't talk, save your strength," Sue said. "Show us the way, Sophia. Bring that brandy, Janet. We may need it."

The Revenue men were still hammering on the door. Sophia took up the lantern and dashed from the room. They heard her shouting downstairs to her mother. As they reached the landing with her brother, she returned to them.

"My mother will keep them talking as long as she can." She smiled faintly. "She can argue a donkey's hind leg off, my father says. Come!"

At the rear of the landing she unlocked a tall cupboard. Inside shelves held clean linen. She swung them out to reveal a cavity in the stone wall, and narrow steps leading down. She handed the lantern to Janet.

"Wait in the cave till I can come," she whispered.

She kissed her brother lightly on the cheek and then pushed him gently after Janet. Sue brought up the rear, her hand gripping his unwounded arm to support him. Sophia closed the shelves on them.

At the bottom of the musty smelling stairway was an iron–bound door, fastened by a bar. Janet raised this and the heavy door swung inwards with a faint creaking. She extinguished the lantern.

Outside it was full dark and stars were appearing between scudding clouds coming off the sea. Like shadows they hurried across the yard and through a gap in the stone wall.

"Make for the stream," Sue whispered. "We'll follow it up the coomb till we're opposite the ravine, then wade across."

They reached the ravine safely. Apart from an occasional half-suppressed groan, Jeremy made no sound. He seemed to be grimly fighting against his pain and weakness.

As they entered the ravine, Janet glanced back. Lights were dancing in the darkness by the farmhouse, as if the men were searching the outbuildings.

Well into the coomb, Janet relit the lantern, and took the lead along the little-trodden path down which they had come a short while earlier with Sophia.

"This is roughly where we first saw her," Janet said presently. "She said the cave was on the left —"

"Shssh!" Sue cut her short. "Listen!"

They froze, supporting Jeremy, straining their ears in the stillness. Far down the ravine they heard the crash of undergrowth and the faint sound of voices.

"They're searching the ravine," Sue said. "Quick, Jan — find that cave!"

Moments later, the lantern light revealed the low entrance to the cave, almost hidden by the scrub. They had to crawl in on hands and knees, dragging Jeremy as best they could. They made him comfortable on a bed of sand, and Janet pressed the bottle of brandy into his hand.

"Sip this when you feel you need it," she said. "And try not to make a sound."

Then they crawled back outside again. "What now?" whispered Janet. "They're sure to find that cave if they search thoroughly."

"They mustn't. We've got to decoy them. We'll go on up the ravine, making enough noise to attract them."

"But there's no way out —"

"We'll find a way, Jan — we must make them think Jeremy got away."

A light appeared down the ravine, and they heard the murmur of voices. Deliberately they waited a few moments, then Sue urged Janet on up the ravine, telling her to crash her way through.

In the stillness of the night the noise they made sounded deafening. There was an eager shout behind them, and Janet, glancing back, saw two lanterns dancing. When she looked again she was relieved to see that the pursuers were already past the cave.

The undergrowth was getting thicker and slowing their flight. The sounds of pursuit were getting closer. Presently the scrub became impassable.

"Must be where we fell," Sue panted. "We've just got to try to climb back, Janet. Come on!"

Perhaps it was luck, or perhaps it was the reward of desperation, but somehow they found a track and scrambled up it, while the lights danced nearer.

About thirty feet up they reached a narrow ledge and paused to get their breath. Their pursuers were below them and the light of their lanterns gleamed on pistols and uniform buttons.

Sue glanced up. "Wall overhangs here," she whispered. "We won't get any higher. Just have to lie low and hope for the —"

She broke off. There was an ominous crack from the ledge on which they were lying. Janet's heart seemed to leap into her throat as she felt the solid rock give under her.

Then, with a noise like a gun shot, the whole section broke away. Janet screamed as she felt herself hurtling down.

She was dimly aware of Sue falling with her, of the pale blobs of the Revenue men's faces as they looked up in amazement. Then something struck Janet on the head and a million stars seemed to explode inside her brain. She knew no more.

Janet blinked open her eyes, then closed them again quickly, for the bright afternoon sun dazzled her and her head ached.

Slowly she opened them again and found she was lying in the ditch at the side of the lane beside her bicycle. She glanced at her watch. It was going again and registered a quarter to three.

A few feet away Sue was struggling to sit up, looking dazedly about her. Suddenly an incredulous look came over Sue's face and she scrambled to her feet and thrust her head and shoulders through a gap in the hedge. For a long moment there was silence. Then Sue pulled clear of the hedge and stared at Janet in wonder.

"There's — there's no ravine through there, Jan — nothing but a ploughed field. I must have been knocked out and had a dream."

"A dream like mine?" Janet asked, her skin prickling.

She told her friend of her incredible experience.

"That makes two of us!" Sue gulped. "Either we're nutcases or —" She grabbed up her cycle. "Let's get out of here!"

When they reached Sue's home, they told her father all that had happened — or they thought had happened.

"H'm!" He sucked thoughtfully on his pipe. "You could hardly

Their pursuers were below them and the light of their lantern gleamed on pistols and uniform buttons.

have had identical dreams in which the other appeared, so — well, this might sound crazy, but some scientists think there may be such — er — phenomenan as time-warps. Now if, when you crashed, you fell through one —"

"Back into the beginning of the last century?" Janet suggested eagerly.

Sue's father smiled. "It's only a theory, but — well, it does fit the facts, doesn't it?" He coughed. "But I don't think you'd better tell Sue's mother. She'd want to pack you both off to the doctor's for a checkup. Better let — er — sleeping dogs lie, eh?"

CALLING NURSE JONES

by Doreen Gray

Nurse Jenny Jones goes to a pop concert but finds herself back on duty again when a young scene-shifter fractures his leg.

Her personal interest in the young man is aroused when she learns that he is the outcast son of the most famous actress of the decade.

Jenny sets herself the task of trying to reconcile mother and son – a difficult task indeed!

"It is a super show, Pam!"

The sparkle in Jenny Jones' eyes was a sure sign that she was enjoying herself.

"Yes, rather!" Pam Elliot, seated beside her in the stalls at the Longmere Theatre, was just as enthusiastic.

The theatre was packed, on this evening only three weeks before Christmas. For there was a very special top-of-the-bill attraction. The Weirdies had come to Longmere. They were the latest pop group sensation, who had suddenly hit the charts. They were the next act.

The dimming lights suddenly flashed on again. Through the drop curtain appeared the theatre manager, fingering his black bow tie.

"Ladies and gentlemen, I regret there has been an unfortunate accident," he announced. "If there is a doctor here—?"

Nobody came forward.

Jenny looked at Pam.

"We are nurses —" Jenny began.

"Ah, splendid! Would you please step on to the stage? Your help will be much appreciated."

Jenny and Pam were already hurrying up the steps at the side of the stage. They had responded to the manager's appeal. They were used to emergencies.

"We're nurses from St. Luke's Hospital," Jenny said, as the stage manager hurried towards them. "What's happened?"

"One of our scene-shifters was hit by a falling flat," he replied. "He seems to be seriously hurt. This way, please."

Jenny and Pam found themselves behind stage. The Weirdies — young, looking very startling in their blue and white striped suits — were lined up behind the curtain, ready for their appearance on stage. Behind them two men were carefully lifting up a large piece of scenery — and on the floor lay the inert, overalled figure of a young man.

A brief, expert examination and Jenny and Pam were in complete agreement.

"Please phone St. Luke's for an ambulance," Jenny said to the manager. "His right leg is fractured. We won't move him, or put on a splint. That will be done as soon as he gets to the hospital."

They made the injured youth more comfortable, and then waited for the ambulance to arrive.

The curtain had gone up. The Weirdies were beating out their first number to the accompaniment of screams and shouts from their fans. Delirious excitement out there in the auditorium; pain and suffering here behind stage . . .

Then, through the din, Jenny faintly heard the clanging of a bell.

"I'll go with him," she told Pam.

Minutes later, with blue light flashing and bell clanging, the ambulance was speeding back to the hospital. Inside, Jenny watched her patient. She saw him open his eyes, stare at her, and she smiled reassuringly.

"We'll soon have you at St. Luke's, and then everything's going to be all right," she told him.

"First time I've ever been in an ambulance. All in favour of free travel . . ."

He grinned — then winced as the ambulance went over a rut in the road, jolting his leg.

Jenny continued to talk to him in an effort to take his mind off his accident. He seemed to have a sense of humour. She noticed how the expressions on his good-looking face constantly changed — almost as if it were made of rubber.

"Nearly there now," she said. "Would you like to give me one or two details about yourself? What's your name — and your address? We shall want to know your next of kin for our records. They'll have to be informed."

She thought she saw a trace of bitterness cross his face.

"No need for that," he said. "No one's likely to be interested. I live alone — in digs at three, Chesil Road. My name is Malcolm Venders."

Venders! Even as he said the name it had a familiar ring to Jenny.

Jenny's friend, Dr. Mike Lawson, was on duty in Casualty that night. He stared in surprise to see her walking alongside the trolley being wheeled into an examination cubicle.

"Thought you were having a screaming session at the theatre," he grinned, "so what's the trouble here? Anything serious?"

Jenny told him all she knew.

"Fractured leg? An in-patient then. Right, you've done all you can, Jenny. Better be on your way and get some shut-eye," Mike said. "Looks as if you're going to have an extra patient in Orthopaedic for a while."

The following morning, Jenny was kept busy in the ward and did not have time to speak to the new patient. Her chance came when she started serving the midday meal.

"How are you feeling now?" she asked.

"Oh, hello, nurse!" Malcolm Venders twisted his face into a wry grimace. "Nice to see you again, but apart from that — awful! It's this splint, giving me gyp!"

"I expect it'll be changed for a temporary plaster this afternoon," she told him. "Now, let me make you more comfortable, and then you can try a St. Luke's speciality — tomato soup, followed by steak and kidney pie!"

He made another of his faces.

"You ought to be on the stage," Jenny laughed, and then broke off. "The stage! That's why I thought your name had a familiar ring. I was thinking of Beatrice Venders, the famous actress. No relative of yours, I suppose?"

"As a matter of fact — yes. Beatrice Venders is my mother, though she no longer regards me as her son. I'm out — sort of disowned, you know!"

Curious as she was, Jenny had her other patients to consider. They were waiting for their dinner, and she had to move on with her trolley.

Beatrice Venders! Perhaps the most famous name on the English stage — certainly the most famous dramatic actress of the decade, and her son was a scene-shifter at a small country theatre, living on his own in digs in Longmere. In his own words, she had "disowned" him. What had happened to cause such a situation?

Jenny was to know the answers later that afternoon. That was after he had been taken away to the plaster-room, for his broken leg to be encased in an above-the-knee plaster. Jenny had just re-made his bed when the hospital orderlies wheeled him into the ward.

"Oh, Mr. Venders, there have been two telephone calls asking about you," Jenny said. "The theatre manager wanted to know how you were — and so did Bert Williams, the leader of The Weirdies. Is he a friend of yours?"

"No. Just got talking to him as I was setting the scene for their act," Malcolm said. "Nice chap." He was silent for a few moments, and then in a lowered voice he said: "Nurse, I don't want my mother to be informed that I've had an accident. She's in America at the moment — and the critics are raving about her. Yes, she's a wonderful actress — and I'm one of her greatest admirers, but as I've already told you, she's no longer interested in what happens to me."

"But — but why?" asked Jenny in bewilderment. "Acting seems to be in you. I would have thought —"

"That I'd be on the stage, too? Because you've seen me clowning?"

"I didn't say clowning," Jenny said. "But you certainly make me laugh."

"I used the word clowning and I meant it. I want to be a clown — or a comic. That's what has upset my mother," Malcolm told her. "Here she is — a great dramatic actress. She expects her son to follow in that tradition, and gets him chances to do so but her son isn't interested. You see, I don't want heavy parts, or to try to make people cry. I want to tumble about — make my audience laugh. Well, that's my story, Nurse," he went on, "and now I'm going to rest. Perhaps I should warn you that with this lump of concrete round my leg I shall have to sleep on my back, and that makes me snore!"

At last, Jenny's spell of duty finished for the day. Outside the hospital she met Pam.

"Sister MacIntyre's been on the warpath," murmured Pam.

"What have you been doing now?" asked Jenny.

"It's what I haven't been doing. You're in trouble, too. We're both on the committee that's organising the Christmas concert —"

"My goodness — yes, we must get cracking," gasped Jenny. "I say, I wonder if Malcolm Venders could give a turn? The concert isn't for a fortnight . . ."

She didn't mention it to him until the Sunday afternoon. It was visiting time at St. Luke's. All the patients in Orthopaedic had friends or relatives to see them — except Malcolm Venders.

His gloomy expression faded when Jenny approached his bed; he positively beamed when she told him about the forthcoming concert. Then he looked glum again.

"Sure I can give a turn. But what's a crock like me able to do?"

"You can tell some stories. By next week you'll be walking around on crutches, and there are such things as wheelchairs," Jenny smilingly told him. "Will you do it?"

"It's a booking! I'll prepare some material. Come to think of it, I can sing a little —"

"And I can play the piano a little," laughed Jenny. "You'll have to be a bed patient for a few days yet, but we'll have a rehearsal as soon as you're more mobile."

The days slipped by. Jenny was a nurse by day and a concert organiser when she was off duty. Then came the morning when Sister said it was time for Malcolm Venders to leave his bed and see how he could manage with crutches.

"We'll have a rehearsal this afternoon," Jenny told him. "I'll collect you in a wheelchair."

The rehearsal was a tremendous success. Jenny had wheeled her patient along to the big recreation room where the concert was to be held. One or two nurses were there, and they gathered round as Malcolm, seated in a wheelchair, his plaster-cased leg stretched out in front of him, rattled off a fund of stories and anecdotes.

Watching him, listening to him, Jenny thought that Malcolm Venders had potential as a comic. Once his leg was better, once he became more active, his act would be even more of a winner. The rehearsal came to an end.

"Marvellous," she told him, laughing. "I can see we might have a

*Almost half-an-hour passed – and then Beatrice Venders made her regal
entrance.*

crop of patients with split ribs!"

"Glad you liked it, nurse," said Malcolm Venders; and then, as she began to wheel him out of the room, he produced a letter from the pocket of his dressing gown. "Nurse," he went on, "would you mind posting this for me when you go off duty?"

It was a letter, addressed to Beatrice Venders.

"You've written to your mother —" she burst out.

"Yes, she's back in England now," he said quietly.

"Oh, I'm so glad. Does this mean that everything's all right between you?"

"It means nothing of the sort," he replied with a shrug. "I've written — now it's up to her."

Malcolm Venders did not get a reply. Beatrice Venders did not come to visit her son at St. Luke's.

"I'm furious about it," Jenny told Pam. "It seems so heartless — such a dreadful shame!"

"Now don't get so het up, Jenny," Pam remonstrated. "I know how you feel. But there's nothing you can do about it —"

"Isn't there?" Jenny almost glared at her friend. "I saw the address on the letter when I posted it, and I'm going to pay Mrs. Beatrice Venders a visit!"

So Jenny, on her first free day, took the bus to Westlea, about twenty miles away. Beatrice Venders lived in an imposing house on the outskirts of the village. A maid answered the door and showed Jenny into the drawing-room. Almost half-an-hour passed — and then Beatrice Venders made her regal entrance. She paused just beyond the doorway, as if surveying her audience and preparing to cast a spell upon them. She certainly put a spell on Jenny.

"How do you do, Nurse Jones?" began the actress — how beautiful was that voice! "And why do you wish to see me?"

"Well — er — I — I came to see you about your son —" Jenny stammered.

"Indeed? Malcolm? And in what way does Malcolm concern you?"

"He — he's in my ward at St. Luke's. One of my patients, you know. He's had an accident —"

"So Malcolm has informed me," Beatrice Venders said. "He tells me he is making a good recovery."

"But you haven't been to see him!" burst out Jenny. "Oh, perhaps it's no business of mine, but —"

"Indeed it is no business of yours!"

"Well," Jenny went on desperately, "I wanted to tell you that your son is giving a turn at the hospital Christmas concert, and I thought you would like to come along and see it —"

"Giving one of his absurd comic turns, no doubt. I am not interested, Nurse Jones."

"This is Christmas time. A time of goodwill. Of— of forgiveness," Jenny pleaded. "Your son would be so pleased to see you."

"I have no wish to see my son Malcolm. There is nothing more to be said." Beatrice Vender's voice was inflexible. "Good-day, Nurse Jones."

The Christmas concert at St. Luke's was going with a swing. The gaily decorated recreation room was packed. The Nurses' Choir had sung carols. Two house doctors had given a humorous sketch. "And now — Malcolm Venders to entertain you," announced compère Sister MacIntyre.

Malcolm wheeled himself on to the stage — a solitary figure against a white backcloth. Even as he appeared the expression on his face brought chuckles from the audience. A few minutes later those chuckles had become roars of laughter.

"He's good," said a voice behind Jenny.

She spun round, to see a youth in a startling blue and white striped suit behind her.

"You — you're one of The Weirdies!"

"That's right, I'm Bert Williams," he nodded. "Guess I've sort of gatecrashed. The nurse on the door swooned as soon as she saw me, so I just walked in. Had an hour to spare, and came along to see how my scene-shifter buddy was getting on."

The laughter was getting more and more uproarious. Malcolm had written some new material, and the theme — broken legs and operating theatres!

"Him a scene-shifter?" said Bert Williams. "He's got talent. I'll have a word with our manager about him. Calls himself Malcolm Venders, does he —"

"And who, may I ask, are you?"

Again Jenny swung round. That voice! Standing there, wrapped in a magnificent mink, was Beatrice Venders. Jenny stood tongue-tied — but was conscious of a great elation.

"Bert Williams is the name —"

"Of The Weirdies!" Jenny managed to get out.

"And who are they?" asked the actress.

"Golly!" Jenny gulped. "And this, Mr. Williams, is Beatrice Venders —"

"Who's she?" retorted Bert, and then grinned. "Forget it. Of course I know who you are. Been to see you when I had more time. Great acting — great!"

"And perhaps I have heard of you, Mr. Williams," graciously admitted Beatrice Venders.

Malcolm's act — and the laughter — was still going on. Jenny managed to find her voice again.

"Mrs. Venders, I'm so glad you came —" she began.

"So am I. I did a lot of thinking after you had left," the actress smiled. "I apologise for being rude to you — goodness, I can hardly hear myself speak. Malcolm seems to be going over well. I was wrong — I can see that now. There are many ways of bringing happiness to people — and I realise now that laughter is one of them. If my son wishes to be a comedian — then he shall have my blessing!"

Jenny was radiant.

"Oh, I must go and tell him," she said, starting to rush away. "He's just wheeling himself off the stage. He'll be so excited!"

No more excited than Jenny herself, because after all she had played a part in bringing about this happy reunion! She was even more excited when a year later Malcolm slipped a diamond ring on a certain finger of her left hand — and winked merrily!

PENNY PROVES HER WORTH

by Catherine Bell

Life in Australia was vastly different from life back in England. For instance
— sharks! Penny's heart leapt frantically when she heard the word. Then —
snakes! Her face paled when she saw the death snake coiled on the baby's cot.
One false move and the fearsome reptile would strike. But what could a girl,
fresh out from England, do?

So this was Port Bowering!

Penelope Ware, small, fair, and just sixteen, stood on the deck of the
coastal steamer that had brought them up from Brisbane, past the
great coral reefs to North Queensland. It was the first time she had
ever been out of England and she was thrilled.

It had all happened so suddenly that she could still hardly believe she
was ten thousand miles from her home and in a strange land. Her uncle
had come to England on account of his health, but she had never
dreamed he would sweep her back to Australia with him and her aunt.
She was to stay for six months, everything paid, for her uncle — James
Ware — was a prosperous store owner.

Now, before her eyes, lay Port Bowering, where she was to live.
What would it be like? It seemed charming — a white horseshoe of
sand backed by low dunes with romantic-looking palm trees scattered

against the sky-line, and a little jetty stretching out to meet them.

Would the Australians like her though? She had heard that some of them were inclined to laugh at the accent and manners of the English, whom they called "Pommies".

As the boat tied up, her aunt was eagerly pointing out her family and waving to them. Amongst those waiting on the quay were Johnnie, aunt's eighteen-year-old son; Maud, the eldest daughter, and the latter's fiance, Dick Roberts, who was a doctor.

Penny waved also, and when the gangway was lowered she went running eagerly down it. Her relatives hurried along the jetty to greet her. For a few minutes everyone stood there talking, then Uncle James led the way towards the quay.

"Come on, time we made for home," he said.

They all began to walk down the wooden jetty, the Australians bombarding Penny with questions. In her anxiety to answer them she did not look where she was going, and as a result stumbled over one of the rough-hewn planks. Swiftly Dick Roberts caught her by the arm.

"Steady," he warned. "The water is teeming with sharks."

His tone was casual, but Penny's heart seemed to miss a beat and she stood stock still, gasping. No railing — gaps between the planks — and sharks!

"The jetty is not finished, you see," explained her aunt, turning to her cheerfully. "But it's quite safe."

All the stories that Penny had ever heard about sharks crowded into her brain. Her feet simply would not move.

"Why, she's gone as pale as paper!" laughed her uncle, his voice seeming to come from a distance. "Really, Dick, you shouldn't have frightened her like that!"

She heard them all laughing and so resolutely she conquered her nervousness.

"It's the heat," she managed to say, but she kept hold of Dick's strong arm for the rest of the way.

As they drove through the little town, Maud at the wheel, Penny's aunt explained that there had been a drought for two years and that was why the streets were so dusty and the fields so burnt up.

"Why are the houses built up high on those poles?" asked Penny, puzzled, for she had thought they only did this in swampy countries.

"Partly for coolness," replied Mrs. Ware, "and partly to discourage snakes."

"Snakes?" repeated Penny, her heart jumping for the second time. "Do — do you get many in the house?"

"You would if you were on ground level," said Johnnie, grinning widely.

"Oh, snakes are nothing!" added Dick.

They were both smiling at her, as if amused by the uneasy look on her face. She felt herself colouring with embarrassment and hurriedly changed the subject; but she could not forget what had been said about snakes. They had always been her horror. Even now she shuddered at the memory of a worm being pushed down her back by a malicious schoolboy years ago. Snakes were like worms, only much bigger; cold, slimy, silent and dangerous . . . she would never, never survive if she had to face a snake! Oh, why had she ever left England?

However, Penny felt better when they turned into a shady drive and passed through a garden of flowering shrubs, and stopped at the side of a large house built also on piles, with a verandah running all the way round it. Penny had gathered that she would not meet Alice, the younger married daughter, for she was soon to have a baby, and her station home was some miles inland.

Penny found the house delightful. It consisted of a large central lounge, divided by an arch into two rooms, one a sitting-room, one a dining-room. Off this centre room ran the bedrooms and they all opened out on to the verandah so that a through draught could be obtained. Penny saw a piano in the drawing-room and exclaimed delightedly.

"Do you play, Penny?" asked Maud.

"Only a little — but I know you play beautifully."

"I wouldn't say that!" replied Maud, pleased, but trying to be very casual.

She took off her hat and walked away, but after supper that evening she played to them and Penny was very impressed. It was odd to see this big, athletic young woman play a piano with such skill and tenderness. They asked Penny to play afterwards, but she refused to compete.

Johnnie got out a book on wild animals, and with great relish pointed out all the most horrible things that Penny might see in Australia, especially dwelling on the snakes. One picture fascinated Penny. It was of a death adder — a snake occasionally seen in these parts. It had a horrible thick body and a spiny flat tail; a wicked flat little head and narrow glinting eyes exactly like a cat's. Snake stories were exchanged and everyone laughed. Then, as Penny's aunt showed her to her room, uncle called out jokingly:

"Look' out for snakes, Penny!"

Left alone, Penny quickly put up her feet on the bed and peered a little fearfully into all the corners. She could see no signs of a snake, so hurriedly she undressed and got into bed, pulling the mosquito net over the bed from the ceiling. As she lay there she heard the mosquitoes "zinging" round like small jet-propelled 'planes and hoped the net would keep them out. She lay in the dark for a long time. Outside the crickets chanted monotonously and occasionally a frog croaked. Then she fell asleep.

Some time later she woke with a frightful start. Something cool had slithered across her face. She lay rigid, trembling. It must be a snake! Yes, it lay on her forehead, cold and heavy. She drew in a horrified breath —

Her scream frightened her even more. She went on screaming, and started clawing at her net to get out, but one of her arms was helpless. She had been bitten! The poison was working. The door opened, light flooded the room.

"I've been bitten by a snake!" she sobbed. "My arm's poisoned!"

In a minute she was standing on the floor between her aunt and cousin Maud, and Johnnie was scouring the floor with a torch. Mr. Ware came in and examined her arm carefully; everyone was talking at once and asking questions.

"Why, my arm is all pins and needles," she said suddenly and then stopped short.

They all started to laugh for it was quite apparent that she had had her arm above her head and it had "fallen asleep." Frightened imagination had done the rest.

Penny got into bed again, and her relatives departed, but they left her door open and the light on.

The next morning they all teased her about her "snake." They continued to do so and Penny set her teeth and determined to be a sport and perhaps one day prove that a Pommy could be as good as an Aussie.

Every day after tea, when Maud and Johnnie got back from the store, they would play tennis until the tropical night came down suddenly about seven o'clock. Penny found she could always tell when it was going to happen, for a cloud of flying foxes came across the sky and settled for the night in the mango trees, hanging upside-down like bats, which they resembled closely, except for their furry bodies and little pointed faces, from which they got their name.

After she had been in Australia a week, Dick Roberts took her and her cousin Maud in his car to see Alice. She was very nice and pretty, Penny considered, though she was rather awed by her big, silent husband, George. It was arranged that Johnnie should bring Penny over riding one day the following week.

On the appointed day Johnnie brought two horses, borrowed from the Ezzys, their neighbours, round to the verandah steps.

"Let's see how the Pommy shapes on a horse!" he called, grinning, not attempting to dismount to help her. What he did not know was that riding was one of Penny's accomplishments. She had learnt young — and bare-back, too — when she was a child. So she was up in the saddle in a twinkling, gathering her reins with a very professional air.

"There you are, Johnnie!" cried Mr. Ware from the verandah. "She'll have the laugh on you this time. I can see Penny is a horse-woman!"

Plainly astonished, the Australian lad rode off with his cousin, warning her that it was twelve miles to the station and she would certainly be saddle-sore the next day. They by-passed the town and were soon out on the track in the bushland, where Johnnie set his horse into a rolling trot, bumping in his saddle. Penny, of course, rode in English fashion, rising up in the saddle. He soon noticed and grinned.

"It looks all right, Penny," he said, "but you'll get tired of it!" But he kept glancing at her admiringly.

She was a trim little figure, sitting her horse with shoulders square, knees and toes in, while he flopped up and down like a sack of potatoes. Johnnie was plainly impressed.

As they rode the sky became overcast and the horses threw their heads up and sniffed the wind that had risen and was blowing in their faces. Johnnie was puzzled and urged the horses on, in case there was a storm brewing. At last he reined in.

"Something's wrong," he admitted.

Penny stared at the overcast horizon. Columns of what looked like dust seemed to be rising into the air; a reddish glow appeared, as if the sun were setting . . . but it was noon!

Her horse neighed and started to rear; at the same time a flight of

It was the fastest ride she had ever had in her life.

cockatoos flew low over them, screaming excitedly; then a wallaby, with her young in her pouch, scuttled into the bush, going the way they had come.

Suddenly Johnnie leant over and gripped the bridle of her rearing horse, checking it. As she opened her mouth to protest he spoke, his voice strained and hoarse.

"Penny," he cried, "it's a bush fire — and it's heading straight for us!"

Penny's heart seemed to jump clean out of her mouth as the full meaning of her cousin's words penetrated her brain. She stared fearfully ahead, to see now smoke and the glare of flames.

"Hold on to the horse!" said Johnnie urgently. "He'll bolt if you give him half a chance!"

Penny tightened her reins, making soothing noises as she did so. The horse was capering madly, despite Johnnie's grip on the bridle.

"What about Alice and her husband?" she called.

"Safe — their place is beyond the valley!"

Johnnie's grip was torn from the bridle as his own horse wheeled right round, ears laid back, raring to be gone.

"We'd better ride to Peterstown and warn them!" he called, struggling with his mount. "It's only a couple of miles over there — we just passed the track. If the wind veers, it'll be on them in no time."

Penny looked in the direction he indicated, but she could see nothing but bushland. Suddenly there was a terrified whinny and a scamper of hooves. Johnnie's horse, the bit between his teeth, had bolted back the way they had come.

Penny's mount made to plunge after the other horse. Penny let it go at a tight gallop after the disappearing figure of her cousin, but she kept thinking of what Johnnie had said — that Peterstown should be warned.

Coming to the track he had spoken of, she turned her horse sharply. Once on the new track she let it go, and go it did, ears flat, head down, all out. It was the fastest ride she had ever had in her life and, but for the panic that clutched at her heart, the most thrilling too!

Various animals kept passing them, some cutting across their path, some running along in the bush beside them. There were wallabies, wombats and opossums — and several snakes, zig-zagging along at incredible speed. While Penny dimly saw them, it never occurred to her to feel any alarm, nor did her horse shy at them as he would have done at any other time, for each living creature was concerned only with saving its own life.

Suddenly, with a gasp of relief, she saw before her signs of life. She passed a stockade and then a few scattered houses raised on posts. Her horse was snorting with exhaustion, but still going gamely. In another minute they were clattering through the only main road of the little town, a few inhabitants pausing in the heat of the midday sun to stare at the galloping stranger.

Penny drew up at the largest building she could see — a two-storeyed hotel. Flinging herself off her horse, she called "Tie him up, please," to an amazed youth who was lounging against the verandah post and ran into the main hall.

A large man in shirt sleeves turned from an office door and frowned at her flying entrance. She went up to him, her breath coming painfully, partly from the ride, partly from the hammering of her heart.

"Bush fire!" she managed to gasp. "Only about three miles away. I was riding with Johnnie Ware from Port Bowering and his horse bolted back the way we came . . . he said to warn Peterstown."

She stopped short and dropped into a chair, struggling with a strong desire to burst into tears.

The combined effect of her youth, her English accent and smartly cut riding clothes and her astonishing news, produced an effect rather as if a bomb had landed in the quiet lounge hall. Several visitors who had been proceeding up or down the stairs gathered round, excitedly commenting and questioning. The large man, who was the hotel proprietor, acted at once. He ordered two men out by car to see what they could see. Then he telephoned the local police.

In a very few minutes the hotel was fairly humming.

Penny found herself drinking a cup of tea in the hotel kitchen, the centre of an admiring staff. They all seemed amazed that she had controlled her horse after her cousin's mount had bolted. In common with Johnnie, they had no idea a Pommy could ride so well! From their comments Penny gathered that they were more worried about the cattle belonging to the stockade she had passed than about the fire. The town was well cleared of bush — but the cattle were out grazing, and if they got wind of the fire before they were safely rounded up, they might stampede into the town and cause appalling havoc.

Penny asked if she could telephone her aunt and uncle. They would be beside themselves with anxiety when Johnnie returned alone. One of them took her to the manager's office, but when he heard her request he shook his head.

"All lines commandeered by the police for the time," he informed her. "The fire's sweeping inland."

"How do you think it started?" asked Penny.

"The sun," replied the manager, whose name was Smith.

Penny stared, round-eyed. He went on to explain that when the bushland was as parched as it was now, after two years of drought, the sun acted like a burning ray and could smoulder dry ferns into a fire — a little wind added, and you had a bush fire.

Penny was anxious to be off back to Port Bowering, but Mr. and Mrs. Smith made her stay to eat a meal. About three o'clock they said the fire was clear of the track she must return on, and that they were sending their son, Bert, to escort her.

When they started off, the entire staff and some of the residents of the hotel turned out to see the Pommy who had ridden to warn them of their danger. Penny's heart swelled as they gave her a rousing "Good luck!" and she couldn't help secretly wishing that Johnnie had been there to witness the scene. Perhaps he wouldn't laugh at her so much then!

She was glad Bert was silent, for she felt more tired than she cared to admit. They rode at an easy pace, expecting to reach Port Bowering about six o'clock. The only signs of the fire were a curiously over-cast sky, the uneasiness of the horses, and the complete absence of bird or animal life. The whole landscape seemed deserted and empty. Suddenly Penny exclaimed with pleasure. A small tree they were approaching seemed to be covered in the loveliest pink blossoms she had ever seen — a veritable garden in the grey bushland.

"Look at those lovely blooms!" she exclaimed.

Bert laughed shortly.

"Watch them," he said, as they approached.

Suddenly with a squawking and fluttering the "blooms" rose in the air and flew away. They were, Bert said, birds who always flew in bunches and settled on small trees in this way.

As they were talking, Bert suddenly reined in and held up his hand for silence, leaning forward in his saddle with a look of intense concentration.

Penny, listening also, gradually became aware of a curious drumming sound.

"Cattle, coming fast," he said, frowning. "Maybe they've been rounded up."

But he seemed uneasy. He wetted his finger and held it up.

"Wind blowing our way now," he added thoughtfully. "I wonder if that darned fire —"

He got no further, for over the low ridge before them appeared a dark, moving mass.

"It's cattle all right," he said quickly, his eyes roving. "And I can't see any stockmen with them. Gee!" His voice rose in excitement. "Come on, miss — this is where we ride like the devil himself!"

He caught hold of her rein, wheeling the horses round, then, thrusting his heels hard into his horse's side, they were off, riding back towards Peterstown.

"What is it?" cried Penny, the wind catching the words and flinging them back into her mouth.

"It's a stampede!" Bert yelled back. "There's two or three hundred head of cattle coming up behind us on the track for the town!"

Penny remembered the faces of the staff at the hotel who had discussed this very possibility and her heart sank.

"Can we beat them?" she called back, the breath nearly shaken out of her body by the pace they were going and the roughness of the track.

"We'd better!" was the reply.

A thrill of sheer fear ran through Penny's heart. She tightened her knees and crouched low in her saddle. Her escort still had her horse's rein in one hand and his big horse was racing the smaller one off its feet.

"Let go!" called Penny. "My mount's tired. Let go!"

Bert took no notice.

Penny glanced over her shoulder, aware of a noise like distant thunder. She saw to her terror that the cattle were gaining on them — they seemed to be only a few hundred yards behind them, in a solid, maddened mass.

"The town!" she gasped. "People will be hurt if they stampede into the town! Can't we lead them into the bush?"

"Into the bush?" he roared back, not seeming to understand her meaning.

Before she could explain her hat flew off and she could feel her horse heaving under her. He couldn't keep up this pace; he would be down if the other horse didn't ease up. The Australian didn't seem to realize the danger that threatened the nearby town.

"Oh, let go!" she cried again.

He still took no notice. She raised her riding crop and brought it down smartly on his hand. He let out a cry and let go. At once the smaller horse dropped behind. Bert reined in for a moment but Penny took no notice of him and swept off the path into the bush, her little chin set in a determined line, her blue eyes curiously hard and glinting. If he wouldn't risk going into the bush, she would . . . and perhaps the cattle would follow. She must make them follow her, somehow!

She tore off the scarf round her neck and waved it, shouting out in a strange war whoop, hoping to attract attention. Her voice seemed thin and powerless, but she went on whooping madly and waving her scarf; at least it had the effect of galvanising her spent horse to a last effort. He went gamely galloping over the treacherous scrub, with its stunted, withered bushes and uneven ground.

She glanced hurriedly over her shoulder. Were the cattle following? They certainly were. In fact, they were so near that she could see the whites of their rolling eyes and feel the shaking of the ground under their rush.

She whooped almost exultantly as she realized that she had succeeded in her intention of leading them off the track to the town, but now her game little mount was almost finished. Twice he stumbled and struggled on and then, while she was shouting encouragement, her heart beating a tattoo that almost shut out the thundering of the herd behind her, she was down.

Almost as she touched the ground, aware of a jarring pain in her shoulder, she wrenched her head up and looked back despairingly.

The maddened herd of stampeding cattle were almost upon her!

In the seconds that followed her fall, Penny died a dozen times. Burying her face in her hands and hugging the ground as if it could hide her, she lay rigid, her whole body cringing as she anticipated the savage blows of galloping hooves.

The ground trembled, the whole air seemed full of noise and

confusion. Frantically she tried to think, but it was not possible — her mind was concentrated solely on fear of a terrible death under the hooves of the stampeding cattle. The seconds passed, and though the earth still shook and she could plainly hear the snorting of the beasts, she remained unscathed.

She dared not move, but lay exactly as she had fallen, her breath which she had held for untold ages, now coming and going in little gasps. Would it never end? How much longer was she to lie there?

Suddenly her ears, sensitized to the least sound, caught the cry of a human voice — a man screaming at the cattle . . . then another; but still she dared not move.

It seemed a long time before a deep, twanging voice said: "It's all right, kid."

Strong hands pulled at her shoulders and lifted her to her feet, and she looked into the face of two strangers. There was a third face; it was Bert's.

"All right?" repeated Penny weakly, her knees not seeming to belong to her at all.

The sky and the faces of the three men went swimming round her. From a long way off she heard them talking.

"A Pommy!" one of them said.

"She's all in!" replied Bert's voice. "She never ought to have ridden into the bush like that."

"What made her do it?" asked one of the strangers.

"I don't rightly know. She kept shouting something — I had hold of her horse's rein — then she gave my hand a bash with her whip and I let go. Reckon she thought her horse couldn't keep up."

"That's so, I guess." He whistled. "But a Pommy! She's got courage."

Her head ceased whirling and, finding that she was sitting on the ground with her head held down by an uncomfortably strong hand, Penny struggled to rise.

"I'm all right now!"

They helped her up, regarding her with curiosity. She turned abruptly to Bert.

"I'm all right," she repeated. "Where's my horse? I must get home."

"Reckon the horse cut along home by himself," replied Bert. "Sure you're O.K.?"

"Of course I am," replied Penny, tilting her chin high.

"Then you'll have to ride behind me, I guess," replied Bert, grinning.

Penny didn't much like the idea, but it seemed to be the only solution. As they went to the horses, she saw the cattle; to her astonishment they were moving quietly away towards Peterstown, several stockmen in attendance.

Bert then explained that these men had arrived in the nick of time and, under his direction, had turned the cattle and rounded them up. The fire had apparently gone roaring in two directions and the herd had got caught between the two and panicked, though there was no real danger, as the wind had died down. All stations and towns nearby were safely cleared and by tomorrow at the latest they expected to have the last of the flames out.

One of the strangers, a very tall, lanky stockman by the name of Frankie, insisted on coming with them. They rode quietly, the air gradually clearing as they left the scene of the conflagration.

Reaching the top of the rise, Penny could see the little town of Port Bowering below, nestling in the hollow. As Frankie turned and left them, waving a good-bye, the sun touched the horizon. Night was on them before they reached the centre of the town, for which Penny was very glad, for she did not wish to be seen sitting behind Bert like this.

By the time Penny had slipped off the big horse and started for the verandah steps of the Wares' house, she knew she was going to be stiffer than she had ever been in her life. Somehow she managed to struggle up without help — then the family were upon her.

After excited explanations, scoldings and supper, Penny was whisked off to bed by her aunt. Bert had declined their pressing invitation to stay for the night, for he had friends in the town. Johnnie, rather sheepish, had been silent as to how he had first become separated from his cousin, and the impression was that both their horses had bolted in different directions. Penny said nothing to the contrary.

For the next two days, despite all the arnica her aunt rubbed into her back, Penny could not move off her bed. Her cousins thought it very funny; her aunt and uncle scolded her affectionately for having foolishly risked her life by galloping into the bush against Bert's instructions. Penny did not like to tell them why she had done it, for it would certainly be taken for boasting.

A few days later, when Penny had just struggled up — her

wrenched shoulder was still painful — Dick Roberts telephoned with the news that Alice's baby had arrived — and it was a fine boy. The next morning Mr. and Mrs. Ware went over in the car to see their first grandchild. On their return they told the others that it had been arranged to bring the whole family over in a fortnight's time.

It was unusually hot in the days following; worse than the Wares ever remembered it. Penny, more shaken by her adventures than she admitted, was pale and listless and not in the mood to take Johnnie's constant teasing with her usual good grace.

He was never tired of trying to frighten her — by pointing out some huge spider in a corner — or yelling out that a frog was about to leap on her, for in this drought they did sometimes come into the house.

Once, after such an episode, Penny ran into her room and had a quiet cry; but she very soon recovered herself, determined that she would not let this tough Australian family have the laugh over her.

One of the daily jobs that Penny liked was to look after the canary they had bought at Teneriffe on their trip from England. Its cage hung on the side of the verandah and every morning Penny would go out before breakfast and lift down the cage, exchanging cheery greetings with the little yellow bird.

On the morning they were going over to Alice, everyone was up early bustling about, packing a hamper, cleaning the car, putting on their best clothes, determined to be off by nine o'clock to avoid travelling in the heat of the day.

Penny got up very languid after a sleepless night fighting mosquitoes. She did not look forward to the journey by car. Having dressed, she remembered the canary and went out on to the verandah, pulling over the chair on which she always stood so as to be able to lift the cage from its hook.

Pursing her lips in a whistle, she lifted it, and immediately she became aware of its astonishing weight. At the same moment she heard a strange hissing sound.

She leapt off the chair, dropping the cage with a bang, and the scream that came from her lips brought everyone running. This time Johnnie was the first to appear and he did not laugh at her. He stopped short and called urgently to his father. Mr. Ware followed, then he said quite coolly:

"It's only a carpet snake — and it can't get out. I'm afraid it's swallowed your canary."

It was true . . . the poor little bird was now only a bulge in the snake!

Everyone in the house gathered round while Mr. Ware fetched his gun. He knelt quite close to the cage and aimed carefully. Penny turned away, shutting her eyes and holding her ears. Even so, she jumped when the gun went off.

Johnnie's roar of laughter followed; and even Maud and her aunt smiled.

Penny felt angry and helpless. Tears stung her eyes.

"It's all very well for you!" she cried, more fiercely than she had ever spoken in her life. "You've been brought up with this sort of thing. I haven't!"

She walked away with her head in the air, biting her trembling lower lip.

At breakfast they were all very polite to her, though she was sure they were still amused. How could she ever make them understand that snakes were just the worst thing she could think of? She wasn't so much afraid of being bitten . . . it was the thought of their cold, slimy flesh touching hers.

By nine o'clock they were all packed into the car, with the picnic hamper in the luggage boot and numerous gifts for the new baby.

The car slid smoothly down the gravel drive, round the rose garden, now sadly parched, and past the flowering pink and white oleanders and under the shady gum trees that made an avenue to the gate. Penny sprang out to open it. She swung it back, jumping on to it to give herself a ride.

"Penny — quick!" It was Johnnie's voice, low and urgent. "Get this side of the gate — quick!"

Penny, surprised at his anxious tone, glanced carelessly over her shoulder. It was to see a black bull standing close behind her. She felt horribly frightened, but she did not lose her head. Stepping off the gate, she quietly walked round to the far side, then let the gate swing to.

Determined that her Australian relatives should not guess how panicky she felt, she forced herself to clamber unhurriedly into the car. As she did so, there came a furious snort, then an agitated cry from Maud.

"Oh, look!"

The bull was heading towards the gate and kicking up the gravel with fury, his little red eyes flashing wickedly. Penny's heart jumped to her throat as she saw how close she had stood to the beast, but she pretended to be quite cool.

Johnnie swung the car round to the left. "We'll have to tell the Ezzys to collect it before it does any damage," Maud said. "Oh, Penny, I don't know how you could be so brave!"

"I don't mind bulls," replied Penny.

It wasn't true, but — well, a bull was better than a snake!

"You Pommies are the oddest mixture," put in Johnnie, shaking his head.

Mrs. Ware turned and patted her niece's knee.

"It's just as Penny says," she said. "It's what you're used to. You see, one day Penny will meet a snake and find she's not a bit afraid!"

"Never!" exclaimed Penny fervently. "Oh, never!"

Alice's home was not built up on piles, as were so many at Port Bowering, but it was enclosed by the customary netted verandah. It had a slate roof, an unusual thing in Queensland, where corrugated iron roofs were mostly used; but then, George Johnson, her husband, was a well-off man.

As they drove up before the house, George, clad in white shirt and flannels, came out to greet them. Penny hung back shyly as they all went in to see Alice and the baby, and had an opportunity of looking round the comfortable lounge.

The small grand piano took her attention. It stood open, placed near the door to Alice's room. Penny fingered a note tentatively, wishing that both her cousins were not such good pianists, for their skill made her feel too shy to play. Just then her aunt called to her to come in.

The baby, only a little more than two weeks old, was adorable with its tiny, screwed-up face and its tuft of dark hair. He was asleep, the long lashes lying peacefully on his flushed cheeks.

When the baby had been inspected, they all had cold lunch, Mrs. Ware producing the hamper they had brought with them and taking out cold chicken, salad, tomatoes, home-made mayonnaise and cakes for tea, including a huge iced one for the baby's christening, which was the following week.

A little later they all strolled out to the tennis court, except Mrs.

Ware, who stayed to help the daily clear up, and, of course, Alice, who was as yet only allowed up a short while; she now returned to her room to lie down.

Penny, whose shoulder was still a little painful, had not brought her tennis racket, and she was quite happy to sit out while her cousins, George and a girl from another station nearby made up a four. Mr. Ware was wandering round somewhere, looking at the sheep in the stockade. She was lazily watching the game and half dozing when she heard someone approaching. She looked up, expecting to see her uncle, or perhaps Dick, who was expected whenever he could get there, and was surprised to find a tall, dark man staring at her . . . and to realize that he was no stranger.

"Hallo!" he said, smiling. "If it isn't the Pommy kid!"

Then she remembered him.

"You're Frankie — who saved me from the cattle!"

He sat down beside her and immediately asked her how she was, and many other questions.

"Why did you ride your horse into the bush?" he demanded suddenly, his blue eyes fixing her keenly.

She hesitated, for she knew how the Australians disliked showing-off of any kind. She really did not know how to reply and flushed awkwardly.

He seemed to be examining the ground now.

"Them cattle could've done a lot of damage in the town," he remarked. "Maybe you didn't know that?"

"Oh, yes, they told me at —" She stopped short.

"Who told you?"

She flushed a deeper pink.

"The staff at the hotel in Peterstown — they were talking about it."

There was a short silence.

"So you turned your horse and led 'em off," he said quietly. She didn't reply. "Gee," he added, "that's just about the swellest thing I've known a kid do!"

Penny's cheeks were now fiery.

"Oh, but I didn't know how dangerous it was," she protested honestly, "or I couldn't have done it!"

He started to laugh. The set broke up at that moment and everyone demanded to know what the joke was. Despite Penny's embarrassed protests, the stockman told them. Her uncle, who had joined them, listened in amazement; as for Johnnie, his jaw positively dropped. When Frankie ended the story with her avowal that she wouldn't have done it if she had known how dangerous it was, they all laughed.

Penny, unable to understand whether they were laughing at her or not, and covered in confusion, made some excuse about wanting to see the baby, and fled.

Finding her aunt in the kitchen helping with the washing-up, she begged her to go down and watch the tennis and said she would rather stay in the house, as she had a headache. Mrs. Ware put on her hat and went willingly enough. Penny finished the drying-up, listening half-heartedly to the loquacious Australian girl.

When the girl had departed Penny went into the house. Alice was resting, so she thought she would find a book and read, but first she decided to peep in at the baby.

She passed the piano, regretting that she couldn't amuse herself by playing it, but, of course, it would disturb both Alice and the baby; then she pushed the bedroom door open a few inches and looked in.

The big bed faced the door. Alice was lying propped up on pillows, but she was not asleep. Her expression was so strange that Penny stopped and stared. Something was very wrong! But what? Alice's horrified gaze was concentrated on the baby's cot. Penny took a cautious step forward, her mouth open to ask a question, but the words were never uttered.

The baby was asleep, but coiled on the blanket was a large, fat snake with dark markings, its small, flat head thrust forward towards the baby's bottle, which lay so near the little face. The whole danger flashed on Penny like a lightning stroke. The snake was after the milk, and if the baby woke or moved —

Instinctively she jumped back and the snake's head came round. Penny only just bit back a scream as a pair of cold green eyes glinted at her. There was a low hiss. A spiny, pointed tail threshed angrily; Penny stood, turned to stone, able only to stare. She knew that death was in the room, for the snake was exactly like the picture Johnnie had shown her of a death adder!

For a second the floor seemed to rock under her feet, then she moved her gaze to Alice's. The appeal in them did something to steady her. Her brain started to work. If she moved backwards out of the door behind her, the snake might follow, away from the child.

Forcing her frozen limbs to action, she stepped back, reaching the door, the snake kept its terrible eyes on her, but did not move. She stepped back again. Still it did not move. She took another step back, and then another, but the snake was motionless. A cold perspiration burst out on Penny's face. She was in an agony lest the baby should wake!

Something touched her back. She went colder than before, but, of course, it was only the piano. She flushed with relief, and then an idea came to her. Snakes were supposed to like music — it mesmerized them, so it was said; supposing she sat down and played?

She licked her parched lips, trickles of perspiration creeping down her cheeks. She sat. Now she could not see the snake. She must play, play, play! She raised her shaking hands. If only she could entice the snake out of the room, she knew Alice would manage to get up and shut the door. Her hands were cold and stiff — the music in front of her swam . . . no use trying to read it — she must play from memory.

She started a Brahms waltz she learnt for an examination at school, stumbling, feeling, playing softly, rhythmically, her eyes on the door so near to her.

The cold beads burst out anew on her forehead as she thought the sound might wake the baby . . . but there was complete silence from the bedroom and the piano notes seemed to stab the moist, hot air.

Now she was trembling all over. Her foot, as she tried to manipulate the loud pedal, leapt uncontrollably, so she kept it pressed down and played softly, repeating phrases where she had forgotten how to go on, then remembering more, then forgetting again. . . .

Something moved on the carpet. She had not been looking at that moment, but she felt that it was the snake. She dared not turn her head, for she knew if she met those eyes at close quarters she would be powerless to continue playing; but the death adder was there, within a few feet of her.

She strained her ears for sounds from the bedroom, then played louder to encourage Alice to move. But the door did not shut. What was happening? Had Alice fainted? Then she remembered the verandah window. Of course, Alice had picked up the baby and run out by the verandah.

Relief flooded her; she missed her fingering and played a series of discords; then she picked up the tune and went on. It seemed she had been sitting there for an eternity and now she could not remember any of the waltz she had started, but kept playing the same opening phrase over and over again. Her head felt as if it was on fire, her hands and feet were like ice.

Surely Alice would fetch someone — or had she collapsed on the way? She couldn't keep on playing much longer; spots were floating before her eyes; there was a strange buzzing in her ears. . . .

"Don't move, Penny," said a man's voice quietly, from some distance. "We're going to shoot."

The snake shifted suddenly. It was so near to her foot that only with the greatest effort of will did Penny avoid leaping for her life; somehow she kept her fingers moving, her body going rigid as she anticipated the explosion.

When it came it was ear-splitting. Not until later did she learn that George, Frankie and Dick had fired together, having to make absolutely certain that the death adder was killed at once. The noise was appalling. Penny never remembered what she did, but they told her she leapt about four feet sideways and then rushed into her uncle's arms and burst into hysterical tears.

A few minutes later they all gathered round the dead snake, pale, shaken, but relieved. Alice, holding the baby, was seated in an easy chair, and Doctor Dick had insisted they all have a sip of brandy.

"What a hideous creature!" shuddered Penny, looking down at the motionless reptile.

"Pick it up, Penny," encouraged her aunt. "Then you'll never be afraid of a snake again."

Very gingerly Penny leaned down and touched the spiny tail. It flicked.

The scream that rent the air made all of them start; then they laughed. After the tension, to have something to laugh at was just what they wanted.

"Snakes," spluttered Johnnie, between gales of laughter, "often move by reflex muscular action hours after they are dead."

At this Penny started to giggle herself, and soon she was laughing as much as any of them.

When they had somewhat recovered, George picked up his glass and raised it.

"To the greatest little Pommy who ever came to our country!" he said.

They toasted her; they hugged her; and Penny never minded how much they laughed at her after that, for she knew she was one of them.

BROTHER — DEAR BROTHER

by Linda Blake

Looking after little brother Joey could be fun in lots of ways. Vicky loved the way he chuckled when she bathed him and was proud when people admired him in his push-chair when they went shopping.

But when Vicky's mother was called away from home for a few days, and Vicky had to look after little Joey, she began to regard her baby brother with growing disfavour.

"Don't see why I should!" muttered Vicky under her breath and she jabbed crossly at the last piece of sausage on her plate.

"Maybe you don't, dear," said her mother, "but you will have to look after Joey for a little while. I shall only be a few days at your Grandmother's, just while she recovers from her operation. Dad will be here in the evenings to help but someone must look after Joey during the day and your holidays couldn't have come at a better time."

"But the girls have made great plans for the holidays," pleaded Vicky. "I couldn't possibly take Joey along, too."

Mrs. Johnson sighed but she was adamant. "I'm sorry, Vicky. But Joey will be good, I'm sure and you know how he loves you to play with him."

Vicky leapt up and tore out of the house in a boiling temper.

Joey was Vicky's baby brother. She still woke up some nights and couldn't believe she was no longer the only child. Joey was just eighteen months old and from the moment he had arrived everything had changed.

Vicky mooched along, gazing into the shop windows. She remembered one of her aunts saying to her mother, "Watch out that Vicky doesn't feel jealous when the baby arrives." She had thought it a beastly thing to say. When Mum had told her Joey was expected, she had been thrilled.

But he was such a disruption. She had had to move out of the little front bedroom that had always been hers. The bigger room at the back was nice but it was the guest room, not her room. But Mum and Dad didn't seem to understand that.

Looking after Joey meant being with him all the time, especially now he was walking, or staggering to be more precise. What a boring way of spending a holiday.

She wandered along the street, kicking moodily at little stones until a yell spun her around. She grinned. The group of girls coming down the road were all from her form at school. She hadn't known them very well last term but this year they seemed much better fun than her old friends.

Especially her old friend Anne. Vicky felt funny inside when she thought of Anne. They had been friends since infant school but this term all Anne had wanted to do was work and think about exams and answer questions in class. She had gone dreadfully serious and didn't like Vicky's new friends at all. They hadn't actually quarrelled but everything was prickly and horrid when they spoke to each other these days and somehow they had stopped going round to each other's homes in the evenings.

"What on earth's the matter with you?" Gillian Baxter, the leader of the group, strolled up to where Vicky was waiting on the corner. "You've a face as long as a mile."

"Oh, everything's wrong. My Mum is going to look after my Grandmother for a few days and I'm stuck with looking after Joey!"

Gillian pulled a face. "Oh, poor you. How long for? Don't forget we're all going skating on Friday."

Vicky's heart sank. She wanted to go skating more than anything at the moment. "Mum might be back by then," she said wishing she felt a fraction more hopeful.

Gillian looked bored. "Oh, heavens, you'll just have to dump the kid with your neighbours. We don't want a snivelling, sticky baby dragging along with us. Our boy friends down at the ice-rink would laugh their heads off if we arrived with a baby in tow."

"He's not a sniveller! And only occasionally is he sticky," Vicky said surprised to find herself flying to Joey's defence.

"Oh well, if you're going to play nursemaid, we won't bother you any more. Come on, girls."

"But I'm not looking after him now . . ." Vicky began but they had brushed past her and gone giggling down the street.

Vicky watched them go, stunned that they hadn't asked her to go with them. A little voice in her head said it wasn't surprised but Vicky squashed it flat and decided it was all Joey's fault.

Mrs. Johnson left the next morning and Vicky spent hours bathing and dressing the wriggling Joey who was cross that his Mummy wasn't giving him attention. Vicky gave him his breakfast and played with him for the rest of the morning. In the afternoon she pushed him down to the park and sat on a bench throwing a bright red ball for him to scramble after. A little way away she could see Gillian and the rest of the girls talking to some boys from school. They were all laughing and joking and seemed to be having a marvellous time.

Once they had all looked in her direction and then laughed. Vicky felt her face flame with embarrassment and annoyance. She scooped up Joey and strapped him into his push-chair. But all the way home the sound of that laughter seemed to be ringing in her ears.

On Friday, Vicky was resigned to looking after Joey. She had to admit it was fun in lots of ways. She loved the way he chuckled when she bathed him and felt proud when people admired him in his push-chair, when they went shopping. Dad did most of the work in the evening and kept on saying she should go out with her friends to a cinema or disco. But Vicky just shook her head and sat watching the television or reading. She didn't want to tell him that, at that moment, she didn't think she had any friends! Obviously, Gillian didn't want to know her and Vicky just didn't feel brave enough to ring Anne and have a long cosy gossip with her about everything.

The shops were crowded on Friday morning. Vicky felt exhausted and bad-tempered by the time she had pushed Joey round two super-markets and struggled to get everything on the list Mum had left.

Once they all looked in her direction and then laughed.

She was still two or three things short when she reached the last shop. She groaned when she looked at the crowds inside. Joey was yelling to come out of his chair and she knew he would run off as soon as they were inside the shop. She knew, too, that if she didn't unstrap him, he would scream.

She gazed round in despair and then caught sight of Gillian coming out of the record shop, looking very smart and attractive in black trousers and a ski jersey. She was obviously just off to the skating rink.

"Hi Gillian. Can you help a sec?"

"What's up?"

Vicky swiftly unstrapped Joey who stopped yelling immediately. "Look, just hang on to him for a little while, will you. I've some more shopping to buy and I can't take him in with me."

"Oh heavens. I'm late already," Gillian pouted.

"I won't be a minute," Vicky begged and, thrusting Joey's hand into Gillian's, she dived into the shop.

She was half-way down one of the aisles when an elderly lady in front of her knocked over a pile of tinned pineapple. The tins rolled and crashed everywhere. In that crowd there was an immediate jam and Vicky took ages getting to the pay-out desk. She kept craning her neck to see if Joey was all right but she couldn't see him or Gillian anywhere.

Fuming and furious, Vicky finally paid for her shopping and raced outside. The push-chair was still parked by the door but there was no sign of Joey or Gillian!

For a second Vicky felt as if cold water was running down her spine. Then she pulled herself together. Gillian would have taken him for a walk. Probably to look in the toyshop window if she knew Joey.

Pushing the empty chair, Vicky ran down the street. There was no sign of either of them. She began to feel hot and cold all over at the same time and her knees wouldn't stay still. Joey must be here somewhere.

Suddenly she saw one of the girls from school. "Have you seen Gillian," Vicky called, desperately.

"Yes. She's up at the ice-rink. I've just left her."

"Does she have my baby-brother with her?"

The girl giggled and shook her head. "The only boys Gillian has anything to do with are much older than your brother!" And she raced off, laughing.

Vicky felt the world spinning round her and wondered vaguely if this was what fainting was like. But then a voice in her ear said: "I have him here, Vicky."

She spun round and there stood Anne, gazing at her solemnly through her spectacles. Joey was drooped over her shoulder, fast asleep, clutching a very sticky lolly in one hand and his teddy in the other.

"W . . . what . . . Anne! I don't understand. . . ."

"She just dumped him back into his push-chair the moment you went into the shop and vanished. I was across the road in the coffee-bar. I saw everything, so I dashed out and took him in for some milk. I thought I'd catch your eye when you came out but you were an age and then I must have missed you when I paid the bill. I'm sorry, Vicky. He's been as good as gold. You are lucky having a brother!"

Vicky held out her arms and took the sleeping boy from Anne. For a long moment she gazed down at him and wondered how she could ever have wished he didn't exist and then she looked up at her friend's face. The beginning of the term vanished as if it had never existed.

"Yes I am," she said from the bottom of her heart.